Jessica F. Woods, Attorney of Record

Victoria King Heinsen

PAGE PUBLISHING, INC.
New York, NY

First originally published by Page Publishing, Inc. 2018

This is a work of fiction. Names, characters, locations, and events are fictional. Any similarities to people, living or dead, occurrences, or places is coincidental.

ISBN 978-1-64462-192-9 (Paperback)
ISBN 978-1-64462-193-6 (Digital)

Printed in the United States of America

Friday, Late April 2013
The Weekend of Week One

Fighting another wave of nausea, Jessica reached behind the driver's seat of her red 2010 Acura to retrieve her briefcase. Yes, it was a Coach; no, she really could not afford it, but at the time she selected this treasure, she considered it essential to her appearance as both an established attorney and one who represented the prestigious firm for which she worked. Besides, what better Band-Aid for a broken heart than a designer briefcase? This innocuous gesture followed others, certainly better than fretting over Andrew yet again. What was done was done. A boyfriend, a love from another life. Jessica's common sense intervened. Moving forward, she congratulated herself. Just moving forward.

Her cell phone chimed. "Hey!" she chirped. "What's up?" It was Lil, Jessica's personal assistant, friend, and moral compass. How Lil had gravitated to Jessica for an interview and subsequent hiring was a gift from the universe. Three years ago, Jess, a newly minted attorney fresh from passing the Ohio bar exam, well, fresh from finally passing the bar exam, had been hired by the Cincinnati firm of O'Malley, O'Malley, and O'Malley. Their plan, and it was a business decision, included breaking into the Columbus market. Eager, intelligent, the daughter of an attorney, Jessica must have conformed to the profile they wanted. She did her best to execute their motto: *We make it right for you, because whatever the case we are right for you.*

With sun-streaked blond hair stylishly cut to shoulder length, a barefoot Jessica stood at five feet eight inches. Because she sedulously exercised, usually running, she maintained her weight of 120 pounds. True, Jess worked hard at looking good; it was her nature. But she also possessed a good head on her shoulders and a kind heart. Smart business people, O'Malley, O'Malley, and O'Malley certainly must have looked beyond the young, somewhat diffident attorney who interviewed for the job to envision the lawyer they wanted as a symbol of their office in Columbus, the state capital of Ohio. Her beauty was not only a plus; it conformed to their business plan.

So Jessica signed the Triple O contract, joined the firm, and subsequently set out to search for a secretary. Or *personal assistant* in the current vernacular. At the same time, enjoying a break from online shopping, Lilly Taylor scrolled through employment opportunities in Central Columbus. A few days later, in she walked to a brand-new downtown office with no furniture except a swivel chair Jessica's brother had hauled up to the second floor. The elevator needed readjustments, he was told; could he wait? No, excited for his sister's success, Robbie Woods had dragged his father's chair up the not-yet-painted stairway so that Jessica, when she chose, could sit down. As it happened, Lil sat down while Jessica asked the questions. Or to be precise, having no experience except as an intern in law school interviewing felons and other attorneys' clients, Jess listened while Lil outlined the requirements of the job. All that was three years ago; Jessica and Lil had become not only employer and employee, but friends.

"The Woolseys are here," Lil offered.

"Shit! They're an hour early!"

"I know," an unflappable Lil responded. She knew from the Woolseys' contrived postures in the waiting room on the other side of the divider that the couple pretending to read magazines were instead tuned to every word. For elderly people, they had the hearing of canines as both Lil and Jessica had discovered from the considerable appointments both scheduled and unscheduled with these holdovers from Jessica's deceased father's estate. Oh, the Woolseys had plenty of time—yes, they did, time—and, as months rolled into years, determination. Like a dog with a bone, Clara Woolsey did not forget, nor did she let go. Her husband, Mel, was just as bad, if not worse. How, Jessica wondered, as the Woolseys traipsed in for yet another visit, had her dad put up with them? Well, for starters, a year into the case her dad had died, an event Clara and Mel too often referred to when adumbrating some kind of accrued interest on the money the insurance company owed them.

"Your dad certainly chose an unfortunate time for his heart attack," Clara somehow managed to insert with each meeting. "I know you are doing everything you can, but closing his estate has really affected Mel and me," she droned on. "Is there anything I can do to help?"

Yes, thought Jessica, *you could not talk, you could let me handle things.* Words she chose instead were much kinder although succinct. They usually flowed something like this: "Mrs. Woolsey, I really appreciate your patience and your time. I know it's difficult for you and your husband to come to Columbus from Ostrander, so just the energy you use to visit me shows how invested you are, as am I. I am working with the insurance company, as you know. We'll get things cleared up sooner rather than later." At this point Jessica would rise from her desk, walk around to Clara, while pleasantly yet firmly pressing the woman's elbow forward, and slowly guide the older lady to the office door. Mel, issuing any number of groans and huffs, tagged along behind, if hanging on to a walker while inching forward could be termed tagging along.

Jessica had indeed inherited the Woolseys while they still visited the Upper Sandusky office Jess's father had unexpectedly vacated when his heart attack at an Ohio Academy of Trial Lawyers dinner proved fatal. Mrs. Woolsey had come to Bob, Jess's dad, almost a year before. She and her husband had been traveling on a Super Bus throughout the South. Any number of causes from the condition of the bus driver to the condition of the bus resulted in an accident in Kentucky when the bus hit an embankment. All of the passengers except for Clara and another woman, Gardenia Pulchinski, about the same age, managed to survive the event with minimal bumps and bruises. Mrs. Woolsey, however, along with the other lady who had by now become her best friend, sustained head and neck injuries, the extent of which Jessica was still unsure. The MRIs read one way, her client said another, and the insurance company doggedly maintained another opinion.

As Lil waited patiently for her boss's instructions, Jessica cast back into her mind for how to buy time, mollify the Woolseys, and hammer on the Super Bus attorneys for a settlement. The accident had occurred nearly four years ago. No one, including Jessica, was getting any younger. Recently Mel had hinted that a wheelchair might be in his future; Clara had presented bills Medicare did not cover. Evidently, purchasing secondary insurance policies seemed to have slipped their minds. If their lawyer were less optimistic, with more cases than she actually had, the Woolseys might have been handed over to another needier attorney by now. The poor devil upstairs, Michael Ritter, doggedly unlocked his office daily, sitting alone most of the time as he waited for clients to find him. However, such was not the option. Jess needed the income; she had the knowledge and the skill to win this one. Because of the years, she certainly had the contacts.

"Lil, let me think. I'll call you right back. Just hold on to them, will you?"

"Certainly, Ms. Woods." Lil liked to use a more formal name for her boss when she knew the clients were eavesdropping. That Clara Woolsey missed nothing, including how her young, inexperienced attorney reacted to her inherited clients' unexpected visits between scheduled appointments. Oh yes, it was fun for the older woman to surprise her lawyer, even more fun to grumble and harrumph about how the new best friend, Mrs. Pulchinski, fared with her own lawsuit against the Super Bus. It would seem, according to Clara's version, that Gardenia's attorney was close to reaching a settlement. The continual phone conversations, Mrs. Woolsey had written them all down by hand, adumbrated that an end was near. Her best friend of nearly four years now would live in comfort the rest of her life; the attorney would receive his fee, which he had reduced considerably because of his high regard for Mrs. Pulchinski. During these attempted forays, Jessica privately called them scare tactics; after a lengthy pause, Mrs. Woolsey sometimes wheezed. Or most likely in a practiced rehearsal had had Mel shift uncomfortably in an adjacent chair as he toyed with his walker. Following the wheeze or the shifting, one or the other of the couple would ask, wonderingly polite, if they were too much trouble for Jessica. Perhaps they should just bother someone else; they knew she was busy.

Of course bothering someone else meant, as all three understood, that the Woolseys implied that they just might—they hated to, of course—jump over to Gardenia Pulchinski's lawyer. Now there was someone who could get things done, unlike Jessica.

What Clara and Mel did not know, Jessica did. She and Gardenia's lawyer Jay Rossford engaged in continual conversations regarding the developments in what they both referred to as the Case of the Super Bus Seniors, SBS in texting. Jay was no farther along than Jessica; his client, every bit as recalcitrant as Clara, possibly more so. After yet another row with her slovenly husband, Gardenia's adult daughter Violet had moved in with her mother two years before, listened to the older woman's complaints, and seen the opportunities that a handsome settlement afforded. Of course she would care for her mother; the occasional tearful whimpering about a rest home should stop. Violet would be both nurse, friend, and caregiver. Yes, Violet had plans for that settlement; indeed she did.

Jessica clicked her phone to handle an incoming call. Max, her boyfriend. "Hey, Hon," she said, smiling into her cell. Thank God she did not use FaceTime, which would certainly have transmitted her pale face, less-than-clean hair, and glasses. Yes, Jessica was hungover. No more Lemontinis ever again for her, absolutely no more. Max loved her; she was pretty sure she loved him. In fact, hungover or not, hearing from him less than an hour after he had pulled himself out the bed they shared at her cottage added sparkle to her day, aspirin for the psyche.

"What's up?"

"I just got picked up for speeding," he was as hungover as she and now depressed as well.

"Oh, I'm sorry," she genuinely sympathized. Jessica knew all too well about speeding tickets. Only in movies were attorneys' peccadillos with speed traps overlooked. Jess routinely paid, adding up OBMV points as she did, in anticipation of driving school for exoneration in the near future.

Max sounded miserable. "The guy got me right outside of Huron. Sixty in a thirty-five zone."

"How can I help?" asked Jess.

"I don't know. I'm glad he didn't make me take a Breathalyzer test. I think I'm still hungover."

"Listen, I'll think of something. When is your court date?"

"Next Friday in Huron. Aren't we leaving for a wedding that morning in Pennsylvania?"

"I'll handle it, Hon. Settle down, go to work, drive safe, and I'll call you later. Love you." Jessica clicked off.

Poor Max. He had driven the night before from work in Cleveland to meet Jessica at her cottage in Fischer's Beach, yet another inheritance from her father. Unlike any number of boyfriends, really not many if one did not count flirtations, Max was both attentive and kind. It was he who understood Jess's exhaustion, her demanding schedule, her grief, even after almost four years, for her father. True, Jessica could function independently without a man. She had done so often enough through most of college and in that awful time after failing the bar the first time before hiring into O'Malley, O'Malley, and O'Malley. Still, it was very nice to rely on a broad shoulder other than her brother's, a sympathetic voice other than her mother's—all that from a man who loved her. For his efforts the night before, Max had earned a speeding ticket and a hangover. Jessica would call the Huron Police Department to see what she could do. Max deserved that and more.

So back to the Woolseys. Nausea struck momentarily as Jessica leaned against the Acura, her head lowered between her arms. Straightening up, shaking it off, her father would have urged that Jess call the office.

"O'Malley, O'Malley, and O'Malley. Lilly speaking. How can I help you?"

"I need some damned aspirin. Tell the Woolseys I am still in court, that I can meet them this afternoon. What does my schedule look like?"

"Yes, Ms. Woods. I will relay your message. They have been kind enough to wait." Lil loved dripping professionalism especially when she did not mean it. A pause ensued while Lilly switched from the online shopping site she had vowed for Lent not to look at in the office. Well, Lent was over; Easter had come and gone. Still, she shouldn't steal her bosses' time; one of the Triple Os had a habit of checking the access sites from his computer in Cincinnati. In the longer view, it wasn't actually stealing if you considered the time she spent thinking about the office on nights after work and on weekends. "Ms. Woods, you have a client at one today, but 2:15 is open." The understood message of the additional fifteen minutes let Jessica know that no client was scheduled for one o'clock; she had until 2:15 to get back from the lake.

"All right. Thanks. See you then."

She called Jay. "Hey, where are we on the SBS? Clara and hubby burst into the office this morning, no appointment, hell bent on a settlement."

Unfortunately, Jay had just hung up from a nasty conversation with Gardenia's daughter. Violet's Bingo binges at the Legion had gone south. When formerly she won more than she lost, recently her positive karma had retreated, to India probably as far as Violet knew. Anyway, she needed money and now.

"Jess, how is my favorite Bobbsey Twin?" A generation older than Jessica, Jay liked to make references to literature, art, music, anything from his youth. He enjoyed trumping Jess if he could with details she might not know. Ah, competition, friendly as it was, was fun; beating a competitor was even more so.

"Look, I think Clara might fire me and get someone else. No, and not you, so forget it. What have you heard on your end?"

"Bobbsey One already has more medical issues than Bobbsey Two." Speaking in code had its pluses because code meant another lawyer was eyeing up the items on Jay's desk as well as listening, while trying mightily to look inattentive. "So the hospital reports are different. Why in the hell she went to that backwoods country place is beyond me. Those clowns run a vet clinic [animals, he meant, not veterans] in the next county. Sometimes I think they mix the dog X-rays up with the people X-rays."

Visiting lawyer had be laughing inwardly by now as Jay conducted what his colleague viewed as a most interesting professional consultation. Let's see, who got billed for this one and how much. Office guest figured it was a split.

"Okay. We need to get together with Super Bus attorneys and go from there. We talked to them over a month ago, and they said they were working on it. I keep telling Clara not to call them directly."

"Same for me with Bobbsey Two." Both Jessica and Jay knew Super Bus attorneys loved clandestinely recording conversations from irritable usually injured travelers. Doing so helped the company while better yet compromising the case against the allegedly hurt parties.

"I'll call," Jessica offered. She knew Jay on a Friday might not follow up until Monday, and she needed to move forward. Financially, Jay was already comfortably settled in Worthington with a wife, two children, and a membership to a golf club that demanded his attention, particularly on sunny spring afternoons. Sufficiently attending to the game, the children, and the wife occurred in order of importance, as it should: tee times first.

Jessica placed her briefcase on the passenger side, started her car, and backed out of the grassed-in parking space at the Fischer Beach cottage she now owned. It was ten in the morning on a sunny Friday in late April. Despite a hangover, a pleasant early morning rendezvous with Max, and several phone calls, she had already logged a good two hours for O'Malley, O'Malley, and O'Malley. Her father used to comment, "With a fax machine you can go everywhere." That was years ago; even Bob Woods had transitioned with the times. Jess's mother Alexandra hinted often enough that her husband's social life post divorce provided the incentive to adapt to the electronic age.

Jessica sighed, partly out of remembering how it used to be, and partly out of exhaustion, from feeling overwhelmed at the surprises, pleasant and unpleasant, life had handed her. Jessica gazed back at the asphalt road in front of her cottage. It was on this road, now called Peach Tree Lane, where she had learned to ride a two-wheeled bike. She and her brother spent summers with their mother up here while their dad drove up from Upper Sandusky every Wednesday and weekends. A white sand beach stretched along the lake, just one block down the path from their cottage. As Jessica and her brother grew more proficient on their bikes, both kids rode over a bridge to the North Coast Yacht Club. They swam in the pool; their mother swam or lay in the sun.

The club offered a lovely restaurant, but what Robbie and Jessica liked best was the outdoor snack bar with picnic tables right by the pool. The rule handed down from their parents went something like this: during the week, one drink and one snack per day per child, no more. On weekends her dad relaxed the stringent requirement; Mom and Dad's beer and cocktails seemed outside the boundaries and therefore didn't count. Seminal behaviors for what Jessica would, as an adult, later term *austerity* caused the One Drink One Snack Law in the first place.

The reason for the rule, a simple one. At home in Upper Sandusky, her dad had received yet another outstanding bill from the North Coast Yacht Club, opening it alone some hot July evening as she, her mother, and her brother "played at the lake," he had exploded into the phone. "Five hundred dollars for snacks!" he bellowed. "I work my ass off down here for you kids to drink pop and eat potato chips all day long! That's going to end right now!" At age eight Jessica did not feel it was in her best interests to correct her father. She preferred ice cream sandwiches to potato chips, so his statement was somewhat incorrect.

Anyway, the One Drink One Snack rule held rather firmly those ten years the family had enjoyed near perfection at their cottage on Fischer's Beach. It must be the effects of alcohol and exhaustion that brought tears to Jessica's eyes now. She sniffed, wiping the tears from her face with the back of her hand. No tissues, of course.

Ten years of bliss. She and Rob played baseball for a local kids'
team. They walked down the road to roller-skate when games didn't
interfere. Robbie kissed his first girlfriend on the roller rink as they
skated to recorded organ music during Couples Only. Unfortunately,
he had made the puerile error of telling his teammates the previous afternoon what he planned. Apparently, the girl got word, long
before cell phones. She must have enjoyed the experience, although,
her prerogative, she refused to talk to poor Robbie after the anticipated skate and kiss. Relegated to sitting on a bench on the other
side of the rail that separated the rink from the onlookers, Jessica had
watched most of the scenario, except where her brother and the girl
glided into a far corner just outside the light of the rotating overhead
mirrored globe. Where was the girl now after nearly thirty years?
Probably married, Jessica thought, with children, probably holding a
good job somewhere. Where was Robbie? Not married, no children,
job situation flexible.

Reveries for Jessica did not take long. Her Acura rounded the
corner where a fence used to be. The first major renovation she exe-
cuted after recording the deed was to tear down the chain link fence
that she had always hated as a child. As a little girl, she felt like a pris-
oner; as an adult, she loathed trimming the wild garlic and dandeli-
ons that year by year encroached along the fence line into the grass.

Her cottage at Fischer's Beach used to be one of the better homes
when she grew up there. In 1983 for 53,000.00 dollars, her parents,
their names entered on the deed as Robert and Alexandra Woods,
had purchased the two-bedroom, one-bath ranch with an additional
half acre of yard. At the time on Peach Tree Lane all the cottages, in
fact, even those on the other streets, except for minor improvements,
looked similar. A marina, a miniature golf course, a skating rink, and,
in previous years before Jessie arrived a dance hall, completed the
1950s development.

However, the marina owner for whom the eponymous Fischer's
Beach took its name, eventually engaged in an unhappy dispute over
water issues with the cottage owners. As a kid Jessica paid no attention to the dispute. As a lawyer, she understood it quite well. Lou
Fischer owned the water plant that supplied all the water to the cot-

tages. He turned the water on the third weekend in April; he turned it off the third weekend in October. He also insisted that he owned exclusive rights to the beach that ran along the other side of the main road in front of the cottages. Two arguments, water rights and beach privileges, engaged cottage owners as well as pitted them against Mr. Fischer. In the end cottage owners, who had long since banded together in an association, won rights to use the beach. It did not per se belong exclusively to Lou. What did belong to him was the acre of grassland that bordered the beach. Cottage owners were more than welcome to enjoy the clean white sand; oh yes they were welcome. Getting there, however, might be a problem as the recalcitrant Lou had erected a chain link fence adorned at the top with coiled barbed wire. A padlocked gate was meant only to keep the area secure from, as Mr. Fischer testified in depositions, vandals. He truly thought he had provided keys to the cottage owners. Well, he sincerely apologized for the confusion.

Back to court the Fischer's Beach Association scurried along with the petulant Lou. Because cottage owners paid a flat yearly fee for water use, they began to water their lawns and their gardens, to wash their cars and their driveways as often as they felt prudent. After all, on hot days what better way to maintain an attractive home than to keep the hose running from 8:00 a.m. to 8:00 p.m.? Surely Mr. Fischer understood how they collectively were committed to upholding the values of the resort named after his family?

Eventually, Lou and the association reached yet another agreement. As one of the attorneys for the FBA, Jessica's dad enjoyed the additional opportunities meetings and depositions afforded. He could come to the lake on Thursday night! In fact, why not stay over from Wednesday through Thursday for research? Lou's attorneys, some from the county seat and therefore county courthouse in Haines Landing and some from Toledo, acquiesced. If the Friday meetings ended unexpectedly before noon rather than dragging on until five o'clock, how were they to anticipate such agreeable outcomes? Time to fish for perch, to take the boat to Kelleys Island; this was serendipitous.

In the end all aggrieved parties in Fischer's Beach Association vs. Louis Fischer reached a peaceful resolution. Mr. Fischer would remove a section of the chain-link fence so that cottage owners and their guests could have beach privileges. Cottage owners would pay Mr. Fischer to clean the beach as needed. A joint committee composed of two cottage owners and two representatives from Fischer's Marina would meet on Memorial Day, Labor Day, and when exigencies demanded. At the time of the second resolution, Jessica worked as a private investigator for, of course, her father's girlfriend of the moment. Attorney Robert Woods's unexpected demise was neither anticipated nor planned for. That Jessica would represent FBA lay suspended, unrealized, far into the future. Now she owned the cottage, her dad was dead, and her mother remarried for nearly ten years.

Time flies, mused the attorney for Fischer's Beach Association, when you are or are not having fun. She scarcely remembered her parents' divorce although horrible struggles with property and custody stretched for her from late childhood through adolescence. The cottage, once a show piece of sorts at Fischer's Beach, waited—neglected and deteriorating. In the spring and summer Bob paid somebody to mow occasionally; mowing did not include trimming or weeding. In late fall dead leaves from the oak tree in the corner of the chain-link fence piled up in drifts and mounds. Jess and her family, when together, used to drive up for one last weekend. Together she and Robbie raked the leaves, arguing as they did so, while Bob winterized the boat and their mother cleaned the cottage one last time before winter. Sometime around late afternoon Bob would return with marshmallows and pizza. As the leaves burned, the family ate s'mores, graham cracker sandwiches with roasted marshmallows and melted Hershey bars. Those times, mused Jessica, had been wonderful indeed.

Well, they were over. As part of the property settlement, the cottage remained with her father. Both parents remarried. Rob and Jessica read books and articles on how children of divorces could be expected, whatever the circumstances, to go on to happy successful lives. Of course they would; everyone said how resilient and smart the Woods children were.

The damned hangover was making her miserable: *saturnine, jeremiad,* her mother turned amateur philologist, would have supplied, whether a listener showed interest or not. As long as Jessica dwelled on her father, she might as well keep thinking about him. Because of Bob, Jessica F. Woods had become the attorney of record, not only for Fischer's Beach Association but also for the delightful Woolseys, apparently for Max, and certainly, if O'Malley, O'Malley, and O'Malley hadn't yet fired her, the only attorney representing the Cincinnati based firm in Columbus, Ohio. Call her Fortunate or Unfortunate, the *F* stood for Florence, not Failure, not Fired. Jessica Florence Woods. Named after the city where her parents had honeymooned years before, Firenza, Florence Italy.

And *Father* maybe? What roles her parents played in Jessica's life as her own and Robbie's own lives unfolded!

Her mother Alexandra, *Trickster Alex* Jess liked to call her, more an epithet than a sobriquet, Alex felt, occasionally supplied Jessica with tales of Bob as a younger attorney. With Bob's death, instead of evanescing, the stories tumbled out. What her father had not already told her, her mother supplied. It worked best, Jessica and Rob conspired, when Alex enjoyed a glass of wine or better yet a vodka martini. Then the tales spilled out.

According to Alex, Bob had not been one of the lawyers who embraced advertising when that ban was lifted for attorneys. In fact, for all his bravado, he feared that advertising could vitiate truth. Reputable honest lawyers could lose the clients who so badly needed them as television and print drove desperate people to firms that paid the most for large ads in telephone books, on huge billboards, and in riveting TV commercials. No matter the skill of the attorneys or the sincerity of their concern for their clients. Get the bodies; the rest would follow.

As for computers, in the late 1980s Bob paid his aging secretary to attend classes. Everyone balked, mostly Bob. He neither typed, faxed, nor e-mailed. Still, he was a competitive fellow. Jokes and restaurant menus rolling out of the fax machine piqued his interest. Other lawyers in a small town with too many lawyers already and more coming out of law school to join their fathers, those lawyers used the whole kit and caboodle. Time to get on board. After his divorce, even more incentives, social as well as professional, drove Robert Woods, Esq. to embrace the electronic age

Before he died, her dad had written and returned e-mails along with the rest of his colleagues. Oh, he hunted and pecked because he had never learned to keyboard. Typing class in his high school days was for kids planning to go into business, secretaries, girls. At Upper Sandusky High School on Houpt Drive, Bob, a college prep student, did not need typing. Who knew back in 1965 that familiarity with computers would direct—no, control—a person's career? In fact, as a high school senior Bob's vision of the future stopped short of acceptance at the University of Notre Dame. Law school had not entered his imagination. He was too busy enjoying football. The previous year he had co-captained the Upper Sandusky team toward a state championship.

Well, thought Jessica, the picture on her mother's piano showed a man Jess did not know. She saw tears sometimes in her mother's eyes as Alexandra looked at a black and white photograph from long ago. Bob, smiling, confident, held a football ready for a pass; his whole future lay ahead of him. Like his future, her dad controlled the ball; the world welcomed his next play.

By the time Jessica was born, her father had long since abandoned playing football. An injury his freshman year at Notre Dame took him off the team. He graduated, not with honors, but certainly with hours of fun those four years. His high draft number scared him, but that same football injury kept him from going to Vietnam. As an afterthought, really with nothing else to do, Bob applied and was accepted to law school at Ohio State. A brilliant student, he applied himself just enough to graduate, pass the bar, and join his father in the hometown firm of one.

Between his junior and senior years of law school, Bob married Jess's mother, their marriage of nearly twenty years surviving crises large and small while his practice grew. By the time Bob died, he had tangled with the railroads at their own intersections, figuratively bashing through legal crossing bars to win. From accepting any kind of work those first few years—drunks, divorces, property disputes—

Bob had honed most of his practice to personal injury cases, worker's compensation, and, of course, disputes with railroads.

Among the stories Bob liked to tell and retell, the tale of the Bluetick Hound remained salient. Back in those days a much younger Bob was certain that his children would not face animal situations of any kind if they entered the field of law. Intelligent as he was, Bob's prescience was not his strong suit. In her years as an attorney, brief as they were, Jessica had already encountered animal disputes and interventions even though she represented a big city firm. She suspected that there would be more.

To steer her mind away from her nausea, Jessica fondly remembered the Case of the Bluetick Hound. Apparently, and her dad was inclined to embellish, two farmers from Crawford County disputed ownership of an expensive hunting dog. Formally named the Bluetick Coonhound—Rockwell, as Farmer One called him, and, Sherman, as Farmer Two called him—lived a sketchy history. Joyously scampering between the adjacent farms, Rockwell/Sherman successfully impregnated several receptive female canines owned by unsuspecting Farmers One and Two. Both men believed that they were entitled to ownership of Rockwell/Sherman.

The dog had become a valuable asset, an intelligent hunting dog with a soft mouth. This meant that Rockwell/Sherman spotted birds, retrieving them without crushing the bones of the prey. Many hunters had at one time or another owned dogs that, once they tasted blood, were of no value in the field. Bob had heard Farmer One's tale of a previous Springer Spaniel that, although handsome, was worthless as far as hunting. Retraining attempts, wrapping barbed wire around a corncob, only annoyed the dog but did not teach the intended lesson.

True, Farmer One fed and trained Rockwell, but Farmer Two had rescued Sherman when the feckless creature had had the misfortune of racing down a county road toward love. Like all dogs, Sherman thought in the present; that did not include cars. He suffered a broken leg. Farmer Two paid for the operation to set the leg, fed Sherman, and believed that because of this expensive act of kindness, he should have custody of the dog. Besides, as recovery satisfactorily progressed, Shermie felt the urge to celebrate. Two more-than-willing female dogs in Farmer Two's barnyard happily responded; pups followed, and both farmers wanted the offspring as well.

Rockie/Shermie was a gold mine! Not only did he fetch and retrieve, he successfully procreated. With no effort on either farmer's part, a dynasty of Bluetick Coonhounds was born. Unfortunately for Farmer Two, Farmer One had papers proving Rockwell's heritage; both sire and dame were purebreds. The pups born in Farmer Two's barn to a yellow lab named Shasta were not purebred. They did, however, have the potential to be coveted hunting dogs. Pups born to a second dog, Angela, who appeared to Farmer Two to be a Bluetick Coonhound, could very well have been purebreds. Farmer Two had access, he was pretty sure, to papers at his son-in-law's. Where son-in-law resided currently could be a problem, but Farmer Two with time could solve it.

First-year attorney for Farmer One entered the dispute about midcrisis. Mediation proved unsuccessful to all parties, so a trial was scheduled and took place. Although Robert Woods, attorney for Farmer One, had considered all aspects of the case, he had not foreseen Farmer One's next move. The day of the trial Farmer One was late. Attired uncomfortably in a somewhat ill-fitting suit, Farmer Two had arrived thirty minutes ahead of time.

There were no cell phones in those days. Young Bob was nervous; where in the hell was his client? The judge certainly wondered. Farmer Two smirked; attorney for Farmer Two shuffled papers. What next? Close enough to being right on time in his own mind, in strolled Farmer One, dirty coveralls, muddy boots, the undeniable smell of pig wafting off him. With him, on a leash, was Rockwell.

"Shall we begin?" the judge drolly asked, neither expecting nor receiving an answer. It was an order.

The quick thinking attorney for Farmer Two requested to approach the bench. "Your Honor, there is one witness, which I had not anticipated. With your permission, may I call him at the appropriate time?" The judge granted approval.

Jessica knew the outcome; she had heard it many, many times. Attorney for Farmer Two called Sherman to the stand along with the disputing farmer.

"Raise your right hand," the bailiff stated. Both dog and man raised a paw/hand. The judge, whose lack of humor had resulted in the epithet of Sober Sides, convulsed into outright laughter; Bob put his head on the table. Attorney for Farmer Two stood motionless.

Jessica's dad was somewhat vague about who received final custody of Rockwell/Sherman. In the end, he recalled, the warring farmers reached some kind of agreement. Farmer Two's itinerant son-in-law returned, divorced his then wife, and started dating Farmer One's newly widowed fairly attractive daughter. Bob was paid eventually, partially in venison from deer that had dined on Farmer Two's soybeans and partially in cash from the sale of Rockwell/Sherman's offspring.

Jessica's chiming cell phone interrupted her reveries. It was her brother Rob. Now what?

Robbie. God, as the years progressed, her brother's physical and mental traits continued to be devolved from both his father, Alex's dad, and Alexandra herself. Alex would observe that her son's personality and demeanor were both syncretic and oxymoronic. *Moronic* was more like it, Jessica reflected, on one of Rob's particularly bad days. If her dad were still alive, Rob would now be taller than he, at six feet five inches. He was slimmer too, than Bob, about 165 pounds. His grief over the sudden loss of Bob had affected her brother's weight, but time brought healing too. As Robbie's good health and better moods returned, so did his appetite. Once again, Robbie liked to eat.

He had a beautiful smile, thanks to Bob's great teeth, but the smile itself, that was Alex's dad: quick, a person wondered if it was forced. But, as Robbie yelled at Jessica when their mother posed the two for photographs, "That's *my* smile!" Robbie, Jessica too for that matter, owed his thick blond hair to their mother's genes. Jessica, Alex, and most of Robbie's female friends wished he cut his shoulder length hair more often than he did. Still, on Robbie Jess guessed you could term the look *sexy*.

"I like to keep it that way, so that when I walk into an office, people think I'm a hick from the country, a guy who doesn't know much," Rob countered. "Then I ambush them with my skills and knowledge." To look at Robbie as he entered a room, people like Alex who had known Bob Woods before he died sometimes, sometimes caught themselves believing even as they knew it was impossible, that Robert Woods, attorney at law, had returned. Rob carried himself just as his father had.

On a good day, as Robbie overcame his grief, on a good day Robbie exuded enthusiasm and joy. On what Jessica and Alex termed a bad day, Robbie could be a jerk. Still, what sister didn't surmise that about a brother at times. Robbie probably tossed a comparable term out for her as well, in the feminine gender so to speak.

As for the brilliant mind, he had inherited that from his dad, along with the good teeth and the height. However, this same mind crafted a personality that could be, could be arrogant. Come to think of it, Jess guessed that arrogance made him successful too. Walk into a room, meet a client, ignore the mistakes, the pitfalls. He was good at that.

"Hey," he greeted his sister, "I owe three hundred dollars to Verizon. Can you put some money from Dad's estate into my account, just until I can pay you back?" Robbie liked to refer to himself as a guy living on the edge; one who took risks, which always worked out in the end. Borrowing money from his sister did not fall into the same category as asking his mother for money. His dad might have paid Rob's bills, pontificating on the boy's lack of responsibility, but Bob would have paid them. Now Bob had been dead for more than four years; Rob was being retrained. A corncob wrapped in barbed wire never worked for Farmer One's Springer, but Jessica idly wondered if a barbed vegetable down the throat of a sometimes impecunious sibling might teach a lesson. Mean thoughts. Her brother paid his bills; Jess just didn't feel charitable.

"Dad's estate is closed. You know that. Why do you owe Verizon so much? I gave you two hundred dollars last month for what you said was your phone bill."

"I broke a filling, Jess. Come on. You know the dentist wants his money up front now. I was in pain." Her brother sounded as if he might cry. Jessica visited the same dentist who, for all her fillings, crowns, and root canals allowed her to make monthly payments. Rob must have fallen behind with the dentist as well as with the phone company.

"What happened to the reimbursement check you got from the insurance company?" Jessica distinctly remembered pressuring her brother's insurance agent and then Brogdorf agency for a collision that most likely was Rob's fault but, thanks to Jess, was eventually construed as weather related. Sometimes January blizzards were heaven sent.

"Never mind. I'll handle it myself." Without the courtesy of a goodbye, Rob silenced his phone.

"Way to start the weekend," a self-chastised Jess reflected as she neared the main intersection in Bucyrus. "A hangover, one mad client, a case that might never end, and a fight with my brother. Good job, Jess." Just then she looked into her rearview mirror to see the bright red and blue swirling lights of a police car. She pulled into a convenience store lot, rolled down her window, waiting.

"Good morning," a Bucyrus police officer greeted her. "Are you aware that you were driving through the center of our city?"

"Good morning, Officer. Yes, I am driving through Bucyrus." Jessica's heart beat too quickly; her palms sweat.

"The speed limit is 35 miles per hour. May I see your driver's license?"

Jessica hoped the officer did not recognize her Coach bag and wallet for what they were. If he did, he would know how much she paid, several times over what a speeding ticket exacted. Maybe he figured the bag and wallet were knockoffs. A young woman in an older Acura with a bashed in left fender most likely could not afford designer accessories. She waited quietly as the policeman returned to his vehicle, lights still flashing, to check her license. Jess's cell phone chimed: her brother again, probably to apologize. She wisely decided talking on her phone while being called over by law enforcement would only make matters worse. She let voice mail take the message.

"Here you are, Ms. Woods." The policeman remained respect-fully polite as he returned her license. "I'm giving you a warning this time. Sixty in a thirty-five zone is a little fast. Try to slow it down next time."

"I will, Officer. Thank you." She glanced at the yellow warning slip before jamming it into her purse: 43 in a 35 zone, good weather, good road conditions. Her quizzical expression invited further com-ments. It was hard to read the scrawled signature, something like Frederick Howell or Howard Jr.

"Ms. Woods, I grew up in Wyandot County. Some friends and I got into a little trouble back in high school, your father helped me out. It was a long time ago, but I haven't forgotten. He did an obnox-ious kid a real favor. I'm here today in law enforcement when at that time in my life, no one, most of all my family, held out much hope for me or my future." He paused, reflecting, Jessica thought, on what might have been. "I'm returning the favor, a bit late, but consider it a debt paid." The officer straightened up, nodded his head, apparently ending the discussion.

"Well," Jessica nodded back in acknowledgement, "thank you again." She was shaken as she always was when another insight into her father's past emanated.

"Oh, Ms. Woods, one more thing before you go on your way." The officer's additional comment surprised her. "When you inter-view clients, you might want to take note of the effects of the sur-roundings. The smell of alcohol can permeate the clothes of a lawyer as well as a client. Just be cautious."

Jessica tried to maintain a noncommittal look. "I certainly will, Officer. And again, thank you."

Jessica's mornings had certainly gone much better than this one. Still, vicissitudes comprised her days and weeks, common, she assumed, for young female attorneys. Returning to North Sandusky Street and out of town toward Columbus, she traveled the familiar roads of Northwest/Central Ohio.

Jessica rather enjoyed the two-and-a-half-or-more-hour drive from her cottage to Columbus. Bucyrus on Route 4 marked a distance of approximately halfway. In town Route 4 became North Sandusky

Street, but out in the country the road connected Sandusky on Lake Erie to Springfield near Dayton. Fischer's Beach lay about fifteen minutes off Route 4.

Years ago someone had cut down peach orchards and in order to develop a resort, complete with a marina, dance hall, and skating rink. By the 1950s a small community of second homes arose, although the term *cottages* was more appropriate. Even back then people from Tiffin, Upper Sandusky, and Marion realized the opportunities that a nearby vacation home on Lake Erie offered.

Most folks' dreams were modest: a two-bedroom, one-bath ranch, no heat or air conditioning back then, worked just fine. Eventually some husbands, most likely with strong encouragement from their wives, added propane heaters. A few of the wealthier families even stuck window air conditioners in. It was a cottage like this that Jessica and her brother had inherited. With Bob's death Jessica eventually assumed the deed for the property; Rob got the house outside of Upper Sandusky. What he did with the sprawling contemporary home in Wyandot County was his business. Jessica enjoyed the peace that her cottage brought her; she retreated there as often as her schedule allowed, which was never enough. Now with a boyfriend and a business, she needed time to relax as well, time to think.

Jessica and Rob were native Ohioans, Buckeyes, as residents of the state were often termed. To be honest, she and her brother liked where they lived. Right after Bob died, both siblings talked about moving; Jess to Colorado, Robbie to Florida. That was only talk. Jessica had taken the Ohio bar exam the first time; she and Rob waited for the results which, unfortunately, came in as failing. In the summer following her father's death, she studied even harder, took the exam on the second round, this time passing. No, moving to Colorado with the boyfriend of the moment would be a mistake. As for Rob, he needed time to heal and to grieve, time in the home where his father had lived, time to remember.

Jessica's work as a fledgling attorney took her farther and farther into her native state. Counties she had seen on road maps became places with county seats and people. Judges presided in courtrooms;

recorders in courthouses provided documents; attorneys protected their clients and filed briefs. So Ohio it was for Jessica.

In the past, describing her state to her college friends from the East required rhetoric that would keep their interest. That meant leaving out the glacier era, which had caused the formation of the Great Lakes and skipping directly to "the lake," as it was termed by most people. Actually, "the lake" was Lake Erie, one of the five lakes formed when the glacier retreated ten thousand years ago at the end of last ice age. Gifts from that long ago era provided Ohio with rich soil for farming, salt, coal, rivers, and streams.

However, the glacier did not descend completely down into what would be Ohio. Designated the Unglaciated Plateau by geologists, this area of Southeastern Ohio included the counties of Belmont, Hocking, Athens, Washington, and Logan. Because millions of tons of ice had not ground out or flattened land in this part of the state, the hills and valleys of what would be part of Appalachia remained. As a college student at Miami University, Jessica became familiar with the Hocking Hills area where she camped, hiked, and canoed with friends. Trails, waterfalls, striking rock formations, and caves sharply contrasted with the lake where she and her family had vacationed. As Jessica experienced more and more of the career she had chosen, she knew too that Southeastern Ohio was also the poorest of the state's economic regions. The region contained few large cities. Mostly scattered rural communities, many impoverished, lay sprinkled among the hills.

Jessica's firm required that she meet clients often at their homes. Driving south to Morgan or Muskingum or Jackson Counties cemented the sympathies she already felt for Ohio's poor. Down here people broke the law too, but they were not like many of the scofflaws she encountered in wealthier towns and cities. These people usually had no other choices; moonshining and heroin brought income to families desperate for food.

Well, today she was not in Southeastern Ohio. Where she was driving on Route 98 south, off Route 4, led in about one hour to Route 23, then into Columbus. Luck and a fortunate connection from the past, thanks to her father, had kept yet another speeding ticket out of her driving record. A few reminders, her mother called them driving lessons, from the Ohio Highway Patrol coupled with greetings from the Marion and Delaware County sheriffs among others had added difficulties with insurance companies, but that would not be today.

Jess's cell phone chimed, her brother again. "Jess, I'm sorry. I'm just stressed. My tooth ached for a week. I couldn't stand it anymore. I had some other bills. Look, just put the money in my account or meet me. You know I'll pay you back. I need my phone for business."

Jessica sighed. Her brother, whatever phase in life he embraced, had a good heart. "Okay, but you have got to pay me back. I cannot keep you afloat while your investment company or financial advice corporation or whatever the hell you term it finds a cruising speed."

"Nice metaphor, Jess. Thanks. Hey, you coming back from the lake?" Rob did not miss much where his sister was concerned. Older than she by three years, he voluntarily assumed a stance between father and big brother. At least as brother and sister they balanced each other, willing to admit it or not.

"I'll transfer two hundred dollars into your account when I get back to the office. Right now I'm running late to a pretrial."

"Thanks again, Jess. Say hi to Max for me."

Before turning onto Route 23 south for Columbus, Jessica realized how hungry she was. She had enough time for breakfast, lunch, something, as the hangover seemed to be dissipating. Texting Max a greeting to keep his chin up and his speed down, she pulled into a mom-and-pop dairy bar outside Waldo. Across the street and down one block, the famous G&R Tavern offered thick fried bologna sandwiches with mayonnaise, onions, and pickles. People traveling between central Ohio and the lake frequently stopped there as well as locals from Marion and the adjacent Delaware County. By this time in the late morning, the restaurant would be open for early lunches, but Jessica was a vegetarian, had been since her senior year in high school.

Peering through the tiny screen window at the dairy bar, she ordered. "A BLT please without the bacon. And water please." God, another wave of nausea hit her. An involuntary retch escaped.

The attendant, a man in his fifties, probably the owner, took the order but asked with some concern, "Are you feeling all right, Miss?"

"Morning sickness."

"My wife had that with our second child. She was miserable. I'll fix you up."

Jessica sat down to wait on a granite rock someone had placed on the corner of the graveled lot in a common sense approach to keep cars from cutting across the parking area. It was nearly noon. She had hoped to be closer to Columbus by now, but the little encounter with the Bucyrus police officer had intervened. Looking across the street, she watched a robin feed its young. Daffodils bloomed in the yard of the two-story frame house. Up at the lake, spring followed about a week after Upper Sandusky and two weeks after Columbus. Lake Erie acted like an air conditioner in the spring and a space heater in the fall.

Similar to that robin, Jessica mused, she could be feeding her young in the nest she and her mate had built. Life certainly brought changes. She and the mate everyone expected her to marry parted ways during law school. True, she had Max, but that was only recently. Who knew where their lives would be this summer let alone in a year or two?

The owner called out from the screened window. "Your order is ready."

Jessica thanked the man, retrieved her lunch, and got back into her car. She was so hungry she tore the white wrapper off, bit into the sandwich, and stopped before she swallowed. Something smelled horrible: bacon grease. "Oh, help me get away from here before I vomit," she prayed. The poor old guy thought he was doing her a favor by adding meat; instead, he made her sick. She got as far as the stop sign, opened the door, and threw up. So much for lunch.

Her cell phone chimed again. Lil. "You had better call this guy." The assistant must have called from the back office to avoid the far too interested Woolseys.

"What's up?"

"He says he got our number from the last TV commercial and needs to see you ASAP. He mentioned a liquor license, the state, wanting to open a restaurant, and a family history in moonshine." Lil paused. "Sounds fun," she added.

"Can't it wait until I get to the office?"

"I suppose so." Lil's voice dropped to a whisper. "Clara is driving me crazy! I had to get away from her! Are you close?"

"Close enough. I'm halfway there, Waldo. Get Clara some more herb tea, flirt a little with Mel, tell them I'll be there as soon as I can. They're an hour early anyway for Pete sakes. They ought to be a little understanding."

"Mel is, Clara isn't." Silence from Lilly. Then, "Oh, my God, I've got to go. Mel is making moves about getting up. He's started to rattle the walker. That means he's headed to the bathroom!" Silence. "Clara's already in the bathroom. Shit! I'm going to have to help him!"

"Don't let him fall, Lil! Triple O won't like that at all. A client falling in our office." Jess sounded every bit the boss here. Stern, visionary. She was in charge now even from her car fifty miles away.

Lil's confident riposte: "You're the woman. No falls here." She echoed her boss's sentiment. "Gotta run. See you soon."

In less than an hour Jessica drove from rural areas to city, passing wealthy farms, a university, urban sprawl, and into Columbus. Wyandot County, where Jess still kept her dad's office, for tax reasons she had been advised, was where Jessica grew up. Bob's office lay one block from the county courthouse in Upper Sandusky, a city of 6,600 souls surrounded on the outskirts by rich farmland. When Jess's parents married and her mother moved from Haines Landing to the city, some people in rural areas still used outhouses. That practice disappeared over the years, but occasionally on back roads an experienced eye could still discern abandoned out buildings that served practical purposes. Some farms too had been abandoned as the owners aged, their children preferring less arduous work.

Jessica had been told that farming was in your blood or it was not. A few of those farmers had sold some of the land adjacent to the road to gas stations or chain restaurants. A McDonald's stood just off Route 53 where Holstein cows used to graze. Probably the same farmer who sold the field still returned to what was once his property, this time to sit with old friends, drink coffee, and be congratulated on getting out of farming. It was rough work, thankless too. A man could plant his soybeans, *beanies* old timers called them, over the summer, watch his crop mature to a field of low lying beauty, and then after a storm of a few minutes be ruined by hail or drought. Crop insurance paid, but the damage to the soul over the years cost a man more than could be compensated by a check. Many farmers drank, secret alcoholics. Many divorced. The rural life the media portrayed was not what Jessica and her father in their practices knew it to be.

People died too or were maimed in farming accidents of one kind or another. They also killed each over property. Another case reached back into decades long before Jessica was born or, for that that matter, before Bob entered college. As Wyandot County prosecuting attorney, Bob's father entered the case at the beginning. Years later, Bob served as executor for one of the estates. Within the practice of law, as with life, nothing is simple. A newspaper editor friend of Bob's used to wryly comment, "It's not about the money." The editor usually paused to allow his listeners to reflect, *cogitate* he called it. The editor then dryly continued, "It's about the *amount* of money." Such was one of the most shocking cases in the history of Wyandot County. People now in their seventies still sadly mulled over the events that long ago summer of Two Sheep Farmers and a Murder.

In the late 1960s sheep farming in Wyandot County was a more viable industry than it is now. The Buckeye Sheep Association, organized in 1949, had just changed its name to the Ohio Sheep Improvement Association. Two men, Bill Whitaker and Fred Howard, owned adjacent sheep farms on the western edge of the county. Instrumental in the reorganization of the professional association, both men served as officers of the group as well as usually friendly rivals. Although sheep were their main income, the two men both also raised field corn, soybeans, and winter wheat. But their love, one might term it their *passion* in the next millennium, was sheep.

At the time of the murder both men were in their early forties: strong, not particularly even tempered, but well liked in the community. Second generation they were; their parents had emigrated from the Old Country. Within the Ohio Sheep Improvement Association, both men served as trustees; both were reasonably expected to continue farther up the ladder to president.

However, one farmer, Bill Whitaker, harbored a long standing jealousy of his neighbor, Fred Howard. With time, the heat of the summer, the long hours and built in hazards of farming, this jealousy crept stealthily into Bill's psyche, eventually overcoming his common sense and decency. Actions, peccadillos Bill never would have performed against his neighbor, became routine. A missing newspaper here, a letter or two occasionally pilfered from the mailbox that stood across the road next to his. These little things scarcely mattered.

As for Fred, well, actions spoke louder than words. The sports section missing from the paper, his neighbor's mailbox accidentally backed into during harvest. My God, that combine had a mind of its own! Middle-of-the-night phone calls, hang ups with no one on the other end happened to both men during lambing. These were surely coincidental. Neither Fred nor Bill could understand how one problem after another kept happening. Occasionally, one or the other of the men let his moldboard plow make an overlapping pass into the other fellow's field. Farmers did it all the time; it wasn't a problem, was it?

Back down by the stream that separated his property from the farmer's to the south, Bill cut some brush. He was not paying much attention, although he should have. The young black walnuts he clear cut to the west, on Fred's property, would grow back soon enough. Mistakes, all of them.

These minor problems, and minor they were if one considered the tempers of both men, might have dwindled through entropy during the winter. Essentially, both Fred and Bill were good men, but money has a way of bringing out the worst in people, especially when two neighbors sell similar parcels at disparate amounts.

Jessica was many years from being born, but the way her father told it, a group from the newly formed Wyandot Golf and Country Club offered to purchase ten acres each from both Whitaker Farms and Howard and Sons Farms. A creek that eventually fed into the

Sandusky River ran behind both men's properties; the acreage the golf course hoped to purchase would provide a beautiful setting for what frequent golfers would refer to as the Back Nine. Not only that, but a friendly competitor, Eagles Bend in Crawford County to the north, possessed a water hole or two but no stream. Oh, the acquisition promised to be a profitable one for all parties.

Mr. Frederick Howard, ignoring his wife's suggestions, listened to the advice of his attorney and agreed to the settlement; Mr. William Whitaker, ignoring the advice of his attorney, chose to follow the advice of his wife. He held out for a larger sum, considerably larger. Howard and Sons Farms sold ten acres in 1965 to Wyandot Golf and Country Club, Inc. for one thousand dollars per acre. Farming being what it was, Fred knew that plans to bring water from the stream at the back of his farm to irrigate his crops in case of a drought would not come to fruition. Most farmers, except for a few, understood that once expensive irrigation equipment was put into place for a summer drought, the weather man brought rain for the next five years. Fred really didn't miss the parcel; he hunted at his cousin's about a mile down the road most of the time anyway.

With half of the money received from the sale, he accomplished three goals. First, he paid for the four-row planter and most of the drill he had bought from Wyandot Implements a year before. Second, he and his wife Ruth traveled to Columbus one afternoon in October where—and this was his wife's goal more than his—he bought his spouse a mink stole, *autumn haze* they called it. Finally, he invested the remainder with his high school friend and classmate Myron Steinhauser at the Edward D. Jones office in Upper Sandusky for "when times got tough," then forgot about it. Meanwhile, Bill Whitaker held on to his property, certain that those rich folks at the country club would come around. They needed his ten acres, of that he was sure.

Intermittent conflicts, you certainly couldn't call them wars, continued over the next winter, one of those in central Ohio, which recorded record snowfalls for the season. As with their neighbors in town, farmers, Bill and Fred included, often plowed each other's driveways. The in town folks, unfamiliar with how farmers occupied themselves in the winter, naively believed that their rural cousins spent the long months between harvest and planting working on equipment. It would be unfair to say that farmers promulgated this disingenuous myth; they simply did not correct their urban relatives. Wives could tell you differently, but in the 1960s most farmers' wives remained silent, occupying themselves with raising children and doing good works with church activities. Only among their very close friends did a few of these same wives even hint at husbands' alcoholism. The term *domestic abuse* had also not entered American vocabulary yet.

On one of those wintry mornings following a two-day blizzard, Fred Howard, in a gesture entirely designed to show forgiveness, to mend fences so to speak, drove his Ferguson, snowplow attached, over to Bill's. To be fair, it was cold, bitter cold, at ten degrees with a wind blowing from the east. There was no term for wind-chill factor back then, but it sure as hell felt colder than ten degrees. During one of those moments when the wind shifted, blowing across sleeping fields of harvested corn, snow flurries blinded Fred. He backed up the tractor, but too much, right into Althea's Ford. Why Bill's wife parked her car in the driveway when she usually used the little barn as a garage was a mystery. But dent the front end Fred did. Venomously shouting with the fervor Jack Daniels fuels, Bill shot out of the big barn. Carrying a pie basket of goods for the church bake sale, a screaming crying Althea hurtled out of the farmhouse mud room. In the end, Fred used cash from the wheat account to pay for repairs. He and Bill grabbed a nip or two from the bottle in Bill's barn, shook hands, and dismissed the incident. That is, in Fred's mind, not Althea's or Bill's.

By Easter, Ruth continued to wear her mink stole to church services; Althea drove her not-so-brand-new Ford to the Sarah's Helpers Ladies' Auxiliary, which met in the Methodist Church basement. The two women worked together companionably enough for funeral luncheons. Christian women, both farm wives tried their best to forgive and forget.

With spring Bill anticipated the sale of his ten acres to Wyandot Golf and Country Club, Inc. Unfortunately, the investors, mostly

Wyandot Countians along with two from Delaware County, had suffered vicissitudes themselves over the long winter. The wife of one
of the financial backers from Delaware had fallen in love with one
of the Wyandot investors. It happens. Why the two lovebirds had
nested right on the outskirts of the county seat of Delaware County
in the Circle K Motel along Route 23 was a mystery, not to mention
a terrible mistake. An impending blizzard had curtailed plans to meet
in their usual location in Worthington. Althea's cousin worked the
motel desk that afternoon, whispering about a clandestine tryst to a
friend at church choir practice the next evening.

A divorce would have happened anyway. However, the super-
cilious matter of the Circle K impacted the purchase of Whitaker
Farms' ten acres. Delaware Investor One deemed it prudent to hold
on to his assets including his money, just in case. Wyandot Investor
Five refused to participate, citing unanticipated health problems. As
they used to say back in the 60's, the Scandal of the Circle K queered
the deal. For Bill that meant no sale. Largely forgotten, Fred's investments with Edward D. Jones, with Myron Steinhauser carefully
monitoring them, continued to grow.

As sometimes occurs in Ohio, summers following harsh winters
try to make up the temperature difference by supplying record heat
waves. Thus, July of that year brought periods of drought with the
thermometer on the north side of Fred's barn spiking to 100 degrees.
He should not have sold the back acres; he could have pumped water
from the stream for his beans. Dammit anyway; he should have listened to the voice of his common sense. Why the hell did Ruth need
a mink stole in the summer? She could only wear it half a year at best.

Mid July, too, was the annual convention of the Ohio Sheep
Improvement Association in Haines Landing. Board members Bill
and Fred planned to drive the seventy miles north together, to save
on gas mainly. They could certainly get along in the car for the hour
or so it took to get to Camp Perry where the meetings would be
held. About a week before the anticipated trip, Bill took his evening
walk down to the woods by the stream. Out of habit he carried his
shotgun. A few shots here and there at doves or blackbirds never hurt
a guy who wanted to blow off a little steam at the end of a long day.

Besides, later on he could clean a few doves, quite a few, for Althea's and his dinner the next day.

Another record heat wave, miserable sheep, soybeans drying in the fields waiting for rain. Bill reached the woods, looking once more at what remained of his neighbor's beloved black walnut trees. Maybe he had made a mistake. Stumps, jagged, a few little shoots barely two inches long with a couple of leaves trying bravely to recover. At the same time Fred happened to wander onto the five acres that no longer belonged to him. This kind of weather brought back memories, reflections of days and evenings in the woods, a haven he could no longer call his own. It just wasn't the same. The Wyandot Golf and Country Club would clear the woods. No deer would nestle among piles of dry oak leaves; the eagle's nest he had told no one about would be gone with the felled trees. Wealthy golfers in their madras shorts would curse the stream where he used to fish. Nausea followed by tears of regret overcame him. He did not know of the botched deal; Bill in his shame had not bothered to tell his neighbor.

A gun, two neighbors, heat, farming. Who would ever know what started the argument? Both men were hot tempered, Bill more than Fred everyone agreed afterward. Why Bill raised the shotgun, why he fired at his friend/rival's arm and missed, why he killed him instead, no one fathomed. When asked about it afterward he told the arresting officer, "I just wanted to tickle the guy. I didn't want to kill him." Some tickle. Leaving his bloodied neighbor lifeless among piles of oak leaves, Bill trudged back to his home, used the phone in the barn to call the sheriff, and waited in the silence for his future to unfold.

A brief trial followed in the Wyandot County Courthouse. Prosecuting attorney, Jessica's grandfather, convinced the jury that the actions of Mr. William Whitaker were intentional. Bill was sentenced to life in prison. Out of compassion, the judge chose Marion Correctional Institute in the next county for the incarceration. Althea could visit regularly; she did not. Bill played basketball with the other MCI prisoners: rapists, murderers, thieves. He was, after all, only in his early forties: strong and healthy. Eventually his wife divorced him, sold the farm, and moved into Upper Sandusky where their children could walk to school instead of riding the bus. Because of the scandal she lost heart to participate in her ladies' auxiliary. She saw Ruth sometimes in her neighbor's regular pew in the Methodist Church but not much.

Ruth tried to keep the farm going, but without a husband it became more and more difficult. She sheared sheep, combined, drove the tractor, all the tasks she had performed alongside her husband. It just was not the same, even with hired hands. Occasionally, after a few years as the boys played basketball on the second floor of the barn where Fred had installed a hoop, she walked down to the woods by the stream where it all happened. She gazed at the nests where deer still slept during the day, nocturnal creatures. She looked across to her neighbor's, then at walnut trees that slowly grew despite the awful clear cutting a few years before. She cried, no, she fell to the ground screaming in grief. After one too many of these horrible episodes, Ruth returned to the farmhouse, called a realtor, and listed the farm. What remained of the family moved into town, a few blocks from Althea.

Without a father to restrain Fred and Ruth's sons at a time when most couples remained together, both boys got into difficulties other kids avoided. Late on a Saturday night an Upper Sandusky police officer knocked on Ruth's door. Freddie Junior was being held at the station for underage drinking, driving while intoxicated, and speeding. Would Mrs. Howard please meet her son there? Shaken, she still had the presence of mind to call her attorney first, Jessica's father.

Fortunately, in those days law enforcement officers tended to overlook intoxicated lawyers, particularly when those attorneys visited clients late on weekend nights. Alexandra brewed Bob, fresh from passing the bar, but not from passing Holenborg's Dew Drop Inn, better known as the Dew Drop, a cup of coffee. He carefully navigated a few blocks to the jail, where he arranged for Freddie to go home with his mother. Monday morning Bob met the prosecutor, asked for a reduced sentence due to the family history, and got it. Frederick Howard, Jr. worked three days a week after school and all the following summer months without pay for Wyandot County. He hadn't learned to run a tractor on his farm; he was too little when his dad died. But he learned on the county road crew. A couple of the men taught him how to drive too, on the rural roads past fields of winter wheat, popcorn, and soybeans. Not particularly bright but somewhat attentive, sheep placidly gazed at what looked like a big rabbit hopping machine as Freddie tentatively shifted gears in the county dump truck. Left foot pressed on the clutch, right foot off, hand executing the iconic H, the teenager learned to drive.

He managed to graduate from Upper Sandusky High School, but no one, especially his teachers, could recall that he had earned much above a *C* in most classes. Frederick Howard, Jr. along with the rest of the boys in his class, registered for the draft. With the war in Vietnam, Fred's low draft number qualified him for what his friends called Hanoi University. Upon graduating from boot camp, the US Army asked him what job he would like. He replied that he preferred office work; they gave him infantry. As everybody who ever worked for their Uncle knew, you ask for one, *They* put you in another.

For some reason, and Ruth related this to Sarah's Helpers more than once, God took care of her oldest son. After six months in Vietnam Corporal Frederick Howard Jr. was sent back to the United States, subsequently transferring to the Military Police. Hardly office work but definitely not stuck in the jungle. He had some familiarity, he told the US Army, with law enforcement; those summers of driving everything for Wyandot County from dump trucks to garbage trucks to front end loaders qualified him to drive for Uncle Sam. After what his mother's friends referred to as a false start in high school, Fred made his mother proud. Honorably discharged, he returned home, where he enjoyed a long distinguished career as a police officer.

Her oldest son having settled into a respectable life, her other boys married and farming, Ruth lived quietly on into a respectable old age in her white two-story frame home in town. Myron Steinhauser had invested the funds from her husband's sale of those ten acres well. Ruth didn't need much; money from the interest along with a few thousand dollars each year more than provided for her needs. For Christmas Eve services and Easter, if it was late, she pulled her autumn haze mink stole out from the closet, draped it over her shoulders, and walked a block to church with her family. How well she knew the cost of the fur that long ago time when Wyandot Golf and Country Club, Inc. changed the Howards' lives forever.

At the age of eighty-five after a Wednesday night prayer service, Ruth returned home, sat down in her recliner to watch the news, and died. As part of his usual morning route, Chief Frederick Howard stopped in at his mother's where he found her, peacefully asleep, a smile on her beloved face. After the funeral he called the family attorney, Robert Woods. Although circuitous circumstances sometimes impacted the time it took to settle estates, this one was easy. The Howard brothers didn't quarrel; the estate closed within a year.

With his inheritance Fred could have retired, but his wife had made it clear she did not want him around the house. Besides, she drove him nuts. If she had not died of a heart attack the next year, he might still be writing tickets in Upper Sandusky. Life, as Chief Howard understood it, had a way of intervening. A widow from Bucyrus, Diane Mulchasa, chose the wrong time, *right time* she called it, for a fender bender in front of the restaurant where she and her sister had enjoyed lunch. Life being short, Fred and Diane married in a quiet civil ceremony within three months of meeting.

Fred retired from the Upper Sandusky Police Department to move to Bucyrus where Diane's friendly yellow lab welcomed him to the three-bedroom brick ranch with attached garage a few blocks from the center of town. Still a relatively young man, Fred busied himself converting a screened in porch to a family room. He purchased a brand new La-Z-Boy for his wife, surprising her one afternoon by placing that and the recliner he had held on to from his mother's home in front of the new television he had received delivery on that morning. Diane's recliner stayed as did the television. *Mom's chair* as the new Mrs. Howard politely termed it to her husband, *that wreck of a chair* to her friends, had to go.

Come spring Fred planted a garden. Beyond mowing and pulling weeds, after reading *USA Today* and the *Columbus Dispatch*, there was not much else to do. With his wife at work, Fred's day yawned before him.

Over a cup of coffee with some new friends, he learned of a part-time position with the Bucyrus Police Department, the BPD. *Why not?* he thought. Diane still had that part-time job three days a week; he might as well jump back into the game too. His friends called it chasing speeders; he called it heaven.

Dropping her reveries, Jessica sped toward Columbus and the waiting Woolseys. A lurking highway patrol car sitting in the Walmart parking lot on the south side of Delaware brought her back to her senses and the reminder of a near miss with another speeding ticket. The chat with the BPD coupled with the now tossed lunch in Waldo had cost her time. She had better call Lil for that number of the man who seemed to desperately want a liquor license.

Dammit! Her cell phone dropped, gliding under the seat. With one hand on the steering wheel and the other under the driver's seat, she retrieved her phone. Reaching into her purse, she pulled a pencil out along with some paper. Yellow. The warning ticket from her new friend in Bucyrus. Well, she could write the liquor license client's number on that as well as on anything else. Jess glanced at the scrawled signature on the bottom of the ticket. Years of reading her dad's train wreck of a signature had schooled her in deciphering most people's handwriting. She looked again at the name on the ticket: Officer Frederick Howard. *You might,* Jessica thought, *yes, you might just know.* She smiled.

Jess punched the contact number for her office. "Hey, Hon, can you give me the number of the liquor license guy?"

"Certainly, Ms. Woods." The Woolseys must have graduated from the categories of minor distractants to serious annoyances. From Lil's laconic reply, Jessica understood it was cocktail hour after work that night with attorney of record buying personal assistant's choice for as long as personal assistant preferred to accompany employer. So much for Jess going home to bed right after work, hangover or not. Silence. Jess waited for Lil's text. Jessica was certain Clara's hearing rivaled that of an owl; despite Mel's trouble with his walker, he had a hawk's eyesight. Yes, texting was the best communication, all things considered.

Leonard Warren, 213 W. Liberty Street, Canal Winchester, Ohio, let his landline ring so long Jessica considered that she had the wrong number. Then, a self-assured voice with only the hint of a Southern accent responded. "Yeah. This is Len Warren."

"Mr. Warren, this is Jessica Woods from O'Malley, O'Malley, and O'Malley. You had called our office."

"Yes, yes, I just love talking to lawyers. You know, you can always tell the honest ones from the dishonest ones." Jessica had heard the Mark Twain joke so many times she waited in silence for the tag line. Here it was from a potential client who already annoyed her. "They're the guys with their hands in their own pockets."

"Mr. Warren, my secretary said you had called about obtaining a liquor license. Have you had difficulty doing so?"

"Difficulty?" She thought she heard him spit something that she did not want to think about as far as the consistency. "Those bastards at the state don't want an honest man to do business around here!"

"I can have my assistant set up an appointment for you."

"You need to come down here. See the arrangement. Get an idea of what's going on." Jess's firm encouraged her to drive to clients, a practice she neither liked nor disliked; it brought a degree of personal service that most attorneys avoided. Realistically, driving all over Central Ohio cost time and money, which usually resulted in the clients paying for it. Nevertheless, Jess did what she was told both by clients and by Triple O. Anything to please.

"All right. I'll have my assistant Lilly arrange a time next week that is convenient for you. Is there any particular day you prefer?" Jess knew the answer already. Monday, the busiest day of the week.

"Oh, any day really. Well, Monday. Yes, Monday's fine."

"Monday it is." Dammit.

Traffic congested as Route 23 neared Columbus. Why in the hell people drove into the city on a Friday could be anybody's guess. People ought to leave, go home, go to the lake, not hold Jess up on her way to her office. A few minutes later she edged into her spot in the parking garage, ran her fingers through her hair, found a wrinkled scarf in her glove compartment, and declared her grooming for the day complete. Now, on to the Woolseys.

Lil smirked, turning her face from the vigilant Mel and Clara. "I trust the hearing went well. Mr. and Mrs. Woolsey are waiting." As if Jess didn't know, since the couple glared at her from their chairs fifteen feet away.

"I'll be right with you," Jess smiled. "Thank you for waiting. I was held up in court." Lil busied herself with the keyboard, a professional through and through.

Mel unsteadily rose, his right hand gripping the walker. Clara pulled herself out of the leather chair, collected her purse, and together with her husband, the couple slowly maneuvered from the waiting area into Jessica's office. Ready indeed to do battle with the recalcitrant insurance company, ready as well to light a fire under their, well, Clara's attorney.

For Jessica, her office in downtown Columbus combined professionalism with personal reflections. After all, she spent more time here than she did in her apartment. Besides, Triple O seemed to appreciate how Jess wove good taste with family memories. She guessed this provided a sense of caring that occasionally she really did not feel for her clients. She was not sure if O'Malley, O'Malley, and O'Malley lived a similar paradox. Usually, though, Jess cared very much. How she interwove her love of the law with her sense of justice and true empathy for her clients emanated from her heart.

Rather than stand for the interminable amount of time it took the Woolseys to navigate the short distance from one room to the next, Jessica gratefully eased into her chair behind what used to be her father's desk. Her brother Robbie had reluctantly let go of Bob Woods' desk from the Upper Sandusky office. Not that Rob would use it; the desk was just hard to part with. He had colored pictures on it as a kid; he had assembled Lego people there. Bob had kept a miniature Spider Man in the top right-hand desk drawer years after Robbie had long outgrown playing with toys. Spider Man still rested in the drawer the day Jess and her brother called their mother to drive down from Haines Landing to write their dad's obituary.

Now Jess officially occupied a corner office in the state capital. She glanced out the window on her left, onto High Street and sun beating down on Friday afternoon traffic. Behind her, two floor-to-ceiling windows looked across to the Franklin County Courthouse. On what decorators referred to as a library table, pictures of Jess's family smiled at her: her dad, in a separate frame her mother, and an earlier picture of her parents together. Well, that was gone. Set aside in a Waterford frame, a note on official stationery congratulated Jessica on passing the bar; the note was from an Ohio Supreme Court justice. Adjacent to it, a photograph of a confident Robbie, in suit and tie, smiled from an ebony Pottery Barn frame. For all their brother sister arguments, Robbie always supported Jessica, always cheered her successes. She had, he loved to comment, arrived.

Mel's walker bumping against the door announced the couple's entrance. Jarred from her daydreaming, Jessica stood, shaking hands with Clara first. "Thank you for coming in today. I appreciate your time. Please," she gestured, "sit down."

Clara glared at the club chair; Mel took his time arranging the walker, then himself. As they did so, Jessica glanced over again at the library table with the framed note from her mother's friend, the Supreme Court justice who had cared enough about Jess's progress to send a message of congratulations. Justice Dewey had suffered difficulties too; Jess's fitful verbal wrestling matches with clients like the Woolseys probably paled in the light of some of the judge's legal battles. She breathed in, breathed out; Jessica F. Woods, attorney of record, was ready.

"Mrs. Woolsey, I talked with your insurance representative last week. How are your appointments with the orthopedic surgeon going?"

Clara snorted, then huffed. Drama, if it came to a trial, should be avoided. No one liked histrionics. "Mrs. Woolsey?"

"He twisted me in so many places I thought I would faint! When I went up to the receptionist to make my next appointment my leg buckled out from under me. I don't know how much more I can take."

"I am so sorry. It must have really hurt." Jessica sympathized. "When you first came in,"—Jessica looked at her notes—"you mentioned you were being treated for back trouble resulting you believed from the Super Bus accident. Are you still seeing your physician for that?"

"Yes, yes, I am. The doctor thinks all my pains are related."

"I see. Now are you seeing a chiropractor in addition to your orthopedist? I guess I don't remember you telling me." Clara had not, of course, told Jess about the additional bills. Clients liked to make their own decisions often based on what their neighbors, relatives, and in this case her newfound best friend from the bus accident Gardenia Pulchinski advised. The attorney did not figure into the decision until mistakes or bills occurred, whichever came first.

"Which doctor are you referring to, Mrs. Woolsey?"

"Clara, please, I feel like we are friends."

"Mrs. Woolsey, if you could just keep me in the loop about your medical appointments in advance, I could help you more, and more quickly. I think we would all like to settle this."

"Oh certainly, Dear. I just thought that when I needed to see my doctors, I could go ahead and make appointments without your approval." Mrs. Woolsey reached way down into an oversized quilted purse, for, Jessica wondered, what? "Here is a list of the doctors I plan to visit. My friend's daughter tells me I need second and third opinions."

Having lost interest and with time to kill, Mel stared out the window behind Jessica's desk. He had heard the rehearsal speech first at home, then on the phone to Gardenia, then to Violet, the Bingo crazed daughter.

"Additional opinions can be helpful, certainly, Mrs. Woolsey. I would really like for you to keep me informed though." Jessica smiled, waiting, looking directly at Clara who returned the gaze. Jessica used the realtor's axiom; the person who talks first in a contentious exchange loses.

"So you're saying I shouldn't get additional opinions?" Jessica had won the little skirmish.

"I'm saying, Mrs. Woolsey, that this is an involved case with any number of potential outcomes. I am your lawyer. You count on me to act as quickly and as efficiently as possible. When additional doctors and chiropractors—"

"Just two chiropractors." Now it's two. *When did that happen?* Jessica wondered.

"Yes, when additional medical personnel are involved, I need to know."

Mel shifted slightly toward his walker. He was definitely bored. He appeared, however, to be silently in favor of Jessica taking his wife to task. Clara could be a termagant at home. It was kind of fun to watch the attorney at work. Yes, it was a lot of fun.

"I'm sorry, Ms. Woods."

"Jessica."

"I just thought—"

"I understand. Pain can do terrible things to a person. If you would let my office know when you feel you need additional medical opinions and assistance, we would appreciate it. We want to do our best for you to get you back on the road to recovery and to just treatment." Had she acted more the liar than she was at that point, Jessica might have reached out to pat Clara's hand. However, the ethics she adhered to prevented that gesture.

With unfailing politeness Jessica ushered the Woolseys out, sighed in abnegation to Lil, then slumped into her chair back in the corner office. If she took ibuprofen, now might be a nice time to do so, but she abjured medicine unless absolutely necessary. Birth control pills did not count, of course. She stared at the Woolsey file, wondering who controlled whom here. She needed to resolve the situation or Clara and Mel would fire her. But how to move the insurance company along? How to stop a recalcitrant Mrs. Woolsey from encroaching? This time she vowed to avoid calling Uncle Ralph, no, she would not; she could handle the Woolseys herself.

Her office phone rang. Uncle Ralph. "Jessica." He smiled through the phone lines. "How's it going? I never see you anymore."

Why one of the most talented esteemed trial attorneys in Ohio took time to stay in touch with her remained a question Jessica could not answer. Ralph Edmonton, friend of federal judges and Supreme Court justices, former president of the Ohio Academy of Trial Lawyers, Columbus Citizen of the Year 2010, Uncle Ralph wanted to take Jessica to lunch the next day. She could use a late lunch now, having left hers splattered on the dairy bar parking lot in Waldo.

"I would love to."

"Say 11:30. I'll call right before I leave the office, then pick you up outside of yours."

Yes, Jessica could use the advice and comforting shoulder Uncle Ralph offered. He was not really her uncle by blood or even by years of family friendships. In truth, Ralph Edmonton and Bob Woods had worked together long ago on a railroad case that would eventually alter the Woods both financially and personally. Over the years Bob and Ralph continued a professional association, some lunches, a few dinners, but contact nevertheless. When Bob died, Ralph Edmonton became to Jessica and Robbie, their Uncle Ralph.

It was he and his wife Carolyn who took Jessica to dinner the day she learned she had failed the bar exam the first time. When considerable problems with Bob's estate presented themselves, it was Uncle Ralph Jessica called. Carolyn worked for her husband in the law office; without hesitation she always put Jess through.

The reading public seems fond of novels presenting attorneys as rascals, liars, and thieves. But for the most part, Jessica's dealings with the many attorneys involved in wrapping up Bob's estate and in continuing the cases she eventually inherited were honest, some-times eccentric, sometimes egotistical, but generally good hearted when real tragedy happened. Without Uncle Ralph, Jessica did not know how she could have progressed to the job she held and the cases she settled. Well, Jess could use Uncle Ralph's realism where the Woolseys were concerned. She looked forward to lunch the next day.

Her cell phone rang: Mom. "Hi, Mom! How are you?" Jessica hoped she sounded neither hungover nor unsettled. Alexandra extir-pated misery from bravado like a cat pulled out treats from a night stand drawer, quickly and skillfully. To describe Alexandra's physical appearance would be to describe Jessica, but adding thirty or so years to it. Neither mother nor daughter saw the similarities when they were pointed out.

Alex liked to counter with how different the two women were by adding, "My daughter is thinner, better educated, more intelligent, and younger than I am. Other than that, we're alike."

If Uncle Ralph were in their company, he usually added a riposte: "I've known a lot of women over the years. The only comment I will add is that I agree. Jessica is definitely younger."

"I miss you, Honey. What do you think about my driving down and spending the night? We'll do some shopping, go to dinner."

"Sure, Mom. Next week. When do you teach?" Alex worked at a community college as an adjunct professor teaching beginning English. She certainly would not describe herself as a lifelong learner even though she had earned her doctorate only four years before. Days and hours varied with each semester depending on the number of students enrolled. Jessica did not even try to memorize her mother's work schedule.

"I'll drive down Thursday night after class, stay all night, and we can shop Friday."

"Come down Friday. We'll shop Saturday. I work, remember?" Good old Trickster, glossing over Jess's heavy workload.

"See you then, Honey. I love you so." Alexandra did indeed love her children so, a love that transcended the miseries inflicted on them, miseries not their fault, incurred only through a protracted a divorce. Jessica was very young at the time, Rob a teenager and three years older. Then when the kids were well out of college Bob had died suddenly; life as they say, alters circumstances.

As the afternoon wore on, Jessica busied herself with phone calls and computer work on both her cases and those she had inherited from her father. This new case with Leonard Warren and the liquor permit sounded interesting. Her potential client had offered no information on the phone except conveying anger at the Division of Liquor Control. Jessica had not spent any time in Canal Winchester except to pass by it on her way to Amish country with her mother a few years ago. Next week would be interesting.

So, immediate plans included cocktails for Lil today, lunch with Uncle Ralph the next day, dinner and shopping with her mother on the following Friday and Saturday, and a trip to Canal Winchester this coming Monday. Jessica felt her hangover dissipate. She walked out into the office where Lil may or may not have been shopping online for shoes. "How about a drink after work? I owe you at least one for putting up with the Woolseys today."

"Make it two. Clara outdid herself with the staring."

"Done." Jessica returned to her office to call Max. "Hey, Hon. How are you feeling?"

"Worse. I'm going home early to take a nap." Poor Max. Jessica planned to call the prosecutor's office in Huron to see about the speeding ticket.

How to manage Max, her mother, her brother Rob, her job? Jessica didn't like to think about it. Max loved her; he told her often enough. He wanted more time with her though, but Max lived in Cleveland, almost three hours away. Her mother loved her, missed her, and was now the only parent she and Robbie had. Having suffered the aches that divorcing parents brought to children, Jessica and her brother, always close, had become closer.

But Robbie was not a lawyer. Except for other attorneys, no one really understood the time O'Malley, O'Malley, and O'Malley demanded to execute the job for which she had eagerly contracted. Uncle Ralph did, Alex sympathized, and Max was as wonderful as he could be without knowing what she really did. Then there was Rob, brother and sister both alternating between needing guidance and giving it. Best to wind things up today, have a drink with Lil, then start again tomorrow.

One more phone call to wrap up the afternoon. This time to Mrs. Woolsey's physician, the one Jessica knew about at least.

"Northwest Medical," the assistant answered. "How may I direct your call?"

"This is Jessica Woods. Is it possible to talk with Dr. Schultz?"

"I'm sorry. May I ask the nature of your call?" Jessica tried to avoid mentioning her position, a tactic which seldom worked. Still she tried.

"I am the attorney for Mrs. Clara Woolsey, one of his patients. I was wondering if the doctor had a few moments to talk with me. I know he is very busy, but I would really appreciate it if we could talk." Silence. Jess searched her notes for the name of the usual receptionist, Marilyn, she found scrawled on the back of a folder. "Thank you, Marilyn." Jessica continued to wait.

Bingo. "Dr. Schultz is with a patient." He usually was. "Just a moment."

"Thank you." More silence, then music, maybe from the 70s?

"This is Richard Schultz."

"Thank you, Dr. Schultz. This is Jessica Woods. Clara Woolsey is my client." Jessica hoped he remembered his patient. Considering the woman's temperament, he probably did. "I wondered if I could get together with you to talk about her injuries and treatment." Both physician and attorney truly did not want to take the time to meet, but professional politeness suggested Jessica request a meeting first.

"We don't need to meet, Ms. Woods. I can have my assistant e-mail you the folder on Mrs. Woolsey." Sometimes it worked out, thought Jessica. Even her hangover vanished.

Saturday, the Next Day

Uncle Ralph had chosen Dempsey's Food and Spirits for lunch, a location that pleased Jessica because she felt less a neophyte and more a skilled attorney when she visited. Sean Murphy had been one of her first clients when she joined O'Malley, O'Malley, and O'Malley. What often happens, as it did for Jessica, particularly for new attorneys, is that friends and relatives need help. In truth, Jessica lived the axiom she had learned in law school: "Friends and relatives don't pay." Still, a person had to start somewhere.

Sean's daughter Maureen worked as a nail technician at Ultra Nails on Henderson Road where Jessica frequently had acrylic nails applied. Frequently, because she engaged in a bad habit of tearing her nails off when she was agitated, which at the beginning of her career, she usually was. Conversation between clients and manicurists regularly turned to family events or crises. Maureen confided that her father credibly complained that the bar he had recently bought and closed on ran into difficulty obtaining a liquor license. Sean swore up and down that he could not understand why the Liquor Control Board delayed, stalled, then stopped. Dempsey's Food and Spirits needed a liquor license to open. He lived an exemplary life; he had worked as a bartender in a previous bar in Canton, Ohio, where there were no problems. Now, here he was in the capital of Ohio right in the neighborhood of the board, so to speak, and no permit, not even a D2 to sell beer, wine and mixed beverages.

Poor Sean. Another axiom Jessica had learned long before law school was that everyone lies: clients, lawyers, she hoped not judges. But everyone lies. A trip to Canton actually to conclude a case with an attorney, sometime girlfriend, of Jessica's father provided an explanation for the Case of the Languishing License. Sean Murphy liked the dice; the dice liked him most of the time. Bartending in Canton offered delightful inside information that savvy gamblers made the most of. Granted, a few losses here and there did not amount to much. Sean covered those adequately. He never took money from the register, he closed out each night with correct receipts, and he kept fights at a minimum. No, Sean was an excellent honest bartender.

What he did not do, nor did he report, was to show records for afterhours sales. How could he? His boss provided spirits, wine, and beer regularly to a group of gambling friends, business people he called them, every Wednesday morning at 8:00 a.m. A white van with a magnetic sign on the side, Cora's Cleaning, pulled up to the back door as plain as you please. Promptly at seven forty-five, boss's orders, Sean arrived to oversee the cleaning and do the books. He also kept track of the cases of alcohol leaving the Canton City Tavern. Not cases really, bottles of Seagram's, Paramount, Korski, and not many when you came to think of it. Piles of rags in buckets, a cardboard box or two of supposed cleaning supplies, the operation worked well for a good two years. Besides, it wasn't Sean's idea nor his baby. He took his tips of course as any bartender does.

Unfortunately for the owner of the Canton City Tavern and therefore for the chief employee, Cora and her husband had a falling out. Cora made too good a living cleaning bars, more than the Canton City Tavern it seemed. Her husband suffered some gambling losses himself, which should and could be more than covered if Cora would come around to his way of thinking. Cora did not. A phone call from a disgruntled husband to the Ohio Liquor Control Board took less than five minutes. One sunny summer Wednesday morning a pleasant looking man stepped out of a Ford Taurus in the alley behind the Canton City Tavern. Cora, Sean, and the owner of the bar participated fully. The investigation chewed up very little time as everyone agreed to pay the fines rather than go to prison.

Apparently, because Sean was involved in illegal dealings but neither orchestrated them nor profited (he saw no reason to mention the substantial tips he received on Thursday evenings from special customers), his fine amounted to considerably less. His attorney arranged for Sean's role in the matter to be adjudged minimal, forced by family necessity. At the time Sean and his wife had a little daughter at home suffering from asthma. With no insurance, the spiraling cost of late night visits to the Mercy Medical Center emergency room depleted their small savings account. The Ohio Division of Liquor Control entered a brief notation regarding Sean Murphy, but that was the extent of it. He in turn agreed to five years of employment in places other than those that served any kind of alcohol. He worked as a custodian at the Mercy Medical Center where, being an affable fellow even during his daughter Maureen's asthma attacks, he had made friends.

Five years passed quickly. Sean and his wife divorced. He and Maureen moved to Columbus where his daughter grew up, graduating with honors from Bishop Watterson High School. About the same time, Sean received a substantial inheritance when both parents died in an automobile accident. With some of the money he sent his daughter, now called Mo, to the Ohio State School of Cosmetology where she graduated at the top of her class. Using the remainder of the inheritance, Sean purchased a bar. It should have been relatively simple to transfer the liquor license to his name. For some reason it was not. Thus, over the application of Tropical Tangerine polish to acrylic nails, those to replace the ones Jessica had torn off before a hearing, Mo related in part her father's troubles. After a subsequent appointment or two during which Jessica had her nails balanced, more to gain a rapport with her technician than to continue the rather unlawyerly flamboyant nail lacquer, the attorney of record received the call she had hoped for.

Sean Murphy made an appointment of his own, with Jessica, meeting her first at the offices of the Triple O. Jessica liked the man instantly; unfortunately at times she truly loathed her clients, but this fellow seemed forthright enough. Sandy hair with streaks of red, a cheerful smile, a happy outlook, he seemed as if he truly did not understand how his license could be delayed for more than a year. He paid cash for the building; he had passed the building inspection. He had registered his business with the state of Ohio. The Ohio Department of Commerce had issued him a restaurant license which he proudly displayed behind the bar that he could not open. What was the matter?

Jessica called the Ohio Department of Liquor Control. A rather vague response left her questioning, but Sean was a new client; Jessica, a new lawyer in need of billable hours. One afternoon she left the office about three to drive to Canton. A beer about 6:00 p.m. sounded delicious; it was a Wednesday. The Canton City Tavern had changed, having now transformed into an upscale bar/restaurant boasting tapas. Servers in serapes and sombreros tapped orders in on iPads; silk palm trees decorated with multicolored lights graced what must have formerly been dark corners. Guitar music played instead of what Sean referred to as Redneck music.

Nevertheless, Jessica assumed that some of the former customers still sought their usual hang out. Used to deception, after all she had worked as a private investigator for one of her father's girlfriend's detective agencies, Jessica procured a barstool in Los Palmas Grande and ordered a Corona. It was long enough after five o'clock, plenty of time to allow for patrons to have enjoyed the accumulating effects of alcohol. Besides, what self-respecting, well, confident, man, married or not, wouldn't approach an attractive woman sitting alone?

Thank God Jessica could hold her beer. True, throughout the two hours she sipped Coronas, paying for only the first, she excused herself regularly to use the ladies' room. Eventually the name Sean Murphy surfaced. Jessica related that she and Sean's daughter Maureen were friends. It really was easier to tell the truth, easier to remember what she had said actually, especially after a few beers. In answer to patrons' questions, no, Maureen, Mo they called her now, was fine. No more asthma attacks; she had outgrown them. Yes, Sean and his wife had divorced long ago. He lived in Columbus now.

As the evening continued, Jessica was almost glad for her small bladder, which helpfully removed Coronas in a timely manner. Four beers into the night, Jess returned from yet another visit to the room still labeled Canton Cuties. Time to rename it to fit the setting, she mused. Maybe Chi Chi Chiquitas? As she leaned down from the barstool to adjust her mustard spike heels, which by now were hot and uncomfortable, a wizened man probably in his midfifties plopped onto the stool next to hers.

"You a detective?" he flung out without preliminary niceties.

"I am not. I'm a friend of my client Sean Murphy." Jessica opened her bag, sliding a business card from Triple O over to her new inquisitor.

"How do I know you're not from the law?" Dressed in what Jess believed were construction worker's clothes, worn dusty jeans, heavy industrial boots, and a faded T-shirt, the fellow was most likely more sober than she. Best to speak slowly and truthfully in reply.

"Mr. Murphy is my client. I would like to help him which is why I'm here. You are?" She looked directly at the man.

"Mike. Mike O'Donnell." He stretched out a paw almost twice as big as her hand. "I might as well believe you, looking like you do and driving up here from Columbus. Besides, you can either drink or you're half drunk already. The state boys only pretend."

Half drunk was the answer, but Jessica was too proud to admit it. She didn't respond.

"Sean's still a friend of mine even though he doesn't come back here much. He and the wife had a falling out, kind of over me. I still like the guy though. You know how things happen. I really respect him. What's he up to now anyway?"

Jessica guessed the friendly Mr. O'Donnell had probably been involved with Sean's wife, which was not why Jess was in Canton tonight and therefore of no interest to her. It most likely was why Sean moved to Columbus though, aside from the difficulty with the Liquor Board.

"Mr. Murphy has a business in Columbus. I'm here to help him wrap up some loose ends." Even though in retrospect, Jessica still remembered her embarrassment at slurring her words. She wasn't that drunk, was she? What did the Canton City Tavern/Los Palmas Grande have on the menu other than hot dogs and burgers? She didn't think soy burgers graced the offerings listed behind her on the chalkboard. As she motioned to the bartender for two tacos with all the fixings (she would pick out the ground beef), she waited for O'Donnell to continue.

"Look, like I said, Sean was a friend of mine. Still is. I'd like to help him if I can. What do you need?"

Jessica closed her eyes, thought about her Corona, the glass dripping water onto a widening pool under her beer. How much information to give the man next to her? She had an idea that Sean's old—most likely, former—friend felt guilty about whatever involvement there had been with Sean's ex-wife. If so, he was trying to make up for it. Probably best to be as forthright as possible, attempt to sober up, and leave.

The Taco Twosome arrived. As Jess tried unobtrusively to pick through the ground beef, Mike O'Donnell grinned. "A vegetarian attorney all the way up here from Columbus."

Ignoring his comment, Jess continued, "Mr. O'Donnell, my client is having a little difficulty getting his business started. Maybe you know why?"

"I do. Do you know anything about Canton?"

Jessica knew a lot. She had worked for the Stark County Prosecutor's office when she was in law school, but she was not about to tell her new bar buddy about it. "Some."

Mike finished his sixteen-ounce Budweiser, signaled the bartender for another, then a refill for Jessica though she shook her head otherwise. "So you know there's a little gambling that goes on, maybe some other operations too." Mike's second round along with Jessica's fifth arrived.

"Sean got into a little trouble here a few years ago when the old owner got arrested for illegal sales. Sean knew better from the get go, but he had a lot of bills because of his daughter. I remember the old owner got slapped with a huge fine and lost his license. I think Sean got off fairly light because of the situation. All things considered, he left Canton at the right time. Good to know he's starting over. Tell him Mike from the Canton City Tavern said hello."

"I will. Thank you, Mr. O'Donnell. I will." Jessica managed to slide off the barstool as gracefully as four and a quarter Coronas permitted. Now to get to the car and home. Well, at least out of the parking lot.

So that explained why Sean Murphy had so much trouble getting a liquor license for Dempsey's Food and Spirits. Most likely a notation next to his name, a small fine, nothing bad but definitely a road block should the same Mr. Sean Murphy wish to obtain a license from the Ohio Board of Liquor Control in the future. The future had arrived.

Thank God Jessica knew the area, or departing from the Canton City Tavern, whoops Palmas Grande Something at 9:00 p.m. could have ended unsatisfactorily. Instead, she remembered a rest stop right outside the city, south on I-77. After an hour's nap, Jess had a headache but no DUI. Returning to Columbus shortly after midnight she counted the day as a long but productive one. Somehow Sean got his license, as Jess recalled, without too much difficulty. A phone call followed by a meeting with the Ohio Liquor Control board, which involved Jessica F. Woods as attorney of record, her client, and a couple members of the board who read some notations made nearly twenty years before moved things along quickly. It had, after all, been at least two decades. The state was generally not punitive; in the business to make money like anyone else if former situations were indeed rectified.

Now, a good three years later, as she had lunch with Uncle Ralph, Jess reflected on the lagniappe, the unforeseen pleasant aspects that practicing law provided. Here she sat in a pub that had been named Outstanding New Business of the Year in 2011. Even after three years Sean Murphy treated her as a distinguished friend and advisor, his referrals adding to her list of clients. Yes, Jessica was a preferred patron, always given the best table in the house. Uncle Frank knew that as well. *Occasionally*, she thought, smiling to herself, *occasionally things worked out.* As her mother Alex, Trickster, too frequently commented in what had become a tropism: "Sometimes you get the bear. Sometimes the bear gets you." Jessica got the bear with this one, so did Sean. Which reminded her, time to call Mo for another appointment. With summer coming, acrylic nails glistening with Tahiti Tropics might do the trick. Bears come in all shapes. Yes, thinking of a toothsomely handsome lobbyist she had met at a fundraiser last week, yes, they do.

"So, Jess, how is your brother doing? Hello?" Ralph Edmonton's questions extirpated Jess from her reveries. How was Robbie doing? Let's see, starting a new company that her mother described as smoke and mirrors, still not married. Still her big brother, her friend, her, dammit, one of the few she could truly count on.

"He's good, Uncle Ralph. You know Robbie. Like a cat. Throw him out a window, even one he didn't know was at the end of the hall, and he always lands on his feet."

Jessica looked at the friend across the table from her as she bought time to consider her answer. To describe Ralph Edmonton, people who liked him or did not like him agreed that he combined boyish good looks with an aura of self-confidence. Ralphs's red hair showed more streaks of gray now than the red she remembered from earlier years. Still, as Jess's mother observed, "Redheads don't show their age." Jess supposed if she were to compare her friend's face to an animal's she might use the word *foxlike*. His green eyes usually sparkled with intelligence, but Jessica had seen cunning too behind the demeanor of a man who preferred diplomacy rather than arguments. Attorney Ralph Edmonton had not beaten one railroad giant after another back without cleverness along with skill and hard work. The results: generous settlements for his clients. People sought the offices of Edmonton and Associates not because they liked Ralph, although in the end they always did, but because their lawyer grappled with opposition and won, more often than not using logic, surprise, and careful timing as a fox hunts and devours its prey.

Jessica continued as honestly as she could. "I just don't know most of the time what Robbie really is doing." She worried about him as much as he worried about her.

A server unfamiliar to Jessica approached their table. "Is Sean all right?" Jessica asked worriedly.

The server replied cheerfully, "He's just fine. He left for a cruise yesterday. His first vacation in years!"

"That man deserves some time off," Jess commented. "For that matter, I could use a vacation myself. Tell him *Bon Voyage* from me if he calls in."

Their lunch arrived. For Jess a shrimp salad with olive oil and balsamic vinegar; for Ralph, a hamburger and fries. "Don't tell Carolyn," he spoke rather conspiratorially. "I just had a hunger she does not need to know about." After a heart attack a few years ago almost as deadly as the one that killed Jess's father, Ralph usually watched his diet. Not today though. Rather than hanging on to subjects about Robbie and her, Jessica realized she should ask Ralph what was going on in his own life. From her experience, food for the soul might be an anodyne for troubles.

"Ralph, how are you? You doing all right? You are always so thoughtful of Robbie and me. What is going on with you and Carolyn and the kids?"

Generously sprinkling salt on his fries, Ralph hesitated, then dropped his customary happy smile. "I am in very good shape. The kids are fine. You know James is still with Coleridge and Marks in Lancaster. Rebecca loves being a stay-at-home mother. I keep telling her she could telecommute, but she has no interest right now in continuing to work in advertising. I don't blame her really. That business is tough."

"I know. Dad's friend in Marion wrote the slogan 'Where's the beef?' for a hamburger chain years ago. The guy did so well a Detroit firm snapped him up. He moved up there with the family, then died of a heart attack a year later. Way too stressful."

"Like being a trial attorney?" Ralph capped her comment.

"Like being a trial attorney. But back to you. You did not tell me about Carolyn."

Jessica had stopped by the offices of Edmonton and Associates a week before. Carolyn looked beautiful as always. Slim, black hair expertly cut in a precise shoulder length page boy, porcelain skin with few wrinkles, Ralph's wife belonged in the front office. No fool she, when lawyers wanted to reach Ralph Edmonton, they had to pass Carolyn's criteria. That included professional attire, good manners, timely responses to phone calls and e-mails, and, most important, a show of respect for the profession. Ralph loved the law. He had spent more than two thirds of his life upholding it. The lawyer who swaggered into the corner offices of Edmonton and Associates, acting as if the client/lawyer thing was a damned game anyway, earned Carolyn's trenchant remark that "Mr. Edmonton was not available." Occasionally, later, Ralph learned too late that his wife had turned away a rather good case, but that seldom happened. Besides, Ralph had more than enough clients and their lawyers to offset the very few that Carolyn determined not worthy.

Ralph placed his burger on his plate, then stared blankly at his too-salted fries now heavy with ketchup as well. "Carolyn goes in for surgery Tuesday. She found a lump."

"Oh, God, Ralph. I'm so sorry." Jessica reached out, put her hand on her friend's. "What can I do?"

"Right now nothing." Ralph hesitated. "Actually, there is something you can do. Keep us in your prayers."

Jessica was reluctant to admit that she bordered on atheism. When she quit praying, she did not remember. Sometime around the time her parents divorced.

"I will, Ralph. How did Carolyn find the lump?"

"A routine mammogram. It's been hell. Another mammogram, more appointments. God, when you are on the other side of the medical problems as a patient, not a lawyer, it's different. A whole new animal. Carolyn is taking this better than I am." He put his head in his hands.

"Ralph, you have practiced law for how many years?"

"It feels like a hundred, but forty years. I know what you are going to say."

"Say it for me, then." Jessica had not anticipated being a cheerleader. Ralph Edmonton was supposed to be the strong one, the one who had the answers. She loved Ralph and Carolyn. This thing with Carolyn shocked her. No. It was not how things were supposed to go. How to be the friend now that Ralph needed? Dammit anyway. How to be the adult?

Ralph sat, tears sliding down his face. A server approached their table but quietly retreated, leaving them to privacy. *Say something,* Jessica thought to herself. *I am not good at this. I do not know how.* Without thinking about it, she prayed.

"Ralph, for forty years you know how these tests go. You know most of the scare tactics physicians use. They hedge their answers. They collect more material than they will ever need, all the time dragging the damned procedures out to the misery of the patients who wait for the phone to ring. Last winter Mom was too frightened to call me when she received a letter, a letter, from radiology telling her to return for a second look. They had found something suspicious in her left breast. It was Friday afternoon. You know how that goes. Try to get some answers then. Ha!"

"I know, Jess. This time the tests were right. Carolyn has cancer. The doctor is a friend of ours. She called my wife at home when the last set came back. I'm sick, Jessica, sick." Ralph stared at Jess, both of them reflecting on all that might follow. Two usually optimistic attorneys, one far more experienced than the other, considered the best outcomes but could not push away the worst.

Ralph spoke first. "Well, we're certainly not helping Carolyn now, are we? Let's at least finish our lunch. Do you want another beer? By God, I'm having another." He signaled the waiting server. "Two more of whatever the hell we're having."

Ralph salted his fries some more. "Okay, Jess, you can help. I am a reasonable guy. I trust people as much as I can, but I am a Boy Scout too."

Jess recalled that he was an Eagle Scout; for the past forty years he had also served as legal counsel for the Buckeye District in the northern part of Franklin County. "Carolyn manages the office. I have another girl there, I guess I say *assistant* now unlike the old days. Anyway, Christine knows the office almost as well as Carolyn, so we can do all right for the time my wife is out."

Jessica wondered what her friend was driving at. She hoped he would not ask her to substitute for him. She was not experienced enough. Jess could handle the cases. That was not the problem. For the people who had made her life better, who took care of her and her brother, she did not want to, as she thought of it, mess things up. Jess waited.

Here it was. "Jess, I hope you do not feel slighted. As much as I respect you and see how you have grown into a pretty good attorney,"—he smiled the old Uncle Ralph smile—"I am going to ask Jay Rossford to handle things while I am out. It shouldn't be too long. I just wanted to let you know."

Jay Rossford, king of the golf course. Why in the hell did Uncle Ralph choose Jay? On Saturday, phone calls from desperate clients to the Jayster remained unreturned until Monday, or Tuesday for that matter. Oh, in matters of money Jay could be trusted; in timely matters forget it. The Old Jayster as he bumptiously referred to himself at bar association meetings, the Old Jayster took care of things when he was good and ready, and not until.

Well, Jessica, thought, *there's a paradox for me. I did not want the job I thought Ralph might offer me. Now when he didn't offer it to me, I'm disappointed. Typical. I want what I cannot have and have what I do not want.*

As for the selection of Jay Rossford, Jessica knew the reason behind the choice. Ralph and Jay graduated from the same Columbus high school. In Columbus, ties to a big city school bound people as tight, sometimes even tighter, than marriage. Whetstone graduates stayed together, Columbus East did business with Columbus East, and St. Francis DeSales with St. Francis DeSales. Ralph and Jay had graduated from Watterson; of course Frank would pick his classmate, the old vice president of the senior class when Ralph served as president.

Jessica tried to look thoughtful, accepting would do. She did not want the job anyway, right? Yes, she did. Well, be the actor all good attorneys are. "Ralph, I know Jay from a case I'm working on. He should be fine." He probably wouldn't be, but now was not the time when Ralph was not himself to offer anecdotal evidence to the contrary.

"I hope so. Anyway, how do you know Jay?"

"His client and mine were injured in a Super Bus accident. The insurance companies keep stalling. You know how that goes. Now the two clients have become friends and are trying to play us against each other."

The older attorney chuckled. "Oh, they come to us anxious for help, then turn on us if we don't deliver by the deadline they set. No matter that the clients miss appointments or omit certain details that could move their case along. Oh no. That would be too easy." He dragged a few remaining French fries through the pool of ketchup. "Other than going behind your back, how is your client doing?"

Jessica gazed into her second beer, which on its own seem to have drained nearly to the bottom of the glass. "I think she's lying. I have the feeling that this time the insurance company knows something Jay and I do not. His client has a different company, but still I get the sense that they are withholding funds for good reason. I just don't know what it is."

"Look, Jess, have you met with the adjuster or is this all by phone and e-mail?"

"I have tried to get together with the woman handling Clara's claims. Last week I called again. The assistant said her employer was on vacation in Cancun but would return by the end of the week."

"Stalling." Frank finished his beer, asked for the check, then helped Jessica from her chair. Always polite, he stood when a woman entered a room; Frank held a lady's coat for her: a gentleman through and through. "I know one Clara. She's got to be in her seventies by now, mean as a feral cat. Turned her away about ten years ago for some kind of ankle injury she said she suffered when leaving a restaurant in, where the hell was it, Reynoldsburg, I think. She has a husband every bit as mean as she is. Marvin or Mervin."

"Melvin." Jessica shrieked as quietly as she could considering the surroundings. "Mel! He acts so taciturn when they come to the office! He's mean too?"

"One lies and the other one swears to it. Good luck with those two." Ralph paid the bill, then held the door for Jessica as they walked out into the spring sunshine. "Call me if you need me, but you are one tough cookie yourself. You can handle the Woolsey family all on your own." Ralph grinned the smile of a fox that, Jessica swore, had just conspired with another about a hapless prey.

"Can I drop you at your office?" Ralph offered.

"Thank you, but I need to walk for a while. It's only down the block." Jessica hugged him, then pulled back, looking directly into his eyes. "I'm not waiting for your call if you need help with Carolyn or your office. I'll stop in to say hello."

"Okay, Jess. I'm not going to stop you. I could use a pair of watchful eyes." Ralph grinned. "The Old Jayster can be a handful."

"Give Carolyn my love and best wishes for a complete recovery." Jessica had the name of a florist on her cell phone contacts list. Yellow roses, symbolizing cheer and healing, would be delivered today to their New Albany home.

As Jess walked back to her apartment she thought about the Woolseys again. This turn of events with Mel surprised her. Mel, the silent complying husband might be quiet for a reason. What in the hell was Clara holding back? For that matter, what did those two have planned? What did Jay know if anything? He could at least provide a hint if he had some idea of what was really going on?

As Jess unlocked her office, a text message from Max pinged. "See you tonight?" Shit. She wanted to sleep, to do her laundry, to do, for that matter, nothing!

Max. Jessica did not deserve the kind gentle man who loved her. She knew it too. How many times had he driven after work from Cleveland to Columbus to stay with her? How many more times had he called, hoping she would agree to his visit, and how many times had she turned him down? Max was the kind of man she wanted to marry. At a slumber party years ago Jessie and her friends listed the qualities they demanded in a perfect husband. Jessie kept the list jammed into the bottom of her nightstand; Max had all these traits. Why, why, why did she turn him away?

At a loss for understanding her daughter, Alex reminded Jessie that all men exhibited qualities women needed to overlook. The trick, Jessie did call her mother the Trickster, was to determine the traits we could live with while ignoring as much as possible the behaviors and personality quirks we chose to live without. In fairness to Max, his one negative quality involved distance; he lived in a bachelor's apartment in downtown Cleveland, more than two and a half hours' drive from Columbus.

As far as the qualities Max embodied when Jessie referred to her middle school list, he had them all. Intelligent, tall, blond, weighing between 185 and 200 pounds, midthirties, athletic, dressed well, and kind. Max had graduated valedictorian from Ohio University; he owned his own financial consulting firm, which employed three additional advisors. Blond, Max at age thirty-five had most of his hair, but since Jessica had such thick long hair, balding men attracted her; Max kept what remained of his hair well groomed. Athletic, yes, Max played basketball three mornings a week on an intermural city team. As far as dressing well, the man Jessie called her boyfriend chose J.Crew for casual and Brooks Brothers for dressier occasions. Yes, and Max was kind. Who else, thought Jessica, would and did put up with the vicissitudes of her profession? Who else understood, or tried to, when an unexpected meeting with a client on a weekend canceled the romantic evening Jessica had promised? Thank God for Max, and yet, and yet, Jessie could not bring herself to commit to him completely? What was wrong with her?

She blamed her job. The highs and lows of court and clients were difficult to duplicate in her personal life. Oh, the lows appeared all by themselves: her parents' divorce, Bob's death. Those were the big ones. But smaller problems encroached too, more than enough to cause her misery. Jessie counted fourteen speeding tickets, three fender benders, and one DUI on her record. The cities of Columbus, Cleveland, Lancaster, and Toledo had towed her car to their impound lots enough times so that the managers greeted her by name. Yes, Jessica had no need to look for lows; they found her.

And the highs? How to describe the highs of an attorney's life? Even relatively inexperienced as she was, Jessica had delighted often enough in legal work to be disappointed when the highs of personal life did not match those of her career. It was not that Jessie had to win in court, although she loved that aspect. It was the excitement, the preparation, the awe of walking into the court room, the feeling right between the beginning of the proceedings and the actual event.

When trying to explain to friends in another career how she felt, Jessie used the analogy of a dinner party. It was that ineffable anticipation a host or hostess experiences in the ephemeral moments just before the first guest arrives. The table set with silver and sparkling white plates glows as candles light the room. Fresh cut roses grace favorite vases. The aroma of food perfectly prepared tantalizes just enough to entice good friends to delight in a memorable dining experience. A refrigerator full of cold beer, bottles of top shelf liquor, favorite wines wait to be poured and savored. Down to the last detail, stuffed olives rest in a bowl, maraschino cherries, sliced oranges, and lemons are arranged to garnish on silver trays. Cut glass gleams in fanned semicircles as the bartender, dressed in black tie, stands ready to prepare the first cocktail. Then, then, the doorbell rings; the first guest arrives. The party begins.

That, for Jessica, is how she felt each time before a hearing. She may be hungover, she may be exhausted, she may have had a terrible fight with her brother or her boyfriend. But when she crossed the threshold into a courtroom wherever it was, city, county, the state capital, rural Southeastern Ohio, it did not matter. Every emotion except the thrill of doing what she loved floated away.

That damned phrase her English teacher mother required her students to memorize, requiring too her own children to repeat. What in the hell was it? It almost, almost defined Jessica's wrestling with her personal life. Oh, yes, the definition of Romanticism: the ineffable striving for the unattainable. Well, Jessica would attain what she wanted. She would. Alex the Trickster might be right; each day with people we loved, husbands, boyfriends did not offer the excitement we first felt when we started dating. Life leveled out, Jessie's mother tried to inculcate. Jessica wished, oh, how she wished, she could accept it.

"Hey, Max, Hon, what's up?" she called back instead of texting.

"I'm finished early here. My client canceled, so I can drive down and take you to dinner." He sounded so hopeful. God, Jessica hated to disappoint him, but she was exhausted.

"Max, I just cannot. I have a trial I have to prepare for and I'm wiped out. I'm going for a run, a shower, then going to bed. Sunday all day I'm working."

Silence. She had hurt him, she knew.

"Look, Hon, I'm sorry. Next weekend, I promise. We'll do something fun."

Poor Max. If he broke up with her, she would not blame him, her fault entirely.

"All right. Next weekend it is. The Indians play the Yankees at home. I'll get tickets. Corey Kluber is smokin'! From the way he has been pitching, I expect him to take the team into post season and maybe the Series. Hey, speaking of tickets, what should I do about my speeding ticket?"

Crap. She forgot. "I'll call the prosecutor. Don't worry about it. When are you scheduled to appear?" She forgot that too.

"Monday." They changed it from Friday. Gives us a few more days."

"I'll handle it, Hon. I love you. I really do. I'm sorry about all the crap I have to do down here." She was too, sorry for herself, sorry for Max.

"I love you too." He did not sound particularly convincing. He sounded as if he did not believe her. What if he went out tonight and met someone else? Don't think about it, Jess chided herself. His own man, Max could do what he wanted to, except, of course, Jessica would be devastated when he did.

Jessica threw her designer bag onto the kitchen counter, tossed the bills toward her desk, dragged herself into her bedroom, and slept for three hours. She guessed rightly that a couple of beers at lunch on top of yet another grueling week created the soporific that evaded what she called normal people on a Saturday. Time for a run, then back to bed for her.

Jessie ran the three blocks from her apartment in the Brewery District to Bicentennial Park, her favorite place to work out. As her feet pounded the concrete walk curling along the Scioto River she emptied thoughts about Max, her brother, her job, her personal situation, however one described it. Eventually she would marry, have babies, purchase a home in the suburbs, maybe Granville, yes, maybe Granville. All of that in, her mother would shudder if she knew, all of that in any order that suited Jessica, well, that occurred. An hour later, sweaty, filthy hair hastily shoved under her ball cap, Jess returned to her apartment to shower.

As she unlocked the door, walking through the short hall into her Pullman kitchen, Jessica felt calm, centered, at peace. She loved her apartment. However, at 1,200 dollars a month, she was too savvy financially to keep throwing money at property she did not own. Still, to return to her two-bedroom home on the fifth floor of a renovated building in the upscale Brewery District always evoked in Jessica a certain calm she very much appreciated. Her building, one of continuing development in what Alex referred to as gentrification, belonged to a four block complex of former warehouses and factories, remodeled into residences that attracted young urban professionals.

Because of the central convenient location, Jessica could walk to any number of pubs and restaurants as well as to her office. For an attorney with at least one DUI already, leaving her car in the parking garage was a wise decision if plans included a few cocktails after work or on the weekends. They usually did.

Jess breathed in, enjoying the peace she craved that her apartment, expensive but worth it, afforded her. Perfect for a single woman, her little kitchen with its stainless steel refrigerator and stove to her left, her sink and dishwasher to her right on the opposite counter, made entertaining as well as pleasant solitary dinners a pleasure. Jess prided herself on eating well. Her stocked refrigerator impressed even Max who did not practice a vegetarian diet. Jess bought fresh produce from the Kroger store across the parking lot from her apartment. On any evening Jessica could prepare a meal from the greens, fresh fish, soy entrees, or seasonal fruit that filled her shelves. From her cupboards she could pull not only macaroni but rigatoni, flat spaghetti, Amish-made noodles, and specialty sauces.

And of course, to satisfy the sweet tooth she had inherited from her mother, Jessica kept Graeter's ice cream in her freezer, Cheryl's chocolate chip cookies in her cupboard, and Kit Kat candy bars in her kitchen drawer. Anyone who lived in Columbus knew about Graeter's, the Cincinnati firm that Louis Graeter founded in 1870. Four generations later people continued to crave the frozen confections that the firm offered now in over thirty retail shops as well as in grocery stores. Jessica's favorites ranged from mint chocolate chip to chocolate chip and now dark chocolate gelato.

Jessica loved her Cheryl's cookies too. In 1981 entrepreneurs, risk takers, like Jessica herself and Robbie, Cheryl Krueger along with her roommate from college opened their storefront business in downtown Columbus. They sold six kinds of cookies and soda pop. As a child, Jessica remembered how her dad used to drop into the shop by the statehouse when he had occasion to meet Ralph Edmonton. Bob always brought home a huge bag of cookies. Fresh, they had to be eaten, so Bob said, right away. Cheryl advised within the week, but the kids or Bob, or Alex stealthily devoured chocolate chip cookies long before the seven day time frame. Jessica preferred frosted buttercream, but seasonal cookies, excellent partners to the seasonal fruit she kept, could usually be pulled from the freezer, or the bag on her kitchen counter.

Yes, single or not, Jessica ate well. She often walked home for lunch, and usually during the week she cooked for herself. Tonight, on a Saturday when she had declined invitations from her friends and from Max, Jessie set her dining room table purchased from Pottery Barn, pulled her white plates out also from Macys, lit a Yankee Candle, a gift from her mother, and poured herself a glass of Pinot Grigio. She was indeed tired. Tonight would be linguini with clam sauce, romaine lettuce with olive oil and balsamic vinegar, and for dessert, le piece de resistance, dark chocolate gelato.

Her cell phone chimed. Eric Stewart. Who the hell was that at 7:00 p.m. on a Saturday night? She didn't know anyone by that name. Take the call, Triple O had drummed into her. "Jessica Woods."

"Jessica, this is Eric Stewart. I don't know if you remember me. My wife Allison and I are frequent guests at your mother and stepfather's bed and breakfast."

Jessica paused, *buying time*, her mother called it.

"We met you when I retrieved my cell phone cord I had left at the Marshall Inn. You were kind enough to bring it back with you from Haines Landing."

"Yes, Mr. Stewart. How are you? How can I help you?"

"Well, the crazy thing is, I happen to be calling from a police station in Ft. Lauderdale."

Not crazy at all for Jess. She was used to it. Clients called from all over the state, country for that matter. He continued. "Anyway, my wife and I are on our way to a cruise, and I guess I might have gotten carried away. Um, I had better hand the phone over to the officer in charge." Eric sounded nervous. What in the hell had he done other than probable drunk driving?

"Ms. Woods, this is Officer Ramirez, are you Mr. Stewart's attorney?"

"Yes, I am, Officer." Ever since Jessica had been sworn in, she had advised her friends and family that if they were arrested, they were to give her name as their lawyer. Alex must have handed Eric Jess's business card when he stayed at the inn.

"Ms. Woods, your client has been charged with driving while intoxicated, reckless operation of a vehicle, vandalism, and criminal intent. These actions occurred in the Publix Parking Lot in Ft. Lauderdale, Florida, where Mr. Stewart was apprehended by another officer and myself. Out of professional courtesy to you as his attorney, I will place him on our station telephone. Please understand that your client has given his permission to record the conversation. May I have your permission as well?"

"Thank you, Officer Ramirez," Jessica scribbled notes as she spoke. "You have my permission to record the conversation."

At this point the path of least resistance and therefore the one less likely to annoy the arresting officer was to agree. Someone at the station probably recorded conversations anyway; she might as well give permission to a moot point.

"Hello, Eric, how are you holding up?" Despondent, unhappily slurring occasionally, Eric told his story. "I'm sorry about all this. Thank you for taking the call. I guess I shouldn't have um."

"Stop right there, Eric. Tell me only what happened."

"Ally and I leave tomorrow morning with another couple for a Carnival cruise to the islands. Our plane landed in Miami. We rented a car to drive to Lauderdale, checked into our hotel, drove around a little, got dinner, then planned to buy supplies, you know, food for the trip. We headed over to Publix Supermarket. The parking lot was packed! Who buys groceries on a Saturday night?"

You do, Jessica thought to herself. She could use a damned tape recorder for this story. Instead she grabbed a baby shower invitation off her refrigerator door, more notes. "Eric, just tell me what happened next. Why were you arrested?" Dinner most likely included drinks, hence the DUI. Why though reckless operation, vandalism, and criminal intent? Good Lord, from the one occasion she had talked with Eric Stewart, easygoing bed and breakfast guests of her mother's, he and Ally seemed innocuous enough.

Silence. Did she hear crying? She pushed for him to continue.

"There goes the cruise, right? My twenty-fourth on Carnival." Jessica definitely heard sniffles. Alcohol does that to a person; guilt does too.

"Eric, tell me what happened. Remember, everything you say is being recorded. Just tell me what happened."

"Okay, sorry." She heard him blow his nose, then silence. Settling himself down or did he fall asleep?

"Eric?"

"Yes, sorry. God, what have I done?"

"Eric!"

"Right. Okay. So we bought our supplies for the cruise, loaded the bags into the trunk, and started the car. I rented a white Toyota Camry, which I like for the room. The four of us are not the smallest of people, you know. Besides, a Camry on vacation is fun. We have a PT Cruiser at home.

"People were trolling for parking spaces, so the place was packed. I started backing up. Ally yelled, 'Look up!'

"A guy in a white Taurus was barreling toward me! No way was he going to stop! The guy crashed right into my front fender then sped off! I was so damned mad I gunned it and started chasing him!"

Right in the Pubix lot? Jessica was appalled. On a Saturday night with old people, wheelchairs, little children, shopping carts full of groceries. She shuddered.

"Anyway, some woman with a shopping cart jumped out of my way. Pretty much. I might have dinged the cart. There was a weird metal on metal clunk. Anyway, I kept chasing the guy up and down the lot as best as I could, but he drove off. A teenager, he must have been the grandson of the old lady with the shopping cart, called the police. Every damned kid has a cell phone, for drug deals in Lauderdale I still think."

"Eric."

"So the guy that crashed into me got away. All people in the Publix lot saw or remembered was a white car. That would be me since the other white car was nowhere around, hurtling up and down the parking lanes. Of course, the teenage kid by that time had coached his grandma, telling her I was trying to run her down. You know how that goes."

Jessica did not. She had now filled the baby shower invitation with scribbled notes. Reaching for a receipt from Nordstrom's, she started filling in the white space after shoes, 250.00, tax, 18.75. Let's see, fees at 300.00 an hour, much of that going right to O'Malley, O'Malley, and O'Malley, best to consider at some time in the future maybe branching out on her own. This phone call and the follow up calls she would make, they could pay for the shoes, hell, the matching bag she drooled over but did not buy, yet.

"Eric, did you hit the lady? Did you hit anyone or anything other than the shopping cart?"

"I'm pretty sure I didn't. I would never hurt anyone. I was just mad."

"Okay. Would you put Officer Ramirez back on please?"

"Thank you, Officer. Is there anything else you think I should know?"

"Ms. Woods, an off-duty officer for the Broward County Sheriff's Department also saw the occurrence. He called it in too."

"Okay, thank you for your assistance. If you would put Mr. Stewart back on the phone, I think that should be it for now. I appreciate your help. I assume Mr. Stewart informed you that he and his wife leave on a cruise tomorrow?"

"Ms. Woods, Mrs. Stewart might be leaving. Mr. Stewart is not going anywhere. Until he makes bail, he will be our guest instead of Carnival's." The officer's gallows humor caused Jessica to break into a grin. Just as well neither the Ft. Lauderdale Police Department nor she used FaceTime.

Back on the station phone she summarized the situation. "Eric, I am afraid the cruise for you is out. I don't know what bail will be set, but you need to start thinking. Is your wife there with you?"

"Yes, Ally's here. God, I've wrecked our vacation. I do OK with my job, not many stressors with clay and e-Bay. But Ally needed to get away from those crazies she deals with. I couldn't do her job. Psychologists. I have to hand it to her." Jessica heard sniffles again followed by a horrible honking blast, probably Eric blowing his nose.

"She will need to find a bail bondsman down there. I don't have the numbers of any. I'm going to call my colleague from law school to see if she will take your case. Her name is Kelley Rubinov. If I don't reach her tonight, it is eight o'clock on a Saturday evening, she should get back to you tomorrow. Hold tight, settle down, we'll get a handle on this."

Jessica thanked Officer Ramirez again, then sipped some more Pinot Grigio. People and their problems. It would not surprise her if Ally and the friends went on the cruise anyway. Eric would make bail; he could sit in his hotel room and reflect on the consequences resulting from his cowboy behavior.

As Jessica prepared her linguine with clam sauce, curiosity drove her to Google Eric Stewart. Not much turned up except the usual: ceramics engineer, owner of Broad Street Clay. Facebook might bring up more information. Yes, indeed it did. There was Eric Stewart, sobriquet Flaming Eric, self-proclaimed King of eBay Enterprise. Hmm. After a voice message to her friend Kelley, Jessica settled into a dinner that two blocks away in her favorite restaurant cost twenty-five dollars plus tip. Since that twenty-five dollars included dessert, Jess opened her refrigerator for some dark chocolate gelato, a pleasant postprandial repast as she scrolled for research.

The website for DUI charges in Broward County mentioned that the extent of the costs and charges were dependent on what exactly the defendant had done and the level of the defendant's intoxication. Oh, Kelley would have fun with Flaming Eric who, sitting in a Ft. Lauderdale cell tonight, definitely was not flaming. The referral fee Kelley sent, Jessica hoped it might take the form of a personal gift instead of a check that Triple O recorded, that fee could be substantial indeed. While savoring her second glass of wine, Jessica continued to cruise the Internet: Designer bags/Louis Vuitton/Spring Summer.

Sunday of Week Two

Sunday morning. A run, an hour with the *Sunday New York Times*, a general agreement with her favorite columnist Maureen Dowd, a long shower. As Jessica gathered her briefcase and bag to walk to the office, her cell phone chimed. Maddie, the psychologist Alex had hoped Robbie would marry. Make that one of the many former girlfriends his mother had hoped to reel in as a daughter-in-law.

Maddie was special, more than special: as with the compendium of predecessors, she was a beautiful, intelligent young woman. Half Bahamian on her mother's side, Maddie was slim with silky milk chocolate skin she highlighted with a fashion sense Jessica admired. Maddie's father, a university professor, and her mother, a physician, would have been delightful in-laws. Would have been. Dr. Madelyn Hendricks waited one year for Robbie, loving him, guiding him, and encouraging him to accomplish what she believed him capable of being, a success in business. After a year and a day, the magical mythical standard, Maddie wanted marriage; Robbie did not. To this day, Jessica reflected, although neither one had yet married, Madelyn had long ago found other people. And Robbie? As far as Jessica knew, he still ineffably strove for what might well be the unattainable.

Jessie and Maddie though remained friends. "Hey, Hon." Jessica juggled her car keys, phone, purse, and briefcase as she pulled her apartment door closed. Just as the lock clicked, she realized she had grabbed her second set of keys, the one without the apartment key. "Shit! Sorry, Maddie, I just locked myself out."

"I'll call back."

"No, I have a key in my glove compartment. What's up?"

"I am really sorry to bother you. Can you cat sit Cedric? My regular cat sitter backed out. I have a conference in London. Mom and Dad are on vacation in the Caribbean, my boyfriend is allergic to cats. Make that *hates cats*. I can't bring myself to drop poor Cedric off at Kitty Kaddy and Crew. The last time he stayed there, the poor little guy was beat up and wouldn't eat."

"Maddie, I'm allergic to cats too. You know the building doesn't allow pets."

"Please? It's only ten days. Poor little Cedric just can't take another bad experience."

Jessica's encounters with Poor Little Cedric were never pleasant. He could use a bad experience or two if it helped him lose weight. At age two, the Maine Coon already weighed twenty pounds. Apparently this type of cat did not finish growing until age five; the darling could legitimately be expected to tilt his kitty scale at twenty-eight pounds or more. Fortunately, despite his size, the guy was, to put it in his feline vernacular, a pussycat.

The first time she heard his high pitched meow Jessica thought neutering had been his undoing. No, Maine Coons were known for a paradox: high voices, big bodies. They were gentle too and liked to play in water. But Jessica simply could not keep him, not for one day or for ten days. Whatever the cat, after thirty minutes around one, Jessie's eyes burned bright red, dragon's eyes. She sneezed; her nose ran. No, no Cedric.

"Please, Jessica! Little Cedric is my baby. I have to go to this conference; I am presenting my paper to the American Psychological

Association. If it were just an ordinary meeting, but this is a huge opportunity," Maddie uncustomarily pleaded.

"Okay. Can you drop him off this afternoon?"

"Well, that is a problem too. I have to leave for the airport in an hour. Can you come here?"

"I'll be right over."

No matter that Dr. Madelyn Hendricks lived in a gated community on the east side of Columbus, a good thirty minutes away. Jessica Woods had nothing to do on a Sunday morning other than prepare for a pretrial the next day.

A half hour later Maddie greeted her friend. "Let me kiss my little Schnookums goodbye one more time." The psychologist pulled her cat close, planting a wet kiss on his mouth. "I put fresh litter in his sandbox, I packed up his toys in this yellow bag." The two women carried Cedric, his toys, and his potty out to the car. "Wait! I forgot his privacy screen. He gets compacted if he does not have his privacy when he goes to the bathroom." Maddie rushed back into her house, returning with what looked like a doll's Japanese folding screen. "I just have two cans of Precious Kitty left, here is some money if you would pick up his food. I thought I had more in the cupboard. He eats a can at breakfast and another at dinner: six o'clock sharp both times."

Jessica silently vowed, six in the morning would not happen. Six at night maybe. Little Cedric needed to learn patience. Forbearance! Weren't cats famous for that virtue?

"Bye bye, Honey Bunch. Mommy will see you real soon. Now you be a good baby for Auntie Jessica."

As Dr. Madelyn Hendricks waved both hands in some kind of window wiping gesture, Cedric shifted slightly in his carrier. Jessica rounded the corner, foot a little too hard on the accelerator; the Acura turned sharply, sending Cedric and his carrier smartly into the right side passenger door. A high pitched complaint from the back seat, and auntie and nephew drove off. Next stop, the grocery store.

To her annoyance, the Kroger store in Jess's neighborhood happened not to stock Precious Kitty, the only food Madelyn claimed he tolerated. Jess hastily decided she might as well park in front of her office, run upstairs to retrieve the files she needed, then work from home in case Cedric felt homesick. Or she could drag Cedric and carrier up to the office, work there for a while, then go home. Bad idea. She placed herself at the front of the line for allergy attacks in both places.

With Cedric securely locked into the Acura, Jessica retrieved her files. A high end gourmet food store might carry Precious Kitty; they did. She bought twenty cans for twenty-five dollars plus tax. Gourmet Kitty, Expensive Kitty, *Forget about Finances Feline*, any of those names fit. No wonder Cedric hauled around so much weight. The damned cat ate better than she did.

Back into the car and home. A voice mail from Maddie lit up on her phone, but Jessica ignored it. Trying to drive while sniffing nonstop, Jessica peered through stinging eyes at a blurry street; she had already had enough already of Maddie and Schnookums/aka Honey Bunch/aka Cedric.

Finally in her parking garage, Jessica opened the passenger door to retrieve her temporary roommate. Out hopped Cedric, pausing long enough to sniff his new surroundings.

"Dammit, how did you get out?" Jessica swiftly bent down to pick him up, but not swiftly enough. Cedric scooted under the Acura. Kneeling onto the concrete, Jessica cajoled, "Sugar Plum, come to Auntie Jessica." Cedric's pupils dilated in the darkness under her car. Jess swore he snickered.

"Having a little trouble?" a man Jess knew only as Bruce from down the hall materialized next to her.

"I think it's a squirrel. You know how they act in the spring." She stood up quickly. No need to court suspicion. Bruce could be a friend of the management. "I can take care of it, but thanks anyway." Jess pretended to sort through her back seat, hoping her friend of the moment failed to see the litter box, yellow bag stuffed with toys, or grocery sacks spilling cans of Precious Kitty. Bruce continued on his way while Jessica allowed what she hoped was enough time before kneeling again on cold concrete. No Cedric. Dammit.

From what she remembered of cats, if they sneaked out, they usually stayed close by. For all their reputation of aloofness, cats were usually timid, not the courageous hunters of legend.

"Cedric, Sweetie Pie. Auntie Jessica has your favorite foodie." At least being out in fresh air started to work on clearing up her allergies. She could see through the stinging tears and breathe through her stuffed up nose again. Thirty minutes later after pretending to investigate the trash filled woods behind the garage, Jessica temporarily abandoned her search. Draping her jacket over Cedric's cat box, she strategically placed his toilet under her left arm, then carried her files in her right hand. Her plan was to look like an attorney with evidence that had to be protected for security purposes.

Jessica decided to return every thirty minutes to the garage, acting as if she had forgotten some items. If Cedric nosed around, which she expected curiosity would drive him to do, she would leave her car windows open. He might want to jump in. How in the hell had the darling escaped in the first place?

A live potted palm, eight feet from floor to ceiling, graced the south corner of Jess's living room. Placing Cedric's box along with its accompanying privacy screen behind the plant, Jessica hoped that when the cat did arrive, he might feel more relaxed among the foliage when nature called. She might as well see what additional instructions awaited her on Maddie's voice mail.

Baby talk to Cedric. Then, "Hey, Jess, the little guy sometimes reaches through his carrier door and unlatches his cage all by himself. Just wanted to let you know. Have fun, you two."

Back and forth up and down the elevator, calling with no results for a cat who had never been here, Jessica felt miserable. By three o'clock she knew she had to work on her files or she not only would have lost a recalcitrant cat, she would lose a client. Settling into her couch, files spread onto the coffee table and floor, Jessica turned off her phone. She would try mightily to salvage what she could of a peaceful working Sunday. Instead, exhausted from the week, she fell asleep.

A sharp rap at her door startled her from a dream involving Max or the lobbyist from Kentucky or somebody she had met at a fundraiser. Hard to concentrate. At least the nap had cured her allergy attack. Pushing her hair back out of her face and straightening her clothes, she peered through the peephole. Bruce from down the hall.

"Yes?"

"Jessica, I park my car five spaces down from yours. I think I found the *squirrel* you were looking for earlier. He poked his head out at me from behind my back tire, so I managed to pull him out before he figured out what I was doing." In his arms Bruce held a purring Cedric, the cat's paws kneading his rescuer.

"Bruce, right? Thank you." She reached for Cedric who chose to hang on to the man's jacket. The more she tried to disengage the cat's claws, the more Cedric clenched onto Bruce. "Come on, Honey, let go so Auntie Jessica can feed you dinner." Cedric looked disinterested in food, as he steadfastly resisted Jesse's attempts to remove him from his new friend's protective arms.

"Would you like to come in, I mean, both of you?" She hoped the cat did but Bruce did not.

"I can't," he demurred. "I'm headed over to the gym. Cedric here might want to though." Jess's neighbor smoothly, one claw by one claw, unfastened the cat's grip. "Here you go, Kitty." He handed the somewhat calmer cat to Jessie, then smiled at both of them, although Jess chose to believe it was more directed to her than to Cedric. Surely the four pawed charmer deserved less a smile than a light rap on the rump.

Nice waste of an afternoon: an obstreperous cat that made her sick, a feckless friend who caused the whole damned thing, and a man who seemed more interested in cats than in a beautiful blond attorney right down the hall from him. Best to avoid thinking about it. Jessica opened a can of Precious Kitty, scooping the whole turkey/egg/gravy mess into a Pottery Barn cereal bowl. As Cedric dined, Jesse reviewed her work for tomorrow's pretrial. She refused to allow herself to think about Bruce, not one thought, not one. She was in love with Max. Thus afternoon passed into evening: cat and cat sitter settling into an uneasy peace.

Monday of Week Two

Monday morning plans to rise at 6:00 a.m. for a run evanesced even as the alarm on her cell phone chimed. Jessie hit the snooze, snuggling down instead under the covers on her king sized bed. Now why, Alex had wondered aloud when her daughter had Arhause Furniture deliver the ebony frame, why would you purchase a king sized bed when a queen provided than enough room? For that matter, why ebony? White furniture in a young woman's bedroom would be absolutely beautiful.

"Because I'm not an old maid, Mother!" silenced Alex momentarily. Jessica's Aunt Katherine (Kate) agreed; for fun Jessie called Alex's younger sister her real mother, more like Jess than Alex was, certainly with fashion trends, and, even Alex admitted, more liberal in personal views. Two years older than Robbie and Jess, both of Aunt Kate's children progressed through the social stages that informed Kate who then advised Alex and Jess, and Robbie if he called. Yes, Kate counseled Alex, Robbie's fitful responses to phone calls from his mother were typical of young men. Don't take it personally. No, Alex, Jessica does not need to marry to have children. Yes, Jessica, young couples prefer the Pottery Barn style dark, Shaker furniture to the white wicker some people (Alex) advised. Your mother means well though, so listen to her about shoes especially. I wish I could wear those spikes; I just can't.

A widow for more than twenty years, Aunt Katherine lived in a wealthy suburb north of New York City. While Alex had attended Ohio Wesleyan University, majoring in English, her little sister had followed a different path, preferring to study fashion at the University of Pennsylvania. Alexandra remained in Ohio, returning to her hometown to teach high school English. Kate returned only to visit their parents. With graduation she moved to New York City where she worked first for Lord and Taylor, then as editor of the sports section for *Seventeen Magazine*. Oh, yes, Aunt Kate knew fashion trends. She married Rory, a very attractive stockbroker, then settled down, she thought to raise their children that appeared at well orchestrated times. What Katherine and her family had not planned was Rory's sudden death early one summer from a brain aneurism, making Kate a widow with no source of income except for her husband's gun collection and an insurance policy for fifty thousand dollars that Rory's parents had given him as a wedding gift. Their son was expected to update it, but he never got around to it.

Rory had belonged to a private hunting club outside New York City. As Kate surveyed the guns her husband had collected, she symbolically kicked herself for avoiding insisting that Rory keep bills of sale. All she knew was that the guns were expensive. Raising children and caring for a husband, a mantra of her generation and that of her sister, that was her focus. What to do?

Bob and Alex flew out the day after Rory's death, staying with Kate and the children for two weeks. As Bob sorted through the mess he found of his brother-in-law's affairs, he continuously circled back to one solution: sell the guns, sell the house, start over. For Kate that meant get a job, find a part time sitter for the kids, now in elementary school and junior high. Live like most people in America did, paycheck to paycheck. "You can do it, Kate. I'll handle the estate, and you should be fine." Bob returned to his office in Upper Sandusky; Alex stayed on with Robbie and Jessica to spend another week with Katherine and kids.

Over wine mixed with salty tears, Kate and Alex compiled a résumé; Alex had a contrived company of her own, Wordsworth. In the early 1990s computers, many were still referred to as word processors, were rather scarce in most people's homes. Although Alex earned very little pay for writing her friends' and acquaintances' résumés, she garnered a certain mystique that stay-at-home mothers (they were not referred to as *moms* at the time) did not enjoy. Alex babysat for all four children while Katherine, dressed professionally in a navy blue suit and low heeled navy shoes interviewed for office and sales positions. Returning home after yet another interview, Kate poured a Chardonnay for herself and her sister. "I have several job offers," she explained. "But I just cannot bring myself to send my children to a sitter and to work for hours I cannot set."

Alex waited.

"I talked to Bob. I'm going to work, I have to. But I'm going to do what I am good at and what is good for Graham and Mandy. I know fabric, I know fashion. Through my children's friends' parents, I have contacts with a couple of window treatment companies. I am going to start my own business in home décor, focusing on windows and accessories. I can sew, my basement is huge. We'll shove the kids' toys off into one room, then open up the rest of the area for my work space. I already know carpenters. Rory relied on me to arrange all the home repairs anyway. Actually, I made cushions and table coverings for gifts; now I'm sewing for clients. That way my hours will fit my kids' schedules, and I can do what I'm good at."

Kate sold the house, *downsizing*, a term not yet in use, *moving* it was called, to a smaller three bedroom frame home in the same town. She left a sprawling half-timber, her friends called it Tudor, with five bedrooms, four bathrooms, and three acres of woodlands with an accompanying pond to move into a house in so much disrepair the realtor's pictures made Alex shudder. Abandoned too was the well appointed basement workroom; Kate installed work tables and adequate lighting. Complaining less than his mother expected, Graham dragged a sewing machine down the narrow basement steps. Mandy babysat, sometimes grudgingly but at least reliably, for her little brother while Katherine Madison of Kate's Interiors called on clients.

At the same time Kate developed her business, her sister too applied herself to work beyond the home. She wrote résumés. Few people owned computers then, actually termed word processors. Alex's job, as she called it, with the self titled Wordsworth dwindled through her own entropy as well as the availability of computers with accompanying programs with which people could generate their own employee applications and history. Kate's business, however, blossomed. Oh, Graham and Mandy might have hated arriving home from school as they tripped over cardboard boxes the height of a teenager and just as heavy. Usually they hauled those boxes in rather than wait for their mother's orders to do the same. The boxes and the Fed Ex messages taped to the door meant an income for their mother. She may have dropped out of the book club their friends' mothers belonged to, but she was home; she was alive.

Kate's Interiors paid for two college educations, two weddings, property taxes, insurance, and family vacations to Marco Island, Florida in the winter, and a cottage rental on Nantucket in the summer. Wordsworth paid for nothing. However, at the time, Alex had no need of employment; Bob paid for everything. That would change as suddenly as her younger sister's life had changed. As with Katherine, Alex just did not know it.

Jessica's reveries ended abruptly. Something warm and horridly furry grazed her bare ankle as Jessica reached for her robe. God! She forgot about Cedric! Her newfound friend, the linear relationship extended only one way, wanted breakfast. How had the little dear opened her bedroom door? Typical cat, with time on his side, having no job to get to and nothing to do but solve one single problem, the darling had figured out, over the long night, how to pull down the door handle.

Purring too. "All right, Cedric, you win this one. Do you mind if I use the ladies' room first?" Quickly pushing the door shut, she scurried into her bathroom, not quick enough though. A large white paw reached around the door, opening it just enough to allow a curious Cedric access into, of course, what the English termed The Water Closet.

"I would appreciate some privacy, Ced." Best to be authoritative now, early in a relationship. She picked up the cat, placed him on the other side of the door, then brushed her teeth. "For interloping, Ced Dear, you can wait for breakfast."

A can of Precious Kitty Eggies and Bacon Bities for the Maine Coon, a fruit/almond soy shake for the lawyer, and Jessica left her apartment for the start of another week at O'Malley, O'Malley, and O'Malley. But not soon enough to avoid the red watery eyes and sneezes that accompany an allergy attack.

"Great outfit," Lil remarked when Jess arrived. Jessica did indeed dress beautifully. For court she had long ago abandoned what she termed Banker's Blue. No conservative navy blazer with midcalf skirt for her, no sensible flats either. Today the attorney of record for her client charged with, mistakenly Jessica was informed, burglary, had chosen an A-line chartreuse chemise, a close fitting tangerine jacket, and daffodil three-inch spike heels. To add a somewhat conservative tone, Jess draped a simple gold chain around her neck. Best to leave the Hermes scarf where it would not attract the attention of perspicacious female judge, should Jessica be blessed with one today. Most men, except for Uncle Ralph and her brother Robbie, could not distinguish one scarf from another. Still, if a woman sat on the bench, no need to annoy.

A quick phone call to Lil, then a short walk to court, a quick arraignment, then back to the office. "Hey, Lil. What do I have today?"

"I have you down for an eleven o'clock with Leonard Warren in Canal Winchester, liquor license case."

"Shit! I forgot about that. All right. I'm headed toward an arraignment, but I'll get the case continued, then check in at the office. Anything else?"

"You have a pretrial at two."

"That one I know about. Personal injury. I actually know what I'm doing with that one. Okay. See you soon."

Jamming her cell phone into her bag, Jessica jaywalked across High Street to the Franklin County Court of Common Pleas. A striking building completed in 2010, the structure with its multiple glass windows showcased what architects and judiciary referred to as *transparency of justice*. Seventeen elected judges, nine magistrates, and one visiting judge comprised the judiciary. Facing South High Street, the court provided services for 1.212 million people in Franklin County. Of those residents, approximate 787,000 lived in Columbus, the state capital of Ohio.

Most people, unless they were associated with the legal system or, unfortunately for them, involved on the wrong side of the legal system, did not fully understand the nature of a court of common pleas. In Ohio the court system provides one court of common pleas for each of the eighty-eight counties. Divisions within the courts include domestic relations, juvenile, probate, and general. All criminal felony cases as well as most civil cases if the amount in contest is over fifteen thousand dollars, and most real estate cases involving title questions fall under the jurisdiction of the general division. Because of the charges, Jessica's newest client Ompherous, epithet One Eye Oney, would appear at 9:00 a.m. in the Franklin County Court of Common Pleas with his attorney of record, Jessica F. Woods, Esq.

For all his surreptitious behaviors as far as his marriage, referring attorney Bartram Irving provided punctilious notes. Charged with breaking and entering, trespassing, and burglary, Mr. Ompherous Oney, age thirty-two, had no prior convictions. For the court appearance, no interpreter was needed nor was audiovisual equipment requested.

As most attorneys do, Jessica met her client, Ompherous (One Eye on his Facebook page) Oney in the hall outside the courtroom. Jess usually did not handle criminal cases, having little expertise in these areas, but a fellow attorney had referred Mr. Oney to her due to a circuitous set of circumstances which Jessica assumed involved the lawyer's clandestine affair, a conference at the Greenbrier, and an unsuspecting wife. Jessica's professional association with Ompherous's attorney had involved a brief handshake at a cocktail party with the accompanying exchange of business cards. At the time, the attorney introduced Jessica quickly to his intern who, Jess learned through Lil's gossip network, was also the guy's girlfriend.

Jess assumed that Mr. Bartram Irving selected the services of O'Malley, O'Malley, and O'Malley for any number of reasons, mostly because her firm was not long established in Columbus and therefore probably less likely to share stories with other attorneys all too eager to hear who was doing what to whom. Fine. Jess needed the case load. Lil knew the background. All the referring attorney knew was that Jess would take care of things while he attended a professional conference for required educational credits.

Having only viewed One Eye's pictures on Facebook, Jessica felt uncertain as to whom or what to expect. She had her choice from any number of candidates. On a Monday morning, distinguishing lawyers from clients was relatively easy. Male attorneys dressed in suits, white shirts, and conservative ties. Female attorneys, Jessica F. Woods, Esq. being the exception, generally wore navy blue or gray ensembles of some forgettable style. Clients displayed a panoply of outfits: salient among them jeans, T-shirts with a variety of logos, and tennis shoes. Despite what their attorneys urged, to dress respectfully for court appearances, clients, guilty or not, already believed they knew more than their lawyers.

More than a hundred Facebook pictures, most in settings highlighting beer bottles, women in low-cut cleavage emphasizing shirts, and men with tattoos and tank tops had not prepared Jessica for the man approaching her now. Self-confident, streaked blond hair slicked back, clean shaven, the thirtysomething gentleman extended his hand.

"Ms. Woods? Pleasure to meet you. I am Ompherous Oney."

She recognized a Paul Stuart shirt when she saw one: stark white, crisp starched color. The charcoal gray suit with barely discernible stripes must be Paul Stuart too. The belt? Probably Burberry. And the elegant gray and white striped tie, in a Windsor knot, of course? Most likely Salvatore Ferragamo, 170.00, she thought. Jess hated herself for inwardly drooling, but she had, just had, to look at his shoes. Italian leather, buttery soft, deep charcoal: 700.00 at least.

Trying rather successfully she thought to avoid appearing rattled, Jessica proffered her right hand, which she hoped was not suddenly sweaty. "Hello, Mr. Oney, pleasure to meet you."

She gestured toward what looked like a church pew at the far end of the hall. "Let's talk down there." One Eye, she now thought of him as Mr. Oney, stood politely until his attorney arranged her briefcase and files. "Please, sit down, Mr. Oney."

"I'm sure your attorney notified you that he had to attend a professional conference. I have the file, so we will proceed. I see here you were arrested on the night of April 15 at 2895 Ten Sweep in New Albany. That is a pretty high end community. What, Mr. Oney, were you thinking? Well, let me ask you first, how am I going to approach this? It goes a lot quicker if you tell me the truth." Jessica knew, of course, that all clients lie.

One Eye, now because of his attire Mr. Oney, shocked her. "Everything I am charged with I did. Except for breaking and entering. I was already there."

"Okay. Why?"

"Look, Ms. Woods, I hold an M. Ed. in music education. I graduated from Kenyon University. My family in Connecticut thinks I'm still a band director in Vinton County. The board of education for the little town where I taught, actually a consolidated school system, cut funding. Long story short, I could have looked for another position in another county. I had the experience, the students, and better yet the parents and administration liked me. I liked my job, I just did not earn enough money. Most teachers average 31,800 a year in Ohio. I wish my tastes ran to the conservative, but as you can see, they do not."

"I have to ask you why in the hell you posted those horrible Facebook pictures? You look like a felon even before you walk into a court. Anyone can check you out."

"Stupid, I know. Call it my year of transition. I lost my job. I couldn't face substitute teaching with take home pay somewhere between 65.00 and 100.00 a day, depending on the district, and that not regular. A sub in demand can get in about a hundred days a year with one district, more if you apply to several districts. I will take those pictures down today. I actually forgot about them. For a while there I lost heart, but," he added brightly, "I'm back on top again, except for this little setback."

"Sorry, Mr. Oney, we have to hurry this along. I'll ask you about your background later. Right now I am going to request a continuance due to unexpected circumstances. I don't yet know what those might be, but I'll think of something. Come in with me, sit with me. Be respectful, which I see you can be. Do not say anything unless you are asked to do so. Then, be as brief as possible. My dad used to say, 'If they ask you the time, don't build them a watch.'" Jessica entered the courtroom, her client politely trailing her, performing, unusual for clients, exactly as he had been instructed.

As the bailiff announced "All rise," Jessica silently congratulated herself on leaving the Hermes scarf back in its orange box on her closet shelf. The judge, a female, would most certainly have recognized the brand and probably the design. People who were cognizant of Hermes often knew the year and the season too. Jessica's mother had started her daughter's collection two years ago at Christmas. As a treat after a particularly bad day, Jesse had been known to visit her favorite sales associate at Nordstrom's, even to call her. The beauty of a Hermes scarf, boxed in white tissue in its square orange bed with the signature horse and phaeton on top, assuaged most pains better than a Lemontini, well, generally. Sometimes a situation called for both.

Jessica waited for the judge to speak to her. Then, "Your Honor, may I approach the bench?"

"Yes, Ms. Woods."

Jessica hoped The Honorable Susan Dial approved her request for a continuance. In truth, Jessica was not prepared for a self-confessed mostly guilty client. Trespassing, burglary, but no breaking and entering.

"Your Honor, due to unusual unexpected circumstances I respectfully request a continuance."

"I assume you have discussed this with your client."

Ridiculous, of course Jessica had. What was Her Honor doing?

"I have, Your Honor. My client is in agreement."

One Eye remained silent, doing exactly what he was told, nothing.

"All right. We will continue this matter at another date. The court will be in communication with you."

"Thank you, Your Honor." Jessica waited for the usual dismissal. "Ms. Woods, may I see you in my chambers?"

Oh, my God, what does she know? What have I done? I hate this job. I should never have been here in the first place. Doing a favor for a damned womanizer, so he could go off to the Greenbrier with his intern girlfriend. And who is the client? A felon with an admitted life of crime! I am going to lose my license all because of... Stop it! She halted her circular thinking. *Do not panic. Most likely some minor court protocol only this judge practiced, which would be unknown to anybody who had not enjoyed working in Judge Dial's court before. That would be me, for starters.*

Jessica glanced at Mr. Oney sitting quietly at the table. She cast a look his way, which she intended to convey an attitude of *This is what I usually do.* He smiled.

Judge Dial stepped down; the bailiff escorted Jessica to Her Honor's chambers. *It must be serious,* Jessica worried, *for the judge to remain standing. What am I supposed to do? Stand? Wait to be spoken to?*

"Ms. Woods." Judge Susan Dial smiled at her, certainly a very different persona than the one presiding over court. "I hope I have not frightened you." Of course she had, but best to appear confident on one's walk to the gallows. "Counselor, I was wondering, where *do* you get your clothes?"

The cold sweat Jesse felt staining her underarm sleeves abated. This story would go into her repertoire for sure, most likely to be repeated over Lemontinis which, having recovered from what she now viewed as poorly blended ones rather than over served ones, would grace her table sooner rather than later. Tonight, most likely.

After lying about scavenging thrift shops, a practice Jess never participated in, Jessica returned to her waiting client. "You can go. We have a continuance. Either Mr. Irving or I will call you when we have another court date. In the meantime, stay out of trouble." She intended for the contactor to be Mr. Bartram Irving. Ms. Jessica F. Woods would subsequently bill the bastard for her trouble and his insouciance.

One Eye Oney, dressed better than most of the lawyers that morning, nodded his agreement. "I'll behave, Ms. Woods." He grinned, a smile showing perfect sparkling white teeth. "For you I'll behave."

Being the gentleman he was, her client followed her out, opened the doors to High Street for her, then turned south toward what could be a Lexus as far as Jessica knew. *You meet all kinds in this shit show,* she thought, *all kinds.*

Jessica checked her watch. Time enough to drive to Canal Winchester to meet Leonard Warren. As she returned to her apartment building to retrieve her car from the parking garage, her phone chimed. Max. "Hey, Hon, what's up? I missed you. I should have invited you down."

"I missed you too, Jess. All I did was watch baseball Friday night."

Jessica knew better. Watching baseball meant watching at a sports bar with friends, among them probably women. Her own fault. Max, a bachelor with no baggage at all, no kids, not spousal support, no custody fights, Max was a terrific catch. And she had turned him down, again.

"Did you call the Huron County prosecutor's office?"

"Oh, Max, Hon, I'm so sorry. I'll call right after this. You should be fine. How does this week look for you?"

"Other than missing you, I'm good. A guy at work has tickets for Friday's home game: the Boston Red Sox. Would you like to drive up for the weekend?"

"Sure, I love baseball. I'm supposed to have lunch with Mom on Saturday here, then go shopping at Easton. Never mind, I'll work something out with her. She is pretty flexible; she just wants to see me. I don't think she cares where. Maybe we can switch to Crocker Park. Listen, I have to go. Get the tickets. Love you."

Exactly what she did not need, driving hell bent to Cleveland after a full day of work. Make that a full week of work. Well, best not to think about it now. The fun of driving to Canal Winchester lay right ahead.

The city of Canal Winchester, population 7,101 according to the 2010 U.S. census, bridged the two counties of Fairfield and Franklin. Perched proudly off Route 33 about thirteen miles south-east of Columbus, the little city boasted a history related to the Ohio and Erie Canal. A few minutes' walk took a visitor through the town center, all two main streets, southeast to the banks of what appeared to be a river now. Ohio joined the union in 1803. Twenty-five years later Reuben Dove and John Colman recorded the first official plat, originally naming the village Winchester. Apparently Dove insisted on suing the state of Ohio when the canal ran through his wheat field. Instead, and farmers were financially astute as Jessica knew from Alex's marriage to Jesse's stepfather Jim, Mr. Dove realized the potential that fitful wheat harvests did not offer.

The little village lay between Columbus and Lancaster. Three years later the canal that had first nearly driven Reuben Dove to sue now floated prosperity his way as well as to that of the town he and John Colman had officially founded in 1828. With the railroad in 1869, it looked as if Canal Winchester would continue to grow and prosper as farming and business added profits to residents' incomes. Evidently the town did grow, but not to the degree that neighboring Columbus or Lancaster enjoyed. Of course, nearly two hundred years later, as urban sprawl macerated surrounding farmland, perhaps the city of 7,101 souls would expand its boundaries in order to keep up.

Jessica did not consider why her new client chose to live where he did; Leonard Warren would tell her soon enough. Passing a white highway patrol car hiding in a used car parking area off Route 33, Jesse lowered her speed to 65 MPH. A quick call to Mr. Warren alerted him that she planned to be about fifteen minutes late due to court. She liked to hint to her clients that she had other clients as well and that she worked on their behalf, including going head to head with opposing attorneys. By allowing clients to conjure up images of her engaged in dramatic courtroom battles, Jessica believed she planted seeds in their minds of a strong victorious lawyer, one to trust and, yes, one who would win. Those histrionic courtroom scenes may never have occurred; sometimes all it took were a few phone calls. Clients, however, did not need to know everything. Neither, Jessica strongly ascribed to this opinion too, did O'Malley, O'Malley, and O'Malley.

Leonard Warren answered on the first ring. "Okay by me, Ms. Woods. Got nothin' to do but sit here anyway. The damned state's not about to give me a liquor license till you get here and start shakin' things up." Good sign; he might be angry, but he trusted her.

She had no difficulty locating Mr. Warren's home at 213 W. Liberty Street. Victorian and Edwardian homes lined the few streets included in what residents termed the old historic area. Red geraniums graced neatly mowed lawns. A few early roses bloomed on black wrought iron fences. In one yard a yellow lab napped in the sun as his mistress planted petunias. Jessica felt her blood pressure, seldom high, drop even more as she settled into the peaceful scene she entered after her morning of usual agitations.

Rocking in a white wicker chair on his front porch, Mr. Leonard Warren, age sixty-six, awaited his attorney. Lil had had no luck looking him up on Facebook, although she tried. Triple O subscribed to a computer program that furnished enough information for Jess to pull together some sort of new client profile. Graduated from McConnelsville High School in Muskingum County in June 1966, drafted into the U.S. Army in September 1966, two tours of duty in Vietnam, made captain in 1971, honorably discharged in 1976 with the rank of Major. Married in 1972. Worked for McConnelsville Lumber Company until retiring in 2008. What the hell was the guy doing sinking his pension into a bar? That was not Jessica's business; her business and her income depended on her securing a liquor license.

"Welcome to our fine city, Miss Woods." Major Leonard Warren rose from his chair, a gentleman when a lady approached. He gestured to a rocker adjacent to his. "Wife keeps this froufrou around. Me? I'd just as soon set out back behind the garage. You want a drink or something? Coffee, something stronger?" He chuckled.

Jessica declined, planning to pick up a salad and iced tea later at the McDonald's she saw back on the road to Columbus. She could certainly use the bathroom though. Not a good idea however to request the facilities with a first client encounter, her bosses had drilled into her. At this point, she was miserable. Crossing her legs discreetly but tightly, she opened her briefcase to retrieve a notebook.

"Major Warren, why did you contact me?" Although her new client was sixty-six, except for his weathered skin, it was hard to tell his age. When he unfolded himself from his chair, he stood about six feet five inches or so. He looked like a runner, thin face, sinewy arms, narrow hips. He wore his full head of gray hair, waxed, in a precise crew cut, military style. For the appointment the major had on jeans, no particular brand, a plain light gray T-shirt, and tennis shoes. No surprise there. Jessica loathed tennis shoes on men except for sports, but for many of her clients, jeans, shirts, and tennis shoes comprised the uniform of the day.

"I'll be damned. You *are good*," he leaned forward in his rocker to look her straight in the eyes. "No one's called me Major since I got out of the Army. Except Rachel, and that only in private conversation, if you know what I mean." He grinned. "Hey, Rache, come on out of the house. We got us one smart lawyer!"

The woman who emerged from the house looked exactly as Jessica expected. At least one client/client family avoided surprising her. Sixty-five or so sat well on some people, not, unfortunately, on Rachel. Whereas her husband appeared to strive for a kind of physical fitness, his wife had long since "let herself go," as Alex often commented about classmates. Poor old Rachel must have weighed a good two hundred pounds. As with her husband, the woman wore jeans, a T-shirt, and tennis shoes. On the contrary, unlike Leonard, she kept the shirt out, untucked, in a failed attempt to conceal the adipose or excessive fat between her breasts and her hips. To Jessica she acted friendly enough; Jess marveled at how couples who physically appeared to have grown apart remained together. Maybe that was the impetus for Major Warren planning to open a bar; he wanted a legitimate reason to get away from home. Mumbling an excuse about needing to get back into the house, Rachel perfunctorily welcomed Jessica, then ducked back inside.

"By the way, call me Leonard. I ain't used to a title these days. Haven't been for years. Back then, I was an officer. Sharp. Dressed the part when I wasn't in the jungle. Things change, you know what I mean?" He nodded toward the door his wife had just closed.

"Leonard, obtaining a liquor license in Ohio is not too difficult. I can apply for you, but all the information you need is on the state website. I charge by the hour, 300.00. You probably need an A1A, which covers the sale of beer, liquor by the glass, pitcher, that sort of thing, on your premises until 2:30 a.m., which is the legal closing hour in Ohio. The license runs about 4000.00 the last time I looked. Expect a background check, but if everything is good, you will receive your license in ten to twelve weeks." As Jessica rattled off the requirements, she watched her client's body language and facial expressions. He shifted almost unnoticeably in his rocker.

"Here's the problem, not everything *will* check out, which is why I called you. I have already applied on the website, just like you said. I went to the library this winter and used their computers. I used to have one here, but I only use it for e-mail. The thing broke down after about six years, and the cost to repair it or buy a new one didn't make no sense."

"Why do you think things will not check out?" Jessica silently muttered the mantra her father and Uncle Ralph invoked, "All clients lie. Everyone lies."

"Miss Woods, I truly do not know. I am a long way from broke. I realized I'm too damned young to be settin' on my front porch in a rocker. Hell, I built houses in Nam, burned some down too. Between the retirement Uncle Sam gives me and my pension with the lumber company, I've got me a nice nest egg.

"Sure you don't want a beer or something? Damned hot this time of year. Hey, Rache," Leonard yelled into the front door, left ajar about enough for his wife most likely hiding just out of sight to listen to the conversation between her husband and his attorney. "Bring the little lady and me here a beer."

Rather than decline, the easier path was to accept, although on a fairly empty stomach Jessica promised herself only a few sips. As Jessica and Leonard waited patiently for the beers, conversation turned to more prosaic topics. Yes, Jessica had family in the military. As a young Marine, her grandfather served in one of several Nicaraguan Revolutions, dubbed at the time the Banana Wars. Later he enlisted in the U.S. Army during World War II, then was stationed in Louisiana during the Korean Conflict. During Vietnam he was a member of the draft board in Ottawa County. As a high school senior, Jessica's mother Alexandra had applied to all the service academies but received letters politely refusing admission.

"Oh, yeah," Leonard remembered. "No women then. Christ, my sister had all *As* like your mom, even tried again during the Gulf War. They turned her down the first time her being a girl and all. They took her the next time; she was over forty, too old really, but she was a nurse.

"Mom tried to enlist then too, but age kept her out. I think she wanted to get away from Dad. My brother and I were little kids then. I'm glad she didn't go to Kuwait. She ended up returning to graduate school, earned her Master's degree, then eventually worked on her doctorate."

Rachel arrived with two very cold craft beers, the names which Jessica had never heard of: Spring Chicken and Dandelion Dandy. "Take your pick, Girlie," Leonard offered.

Jessica winced. First Little Lady, now Girlie. All in a day's pay. Dandelion Dandy sounded vegetarian. It also tasted strong, a good 10 percent alcohol, maybe more.

"Cousin brews this swill down in Muskingum County." Jessica's client raised his bottle in a kind of toast to his new attorney. "Bottom's up, Honey. He got a damned license; here's to you gettin' me one too."

"I'll do my best." God, the beer tasted good. Jessica forced herself to concentrate on writing in her notebook. Best to get as much information as she could before the beer hit her. "Major, you were honorably discharged, married, held a responsible job for thirty-two years. I will look into why you are having difficulty with the Division of Liquor Control. Straightening out the situation should not pose too many problems. I'll stay in touch with you."

She placed her nearly full bottle of 10 % lunch beverage on the table next to her rocker, then rose to leave. Not quickly enough though.

"You didn't drink all your beer." Leonard's authoritative U. S. Major's voice replaced the down home good old boy tone he bandied about with her earlier.

"I have to go, Major." It was the truth. She really had to go, at the first gas station she found.

"Sit," her newest client ordered. "It's a shame to waste the nectar of the gods."

Easier to sit and hope for the best, so Jessica dropped back into the rocker. Maybe she could, as she used to do in college, chug her drink. Well, at least down it faster and get away... soon.

"I'll tell you one story, kind of get you familiar with my background. Rache, bring us a couple more! Hey, where are my manners? It's lunchtime."

The front door opened slightly, quickly, Jessica observed. Rache must have been right next to it, listening, as Jess had already surmised, the whole time.

"Rachel here used to be a waitress, whoops, server we call them now, didn't you, Hon?"

Jess took heart in the first real smile Leonard's wife found to offer her guest. Before the marshmallow face, the barrel midsection, and the loose grayed thinning hair a beautiful woman must have enthralled a soldier returning from Vietnam. Either that, or Leonard Warren, thinking with his head, not the one between his shoulders, had entered a marriage contract for other reasons.

"The prettiest woman in McConnellsville, weren't you, Sweetheart?"

Rachel blushed. Those two might still love each other, disparate appearances to the contrary.

"Drink up. Your beer's getting warm, and you've got another to wash that one down."

Jessica chugged, putting into practice a skill that in college earned her the sobriquet Queen of Beers. Of course, she weighed ten pounds or so more back then. Well, it was done. One more beer and she could leave.

"Rachel, Hon, run down to the 7-Eleven and pick us up a couple of those mile-high club sandwiches. You know the ones we like: turkey, ham, beef, cheddar cheese, and mayo."

"That's so nice of you, Major. I have to get back to Columbus. I have a hearing this afternoon."

"A person has to eat. Hold off for a while. I'll let you go after a good lunch."

Leonard pulled a fifty-dollar bill out of his jeans pocket. Handing it to his wife, he smacked her on the rump, "Get going, Honey. We're hungry!

"She didn't always look like that," he sounded wistful. "Unlike a lot of guys, I felt pretty good when I got back from Nam the first time. I was damned lonely though. My high school friends were either dead or married. Take your pick. In the jungle a lot of guys went out; a lot of guys didn't come back. Those were hard times.

"I was between tours of duty. Rachel worked at the McConnelsville Tavern. You know how it goes; she was available and so was I. Back then when you got a girl pregnant, you married her." He put his beer down, surveying Jessica's. "Drink up."

"These kids now do it backwards, I think. The kid goes to school, parents have a couple of different names. Kid wonders why he's different from everybody else. Teacher keeps calling Mom and Dad by the wrong name. Maybe the parents get married later; maybe they don't. It's easier to split up without a certificate holding you together. At least, that's how I see it.

"Anyway, me and Rachel have a quickie ceremony. Honeymoon for the weekend in Cincinnati; I head back to Nam. Baby's born all right. Born but not right. What do you call that, real big head, funny body, hydrocephalic. He would have been about your age now if he lived."

Jessica understood the condition. In her college sorority as one of their social service projects they visited a care center for mentally disabled people. The guide had described hydrocephalus in lay terms, "water on the brain." The mental condition could be the result of trauma such as an accident or through complications at birth. It could also be genetic. Consequences of hydrocephalus caused a steady accumulation of fluid on the brain, which eventually enlarged the head of the afflicted person as well as brought about ensuing mental disabilities. Often enough other developmental disabilities accompanied babies afflicted with hydrocephalus, and shortened life spans for the sufferers were frequently anticipated. The person the guide had pointed out, however, appeared to be in his midthirties. After that visit Jessica had returned to her dorm where she cried most of the night. Yes, she knew about hydrocephalics.

"Anyway, with my boy's condition and me back in the jungle, Rachel had to make all the decisions on her own. I was halfway across the world serving my country. Don't get me wrong. Like your grandfather, I was proud to serve. Still am. I could have done better by my wife, though. I could have come home, pleaded hardship.

"So by the time I got out Benjamin, Benny we called him, lived full time in the Muskingum County Home. He got good care. We visited him often enough. I think sometimes he even knew who we were. I used to get the biggest kick out him. I actually taught him to salute! I'd salute, he'd salute. I'd salute, he'd salute. He giggled too. I swear, he could say 'Mommy' and 'Daddy,' but only in a way Rachel and I understood. It didn't matter though. He was our son, and we loved him just as he was.

"Most hydrocephalics don't live very long, in case you didn't know. Benjamin Leonard Warren died in his sleep at five years old. We buried him in the family cemetery the county maintains even though a shopping mall stands next to it now. With what happened to Benny, we couldn't bring ourselves have more kids. Maybe his illness wasn't genetic, but we didn't want to do that to another human being if it was our fault.

"After our son died my wife and I realized the only thing keeping us together was Benny. We were two different people for sure. Still, Rachel and I just stayed married. It seemed like the thing to do at the time."

Leonard finished his second beer. Returning with the sandwiches, Rachel set them on the table between Jessica and Leonard, then retreated again into the house. Nodding back into the interior, he continued, "Still does."

Jessica finished her beer. "Major Warren, I really do have to leave. I'll do what I can for you." She dropped her notebook into a pocket of her laptop carrier. An officer, a polite gentleman, Leonard stood, shaking hands with her.

She walked down the first step, then turned, going back onto the porch. "Major, a lot in life is a shit show, I'll give you that. Thank you for spending time with me. I'll do my best. We'll get your license for you."

Jessica shoved her laptop into the back seat, pulled her phone out of her bag, and started the Acura. It was very hard to see through her tears. The guy wanted to buy a bar to bring him and his wife together again. If she could, and she would try very, very hard, she would give them that.

Following a badly needed stop at McDonald's, Jess chomped on her salad as she called Lil. "How are things at the office? Still have the herd under control?'

"I checked. Your 2:00 p.m. hearing is canceled, so I can schedule more appointments if you wish." Lil was nothing if not aggressive for her boss.

"Sure. Triple O loves billable hours. I am supposed to be a workers comp/personal injury attorney, but right now except for your friends Mel and Clara, I seem to have everything but."

"I believe, Counselor, your inherited the Woolseys, not me. I choose my friends better than that," Lil sweetly commented.

"Speaking of choosing friends and inheriting, don't you have an upcoming family reunion somewhere in Southeastern Ohio?"

"Every year, the second weekend of June. Want to tag along? My family would love you."

"Can't. Mom's birthday weekend. Where is the event anyway? I think I need your help on that liquor license case I just came from."

"The Dawber Family Reunion always meets at Blue Rock State Park. We book the same shelter every year for the next year. I stay with my parents. Almost everybody gets a cabin. We spend the whole weekend hiking, picnicking, fishing. Some people trailer boats, but we can rent boats too. It's just so pretty down there because summer comes earlier in southern Ohio. I'll tell you, by that time I can use a break. It's just so, so peaceful down there in the hills."

"Is that, I truly hope, in Muskingum County?"

"You've got it. Most of my family come from New Lexington, Athens, Logan, Zanesville. I wouldn't miss the reunion for the world. A lot of those people are getting older, so the crowd isn't as big as it used to be, but we still have fun. What do you need?"

"I just left Leonard Warren, the man that called about a liquor license. He and his wife live in Canal Winchester now, but he worked in McConnelsville for thirty-two years. The poor guy wants to open a bar, but he has run into a stone wall with the liquor department.

I'm wondering why, and I'm thinking somebody in the Dawber family has got to know him."

"You could go with me."

"We'll see. Robbie and I celebrate my mother's birthday with her that weekend. I don't think Alex will be too happy if I cancel or reschedule. I will check though. I promise. Could you maybe start with a few phone calls to see who remembers Leonard Warren? His wife is Rachel Something; I failed to get her maiden name. Major Warren served me two craft beers, which I did not need before lunch. I can barely think straight now. Shit! There's a cop behind me with a flashing light. Dammit. I'll call you back."

Continuing to drive at her same speed, four miles over the limit, Jessica took some deep breaths. As she did, she sent thought waves to the steadily approaching white car behind her. Please, please, don't pick me up. Yes, my alcohol level is probably over the limit. I already have one DUI. Not this time too. Please. As she slowed down, the officer passed her. Jessica's heartbeat returned to normal; her breathing steadied. Fortunately, the adrenalin levels sobered her up too. Back to the office it was for an afternoon of work.

Lil greeted her. "You smell like a brewery. Go rinse with mouthwash in the back bathroom. You have a new client." Nodding toward the waiting room, Lil indicated an attractive man probably in his early thirties, chiseled features, dressed, unlike most of Jessica's clients, in a summer blue shirt with bow tie.

Jess's heart sank. "Lil, hold him off a while. I'm pretty sure that is my old boyfriend from high school. I do not want to meet him looking like this."

"Might I add smelling like this too?"

Friends/employees enjoyed latitudes that typical employees did not. This was a time Jessica would have preferred a more formal relationship.

As quietly as possible on daffodil colored spikes, Jessica retreated to the employees' restroom. A brief look in the mirror returned an image she would have preferred to ignore, were it any other person waiting for her. Jess found a brush on a decorator table, pulled it through her hair, which, she wished now, she had taken the time to wash this morning. After four days, she definitely could use a shampoo. Let's see, pull it up, find an elastic band in the medicine cabinet, wrap the whole mess into a topknot. There, better.

Now, wash the mascara off that had creeped down below her eyes. Rinse the beer out of her mouth, pull some lipstick out, check her nails for chips. Ready.

Jeff. How she had loved him back in their junior and senior years in Upper Sandusky High School. She still remembered parking on country roads in Wyandot County. Back then, she was a virgin. In fact, she insisted on remaining one even with Jeff. Despite the boundaries, they managed to have a good time, so to speak. They attended both their proms together, successfully lying to their respective parents about the after prom events, which they failed to attend.

Instead, for their senior prom Jeff had managed to discreetly remove a bottle of champagne from his father's overstocked bar. With more than a half dozen wines, gifts generally from dinner guests among whom Jessica's parents often numbered, Mr. Rhinesworth would certainly not miss one vintage of a probably forgettable label.

The night of their prom, on a country field under the bright stars Upper Sandusky city lights dimmed, Jessica and Jeff lay on their blanket, delighting in each other. Jeff surprised his girlfriend with two champagne glasses and some cheese and crackers he had purchased as surreptitiously as possible from a convenience store outside town off Route 53. As the two lovers, and they were for all but the final step, sipped champagne Jeff had already chilled in a Styrofoam cooler, they identified constellations in a late spring sky. An August baby, Jeff pointed out Leo the Lion, his guiding Zodiac sign. "See?" She smiled, still remembering his excitement more than ten years before. "It looks like a backward question mark."

"You are a Scorpio," Jeff commented. "Can you find your constellation?" Not used to alcohol, Jessica slurred "no," but her boyfriend had done his homework. "Here. Follow my hand. Look toward Columbus, right above the horizon. See that bright red star?"

She had a little trouble concentrating. "That is Antares. Now look up a little. You cannot see all five stars of the tail, but since we're out in the country, we can see part of it. The stars are really dim but they form Scorpio's tail. If we were out here in July, we could see your constellation better. I'll bring you back then, I promise."

Scorpios and Leos, if one believed assertions from the zodiac, can remain committed to each other for life. For Jessica, born mid November, passionate dramatic relationships predicted intense involvements. However, when they settled on their partners, as Jessica had with Jeff, they remained faithful for years. As for Jeff, born late July, his sign as a Leo encompassed devotion and fidelity as well as good fortune. Caught up in each other that magical after-prom night, neither of the couple wished to consider or to actually remember the potential negative aspects of a Scorpio/Leo pairing. If, as one astrologer commented, a Leo's heart were broken, the Lion might walk away forever. As for Scorpios, with love that goes awry, they may never forgive or forget.

Effects of a full day preparing for the prom, hair done, professional manicure, dinner, dancing until midnight, combined with the champagne to put Jessica to sleep. Occasionally, that magic night, she and Jeff awoke, whispered their love, then fell asleep again. Unlike rural legends, the country is not quiet. Birds chirping and squawking woke the pair up even before sunrise. Along with the birds, a dry mouth and headache greeted Jessica, the first of many aftereffects of alcohol that would pester her in coming years, consequences that she would have preferred to avoid.

For Jessica and Jeff high school graduation meant not so much to them as to many of their friends. True, J&J as they signed their names together at classmates' celebrations, looked forward more to college than to walking across the temporary stage in their high school stadium. Jessica had been accepted at Miami University in Oxford, Ohio, Jeff at Ohio Wesleyan in Delaware. Take Route 42 south out of Delaware, jump onto I-70 W, 130 miles, two hours and twenty minutes—easy to do when you are in love. And they did, borrowing friends' cars, carpooling, that first year was easy. For Jessie, sleeping with Jeff was somewhat more difficult. She did indeed plan to remain a virgin. Plan.

Both universities boasted strong Greek affiliations. Although formal rush officially occurred mid January, tacit agreement with the university accorded fraternities opportunities to recruit pledges almost from the first day young men walked onto campus. Keg parties along with well chosen upper class mentors eventually steered Jeff toward Phi Delta Theta, the Phi Delts. Jessica rushed at Miami, pledging Delta Gamma, DGs, a double legacy of her mother and grandmother. Jeff played baseball in high school; likewise, he played for the Battling Bishops all four years at OWU. Although Jessica had excelled in high school sports, basketball and volleyball, she took a more eclectic approach to college sports: swimming, ice hockey, intermural basketball. Somehow, neither Jessica nor Jeff really understood why, college did indeed gradually, insidiously, intervene.

Sophomore year there was baseball for Jeff, informal rush for both Jessica and Jeff, then sorority and fraternity parties. Over coffee by Christmas vacation that second year the lovers who had truly planned to marry, Jessica already in her mind and body Jeff's wife, agreed to let time deal with their relationship. Neither wanted to date other people; it wasn't that. They longed for weekends without worrying about traveling those more than two hours to sleep together. No, not even that. Jeff thought their relationship had played itself out; Jessica's family had given her a semester in Italy her junior year. Time to say goodbye. For then.

As Alex and Bob hoped, Jessica returned from Italy more an adult and less the still relatively naive young woman they had placed on a plane to Rome fall semester. Mother's weekend at Miami for Alex collided with a formal fraternity party Jessica truly wanted to attend. Her escort was Andrew, a man she would stay with through law school, almost. As for Jeff, DGs still attracted him. After all, over a hundred years before, a Phi Delt had helped his female friends found Delta Gamma in the South. Officially the fraternity and sorority were known as brothers and sisters. In the spring of her senior year at Miami Jessica answered a hurried phone call from a rather distant friend. The acquaintance informed her, nastily, Jessica thought, that Jeff was engaged to "someone at OWU in a sorority like yours."

Memories. Flashbacks. Jessica's mouth stung with the third mouthwash rinse. She stared again at herself in the mirror. God.

Why Jeff? Why now? She was so over him, a term her college friends employed. So over him.

Lil grinned as Jessie's crisp walk announced her return from what Lil had informed the new client, a necessary phone call. Rounding the corner to her office, Jessica could see Jeff without him noticing her. What was her first love doing? Not checking his cell phone, not reading a magazine, although Jessica herself chose to avoid backdated copies of *Fish and Game* or *National Geographic.* Nothing wrong with them; waiting rooms made her nervous. She had difficulty remembering what she read. No, Jeff had the audacity to look at the framed photographs on her library table. He had one in his hand!

Physically the years had been gentle with Jeff. Actually, ten years added distinction to his face, his hair. She saw streaks of gray beginning at his temples, wrinkles at the corners of his eyes. At six feet two inches, he had gained only a few pounds since college, really filled out into what he should look like, a man secure in his appearance. He still had the broad muscled shoulders of a baseball player; he probably still worked out. Although he wore a well-cut tailored suit, she noticed his tan hands, his lightly bronzed face. It looked like he shaved carefully, intending however to keep the short stubble popular on younger men. Why not? He looked five years younger than what he was.

Breathe deeply; pretend not to notice. It was her office, not his. "Own it," as she firmly instructed her clients.

"Jeff." She smiled, extending her hand. "How are you? What brings you here from, where is it, Connecticut?" She truly hoped he and his wife were not divorcing. She also hoped no one was sick or dead. Most other events she could handle.

Ignoring her proffered handshake, Jeff moved too quickly for Jessica to think. Firmly placing his arms around her, he hugged her. "Come on, old friend, we know each other too well for just a handshake."

She successfully fought strong urges to hug him back and, worse yet, to place her head on his shoulder. No. She pushed gently away instead. Not immediately though, but quickly enough, she thought. Owning the moment.

Replacing the framed photograph of Jessica and family, Jeff apparently attempted to own the moment as well. Looking directly at her, he sympathized. "Jess, I heard about your dad. It must have been a terrible shock. I'm so very sorry." The senior Rhinesworth family had sent flowers, but there had been no word, no card, no phone call from Jeff.

"My wife and I were in Germany at the time on business. My company sent me there for a year to supervise their operations. By the time I heard about your dad, it was too late. I should have done something even then, but the longer I didn't, the guiltier I felt. I'm truly sorry."

"I understand." She did not, but it was time to get to why Jeff had invaded her office. "Sit. What brings you here?"

"Well, aren't we both at an age when we think we know more than the people we work for?"

Damned Leos, charismatic, intelligent, egotistical. "I developed a plastic that is far superior to existing ones, especially impervious to extreme heat and cold. It outlasts others, can be used in space, and, as practically, in the home."

Leos did indeed seize opportunities. They were not supposed to look back. Why did he have to come to her office instead of one of his attorneys in Connecticut? Unless. Shit.

"Jessica, no one is getting any younger. You look great, by the way."

Her office phone rang. Thank God. "Hello, Mrs. Woolsey. No, no, you are always welcome to call me."

Who would ever think that a call from the pestering Clara Woolsey would be a welcome one? Jessica decided to extend the conversation. Jeff could have contacted his old girlfriend when her father died. For now he could cool his heels across from her and listen to what she would pretend to be a well-paying client.

"How is Mel? Oh, I'm so sorry. How did he break his walker?"

Jessica held the phone away, whispering to Jeff that the conversation might take a while.

"I can wait." He grinned. "Go ahead with your client." So she was not going to get rid of him easily.

Feigning a concern for the obstreperous Woolseys, it seemed Clara currently suffered from malingering pain in her left elbow due to the Super Bus accident and poor Mel had stumbled headfirst into his walker. Jessica concluded her conversation. "Just have Mel's doctor write a prescription. Medicare should pay for the new walker. Yes, yes. Call me any time."

"I'm sorry, Jeff. Clients need hand holding at times, so we do that too. Tell me, what can I do for you?"

"Jess, my wife and I are coming home, back to Ohio. I married a girl from Bucyrus I started dating at Ohio Wesleyan after you and I..." He stopped. "After you and I kind of fell apart. Maybe you know her? She's a DG too, like you. We already knew each other from working on Greek Week together for a couple of years. In my guy kind of way I tried a few moves on her, but she kept turning me down.

Jessica held on to her blank expression. Good acting.

"Crazy, I thought. Then one of her friends at the house told me she knew about you, a sister Delta Gamma. Even though you were on a different campus, Erin felt it would be disloyal to a sister to date me. When I figured out why she wouldn't go out with me, me, a Phi Delt, a nice guy." He shrugged that old Jeff way Jessica knew so well. "I told her you and I were no longer an item. We started dating. She was Homecoming Queen our senior year. I was her escort since her father had died when she was still in high school."

Why did jealousy of a sorority sister she had no right to feel anything but respect for creep spidery fingers into Jessica's consciousness? Jeff was free to make his own choices; after the end of their relationship, Jess had fallen in love with Andrew, deliberately severing ties, even potential information, with Jeff.

"Anyway, by spring our senior year I asked her to marry me. Maybe you know her? Erin Pulchasa. Her mother ended up marrying a man from Upper Sandusky, Fred Howard. He's a part time police officer in Bucyrus."

"Yes, I believe I have heard of him."

"I had a great job offer with a plastics company in Connecticut, so Erin and I moved to Bridgeport where we fully intended to stay, raising our kids.

"You remember how I liked to fool around with chemistry experiments in high school?"

Of course she did. Damn him. Jeff's presence in her office invoked memories she assumed she had completely forgotten.

"I could not get this one formula out of my head, so I kept altering the combination of elements, more here, less there. I would like to say I accidentally discovered the right formula, but I did not. It took a good four years.

"Jessica, I am negotiating with the owner of a plastics factory outside Gahanna. The equipment needs a little updating, but not much. A couple of friends I work with in the Bridgeport facility have agreed to go in with me. Together if things work out, which it looks like they will, we're going to start our business back here.

"My kids are still little, so for our family returning to Ohio is a good decision. I have a patent on my plastic. What I need from you, actually, what I would appreciate, is for you to file articles of incorporation with the Department of Commerce."

"Jeff, I'll be happy to." She hoped she sounded as professional as she intended. *Remember*, Jessica silently instructed herself, *you are in charge of this situation, mild headache, dirty hair or not. Best to dismiss him first rather than the other way around.*

"Why don't you e-mail me exactly what you want, the name of the corporation, the officers, that sort of thing. I will handle it from there. I'm happy for you." She rose out of the chair her brother had hauled up two flights of steps, her father's old chair.

"Isn't that your dad's old chair?"

"It is. Good memory." Did he remember, too, the constellations he had pointed out to her that night so many years ago when they spread a blanket out under the stars and sipped champagne as they planned their future together? Did he think about the countless drives down Route 42 from Delaware to Oxford so that they could sleep together in her dorm?

As she had twenty minutes earlier, Jessica extended her hand, this time to conclude the meeting. Just as he had, Jeff ignored the handshake, wrapping his arms around her instead. "Thank you, Jess, my friend, my dear, dear friend."

She pulled away. "As soon as I hear from you I'll prepare your articles of incorporation."

"Jessica, it has been wonderful seeing you again. You seem to be doing very well. Corner office, assistant, your name on the plaque. I'm happy for you."

Do not, she ordered herself, *do not look back. Guys are guys. More than ten years have come and gone. You cannot get that time back.*

"I'll walk out with you." Owning it, yes, indeed.

He touched her lightly on the elbow. "We'll have to get together."

"I would like that, Jeff. A sorority sister from Ohio Wesleyan. Why I remembered the chapter I do not know. Alpha Rho as I recall. Your wife sounds like a wonderful person. I look forward to meeting her."

As the heavy oak door closed behind Jeff, Lil looked up from her computer screen, smirking again, Jessica observed.

"He seems like a nice guy," Lil remarked. "He said he knew you in high school."

Jessica mentally listed a compendium of her assistant's positive attributes, among them, intuiting relationships and a sense of humor. Well, Lil could intuit away on this one. Jessica needed time to absorb all that Jeff, and his wife's return to Ohio, meant. Nothing.

"We were friends in high school." She smiled. "Would you retrieve one of the files I did last year for a small company incorporation? Try the Miller file."

"Mr. Rhinesworth left his personal cell phone number on the back of his business card."

"Keep it in the file with the rest of his information." Jessica's trenchant retort cut off further conversation on the Jeff topic. "Anything scheduled for the rest of today?"

"Jay Rossford called. He seems to be observing office hours today."

"No *charity* golf outings today? Gorgeous weather. The sun is out, not too hot on the links. Must be a slow day for the Jayster. What did he want?"

He mentioned something about a call from Gardenia Pulchinski, our Mrs. Woolsey's new best friend. Here's his number."

Turning back to her office door, Jessica brushed surprising tears from her cheek. She used her desk phone to punch in Jay's numbers. "Jay, you're in your office on a great day. Is the club course closed down?"

"I work hard, Jess. You know that. Like an old cow hand from the Rio Grande." His bumptious tone belied his remark. "Hey, Gardenia Pulchinski called me this morning. Do you know anything about Mel going to the hospital?"

"I know he fell onto his walker. Why?"

"Your client seems to have a nasty temper. Violet called Gardenia after Bingo. According to the daughter, who, I know, imbibes a bit at the Legion, Violet witnessed an altercation in the parking lot. Now, she didn't actually see Clara push Mel, but she heard a female voice yelling, then saw Mel slumped onto his walker, the thing slipping out from under him as he tumbled forward."

"Lovely couple. I already talked with Clara earlier this afternoon. Thanks, Jay. I'll look into it."

"You know I'm covering for Ralph Edmonton while he is out of the office with Carolyn's surgery."

"He told me. Let me know if you need any help. Ralph and Carolyn are old family friends. I will do anything I can for them." She hung up, ready, late afternoon, to go home.

"Lil, I have a Pilates class. I'm leaving. Let me know if anything comes up."

Jessica walked home. As she unlocked the door to her peaceful apartment something warm and furry brushed against her ankles. Cedric. What do they say about cats? If you do not particularly like them, they gravitate toward you. Purring, all twenty pounds of cat pushed against her as she tried to maneuver down the hall toward her bedroom. He was probably hungry, but according to her watch, dinner still was an hour or so away.

"Here, have some kibbles."

As she dumped a few into his dish, her cell phone chimed. Madelyn, in London, ten o'clock there. Jessica threw her daffodil bright heels into a corner, then took a load off her feet, so to speak, as she sank down onto a kitchen chair.

"How is the conference? How did your presentation go?"

"Great. They loved my paper."

For a young woman to be invited to present at the international conference of the American Psychological Association was quite an honor. Robbie should have married her as, Jessica recalled, Madelyn had pushed for. Instead, Robbie floundered with what Alex viewed as a harebrained financial scheme while Dr. Madelyn Hendricks cemented her role as a formidable researcher on causes of autism. That the scheme might, just might, come to fruition Alex's clair-voyance seemed to have missed. By all accounts, Robbie was doing pretty damned well.

"How is my little Cedric doing? Is he eating? I worry so much about him. He usually doesn't eat when I am not around to feed him."

Looking at the Maine Coon crunching a bowl full of Precious Kitty Matinee Muchies Indoor Cat kibbles, Jessica assured her friend that, yes, Cedric retained an appetite.

"Can I talk to my baby?"

Jessica held her cell phone up to the ear of the still crunching cat. Ridiculous.

"Hi, Sweetums. Mommy misses her Baby Doll. Are you being good for Auntie Jessie?"

As far as Jess knew, no vomit yet on the beige carpet, no potty problems either. That constituted good behavior on Cedric's part. Apparently oblivious to Dr. Madelyn Hendricks, the cat munched his way to the bottom of the dish, then rubbed against Jessica's ankle and headed in the direction of the couch. "You be a good boy now," Madelyn spoke to air. "Mommy will be home soon to love her little guy."

"No problems then? I really am grateful, Jess."

Best not to mention the excursion in the parking garage. Cedric would certainly say nothing.

"No problems here. I have a Pilates class, so I have to go. Call any time, Madelyn. Your boy is in good hands." Scurrying toward her closet, Jessica slipped on something warm and slippery: kibbles mixed with cat spit. Vomit. Then a trail of what looked like this morning's breakfast, dried, combined with strings of hair. Good boy all right. He did it on purpose. Punishing Jessica for babysitting him when he should have been with his mother. "Oh, Cedric, thanks for the welcome home," she mumbled as she wiped up his work with wet paper towels. "You can just wait for dinner until I am good and ready to feed you."

Curious, the cat circled around her as she scrubbed his mess out of the apartment carpet. Invoking the harshest comments she could think of, Jessica added, "Mommy will not like this, Cedric. Bad kitty."

The Maine Coon stalked away. Not his problem. He did not want to stay here in the first place. Jessica softened; the cat was probably homesick.

"I will be back in about an hour. You can have dinner then. Let's hope you will keep it down." Cedric glared. "Let's hope so, huh, Kitty?"

Maybe she could pick up a toy for him at the pet store in the strip mall adjacent to her class.

Wednesday of Week Two, the Same Week

The next few days passed relatively smoothly if Jessica were to describe the week to her mother. In fact, that is the phrase she used when Alex called the night before to confirm lunch and a shopping trip Saturday, which, of course, Jessica mentioned when suggesting a change of venue to Crocker Park in Westlake, Ohio, rather than at Easton. Only one glitch occurred on Wednesday which Jess wisely omitted discussing with her mother. Generally in a hurry, most young attorneys very cognizant of billable hours were, Jessica quickly pulled into a parking area reserved for buses only. She swore she would be in her colleagues' offices only long enough to drop off papers pertaining to a case on which they held mutual interests. The few minutes expanded to thirty minutes or so as the senior attorney waxed on about his children's weekend successes in soccer. Listening as attentively as possible to yet another parent's stories of always brilliant talented sons and daughters, Jessica inwardly screamed with impatience.

Still, good attorneys were nothing if not good actors. When her colleague launched into a third story, this time about a child's recent piano skills during an elementary school music performance, Jessica glanced at her watch, commenting that she had a scheduled pretrial she had to attend. She did not, but it never hurt to build on one's own successes causing, as she hoped, competitors to wonder just how many cases this relatively new attorney had accumulated/taken from them.

Racing down the stairs from the fourth floor instead of waiting for the elevator, Jessica clipped along as fast as she could manage in her Coach spikes. Thank God she got out of the offices in time, she congratulated herself as she happily surveyed a crimson car. A closer look discouraged her, not her Acura at all, the red Taurus parked two spaces behind where her car used to be. Towed again. A phone call, a cab, and three hundred dollars added to her credit card settled Jessica F. Woods, attorney of record, back into her day, about two hours lost but still in time to return to her office, she decided, without mentioning the little incident to Lil. Maintaining a professional distance between employer and employee was essential.

Friday, the Same Week

By Friday afternoon at three Jessica actually had resolved most minor problems, returned as many phone calls and e-mails as she felt necessary, and effectively wrapped up her week. "I'm headed to Cleveland on a case if Triple O calls," she confided to Lil. "Any urgent messages before I leave?"

Looking up from her desktop screen—which could have been on a shopping site, it was Friday afternoon after all—Lil handed Jessica a stack of white slips torn off from the message pad. "Nothing urgent; you can call these people on your way to see Max."

Was Lil smirking again? "I'm pretty sure you can toss that last message on the bottom. Eddie's Towing and Brake Services called Wednesday, something about your car at their lot." A brief smile crossed Lil's face as she quietly returned to her computer.

"Check out the Kate Spade shoes for me while you're looking," Jessica responded as she scampered out the door of the Columbus offices of O'Malley, O'Malley, and O'Malley, motto, *We make it right for you, because whatever the case, we are right, for you.*

Shoving lingerie, workout clothes, and jeans into her tote, she remembered Cedric. "Dammit," Jessica spit more to herself than to the waiting cat. "What am I supposed to do with you?" She felt a twinge of conscience after swearing at the feline whose only fault lay in his mistress' trip to London. "Here, have a snack while I pack. I'll think of something."

If Cedric were her cat she would leave the little guy in the apartment for the weekend. Plenty of food, water, a clean litter box, and by Sunday evening he would still be safe. Not happy probably, but safe. Well, he was not her cat. One of her best friends had asked a favor. How often had Jessica called Dr. Madelyn Hendricks for informal counseling? How many times over the years they had known each other had guidance for Jessica's romantic vicissitudes unexpectedly interrupted Madelyn's days?

"All right, Cedric. You are going on a trip with Auntie Jessie. We'll just pack you up in your little carrier and off we'll drive to Cleveland. You'll love Uncle Max. I promise."

As she reached for the cat, Cedric deftly scooted under the king sized bed, placing himself dead center.

"Come on, Honey, Auntie doesn't have much time." Jessica scurried around, shoving a frothy little lace number Max admired into an additional tote as she attempted to cajole an obdurate feline. "Okay, how about some nice treats?" Gradually the cat warily moved out from under the bed as Jessica shook a package of Hot Dog Delights

Kitty Tantalizers, just the incentive for a Friday night baseball excursion. Tempted more by the treats than by his caretaker's tone, Cedric followed the trail of goodies toward the open door of his carrier, almost. He balked at the entrance, but not long enough to decide to bolt. Jessica firmly pushed his sizable rump, urging him forward into the carrier. Two trips to the parking garage, the first with her totes, the second with a very annoyed cat, and she was off. North on I-71 toward Cleveland, Max, and, shit, Max's yellow lab. Well, nevertheless, despite the animals, it promised to be a grand weekend.

She yanked her cell out of her handbag. "Hey, Hon, I'm in a little traffic but I'll be there soon."

"Where are you now? The game starts at seven."

"I just left Columbus. There must be an accident or something. The traffic is backed up it looks like for more than a mile. Go on to the game. I'll meet you there." As an afterthought, a few yowls from the back seat reminded her. "Is it all right if I bring Cedric?"

Silence. She had failed to mention the cat in their conversations that week. In a still new relationship, in Max's mind Cedric could be anyone, especially one of Jessica's friends from her past who seemed to pop up inconveniently and unappreciated, at least by Max. "You met Madelyn. I'm cat sitting her Maine Coon. I just couldn't leave the little guy for the weekend."

"Fine." Max's friendlier tone responded. "What about Charles though?"

"Oh, they'll get along fine. As a psychologist, Madelyn has probably tried behavior modification on Ceddie." Jessica glanced into the back seat at a glaring cat crouched in the very back of his carrier. "The little guy should get along just fine with Charlie, won't you, Ceddie? He is a very nice yellow lab. I just know you two will become the best of friends." Jessica took Cedric's silence as an assent.

Max's apartment in downtown Cleveland was perfectly located for a bachelor, criteria which Max, at age thirty-five, no ex-wife, no children, one pet, met. He could walk two blocks to the south to the bank where he worked, three blocks east to Progressive Field and his favorite team the Cleveland Indians, and less than one block in any direction for coffee or beer, depending on his thirst.

Jessica knew as well that sports and beverages were not the limits of Max's interests. Women too liked beer and coffee, no cream or sugar. Professional women, bankers, insurance executives, physicians. Oh, they would be more than pleased to provide companionship for a man whose girlfriend unexpectedly had to work late on Friday or return early Sunday morning. She should not be so cavalier with Max's loyalty; so feckless with her phone calls and after work drinks with *just friends*.

Three hours later, into the bottom of the second inning, Jessica hauled Cedric's carrier up to Max's apartment before hurrying off to the game. Her totes could wait till afterward, but a missing Cedric in Cleveland, Ohio, if her car were broken into, was not an option. Charles greeted his master's sleepover friend with a cheerful bark. By nature, yellow Labrador retrievers are mellow. A few curious sniffs at the carrier satisfied Charles; Cedric rudely responded to his host with hisses and growls.

"Here, Ced." Jess placed the carrier in the only bedroom of the tiny apartment. "You can wait here. Listen to the game!" A roar from the stadium signaled what she hoped was a home run for the Indians. "I forgot your toilet. Well, you'll have to wait. I'll think of something."

Much later after the Indians beat the Red Sox 5 to 2 with Perez hitting a homer in the second inning. Max and Jessica hopefully turned the key to what they prayed was a peaceful apartment. Deeply asleep, Charles needed a few seconds to acclimate himself to his master and his master's nice friend. Jessica cautiously opened the bedroom door to a sleeping Maine Coon. Answered prayers.

Saturday of Week Two

The next morning Max jerry rigged a litter box of shredded newspapers in a plastic bowl. The contraption annoyed Cedric but satisfied him to the extent that no accidents occurred. In her haste to meet her boyfriend, Jessica had failed to pack food, so a can of tuna in Max's nearly bare cupboard fortified Cedric for breakfast. Charles feasted on canned dog food, which might have to make up his new guest's dinner if Jessica and Max failed to find a convenience store downtown that carried Precious Kitty.

A Saturday morning romantic reconnection softened Max's response to Jessica's request that he can sit while she joined her mother for lunch and shopping. Although disappointed in his girl-friend's absence, Max agreed to Cedric's company. Besides, he added, "I have to go into the bank for a meeting with a potential client. Nothing big. Ceddie and Charles here can watch television."

Jessica scooped up a napping Cedric before he realized the out-come, then firmly stuffed him back into his carrier. Placing the car-rier in front of his forty-two-inch television screen, Max scrolled to *Animal Planet*. Allowing a Maine Coon and a yellow Lab, however mellow, to remain unsupervised without confinement in the apart-ment would be a poor decision indeed.

"I won't be long. Alex and I usually finish about three, so I can meet you afterward. Text me." She kissed Max goodbye, a nice long memorable kiss. She could do a lot worse, she reflected. Jessica liked romance, yes, she did, tangibly acted out with techniques that Max, an experienced bachelor, appeared to enjoy using on her. Maybe Alex could wait; Saturday morning traffic snarls in downtown Cleveland were rare, but sometimes construction bottled things up a bit.

An hour later: "Mom," Jessica called from her car as she pulled out of the apartment parking lot, "where are you?"

"Almost there, Honey. Right outside Avon."

"Hey, I'm going to be a little late. I'll meet you right outside Ann Taylor in forty-five minutes."

Alex and Jessica employed shopping as a mutually pleasant avo-cation, really more a reason to get together than to buy. Generally for Jessica shopping also meant a gift from her mother which, as most daughters understood by tacit agreement, included clothing, a piece or two of costume jewelry, and lunch or dinner. Mother always paid. Today as usual when at Crocker Park in fine weather, Alex and Jessica selected a table for two on the outdoor patio of Brio's.

"Prosecco, please," they both ordered. A celebration with the wine they loved, another time together.

"How is Max?" Alex sipped her Prosecco as they toasted each other. Jessica assumed as with all of her boyfriends in the past that Alex would relish planning a wedding. Planning also included a St. John knit evening suit for mother for the rehearsal dinner, a full-length ball gown, possibly lavender for the reception. A Mary Francis bag shaped like a wedding cake for Jessica. Yes, planning a wedding for her daughter would be a delight both for bride and mother of the bride.

"Max is fine, Mom. I just don't know about the future."

Jessica truly did not know; she wished he did not live in Cleveland and she in Columbus. The damned geography separated them more than anything else. She liked his family; they seemed to like her. A well planned plaid blouse with matching plaid chunky heels at Christmas impressed them, that and her mother's ring, which she had borrowed in the last minutes before rushing away to meet Max's family for the first time. Not that his mother, dad, and sister were shallow; Jessica had intended to purchase the attire anyway. It never hurt to look one's best.

"Honey." Alex placed her hand over her daughter's. "I want you to be happy whatever you do."

Not good. Here comes a speech. "You want children. It's a lot easier to be married than to go it alone. I know. I know. Society at least here is changing. Single mothers, especially professional ones like you with a good income, can raise a child alone."

Their chopped salads arrived. "We'd like another glass please," Alex ordered.

What did Alexandra have in mind? Was she sick? Is Jim in some sort of trouble, probably with the IRS or anyone else nosing around in his insurance business? Small farmers like Jim needed extra income; an additional one selling crop insurance worked out well. Here it comes.

"Honey, you are in your thirties. Most of the women your age are married or engaged."

For Jessica statistics were half of that, but best not to argue. Save it up for the next verbal volley.

"You are extremely fortunate that Max has no baggage. I mean,"—Alex sipped her wine—"no child support, no alimony, no former relationships he can't get over."

"Mom, I know that. I just, I just, sometimes he calls, and I don't want to talk to him. Some weekends when we plan to get together, I just want to be alone. I'm busy. I don't want to get together with him. I know I should. I just don't."

"Jessica, in all fairness, do you really believe that married couples work at keeping sizzle in their relationships? Do you honestly think that when Jim pulls into the driveway in the evening I am always thrilled to see him? Come on, Honey, it's reality."

As Alex sipped her Prosecco Jessica silently mused. Maybe Jim was not always thrilled to see his wife. Alex could be a handful. Best not to mention that. For Jess, the *F* of her middle initial could mean too, *Forbearance*.

"Excitement, I guess people your age call it passion, excitement levels out. Jim and I love each other, but fireworks as your Aunt Kate terms it, fireworks don't always light the night sky. Well, sometimes they do."

"Mom. No sex life please!"

"All right." Her mother sipped some wine, then continued. "Instead, we have the joy of dinner together, talking over cocktails, watching movies, going on vacations. Oh, there is still—"

"Mom, don't."

"Honey, be mature enough then to accept that love changes, grows, as you grow together. Give Max the chance he deserves. Tell him what you want. Believe in him."

Was her mother finished yet, before Jessica started regretting her years with Andrew and the disastrous end?

"I believe in you, Dear. Believe in yourself."

Alex retrieved some tissue from her purse, handing it to Jessica. "Here. Wipe off the mascara under your eyes. You know what you need, and I will buy it for you. A beautiful compact. My mother told me never to use one in public. I have to say, she was wrong. Men are attracted to a woman using a compact as she nonchalantly applies lipstick or straightens her hair. Watch."

"Mom, you really do not have to do this. I'm fine." Jessica wiped her eyes.

Too late. Alex, Gucci gold compact in her left hand, reapplied another coat of scarlet to her lips. Did a man twenty years younger try to catch her mother's eye? Jessica was too chagrined to look.

"I have to meet Max, Mom. This time I'll get the check."

She placed her credit card on the tray the server had brought. Jessica tried to glimpse the younger man who, she had to admit to herself, had been attracted to her mother. Black hair slicked back, open-necked Banana Republic golf shirt, madras shorts, Sperry Topsiders shined almost enough to reflect the sun, maybe she would try the compact trick.

"Are you walking out with me? Or staying here?" Jessica signed the credit card slip, adding a generous 20 percent tip. Let Alex leave cash, and the poor server ended up with 15 percent or less.

"I have to make a couple of phone calls. I'll kiss you here. Say hi to Max, Honey. I love you."

"I love you too, Mom. Have fun with those phone calls." Jessica hurried out of Brio's, texting Max as she threaded her way through Saturday shoppers toward the parking garage by Ann Taylor.

Thump. Right into a massive woodsy smelling form. Andrew. Andrew. The man she had lived with for three years, the man she had, to use the vernacular, been in a relationship with for six years. Andrew, thinner, handsomer than she remembered, Andrew, now an attorney, just like her. She had inspired him, he wrote when he applied for law school. Andrew, valedictorian of his class, unlike Jessica who had graduated toward the bottom end of the middle. Andrew, who passed the bar exam the first time through; it had taken her twice, then with a score she would just as soon forget. What in the hell was he doing in Crocker Park? Probably with his girlfriend. Buying her a trousseau. No, mothers did that. Probably waiting while she purchased a dainty little nothing at Victoria's Secret.

Jessica herself refused Facebook either to participate or to look. Well, she might use her brother's password occasionally to update herself as far as her high school friends went. Triple O had an account for business reasons; it rarely ever occurred to clients that their personal affairs, which they failed to reveal to their lawyers, blatantly announced their real lives on Facebook. Let's see, when Jessica had last checked, Andrew had posted a picture of his family and some dark-haired woman at a picnic of some sort. She had had to enlarge the photograph to read the letters on the banner behind the supposed friend next to Andrew: *Congratulations Dr. Karen Edelman.*

Jessica's phone chimed. "Max, where are you, Hon?" She waved at Andrew in a kind of gesture that she could talk in a few seconds. "I'll meet you there in about forty-five minutes. Love you too."

She placed her phone back into her bag. Andrew reached out to Jessica before she moved into him. "How are you? Still meeting your mother for lunch and shopping, I see." Observant as always.

"I am. I still do." Rattled responses, brilliant rhetoric from an attorney much more experienced than the one currently speaking to her. *Remind yourself, Jessica, you are the senior here. Settle down.* "Yes, did you see Mom? I left her back at Brio's."

"Alex still looks terrific, Jess." Andrew hesitated. "You know what they say about daughters. Look at their mothers, and that is how the daughters will turn out too." His smile, the same as she remembered, the same confident aura. "In my considered opinion," her old boyfriend, her lover of more than six years, continued, "I'd say you have a beautiful future."

What riposte for that? The last time they had talked, had it been how many years now actually, the last time they had spoken their conversation concluded with someone in tears. Maybe it had been both of them. Now, here he was. Thank God, the thoughts raced through her mind, her nails were done; she had washed her hair and styled it. Andrew most likely noticed her Coach shoes and Louis Vuitton bag. Yes, Jessica presented well this Saturday afternoon.

"So you saw Mom back at Brio's. Did you talk to her? She still asks about you, you know." Of course Alex asked. Everyone: Andrew's family, Jessica's family, mutual college friends—everyone thought she and Andrew would get married. Everyone but Jessica.

"I didn't, Jess. She seemed caught up in talking to a guy about my age. You know how that goes." Andrew's speculations remained unstated, trailing off for Jessica to draw conclusions of her own.

Mom, what in the hell are you up to? Oh, Alex liked handsome men; yes, indeed she did.

"How are your mother and dad? Your grandmother?"

For six years Jessica had been a part of Andrew's family. Christmas, Easter, birthdays, she was there, taking photographs but never in the pictures. Everyone assumed she would be. Later.

"Fine, Jess. Everyone is fine. I take it your mother and Jim are good too. How is Robbie?"

Good old Robbie. Sometimes impecunious. Actually, her older brother might, this time he actually might, be on the verge of an actual business, not the smoke and mirrors Alex accused him of.

"Robbie, he is Rob now to the financial world, has his own investment company. I honestly think he will do all right. Do you ever talk with him?"

"He called me about a month ago. Asked me if I wanted to go in with him on a business venture involving some developers in Upper Sandusky. Apparently years ago a group of men purchased some property out in the country. The idea was to build a golf course, and they almost succeeded. Then sex reared its ugly head." Andrew laughed. Laughed.

The sex she and Andrew had enjoyed together, even fighting, even when their relationship painfully deteriorated. How could he laugh? Actress she was, Jessica laughed too at the adumbrated silliness of sex ruining lives.

"Anyway, years ago, according to Robbie, the deal fell through. The wife of one investor unfortunately misbehaved with one of the partners. Long story short, the golf course never got built because the farmer who planned on selling his property to the group lost the opportunity when the scandal put the kibosh on things."

How Robbie unearthed a squashed deal and a scandal more than fifty years before impressed Jessica. She had to give the devil his due. Robbie was brilliant. If anybody could pull this off, Robbie could.

"Rob mentioned something about a murder too, one farmer shooting another. You folks in Wyandot County lead quite interesting lives." At least in talking business, Jessica and Andrew had managed to circumvent the former intimacy of their personal lives.

"I live in Franklin County now, Andrew. Not without its felons and philanderers though. I remember my dad mentioning the case. I wonder how my big brother got involved."

"You know how Rob is. He has a nose for business, the more surreptitious, the more it fascinates him. Apparently the widow of the murdered man moved into town. One of her granddaughters dated your brother. The golf course story is a legend in their family, so when Rob heard it, he made some inquiries. The land was never developed. Sheep farming is not the business it used to be, but a few families in that part of the county still raise sheep. The grandson of the farmer who bought the property still has a place and still, according to Rob, turns a profit on soybeans and winter wheat. The last I heard from your brother, farmland in Wyandot County sells for 8,500.00 an acre.

"Robbie met him at a bar; he already knew the story. So your brother being your brother, asked if anyone had approached the fellow about resurrecting the golf course deal. No one had, but the farmer suggested he might be interested. If he could stay on as caretaker. I turned Rob down, law school loans being what they are."

Jessica knew so well her own indebtedness, which she managed each month to knock down payment by payment. Andrew, however, had just started the loan repayment journey. "There, a long answer to your question if I talked to your brother." Andrew's sigh was almost inaudible, almost. Perhaps he too felt as nervous around his former lover as she felt around him. Nervous and, what was the word, *discomfited.* What had happened to them? They lived together. They had started looking at houses in neighborhoods near where they expected to work. Had Andrew asked her to marry him? Jessica, truly, did not remember.

The aftereffects of the two Proseccos she and Alex had cheerfully consumed manifested their presence via a dull headache. Alcohol in midday additionally has a way of bringing on depression. That was it; the wine, not any other events caused a sudden wave of sadness that enveloped Jessica. Best to be the first to leave.

Following a cursory look at her watch, which she really could not see, cloudy contacts most likely, Jessica regretfully concluded, "Later than I thought. Andrew, great seeing you. I've got to run."

He pulled her against his chest, briefly, a friendly brotherly gesture, which lasted longer than it should. "You too, Jess. You too."

Make yourself back away. Do not allow tears to spill, not so that he can see them. She turned her head. "Say hi to your family!" Hurrying toward the parking garage, she ducked into the Ann Taylor store in case Andrew might follow her. Under no circumstances did she wish to continue their conversation. Before she could collect herself, Jessica found tears rolling down her face, definitely ruining her mascara, probably floating her contacts toward the floor as she wiped her eyes.

A salesperson approached, concerned. "Are you all right, Honey?"

"Old boyfriend."

Sniffles stopped up her nose. Jessica pushed her hair out of her face. A nearby mother and daughter duo much like her own pretended not to notice as they randomly sorted through sales racks by the cash registers.

"Dammit." Jessica upbraided herself. "A meltdown, right here at Crocker Park." Her stomach lurched.

"Here, why don't you go into this fitting room?" Lightly touching Jess's elbow, the salesperson gently guided her toward the large corner dressing area. "I'll bring you some tissue. Just rest for a few minutes. I will be right back."

Sobbing full throttle now, Jessica threw herself onto the fitting room bench. Where did any of this come from? She was so over Andrew, so over him. She loved Max. She flirted with the lobbyist from Kentucky. A serendipitous visit from her high school boyfriend still rankled her emotions. Good Lord, even that man that stopped by her apartment with a rescued Cedric drove illicit thoughts into her head. She was a mess! A mess.

A quiet knocking on the fitting room door curtailed Jessica's sobbing. "I brought some tissue for you, Honey. If you prefer a few minutes of privacy, you can rest in my office. I am the manager here, so you will be fine if you need a little more time."

As she dabbed at the black mascara smudges under her eyes, Jessica upbraided herself. Unprofessional it was for an attorney, Jessica F. Woods of O'Malley, O'Malley, and O'Malley to behave like a high school girl after a dance when her secret crush escorted another girl out into the dark. Between sniffs, she told the salesperson, "Thank you. I'm fine." She tried smiling. "Or I will be soon. Thank you again though." Jessica, *Fine Thank you Woods*. Woods breathed in, breathed out.

Patting Jessica's arm, the salesperson continued, "I'll be on the floor if you need me. I brought you some water too. Take a few sips, it should help."

"Thank you." Jessica smiled at the older woman. "I should be all right in a few minutes." She sniffed again, blowing her nose and wiping her tears. Wadding up wet tissues full of ruined makeup, she stuffed them into her Louis Vuitton bag. Jessica realized in a part of her heart she knew as shallow, owning designer items did offer a person some measure of comfort. She pulled the leather drawstrings tight, closing her purse and closing down her memories of what used to be Andrew and Jessica. No more. She had moved on, forward. As a matter of fact, *F.* for *Forward.*

Jessica F. Woods, Esq. stepped out the fitting room, firmly pushing the door until it snapped into place. She found the kind saleslady. "Thank you. I had a little trip back into the past. I appreciate your help."

"I have a daughter of my own. I understand." The smartly dressed expertly coifed older woman gazed directly at Jessica. "Like you, she has her ups and downs. I wish she were closer, but she lives in Columbus, so I cannot be there for her as often as I would like. I'm glad I could be here for you."

Jessica signaled a left turn out of the parking garage, north on Crocker Road toward I-90 and Max. Her phone chimed. "Hey, where are you? We finished our meeting at the bank early, so I'm having a beer at the Winking Lizard. Do you want to stop by or should I meet you back at the apartment?"

"I'll just meet you back at your place. I'm a little tired from the week, so I plan on a huge nap when I get back."

"You sound stuffed up. Fight with your mother?"

"Allergies. Hey, I have to feed Cedric. Can you pick up some cat food? I forgot."

Poor Cedric. He apparently hated her guts anyway; neglecting to bring the only food he allowed himself to eat continued the animosity he already nurtured.

"Precious Kitty Tuna Tidbits or Beefy Bonanza are his dinners of choice. As long as you are there, would you mind horribly getting him some treats? I think the ride back to Columbus might go easier if I stopped occasionally and bribed the little guy with goodies."

"My dog gets bones for which Charles is most grateful. Dinner for you and for Cedric I will buy. Treats are on you, Kiddo."

"Sheesh. The meeting must not have gone well."

"The meeting went fine. Actually, the client is here with me at the Lizard. I'm in line at the bar or I would not be talking like this. I think the guy is clandestinely recruiting me for his new business in Columbus. I'll tell you more later. I have to get these beers back."

"So you will pick up some cat food?"

"Precious Kitty is at the top of the list. Followed by treats. I love you, Jess. Gotta go."

At six o'clock when a fairly drunk Max unlocked the apartment door an alacritous yellow lab barked cheerfully while a saturnine Maine Coon yowled, both animals fervently announcing dinner time.

At 9:00 p.m. Jessica woke up to a snoring Max next to her. Too late for dinner. Kissing him softly on his cheek, she nestled against her boyfriend of the moment. No, the man she loved. Before she fell back asleep she checked her cell phone. A voice mail from Alex. Whatever it was could wait until Sunday.

Sunday of Week Three

By mid Sunday, having wooed Cedric into his carrier with a trail of Beach Blast Temptalots, Jessica barreled south on I-71, four miles over the speed limit. No more than that. With the sun shining, a pleasant early morning rendezvous with Max, and a plan in place to delete memories of Andrew once and for all from her mind, she felt strong enough to return her mother's Saturday night call.

Alex answered on the first ring. "Hi, Honey, thank you for getting back with me." Alex sounded excited. Whatever she had done or thought about doing with the younger Hugh Jackman–type look alike at Crocker Park must have gone well. Her mother was neither in jail nor headed toward divorce. Jessica hoped she was not in a motel. Why think the worst? Jessica upbraided herself for her less than charitable estimation of her mother.

"Where are you, Mom? Are you okay?"

"Home. Where do you think I would be?"

Relieved, chagrined at her uncharacteristic unfounded suspicions, Jessica covered with "Church. I thought you might be in church." To be fair, Jessica had selected an honest retort, for Alex currently bounced among three churches, collectively referring to them as the Holy Trinity.

She and Jim belonged to the Lutheran church; the Methodist church held her loyalties from a childhood of attending Sunday school services, and the priest at the Episcopal church preached the most academic sermon her mother had heard in years. That he weekly invoked seventeenth century English theologians and poets endeared him to Alex, a lifelong learner and student of British literature. Besides, she liked the congregations and for that matter the ministers at all three churches. In the meantime Jessica suspected that all three men hoped Alex did not meet an untimely death. Who among the three ministers she listened to, congratulated, and to whose churches she contributed her offering, who, would bury her?

"I went to the five o'clock service last night at the Lutheran church after I returned from Crocker Park. I'm grading student assignments this morning. Did you have a happy weekend with Max?"

Mother and daughter tacitly understood that *happy weekend* might lead to happy life aka marriage.

"I didn't break up with him, if that is what you want to know." Fun to throw her mother off track.

"I called last night because I kept thinking about the man we saw at Brio's. You remember, the dark haired Eye Candy (her mother liked this sobriquet) fellow on the patio, the one who kept staring at you?"

"Yes, Mom, the Hugh Jackman evil twin."

"Who? Anyway, after you left it clicked with me. I knew I remembered him from somewhere before. He looked just like a man I used to date in college, except, of course, that man had grown up. This fellow was the mirror image of someone I was almost pinned to, Oliver Oney."

"I thought you dated Dad in college?"

"I did, junior and senior years. Oliver was before that."

"Before, between, or during, Mom?"

"I liked you better before lawyer school. Make it *between* if you must know. Your father, as you recall, had difficult committing. Do you know anyone like that?

"Anyway, Oliver attended Kenyon College, which at the time accepted only men. They take everybody now, just like the service academies and the Ohio State marching band."

"Hang on, Sloopy."

"True, Sloopy hung on long enough to be admitted West Point."

"Your point, Mom? I have to call Triple O at noon."

"I just wanted to tell you that Oliver Oney could very well have been your father if we had gotten pinned, and engaged, and married, in that order. We broke up when your dad decided he loved me after all. I haven't stayed in touch with Oliver, of course."

"Mom, not judging." In reality, Jessica listened oh so carefully to her mother's tone. A few years of experience with lying clients came in handy with family too.

"So after you left I approached the fellow's table. You remember he was sitting alone?" Effrontery in Alex's book will get you everywhere. "I said he looked exactly like someone I used to date in college. To make this brief since I know you have a call to your firm, this man was Oliver Oney's son! Oliver Oney, Junior. He has a brother in Columbus, a musician! Small world, isn't it?"

Most likely Junior had avoided further family disclosures. Such as Ompherous aka One Eye. True, Brother most certainly worked as a musician, but he also contributed to his coffer through trespassing, theft and breaking and entering. Whoops, no breaking and entering. One Eye Oney was an invitee to the premises, hired by the host and hostess, usually the hostess, for his well turned out good looks.

Once in the estates and palatial homes of Central Ohio's very wealthy, One Eye easily navigated within the master suite, now mistress's too as builders acquiesced to couples' preferences for separate bedrooms. In a usual frenzy before parties, occupants often neglected to secure jewelry, paintings, clothing, knick-knacks. Expensive knick-knacks for One Eye were the easiest to steal but brought the least return. Demand for Lladro statuettes rose and fell with the vicissitudes of the economy. Waterford crystal broke. Besides, clients or buyers, as One Eye referred to them professionally, were picky about patterns.

An honest seller such as himself could collect a half dozen Waterford tumblers, proudly displaying them to the client, only to learn that the order had been for a Colleen pattern, not Shannon. Had the client failed to tell One Eye? He, usually she, was terribly sorry.

No, for One Eye, women's jewelry, watches, and Judith Leiber purses topped his list of preferred items to obtain on a good night. All fit nicely into his violin case. Carefully curled Salvatore Ferragamo ties fit there too. As for the shoes, shirts, and suits, most men assumed that whatever was missing was probably at the cleaner's. One Eye, Maestro Oney to his students and to the people who hired him as their entertainment, One Eye assured everyone that he needed no help transporting his stringed instruments. They were highly valuable, insured; he did not want to place anyone in difficult circumstances.

Highly valuable indeed. Insured, of course. As for difficult circumstances, Jessica had been brought in by good old Bartram Irving when she met One Eye. All she was supposed to do was introduce herself to Ompherous Oney a few minutes before court, continue the case, and bring Bartram back in when he returned from his conference as he called it at the Greenbrier with his intern. That most likely should have been the last of her encounters with Mr. Oney. However, a grateful One Eye insisted on visiting her at her office anyway where he cheerfully summed up his professional activities. No need to tell Alex about these or about One Eye. Confidentiality.

"Gotta go, Mom. Glad you ran into an old friend, sort of."

"Okay, Honey. Have a good week."

Jessica clicked off first, shaking her head and smiling. Mom.

By late Sunday afternoon on a spring day in Columbus, Ohio, Jess reached her apartment, dumped her clothes from her totes, then tilted the carrier for her precious feline cargo to unceremoniously emerge.

Time for a jog. She retrieved her running shoes from the corner of her closet where she had tossed them. Whew. Best to wash them soon. She worked out sedulously four or five days a week, had done so since middle school as an escape, an anodyne as her parents drifted apart, then separated for good.

Lacing up her less than clean running shoes, she allowed herself one final reflection. Perhaps living through her parents' divorce had impacted her waffling on marriage. Max could be pushed to a commitment; Andrew must have asked her to marry him at some point during their six years together. Well, enough of that. Best to run; let time and exercise work for her as they always had.

"I'm heading out, Cedric. I'll be back in about an hour. Be a good kitty."

Jessica believed in politesse, even to animals. Apparently, Cedric did not. From his crouched position under the potted palm, he glared at his sitter, then turned his furry head toward the corner window.

Apparently, Jessica suddenly realized as she pulled the apartment door shut, a bit too hard, not, of course, in retaliation toward a recalcitrant feline, apparently sometimes one's body adjusted to environmental hazards. Those hazards being cat fur. Without being fully cognizant of when, Jessica noticed as she ran down the five flights of steps to the street, her eyes had stopped watering. Her nose no longer ran. Allergies, for the time at least, seemed to have abated. What did physicians call it? Antigens, specifically to cat dander. She supposed she could thank Cedric for the reprieve. Lovely kitty that he was.

Back in the apartment after a wonderful soul satisfying run, Jessica tossed her shoes into the washing machine along with her running clothes. But not before Cedric, in a burst of energy and curiosity, darted over to the sweaty pile on the bathroom floor. Embarrassing really how dirty tennis shoes achieved a goal both carefully purchased treats and cans of Precious Kitty, not to mention some cajoling, had failed to do. Jessica stared in amazement as Cedric purred, she could call it, maniacally. He sniffed, he pawed, he delicately stepped into one shoe. My God! What was he doing now? He lay on top of the second shoe. As she watched stupefied, Cedric looked up at her, Jessica was very sure, with half-closed eyes, a face full of love. "Oh, Cedric, we cannot tell your mother about this. Not a word."

Fifteen minutes later when Jessica stepped out the shower, she found Cedric still in the same place, stretched regally across the tops of both shoes, in love. "Come on, Ceddie." She picked all twenty pounds of him up. "I have to wash my clothes and you can have dinner while I fix mine. How's that, Honey Bunch?" He nestled underneath her chin. "What your mom doesn't know, we won't tell. Right? Mother's gone seven days and you fall in love with someone else. Not sure if I can return the sentiment, but, Ceddie, I am happy if you are happy."

Monday of Week Three

Monday morning in the offices of O'Malley, O'Malley, and O'Malley. Lil greeted Jessica with a "How was your weekend?"

"Great! Yours?"

"I did some laundry, shopped, cleaned the apartment. Not much. Craig Skyped from somewhere in Afghanistan where he is not supposed to be, and I am not supposed to know about. Sometimes he wants to get married; sometimes he drifts. He talks about how he might not come back, how dangerous it is over there, how he wants me to be prepared in case anything happens."

Poor Lil. Before Craig she and Jessica trolled the Columbus bars on weekends. Well, sometimes Thursdays too. Make that from Wednesday on. A person got used to hangovers. Fortunately Jessica suffered fewer of them now, Lil almost none.

Lilly Taylor had met Craig on one of those long weekends, which started midweek and lasted through Sunday night. Jessica had only been with Triple O for a year or so; Lil described herself at the time as "not in a relationship," although she assiduously hovered around her high school boyfriend's Facebook page. Together that long ago Wednesday after work Jessica and Lil had dropped into the Mohawk in German Village. Just fishing, they called it. While Jessica wasted time scrolling through ads for upcoming shoe sales, Lil began a conversation with a tall physically fit Craig Washington, home between tours of duty. He had graduated from Columbus East; Lil four years later from the same school. Their families knew each other mainly from mutual sports events. Craig and his brothers played football; Lil's brother Henry, Hank to his friends, played on the same team. Salt and Pepper the coach called Hank and Craig, co-captains for the Tigers.

Lil disappeared after office hours those few weeks Craig was home. Jessica had to hand it to her. Even in love Lil kept her mind on Triple O business from nine to five. Jessica secretly upbraided herself for not doing the same, always. Hungover those first years more than she should be, racquetball bouncing through vicissitudes of emotions over Andrew and a few others she picked up along the way, Jessica clandestinely awarded herself a grade of *C* in the Attention to Attorney Duties Department.

Before Craig was deployed, he asked Lil to marry him. No time for an engagement ring though, so instead he circled a silver necklace around her neck. A diamond hung from it, close to her throat. Close enough, he affirmed, to feel your heartbeat. "Wear it always for me, until I return next time to marry you."

They Skyped as often as they could considering time and the secrecy surrounding Craig's deployment. Noon in Columbus, Ohio Eastern Time was 8:30 p.m. outside Kabul where Craig was stationed, or so he said. Distance and time, Jessica knew so well, wreaked havoc on relationships. Now Lil knew it too. Apparently for her personal assistant, the weekend had not gone well. Did living daily with constant danger destroy feelings Lil thought her fiancé had for her? Was he even her fiancé? No engagement ring graced her ring finger. There were only Craig's promises of a wedding soon, right after he returned. Lil had those, but he did not seem as eager to discuss plans as he had been when she and his family waved goodbye to him at Port Columbus International Airport.

Surely their differences in race meant nothing to his parents. The Taylor family raised no objections. African American, Native American, Hispanic. Somalian. Lil's mother and father only wanted their daughter to be happy. Likewise, before he left, Craig's mother invited Lil for a hands on lesson in preparing ham, greens, and sweet potato pie just the way her son liked them. At dinner that last evening together with the family, Craig's dad prayed for his son's safe return as well as for the good health and safety of his future daughter-in-law. No, whatever bothered Craig, whatever seemed to dampen the fire of his enthusiasm, it was not family disparities over race.

"Life, huh? It can be a shit show."

Jessica tried to console her friend. Hardly a profound comment from an experienced attorney. It seemed to work though. Lilly Taylor, soon to be Lilly Washington, brightened.

"He will probably call from the base tonight. Midnight here is morning there, so I keep the laptop on my side of the bed. It's a far cry from sleeping with him, but it's comforting in a way. Warm too, since I keep it plugged in. I'll be fine."

Out of habit Lil touched the diamond at her throat. She seemed to have stopped, however, fretting about bridesmaids or how many of Craig's three sisters and numerous cousins should be in the wedding. Talk too of Jessica's serving as maid of honor had ended.

"Okay, Lil. What is on the agenda for today besides a trip to Canal Winchester? Any Woolsey appointments? My mother is clairvoyant, but not me."

"I don't foresee any," Lil quipped. "I did not know Alexandra could see the future though. Do tell."

"It passes down through the women in our family. My great grandfather Reichert, one of the developers of Haines Landing, never bought or sold property without consulting my great grandmother who read Tarot cards."

"That makes you one of the women in your family." Lil pushed when she wanted to.

"All right. To some extent I am, and no, I cannot read the stock market. Mom's better at clairvoyance than I am."

"All these years and why haven't you told me?"

"The subject never came up. Look, Lil, I ought to be able to predict my own future, which, as you might have noticed, I am terrible at. Everyone predicted I would marry Andrew. Now here I am with Max. No marriage, no kids. I used to select my engagement ring, but I quit doing that too."

"So the canary diamond, two carats as I recall from the website, is no longer part of the plan?"

"I am not even going to ask how you know about that?" Jessica really did wonder. Was her friend and employee snooping?

"You have been known to work on my computer up here too," Lil added before her boss continued. "Not that I would ever, ever go to a bookmarked site. Not me. Colin O'Malley might, but not me."

"Colin, rats, he is not coming up today, is he?"

Colin, of the three partners it was Colin, son of Gerald O'Malley, nephew of Patrick O'Malley. Colin it was who drove the bimonthly trip from Cincinnati to Columbus to consult with, Lil called it *spy*, on his firm's only capital city attorney. Without a doubt, his Irish good looks had at first caused Jessica to catch her breath. With red hair, green eyes crinkling at the corners when he smiled, a cheerful outlook on most things, and the innate ability to drink far more than the legal limit without showing it, Colin O'Malley could have been the one to place an emerald on Jessica's left hand. Or a canary diamond. Two obstacles blocked the road.

Colin did not prefer men. No, far from it. He was, however, Jessica's boss, one who, credible sources assured his employee, possessed a terrible temper. According to a colleague from another Cincinnati firm, attorneys could be counted among the very worst to gossip about each other. Colin had been discreetly but permanently banned from at least six bars in the Queen City. Visits from preholiday leprechauns must have disturbed the normally sanguine Irish temperament, for Colin's escapades usually occurred on or around Holy Days on the ecclesiastical calendar.

A Cincinnati colleague Jessica had run into while killing time at a required CEU course gleefully recounted the first of many such escapades gone wrong, this one dubbed the Christmas Eve Caper. Jessica heard how not so many months before, an intoxicated Colin careened into the driveway of a former fiancée's parents' home. How he learned about his own broken engagement was anyone's guess. Nevertheless, there he was stumbling into a living room of an ex-girl-friend. He drove a fist into his usurper's jaw, kicked the family dog, then slammed the front door shut behind him with such force that a Waterford framed portrait of the newly engaged couple toppled off the grand piano and broke. The family dog recovered quickly enough, biting Colin's rival in misplaced revenge. What upset the former fiancée's family, actually her mother, was not the intrusion. She rather liked Colin in spite of his moods. The ingrate had broken her Waterford frame! No one pressed charges, however. It seemed a pending real estate deal in downtown Cincinnati superseded breaking and entering and assault and battery. The elder O'Malley and the fiancée's father agreed to let bygones be bygones. Boys will, after all, be boys.

Then there was the Easter Episode, laughingly referred to at the downtown Cincinnati Club as the Egg Regious Event. Oh yes, the gated community's children's party had started peacefully enough. Colin's girlfriend of the moment, Colin's trampled heart having recovered sufficiently for the jilted attorney to date/sleep with women in record time, had been invited to join the O'Malley family for lunch on Holy Saturday. Afterward they would all convene at the O'Malley estate in Hyde Park to color eggs with neighborhood children. It was an annual event; everyone brought hard boiled eggs, including Colin's newest love.

The poor girl, nervous among the affluent O'Malleys and their like, dutifully brought the required six dozen eggs. Unfortunately, among those six dozen, three dozen were hard boiled, three dozen not. The reason for the uncooked eggs lay at the heart of the problem. Oh, originally all six dozen were cooked, all right. They were all placed nice and neat on the right side of her refrigerator.

On Good Friday evening, Colin had been commiserating with friends over the Reds' losses to the Indians the previous year. Sure, and he had called his faithful colleen. His excuse: future clients, he said, held him up. He could not come over that night as planned.

Colin's girlfriend needed solace. It was difficult to have such a successful attorney as a boyfriend. What happened next was an honest mistake, which anyone could have made. A lonely husband whose wife was on a business trip happened to stop by. Well, Colin's girlfriend might have called, but still it was nice for him to stop by.

He lived next door, saw the light on around midnight, and thought he should check to see if everything was all right.

The next morning anyone would have hastily prepared a breakfast for a hungry visitor, which is what Colin's girlfriend did, feeding both her new friend and her own children. Mildly hungover, the lonely next door neighbor, also straying husband, helped clear away clutter, thus the misplaced eggs. Six dozen or so, whatever order they were in since he had not been informed, all looked the same to him.

Already running a little late, girlfriend grabbed eggs and children, ran out the door, and drove downtown. Girlfriend realized the error, but her two daughters, eager to help out Mommy's friend who might soon be their new daddy, cheerfully carried the eggs to the O'Malley's backyard.

"We brought these! Mommy and her friend and I all had breakfast together this morning, Uncle Colin. We ate some too, but we saved the best for now!"

"Who?" asked a suspicious Colin. "Who had breakfast this morning with you cute little girls? I thought just the four of us ate together on weekends. Did Mommy's college friend come over?"

"No, Mr. Rittig from next door. He's really nice too."

"Of course he is, girls. I'm going to talk to Mommy for a little bit. You go color eggs." Colin shooed them off. Lavender and yellow checked dresses flouncing toward the egg table, the two little girls happily joined an elaborately attired Easter bunny hired for the occasion, the giant pink rabbit actually being one of the O'Malley clients working off his lawyer fees.

In fairness to Colin, with the revelation, he promised himself to keep his temper in check until he ushered his girlfriend one last time out to her car, a Taurus for God's sakes. In better days he had also hinted at purchasing a Lexus for her. Maybe. That plan shot, the best he could do was control his mood.

"Hon, I missed you last night," his soon-to-be-former girlfriend purred.

Holding his hand in hers, she paraded Colin past the guests, certain of Old Cincinnati matrons' jealous stares. The happy couple, happy only in girlfriend's eyes, reached the egg table.

"Here, let's join the kids. You color an egg for me, I'll color one for you." Her tone sounded sweetly lascivious. "I just bet the Easter Bunny might have something special for you tonight."

As she handed him an egg from their carton, a hangover and possibly some guilt drove her to lose concentration. Colin reached for the egg. Hands colliding, the egg dropped, raw, onto Colin's shoes, soaking through the soft Italian leather into his socks. Poor Colin. Grabbing one egg after another, he hurtled them toward his startled, now former girlfriend's PayLess spiked sandals. Horrified parents, attorneys in the majority among those professionals, delighted children, and one entranced Easter Bunny who removed his papier mâché rabbit head for better viewing, watched what later became the Egg Regious Event.

A staunch Roman Catholic, Colin observed all Holy Days equally. Were it not for his father's and his uncle's interventions on that particular occasion and others, Colin may have observed them in jail.

However, the All Saints' Day Disaster, as snickering attorneys both in the offices of O'Malley, O'Malley, and O'Malley and in offices of competing firms referred to it, might have been the worst. Colin himself called the whole mess a Wicked Halloween which unfortunately morphed into an Evil Event. Or Disaster. By the time the All Saint's Day Debacle occurred, Jessica had been with the firm less than six months. Triple O required her presence at monthly meetings, a not too difficult task. Usually lunch was brought in, roast beef and ham club sandwiches for the other lawyers, a vegetable wrap for Jessica. Occasionally if the meeting lasted into the afternoon, Jessica joined her colleagues for a drink before driving back to Columbus. One drink, no more.

It was more than one, however, on this occasion, Halloween. Earlier that morning, the only attorney in costume, Colin sat next to his father, two senior O'Malleys in Paul Stuart tailored dark pinstripe suits, the junior O'Malley as a leprechaun.

Tipping his high top Kelley green hat to no one in particular, he observed, "It's the right thing to do at the right time. My alma mater Notre Dame plays at home this weekend. I have tickets, so I thought

I would dress in appropriate attire. I picked this up at a little costume shop down the street. I just might wear it to the game too."

Usually saturnine, on this particular day the older of the two senior O'Malleys enjoyed his nephew's humor, his joie de vivre, inappropriate at firm meetings as it might be. Without warning then Patrick O'Malley, older than his brother Gerald by two years, excused himself from the long polished cherry table to retreat to his office. Partners, interns, personal assistants, and additional assorted attorneys waited thirty minutes for what they hoped was not the beginning of "the old man's wanderings."

Old man indeed. As the collected team of O'Malley, O'Malley, and O'Malley squirmed ever so surreptitiously, occasionally texting underneath the polished conference table, the senior partner made his grand entrance. Dressed in a ragged, pilled costume complete with snapping jaws which still worked in the chicken wire head gear of an angry University of Michigan icon, a wolverine, Patrick O'Malley gleefully jabbered through the open mouth of the symbol of Ohio State's hated rival. "Hey, gang. You didn't know I served our fraternity as mascot, back in the day, did you? Ha!" He pranced around the aghast group. "Thank God, I kept it here," he continued. "My ex-wife threw out everything I had from Phi Kappa Psi. Not my fault she didn't like us."

Jessica, seated demurely between two stodgier associates, smiled politely. How in the hell did she handle this one? No bar exam training had prepared her for a 180 degree change in her senior employer. "Hey, there, Little Red Riding Hood!" he breathed over her shoulder.

Off Patrick O'Malley, Esq. pranced, down the sedate halls of Triple O, up to the elevator and off to offices below and above him in one of the tallest buildings in downtown Cincinnati. "Apparently our partner has a pressing engagement," Patrick's brother observed. "You might wish to accompany him, Colin." Definitely not a wise choice for the son who had triggered the episode. As the youngest of the partners excused himself, Jessica, along with the remainder of the group, politely shuffled papers, while everyone waited for the meeting to begin.

Begin it did. Gerald O'Malley covered the entire agenda: status of cases, cheerful reminders of the importance of billable hours, and announcements of upcoming classes for CEUs, Continuing Education Units necessary to retain one's license to practice law. As the meeting concluded, Jessica felt her cell phone vibrate. "Meet us at the club when UR done." Colin. She hoped he didn't mean Patrick too.

Had the senior O'Malley, aka Uncle Patrick, not donned an incendiary Halloween costume, perhaps the events which unfolded would not have occurred. But they did. Ohio State fans, however well educated and from whatever walk of life, are famous for rabid outrageous behavior regarding their hated rivals, the University of Michigan. Generally residents from all parts of the Buckeye state hold strong allegiance to Ohio State, but particularly in Central Ohio, and almost certainly in Columbus, home of the Ohio State University. The fever spreads as far as Cincinnati too, causing normally reasonable adults to break out into heated sometimes violent disagreements. Although the actual game occurs in late November, tension builds throughout football season, reaching a climax on Game Day.

People dress in scarlet and gray the week of the game. Even elementary school children as far north as Marion and Upper Sandusky and as far south as the Ohio River are strongly encouraged to wear the Buckeye colors. Jessica judged the whole overblown hysteria disgusting; she hated Ohio State. Still, on this Halloween, as a newly hired employee, she had to meet her bosses at a bar and feign interest in the approaching annual rivalry. At least O'Malley senior was not sporting a Brutus the Buckeye costume.

Triple O as a firm belonged to the Cincinnati Club, which is where in the bar Jessica found two of the three partners. Although in the dark walnut recesses of the sedate club, residents of the Queen City mitigated their enthusiasm regarding the traditional November game, it was not difficult for Jessica to locate her employers. Loud renderings of "Cheer, cheer for Old Notre Dame" blended cacophonously with "Hail to the Victors." Jessica feared the worst. It would not be long before "Charge, charge on down the field" boomed out too.

As Jessica joined her two employers, one a leprechaun, the other a wolverine, she prayed for a Deus ex machina to extricate her from what would only snowball into a worse scenario. And why not? Sixteenth century audiences believed in the credibility of God from the machine. They still spoke Latin at Notre Dame, didn't they? Why not here in a city with a still strong Catholic environment? German, true, not Irish, but Catholic nevertheless.

The bartender set a martini in front of Jessica. "We know you like these. Drink up," Colin ordered.

"We did our due diligence before we hired you," Patrick breathed a muffled confession through his wolverine head. "Martinis, beer, margaritas. You are one experienced attorney, flexible in any drinking situation."

"Hey, barkeep," Patrick shouted down to the female bartender. He was definitely on his way to a drunk. "Bring the little lady some pretzels. She has to drive back tonight. Wouldn't want our little pal here to get picked up for a DUI," he whispered loudly past a bedraggled paw cupped on the side of his mouth.

An old fashioned bell ringer sounded on Patrick's phone. "Whoopsie. Probably an office crisis." The wolverine paws failed to catch his phone as it crashed to the floor. "No pain, no gain," he offered to no one as he scooped up his phone with the now cracked face. "Have to leave anyway." He signed the tab. Then with one last howl, he exited the prestigious Cincinnati Club.

"Well, you and I can stay, at least."

Please, no, Jessica prayed. *Come on, Deus ex machina. Rise from the floor. Drop from the ceiling. Help!*

The landline behind the bar rang. "Folks, I'm sorry. We have to evacuate the club. Someone pulled the fire alarm outside the men's room. I'm relatively certain that there is no fire, but to be on the safe side, we have to leave." Concurrently, alarms screeched throughout the club as bartender, cleaning personnel, members, and guests quickly moved outside into the hot sun of a Halloween afternoon.

Jessie thanked heaven for an answer to her prayers. With a hasty goodbye, she wove away from the club premises before it dawned on Colin that his employee had escaped. An hour's nap in the firm's parking places, then back home for attorney Jessica F. Woods.

Meanwhile, the junior partner of O'Malley, O'Malley, and O'Malley led an assortment of assembled club attendees and curious bystanders in repeated choruses of *Old Notre Dame*. Not surprisingly, Colin being Colin, celebrating Halloween transitioned at 12:01 a.m. to the paradoxical celebration of All Saints Day. What should have been a serious occasion for him was not. Wandering happily down a few streets to a less dignified setting than the Cincinnati Club, Colin encountered University of Michigan graduates. The annual September game between Notre Dame and Michigan rivals to some lesser degree achieved a simulacra of the Ohio State vs. Michigan hysteria.

Colin's temper obscured his better judgment yet again. The probability of one lone leprechaun inciting four wolverine fans, not in costumes but in maize and blue sweatshirts just, just, just was too high. Make it a one, to be mathematically correct.

Later that day on November 1 Colin's family attended five o'clock mass together. Patrick nursed what he referred to as a migraine due to office stress. Gerald sat with his wife and two teenage daughters from his second marriage, make that his third. From his cell in the Cincinnati City Jail, Colin observed the day as well. A grateful but exhausted Jessica Woods napped fitfully November 1 in the offices of the Columbus branch of O'Malley, O'Malley, and O'Malley.

"No." Lil brought Jessica back from unpleasant recollections of days gone by with Colin and family. "You don't have a meeting with Colin today. At least nothing on the calendar. You do have an eleven o'clock appointment in Canal Winchester with Leonard Warren though."

"Right, I know about that one. Thanks, I'll get some things together in my office. You can transfer any calls in before I leave." Jessica's case load exceeded that of the two attorneys on the floors above her. Robbie seemed to have pulled that bit of information out of one of his friends who played intermural basketball with one of the lawyers from the competing firm. Worried, those two on the fifth floor in separate expensive offices were, about their own billable hours. Jessica actually felt overwhelmed with the number of ongoing cases she had, but she was not about to relinquish any of them to her rivals/colleagues. At least when Bartram Irving returned from the Greenbrier, she could pass Mr. Ompherous Oney back to him. Better yet, she could expect payment for her services as the senior and only living partner of Irving and Irving, LPA concluded the case. Bart may be a philanderer, but he paid his bills. That mattered more than marital fidelity where Triple O was concerned.

The phone on her desk rang. "Ms. Woods?"

"Yes, this is Jessica Woods."

"This is the Huron County Sheriff's Department. We have a Maximillian Edwards in custody. He says you are his attorney. Is that correct?"

Shit. What had Max done now? She just left him yesterday. "Yes, officer, that is correct. May I speak with him?"

"Jess," Max sounded shocked. "Jess, Dad sent me out here to deliver some equipment for him."

The Edwards family owned a construction company in Lakewood on the west side of Cleveland. Surely, Mr. Edwards could have sent someone else. "They got me for going 55 in a 35 zone. They said I had a past fine I hadn't paid and hadn't appeared for a scheduled court date." He paused, waiting for Jessica's confirmation that she had indeed handled the speeding ticket from a week or so before.

"Shit. Max! I am so, so sorry." Words every client, paying or not, dreads hearing. "I forgot. Put the officer back on the line. I'll see what I can do."

"Yes, this is Officer O'Reilly."

"Officer, is there any way to release my client for work? As his attorney, I understood that my office had taken care of the prior speeding ticket and that the court appearance was not necessary."

"I am sorry, Ma'am. We do not have such information on record."

"I can be there in about two hours. Would it be at all possible to release my client so that he can return to his job in Cleveland?"

"No, Ma'am. I do not have that authority."

"Thank you, Officer O'Reilly. I am in Columbus now, but I will drive to Huron shortly and be there in about two to three hours. May I speak with my client again?

"Hey, Hon. I'm on my way. I'm truly sorry about this. It's all my fault."

From Max's tone he seemed both contrite and resigned. "I'll be here. You know where to find me." Poor Max. Until she arrived to change his situation, her boyfriend, the man she might very well marry, would sit in the Huron County jail.

"Lil, could you call Leonard Warren and see if we can reschedule? I have to drive to Huron."

Lilly looked up from the online shopping site, this time women's hats. "Sure. Let me check your schedule. How about tomorrow or Wednesday for Canal Winchester?"

Rushed, disgusted with herself, she said, "Whatever. I messed up seriously with Max. I forgot to talk to the prosecutor's office. Max just was arrested for speeding. He's in jail, thanks to me. I'll be back this afternoon."

"Drive carefully, Jess. I'll tell Mr. Warren you have a trial that lasted longer than expected. Clients love to hear that their attorney goes to court."

Two and a half hours later from the wrong side of the jail cell a miserable Max greeted Jessica. Having paid his bail, arranged his release, and set up a time for him to attend driver's school, Jessica attempted to kiss her boyfriend. Max turned his head, offering his cheek instead. Jessica shrugged off the rejection. In his situation, she would have done the same. Smiling, offering a quick hug, she waited with him as he collected his wallet and retrieved his shoes, "I have to run, Honey. I really am sorry about all this."

Understandably a distant Max escorted her to her car, opened the door for her, but held back on returning gestures of affection. "Thanks, Jess. Say hi to Cedric for me. No, "I'll call you tonight" though.

Jessica deserved the cold shoulder. Yes, she did, she told herself. It was one thing to think about other men, certainly one thing to wonder if she loved Max at all. Quite another to be politely but firmly rejected. Well, he could cool off for a day or so. After all, she and Max had just enjoyed a perfect weekend. She planned to call him that night anyway to attempt to make up.

Back in the Acura, a wasted day thanks to her own lack of organization, Jessica called Lil. "Did you change the appointment with Mr. Leonard?"

"Done and done. You meet him tomorrow morning, same time. He acted relieved actually."

"When is that family reunion? I would really like to find out why Warren has so much difficulty getting a liquor license."

"Next month. You should go with me."

"We'll see. I might have to take my boyfriend to Newport Rhode Island to Aunt Kate's condo. I really made him mad this time." Jessica checked her cell phone for a text from Max. Nothing. "He went to jail because of me."

"Nice" was Lil's simple riposte. "Want me to check flights?"

"Not yet. If he breaks up with me, I hate to waste the money on unused tickets."

"I could go instead," Lil offered.

"You have your family reunion. Besides, you definitely do not look like Max Edwards, so forget it. I'll see you in a few."

The remainder of the business day, brief as it was due to her unexpected round trip to Huron, passed relatively smoothly. Jessica sent Lil home at 4:30, a gift, for all the extra time Lil put in on other days. "If you see some shoes I should have at DSW in my size, call me," Jessica suggested as her assistant scampered out the door.

"Do you want me to lock up?" Lil asked. "I really do not like to have you up here by yourself after hours. The neighborhood isn't the best, you know."

"I'm good. I have two attorneys a few floors above me and an insurance agent below. If I scream, at least one will come to my rescue."

"Maybe the insurance agent. I doubt the lawyers will. They might save your files, but not you." Lil laughed. "By the way, I hid the information on Clara Woolsey in the backroom refrigerator. You can refresh yourself with a container of vanilla yogurt as you spend time with your friends and mine, Clara and Melvin. A person never knows when to expect them." With that Lil let the door shut. Jessica heard the elevator door open for Lil, then descend to the street. Lil should have used the stairs, Jess reflected. Her friend had put on ten pounds or more since Craig's deployment.

Poor Lil. Blessed with a 5'8" frame and ingrained habits of exercising along with healthy eating, Jessica forgot that many people, women especially, did not practice her lifestyle. With the onset of each new year, Lilly joined a fitness center, even accompanying Jessica to Pilates classes. However, the cold, snow, and icy rains of winter in Central Ohio successfully chipped away at Lil's determination to exercise.

Her assistant stood about Jessica's height, 5"6", but even at Jessica's age she was beginning to develop a barrel shape between her breasts and her waist. Exercise and watching her food intake could remove that spare tire. Lil had to want to, however. Maybe Craig liked her shape just as it was though.

Despite her rounded middle, Lilly Taylor was attractive. She emphasized her heart-shaped face by wearing her ebony hair in a contemporary French twist, teased at the crown. Lilly liked makeup, which she deftly applied; in fact, between Lil and Alex, Jessica learned the most recent updates for lips and eyes. A few tubes of Lil's current favorite, an arresting red called Roman Candle, lay in the employee's restroom as well as in the assistant's top desk drawer. On a good day, and there were many, Lilly's porcelain skin, midnight black hair, and deep ruby lips caused clients and attorneys to take a second and third look at the woman who guarded the gate to O'Malley, O'Malley, and O'Malley.

With Lil's departure, Jessica retreated to her office, intending to close down for the day. Tomorrow promised to be better, she was sure. She stared at the hodgepodge of papers she had left when she hurried up to Huron. Lil had placed the day's messages neatly on top of open manila folders, a calculator, and last week's *New York Times*. Jess started shuffling through messages, nothing urgent so far although she tried hard to return phone calls the day she received them. Her father was terrible at that office detail, but Jess prided herself on keeping up with most business matters. Of course, her dad was his own boss. Jessica had three, Colin O'Malley being the most punctilious.

She heard a man's footsteps in the hall; then the door opened. "It's me, Honey, I'm home!"

Acting as if he belonged, as if a day or two had passed, not a chasm of more than ten years, her high school boyfriend strolled smiling into her office. "I happened to be downtown and thought I'd save you the trouble of mailing me those articles of incorporation." God, he looked good. At least today Jessica looked good too despite the round trip to Huron County. She had washed her hair and styled it that morning. No stringy greasy mess for her. She had dressed well too.

Unlike so many of her female colleagues who donned pantsuits, Jessica preferred a feminine look: dresses and skirts. This afternoon the tangerine colored linen sheath from J. Crew still held up well despite a few wrinkles. Multi-strands of chunky amethyst and turquoise colored glass hung just below the boat neck. For fun that morning, Jessica had picked out her favorite Kate Spade spikes, emerald green with cotton candy colored heels. Jessica's shoes took a beating; sometimes they were so scuffed she had to throw them out. That hasty car trip hadn't helped the backs but she apparently had not yet wrecked one of her newest purchases.

"Jeff, what are you doing here?"

"Just what I said. I was over at the state house kind of reacquainting myself with Ohio. It doesn't hurt to relearn information about my new home, old home really."

He smiled. Those teeth. That mouth. Those hands.

Stop it; Jessica brought her thoughts back to professional ones. "I'm sorry, Jeff." The second time today she had apologized to a lover. No, just one time to a lover. The man casually standing in front of her desk was a client only. Best to keep those billable hours in mind though.

"Jeff, I sent in your articles of incorporation. I have not received them yet though. It's been less than a week, but the Secretary of State's office is timely so it shouldn't be too long. I'll have my assistant call you when they come in." She smiled, a professional smile, quick, firm, nothing more.

"Lil can call me, but it's you I prefer."

"Jeff, Lil is here all day," Jessica parried. "She can call you or drop them in the mail. Whatever is easier for you."

"Look, Jess, I would like us to be friends. Lil can handle the details if that is what you want. I'm happily married." As if Jessica had jumped to conclusions. Dammit. She felt like she had been upbraided by her high school principal. When had she lost control of a conversation she did not start nor wish to continue? "It's almost five o'clock. Let me buy you a drink. We can catch up on ten years' worth of gossip. How about it?" He checked his gold Rolex.

Jessica checked her silver one. Mrs. Jeffrey Rhinesworth probably wore the woman's watch with diamonds. Ridiculous investment really. A person couldn't water ski or play golf or engage in any strenuous activities with that damned watch. Jessica was just fine with her silver one with the gold interspersed in the band and on the dial.

"All right. I have two calls to make. Where do you want to meet?"

"How about down the street in the Irish pub–type tavern? Twenty minutes." Jeff turned and left before Jessica could reply. The door shut. No elevator this time; Jeff walked.

Now what had she agreed to? Catching up with an old friend, that was all. Billable hours and what could very well be a big client. Nothing more.

Just to be sure no clients had texted or e-mailed her, Jessica checked her cell phone as she walked down the street to Dempsey's Food and Spirits to meet Jeff. Nothing.

Jeff stood to greet Jessica as she approached the table. A gentleman, he always had been. Women notice. Alex liked to tell and retell the tale of a former college friend, also currently a former county commissioner in Tennessee who had lost his bid for reelection by only a few votes. Those lost votes? The defeated official had failed to stand when women entered the room. He neglected to open doors. In short, arrogance and ignorance defeated him. Apparently he still sold insurance although there too arrogance caught up with him. There was some problem with him being accused of selling insurance from his office in the county courthouse. Nothing was proven, of course. Well, as Alex had commented, he could sell insurance back in his office wherever it was and stay seated while he did so. It might work out for him yet. He certainly had more time now. Jessica assumed the unfortunate fellow had also been a former boyfriend of her mother's, probably the one to break up with her instead of the reverse.

Before she could think, Jeff leaned in to kiss her on the cheek. "Thank you, Jessica, for meeting me here. This tavern is very nice. I met the owner, Sean, who told me you had helped him get his liquor license."

"He did most of the work himself, but I tweaked it a bit for him. I am glad it worked out."

"You are too modest. I'm proud of you, Jess. You have done very, very well. Here,"—he helped her with her chair—"sit. By the way, those shoes are beautiful. My wife loves shoes too. You will really enjoy getting to know her. Sorority sisters too."

Any former girlfriend truly enjoys hearing about current wives and girlfriends. Acting, for attorneys, came in handy. "I can't wait to meet her. We should all get together soon. You didn't mention if she is here now or back home." Jessica garnered so much interest and enthusiasm that Jeff believed her.

"She and the kids are staying with my mother-in-law in Bucyrus. In fact, we will all live there until the house in New Albany is ready to move in to. I told you we bought a home, didn't I?"

New Albany, a city blessed by Limited founder Les Wexner. Jessica's mother Alex had stayed close to a friend from Upper Sandusky whose family business had grown so successfully over the years that the logical choice was to expand and to move to Columbus. As they relocated the container labeling factory to the east side of the city, they also purchased a home nearby. Hallmarks of Georgian architecture, homes off Greensward Road in the perfectly planned development varied in price from 1.5 million on up to 3.5 million dollars and more. Almost all brick homes boasted at least five bedrooms with seven to ten bathrooms. Alex's friend had chosen one of the most beautiful estates in what was termed the Original Crescent.

With swimming pools, landscaping seasonably highlighting two or more acres, these red brick mansions were usually occupied by upper level executives and other wealthy business people, quite often entrepreneurs who had taken risks and succeeded.

Maybe, thought Jesse, *Robbie might live there some day too. He could certainly claim to be a risk taker.*

Les Wexner was one, Alex's friend another. Evidently Jeff had also joined that group. And more power to him. In all fairness, however, she would not recommend One Eye Oney's ensemble, better known professionally as Tuxedo Bandsmen, for the house warming party.

As long as she continued her charitable thoughts, Jessica might as well follow up with more innocuous conversation. "I hope your wife will be able to relocate with her job." Whatever she does, Jessica thought, probably nothing except flash that gold Rolex around in tennis matches.

"She shouldn't have too much trouble. While I stumbled through college, partying more those last two years than studying, Erin kept her grades up and was admitted to medical school. She has had a couple of interviews with some hospitals here: Grant, Riverside, and Ohio State University Medical Center. It looks like the position with Ohio State might work out best. Plastic surgeons can usually find a job wherever they go, and my wife is an excellent one. You will really like her."

Definitely, thought Jessica. No lines on her forehead thanks to self-injected Botox followed a week or so later by Restylane. Most likely the skin of a woman ten years younger: blooming, shiny. Why not add a flawless neckline too. Oh, Jessica couldn't wait to meet the woman, physician, millionaire wife of the man who got away.

"We will definitely get together. I'm sure Ellen and I will become very good friends."

"I hope so, Jessica. *Erin*," he corrected. Sean Murphy came out from the kitchen to greet her.

"How's my favorite attorney?" He grinned at her. "The first round is on me. What will you two have? You know you've got the best lawyer in town, right? You get into a mess. Jessica Woods here will get you out of it."

"Jess, what about it? Champagne?" Jeff looked at her. Surely he remembered that night after the prom. Damn him.

"Guinness, please. Fewer calories and full of vitamins."

"Make that two. And thank you, Sean. I have a feeling we will be here often." Jeff grinned.

Not with me you won't. Bring the little woman between surgeries. I'm sure you two will do just fine. Sean returned with the beers and a bowl of salty pretzels. Jessica checked her cell phone again. Nothing.

"So here's to the renewal of old friendships." Jeff raised his glass. "Look, the bartender knows how to swirl a shamrock on top, just like they do in London! Fantastic! Anyway, to old friendships."

"And to new," Jessica added. "I look forward to meeting your wife."

"You will love her. In the meantime, let's enjoy each other's company. We have a lot to catch up on." Jeff looked at her left hand. "I don't see any significant rings yet. Anybody in the wings? A beautiful young professional woman like you probably has left a trail of broken hearts. I thought you would be married by now."

"Oh, you know. The law practice keeps me rather busy. Robbie will probably get married before I do. I work all day, then into the evening. Appointments, meetings, hearings. Not much time for fun or romance."

"You need to have more fun, Jess."

She waited for the next line, which usually ran something like, "I do." It seems Jeff really was still a gentleman. Instead he added, "I would like to see you happy."

Dammit, she *was* happy. She would have been considerably happier had Jeff Rhinesworth not returned from the East Coast and tried to interlope.

Occasionally while consuming three Guinnesses accompanied by two large bowls of salted pretzels, Jessica checked her watch. Not a gold Rolex with diamonds. "I have to run; I have a Pilates class."

Rising to pull out her chair for her, Jeff did not urge her to stay. He did, however, place his hands on her slim shoulders. Looking her straight in the eyes, he said, "We'll have to do this again soon. It's been very pleasant, Jess." As he released her, his phone chimed. "My wife."

Switching to a completely professional tone with Jessica, he continued, "Great seeing you. Let me know when you get the papers back from the Secretary of State. I'll stop by and pick them up."

He waved at her as Jess made a beeline toward the door and sunlight. On her way out she heard, "Sweetheart, I'll be back soon. Just finishing up some business here. Feed the kids; we'll have a romantic dinner later. Just us two."

Where the hell was her car? Either in the firm's parking garage for which she paid nothing or in her apartment garage. She couldn't remember. Pilates class was out. Darling Cedric needed dinner. Evidently the beers and pretzels served as Jessica's dinner; she felt both bloated and slightly dizzy.

A can of Precious Kitty Savory Salmon Sliceys with Eggie satisfied Jessica's new best friend. Purring loudly, he nuzzled so hard that she had to gently move him away from his bowl so that she could scoop dinner in. "What Mommy doesn't know won't hurt. Right?" She added another scoop. Cedric attacked his food with relish.

Dammit. She had planned to work at home that night, but in the frenzy to join her old boyfriend, no, the rush to meet her new potentially big client, one that could develop into a lucrative one, Jessica had left her laptop at the office. She decided to walk those few blocks back to the Triple O branch, review some notes for tomorrow's meeting with Leonard Warren, then retrieve her car from the parking garage where her firm paid her yearly fees.

Back in her office she figured she might as well check her phone before organizing the next day's work. She could check to see if Max needed assurance that his legal difficulties were behind him. Nothing.

Jessica dropped heavily into her chair, opened the remainder of her mail, then briefly rested her head against her computer screen. Her eyes still stung occasionally due to Cedric, although she seemed to have developed an immunity because she no longer looked as if she had been on a weeklong drunk.

Tuesday of Week Three

"Jess, are you all right?" Lil's concerned voice sounded close to Jessica's ear. What was her assistant doing in Jess's office at night, for heaven's sakes?

"Did you sleep here?" Morning, 8:00 a.m. Another headache, another dry mouth, another day, another dollar.

Jessica swept her hair back from her face, blinked several times to clear her cloudy vision, and gazed groggily at her employee. "Shit. I came in here last night and must have fallen asleep. Damn! What time is it? I have to meet that client in Canal Winchester."

"You have plenty of time. It's 8:10. I just came in early." Probably to try to Skype her uncommunicative supposed fiancé from the office. Poor Lil. "Go home, shower, you will be fine."

"I think I'm going to run too. I feel awful. I'll be back this afternoon, but call me if anything comes up."

A run sweat out the remainder of last night's Guinness. A hot shower washed it away. Another open can of Precious Kitty Breakfast Bacon and Eggies settled Cedric down. Where the hell was Madelyn anyway? Why had not the doting mother called to baby talk to her darling? Jessica took a hurried look at Cedric's litter box. Yuk. Apparently the Maine Coon chose to punish his new best friend— did he think of her now as Mommy?—for last night's absence. She could clean the box later this afternoon. Make that now, Cedric rubbed against Jessica's legs, then back to his box, then back to her.

"All right, Ceddie, you deserve a fresh bathroom. My client can just wait a few minutes."

Carrying a nearly overflowing plastic grocery bag full of Cedric's work, Jessica juggled her laptop, her briefcase, and her purse as she pulled her apartment door shut. No need to check her phone for a text from Max. He could wait a few minutes too. First the Dumpster, then Max, in that order.

As she pulled out of her parking spot into the spring sunshine, Jess decided to review Max's texts before responding. Nothing. Well, not enough time had elapsed really, less than twenty-four hours. She had more to do than worry about a boyfriend in a minor snit. She planned to call tonight. Thirty minutes to the east her client waited, less than that if she drove a few miles over the speed limit. Twenty-five minutes later Jessica pulled up at the curb of 213 W. Liberty Street, Canal Winchester, Ohio, the town that bridged two counties: Franklin and Fairfield.

Sitting on his porch, Leonard Warren duplicated the same position in which Jessica had left him one week before. However, rocking in the wicker chair next to him a wizened man with faded big overalls smoked a cigarette. He exhibited the same features as Leonard, if one took into account the effects of age, weather, and probably alcohol. Whoever it was—and Jessica loathed the helpful guidance of relatives and friends when she met with clients—had the same thick full head of hair, crew cut, the same broad nose, and the same deep wrinkles at the corners of his eyes. Cheerful enough, if a person did not look past the seemingly harmless gaze into the depth beneath. Whatever troubled one man troubled both. Maybe life.

Leonard had had his share of sorrows. Perhaps the man next to him had too. People in Southeastern Ohio struggled with poverty and addictions of various kinds. Jessica's job did not include fretting over client problems other than those she was hired to solve. Colin O'Malley drummed this mantra into her skull at almost every meeting. "Start trying to change the world, and you've got yourself in over your head," he reminded her. Not to mention out of a job. The business of Triple O was business, no hand holding and bleeding hearts for one of Cincinnati's top firms. How the hell do you think they stayed at the top?

Jessica pulled her laptop from the back seat. Better put it back. Who knows how the older man, guide as it were, would take to what he might call gadgets? As she climbed the porch steps both men stood. Gentlemen, whatever their SES or socioeconomic status. The defeated county commissioner down in Tennessee selling insurance from his office could take a page from their books.

"How are you, Mr. Warren?" She extended her hand.

"I am just peachy, Miss Woods. This here is my uncle John Henry Warren. We just call him Thumper though. I hope you don't mind Thumper here sitting in. He's kind of the family advisor since

Daddy died, so respect your opinion as I do, I mean I hired you and all, Uncle Thump here is my sounding board too."

"I am pleased to meet you, Mr. Warren."

"Call me Thumper. Don't feel right you callin' me anything else but."

Leonard Warren gestured to one of the wicker chairs. "Here, have a seat. The wife will be out with a lemonade as soon as she gets back from her ladies' meeting. I swear those church circle gals do more harm with gossip than they do good at their Bible study, but what do I know? At least I learn who's doin' what to whom when she returns from one of those gatherings."

As Jessica settled into the chair Thumper had placed next to his nephew, she smelled the sharp aroma of burning leaves coming from the house. Like the smoke from bonfires she and her family built at their cottage on Fischer's Beach, the distinctive odor evoked times when she truly had been happy, not rushed or hungover or caught up in romantic histrionics. But no one was roasting marshmallows inside her client's two story frame house; that was pot Jessica smelled. Either Leonard, Uncle Thumper, or Rachel must have been smoking shortly before she arrived. That smell was recent if not current. The Little Woman, as Leonard referred to her, could very well have attended her Ladies' Auxiliary, learned nothing new in the gossip, and returned home for some relaxation. Hell, they could have all been smoking for all Jessica knew. Not her business, of course, as Colin's rejoinder swirled in her mind.

"So, Mr. Warren, I made a few phone calls."

Clients loved to hear that their lawyer took the aggressive approach. Phone calls were good, meetings better, trials terrific. As long as these forays into justice were brief, successful, and inexpensive.

In actuality Jessica had e-mailed one member of the liquor control board who had not replied; the automatic response indicated that Mr. Willard Portland was out of the office for two weeks. That meant he was on vacation. A second e-mail to another board member brought a more satisfying response, however. All papers were in order. Approval of the license dated January 21 would be forthcoming.

"Mr. Warren, as with you, I cannot understand what the holdup is on your license. The liquor board usually moves quickly. You already have your food service license, don't you? The board does not do anything until the board of health comes out, inspects the premises, then grants their approval."

"Got that right after Christmas."

"Sure did." Thumper woke up from what was either a dope induced reverie or a genuine nap.

"Mr. Warren, is there anything I should know? I drove out here to help you, but I cannot help you if I do not know circumstances, which might conflict with your receiving your license in a timely manner." Jessica waited. Allowing clients some time without pressing them often worked.

As she waited, she turned to Thumper who still had his eyes open. "Mr. Warren?"

"Thumper."

"Thumper, have you lived in Canal Winchester for long?"

Wrong question, a question she would berate herself for in the drive back to Columbus.

"Hell, I haven't lived anywhere for long, let alone this town. Gotta keep movin', know what I mean?" Jessica did not, but he was about to tell her.

"While Leonard here decides to tell you what he wants you to know, let me fill you in on how this boy and I here spent much of our lives. Now you could call what we did outside the law. Hell, moonshining ain't a crime if you pay the liquor boys. That's what that stamp on the bottle is for. Means you paid your taxes, fair and square. Thing is, back in the hills when folks are strugglin' anyway, who wants to charge his neighbor more 'en he has to?"

Moot point. Rhetorical question.

"Know why they call it moonshine?" Another rhetorical question. "Because when you're makin' liquor illegally you're sure as hell not gonna make it in daylight when nosey neighbors and nosier Law can see what you're doin'." Thumper lit a cigarette, a legal one this time. "You smoke?" He offered her a Marlboro.

"I never took it up. Mom used to but quit when she was pregnant with me. She still sometimes stands outside with the smokers at the college where she teaches just to breathe in the smell of cigarettes. People say it's a more difficult habit to break than that of alcohol."

"I know that for sure. Gave up drinking ten years ago. Can't give this up though." He inhaled deeply, sighed contentedly, then continued. Jessica assumed he had taken up marijuana as a replacement for the alcohol he missed. Again, not her problem.

"So my dad and uncles and me moonshined most of my younger years. See, during the war there wasn't much to do. You've gotta remember people still were living through the Depression. If you weren't in the service, which at the time I was too young for and my dad and uncles already served or were too old. Anyway, there were only a few jobs to be had and those piss poor as far as pay. In Southeastern Ohio, Kentucky, and West Virginia you could work in a sawmill, a mine, cut timber, pick cotton, or moonshine. Some of our family did all them jobs, but families were big back them.

"People had to feed their kids some way, so a lot of them turned to moonshine. They didn't deliberately want to break the law. They just couldn't think of another way. Besides, all we were doing was beating the government out of a little tax money."

Leonard Warren got up quickly from his chair, retreating through the screen door to the darkened house. Billable hours, Lennie, for me to listen to your eighty-year-old-plus uncle tell stories of the old days. Might as well listen; your dime. God, Jessica had definitely fallen under Colin's dictum: Bill 'em. Boring? Bill 'em more.

Oblivious to his nephew's leaving or Jessica's boredom, Thumper continued. "See, back in those days people thought about moonshine the way they feel about pot now. Most wanted it legalized; some were dead set against it." Jessica listened rather than argue.

"The only way the Law could catch you was to sneak up on you. 'Course the Law had to figure out where back in those hills you were. It was kind of like now. People snitched. Same old thing: jealous neighbors if you made too much money. Jealous husbands and boyfriends if you messed with their women.

"Sure you don't want a cigarette?" Thumper flicked the butt into his nephew's bushes. Evidently Rachel or somebody picked them up; landscaping around the house showed meticulous care.

"Anyway, where was I?"

Too much dope smoking plus years of alcohol wreaked havoc with memory. Jessica reminded herself of that. From now on, limit yourself to two drinks no matter what. There. She felt better already.

Jessica checked her watch. The phone was in her purse, which she had left in the car. No way to make it ring to get her out of this, billable hours or not. Where the hell was her client?

"So I am going to give you a brief lesson in how to make moonshine, in case you ever need it."

No stopping him now. Think of Colin's dictum, then relax and pretend to listen.

"Here's what you need. A large copper kettle, about a hundred gallons, piping, and a condensing coil. The pot has to sit on the fire, so you need to have a container that won't melt.

"We didn't make gin, so I don't know how to do that. We made corn liquor. Whole kernels are okay, but ground corn ferments faster. You have to have a lot of sugar. Mix about five pounds of sugar to three gallons of water. That's why most moonshiners set up their business near streams. You put it together and let it ferment for a few days, about five to a week is good. Then when you think it's just right, you boil it off.

"You have to have a hole in the pot to boil it off, and another container about two feet high with an elbow in it. You see, what you do is boil this off into a condenser. Now before the stuff gets to the condenser, it goes through a thumper which works like a strainer. Separates sludge and junk from the rest of the mixture."

"Hence, your name," Jessica interjected.

At this point the sludge and junk consisted of a conversation she did not wish to be on the wrong end of. Her client seemed to have disappeared while the guide or advisor rambled on.

"Yeah, me. I kept a lot of folks from getting into more trouble than they needed. I guess you could say I separated sludge from junk. You're one smart attorney, Miss." He inhaled, appeared to reflect, then continued. "Of course, I got into a little trouble myself but I always got out of it." He winked. "Could have used you a few times though. Yes, I could.

"Anyway, after it passes through the thumper, it gets to the condenser which is a coil. Looks like a curly-cue surrounded by water. I have to tell you back in those days some folks used a car radiator in the process."

"When?"

Thumper lit another Marlboro, paused, then chuckled. "Radiator held the water that cooled the steam. It was pretty dangerous, but people probably had a lot of junk cars around so they just put the radiators to good use. That was pretty dangerous, all things considered. No matter how well you cleaned the radiator, you ran a huge chance of adding poison to the brew.

"Anyway, after it condenses, it runs off through copper tubing into a barrel. When it comes out, it's about 150 proof, so you need to cut it down to about half and half. Now I can tell you truthfully I tasted it and it tasted horrible, like medicine. Some folks like it strong though, but we still cut it down.

"Then we put the liquor in five-gallon cans and someone came to pick it up and haul it to the distributors. The distributors put it in pints or half gallons and sold it from there.

"Now that's where NASCAR came in. Ya see, no one wanted to get caught. The faster the car, the better chance the haulers had of getting away from the Law. I've gotta tell you, more guys got caught buying sugar than they did hauling moonshine. See, back in the war."

"World War II?"

"Yeah, World War II. I'm not that old! World War I was 1914 to 1918. I wasn't born till 1928." Thumper lit another Marlboro.

"Do you suppose we should check on Mr. Warren?"

"Call him Whizzer. Everybody does."

Jessica did not want to hear a story regarding the origin of that name. Instead she knocked on the screen door. "Excuse me, I will just check to see if Whizzer is all right. Mr. Warren, is everything okay?"

"Yeah, sorry, I will be out in a minute."

No getting away. Jessica sighed, sinking back into her rocking chair.

"I'll tell you, back in those days it was a chore just to try to get something to drink!"

God, another story. Interesting as it might be, Jessica wanted to scream. She heard a door slam, then watched as Rachel gunned out the driveway in what must have been her husband's red Ford pickup truck. Apparently there had been some discord at the ladies' circle meeting to which she felt called upon to return to settle matters. Jessica decided peremptorily to listen five more minutes to Thumper, then leave.

"Some counties were dry, some weren't. Now me being a teenage boy, close to being an adult, I wanted a drink just like my friends did."

"Couldn't you have some of that moonshine?"

"Hell, no. We sold that. You're looking at the beginning of the war. One way or another most of the alcohol made went to the armed services. Besides, I lived in a dry county. My friends and I had to drive to the next county if we wanted a beer. We'd head over to a restaurant that didn't seem to care how old we were. Have a big time, we did, just laughing it up, then drive back. The Law didn't like us drinking underage then any more than they do now, but I never got caught. Never paid a fine for nothing.

"I'd better be honest. Us guys knew about one bootlegger who hid potato sacks with pint bottles in the bushes around his still. We sometimes helped ourselves, but the guy was real mean, so we decided we would be better off just driving to the next county

Leonard returned looking distracted. "I'm sorry. Rachel there does not seem to be having a good day. Look, can we reschedule? I know, you have to drive out here again, but today is not turning out very well. I'll pay you for your time. I just cannot talk any more today."

Thumper rose from his rocking chair to join Leonard, aka Whizzer. Together the two men presented imposing figures. Jessica would get nowhere with them today, but at least they had released her from any more moonshine stories, interesting as they turned out to be. She could tell Max the NASCAR story when she called him tonight.

"It was nice meeting you, Mr. Warren, Thumper." Turning to Leonard she continued, "I'll have my assistant call you to arrange a meeting for next week. We might be able to finish most of this on the phone."

In a few weeks Lil had that family reunion, which Jessica might be attending if Max was still not talking to her. Maybe she could learn what Whizzer had done in Hocking County to annoy someone so much that the license of a Vietnam veteran honorably discharged, one whose record as far as felonies was clear, why that license was delayed.

Jessica waved goodbye to both men, pulled away from the curb, then called Lil. "Anything earth shattering happen while I have been down here in Moonshine County?"

"Ralph Edmonton called. Carolyn came out of surgery just fine. She did have breast cancer, but according to the surgeon, it was contained to a miniscule lump. It was not in her lymph nodes, so she does not need chemo."

Sometimes in this shit show the good guys really do finish first. Without being aware of it, Jessica felt tears cloud her vision. "Thank you, God," she prayed. "Thank you."

"Jess, are you there?"

"Sorry, I dropped the phone."

"Anything else?"

"Bartram Irving called. He is back from his conference at the Greenbrier and wanted to get together with you on Ompherous Oney."

"One Eye. Call Mr. Irving and tell him all I did was ask for a continuance. One Eye is one interesting client, but I just made an appearance. You can hand this mess back to good old Bart and his intern, slash, girlfriend. If you're killing time, you could find out why our client carries this particular sobriquet."

"What?"

"Why they call him One Eye. To me the guy looks perfectly normal."

"I know the answer to that." Lil quite often knew more about Jessica's clients than she did. "Ompherous David Oney plays in a group, the Tuxedo Bandsmen. I used to date one of the band members. It seems your client,"

"Bart's now. One Eye might be too slick for me. I do not want to lose my license over a man that insinuates himself into what could be potential clients' homes, steals their jewelry and clothes, and gets away with it. I have every reason to believe that Mr. Oney's sartorial splendor for court was the direct result of him helping himself to closets not his own, most likely in New Albany."

"Okay, Bart's client was born with vision in one eye only. It is extremely rare, but it happens. Now, if a person is born blind in both eyes, or with restricted vision, most people are not born totally blind, they still recognize light and shadows."

"You know a great deal about vision."

"Another past boyfriend attended optometry school for a while. He hung out with ophthalmologists, so I learned that way. Until, you might know, he went back to his wife. So much for Separated Getting a Divorce Soon Sam."

"Lil! Just stay with the matter at hand."

"One Eye got his name in elementary school. Kids can be cruel, but Ompherous apparently preferred the nickname to his given name. What were his parents thinking anyway? So because the kid had vision in one eye his face and general appearance developed normally. When both eyes are affected, that is when you see the roving eyes. The brain tries to help the eyes to focus, a task which cannot be completed because of the impaired sight. End of lesson."

"I'm about fifteen minutes away from another waste of time. Pull out Leonard Warren's address and send him a bill. For my efforts and my now two visits, I have learned how to construct a still but other than that, nothing. Schedule an appointment at my office for Mr. Warren, not in Canal Winchester. Make it contingent upon receiving payment for the first two appointments. I have had more than enough of Whizzer and his sidekick Uncle Thumper."

"Moonshine stories, huh? I heard a shitload of them growing up in Southeastern Ohio. Will do, Boss."

"I have a beep. Talk to you soon."

The screen on her phone read *Unknown*. Jessica answered anyway.

"Jess, it's me, your long lost friend Madelyn. How are you? How is my little baby? Is he eating?"

"Dr. Madelyn Hendricks. It should be about teatime over there. How was the conference?"

"To answer you in reverse order, it is long since past tea time, we are well into cocktail hour. I'm at the Ritz drinking champagne. You have been here, haven't you?"

Oh, yes, when Jessica was in high school Alexandra had taken her daughter to London for a ten day tour, the first of Jessica's trips overseas. To this day it remained one of the most pleasant vacations of Jess's life. Their tour allowed considerable freedom to explore London and surrounding environs, among them the British Library, the British Museum, and Stratford-upon-Avon.

From their hotel they had walked down Euston Road to the national library of the UK. For Alex and later for Jessica, who like her mother became an English major, seeing original manuscripts continued to be an experience of a lifetime. Together mother and daughter viewed displays of a Guttenberg Bible, Chaucer's *Canterbury Tales*, and the *Magna Carta*. Did this trip influence Jessica's decision years later to become an attorney? As a high school sophomore she seldom viewed life beyond the next week. Now as a lawyer with at least a few years' experience, she thought perhaps that trip, that view of a document signed by King John in 1215, which in writing limited monarch's powers and more importantly promised trial by jury, that trip may have been the beginning of her own journey into the legal system she so revered.

At the British Museum Jessica remembered her favorite exhibits, those collected from the explorations of Captain James Cook and the explorer Howard Carter. Cook's search for the Northwest Passage, a shorter route from England and Europe to China, resulted in his discovery of Christmas Island in the Pacific and the Sandwich Islands, later of course renamed the Hawaiian Islands. George III,

King of England, was the recipient of some of Cook's discoveries which are on display in the Museum.

For Jessica, for her mother, and for many tourists, the Rosetta Stone was among the most fascinating finds. To be so close to it, to see it, Jess still felt in awe of the ancient Egyptian hieroglyphs and Greek scripts, which when decoded brought understanding and knowledge of Egyptian history. Jessica loved, too, the astounding displays of the many sarcophagi, coffins if you will, of pharaohs. Carter's discovery of the tomb of King Tutankhamun supposedly carried a curse. The archeologist opened the burial vault in 1923 but did not die until 1939, so the curse seemed questionable to Jessica. However, the splendor of the museum astounded her.

Serendipity too happened on that trip. The hotel where Jessica and Alex stayed on the tour was within walking distance of Buckingham Palace, the museum, and the British Library. Some streets were far less confusing than others, and Alex, having traveled to London two or three times already, apparently knew the territory although she carried a map as well for reference. The British people are in general a polite lot. Receiving kind assistance required courtesy. Such questions began with, "Excuse me, I was wondering if you could perhaps give me directions to…"

Despite the map and Alex's previous experiences, she and therefore Jessica were somewhat confused as they crossed a park, one of many in London, to where they expected to find the British Museum. At a stoplight, realizing they were lost, they asked a well-dressed man ahead of them for guidance. He turned, politely proffered specific guidance, then added, "Paul McCartney's down there. If you hurry you can see him." Placing his hand on Alex's arm, he looked directly into her eyes and smiled. "Hurry now, you do not want to miss him. He is wearing a blue suit."

The light changed. As the helpful Londoner disappeared into the traffic, Jessica urged her mother to walk faster. A member of the famous Beatles was right down the next street.

"No, Honey, he is not. We just saw him."

Indeed they had. The kind man with the perfect skin and smiling eyes wore a blue sports coat, not a blue suit. Other than that, he was the same Paul McCartney. Earlier that morning Alex had read in the *London Times* that the foremost Beatle was in the city to dedicate a memorial for his wife who had recently died of cancer.

"Why didn't you say something, Mom?"

"Honey, he is still in mourning. It would have been very, very impolite to encroach. We were fortunate just to have seen him, even more so to talk to him." Another lesson, Jessica reflected, her mother had taught her. Silence, discretion, good manners. Graciousness.

Mother and daughter had been to the Ritz Hotel too, to the large main rooms where one could sit at small tables and sip champagne, just as Madelyn was doing now at approximately 7:00 p.m. London time. Jessica could use a drink herself after that most unfruitful meeting with Leonard Warren. Limit though, two. Self-discipline in all things made Jessica a healthy person. So far on Day One of the self-imposed Abstemious Regime, she was doing quite well.

Madelyn rattled on about the conference of the American Psychological Association. Apparently her presentation was well received. Attempting to pay attention, Jessica let her thoughts wander to her trip so many years ago with her mother, her decision to enter law school after a year as a detective, her love for Andrew, her dad, Robbie. Her brother should be the attorney; no, the physician. Every bit as intelligent as Bob, more so, after graduating from Notre Dame, Robbie could have any job he wanted. A risk taker like, well, their dad, Jeff, oh, shit, like herself, maybe her big brother's visions embraced more than he let on. Jessica prayed they did.

"Listen, Jess. I was wondering if you could keep my little Cedric for a while longer, just a week or so until I get back."

"I can, but what about your clients?" Madelyn managed her practice herself, receiving people in her home. She had recently purchased a house from a retired music teacher who tutored students in an office he had converted from a breezeway between his home and the garage. Along with many situations Jessica had encountered, the music teacher turned tutor had been encouraged by the Reynoldsburg police to retire completely from the business of engaging with children. As a friend, Jessica checked the title for Maddie. Discovering no clouds, except for those raining on the man darkly hinted as a pedagogue, Jessica F. Woods, attorney of record, represented both the buyer and the absent seller, seller having been advised to leave Central Ohio for good. Faxed contracts and agreements readily signed by the seller from a rural location somewhere in Missouri moved the sale forward in a timely manner. In Ohio a deed is not a deed until it is recorded. Jessica duly recorded the deed at the Franklin County Courthouse. Shortly thereafter Dr. Madelyn Hendricks moved her practice and herself into a gated community off Greenleaf Drive.

"I am so grateful, Jess. You know I do not ask for many favors. It's just, well, something has come up."

The many favors were snowballing into an avalanche. Cedric had turned out not to be a problem, but Jessica waited for the next request.

"Do you think I could persuade Lil to call my clients? She is so much better at cancelling appointments than I am."

Nice turn of phrase for a psychologist. Indicating that Lil had considerable practice in cancelling appointments for Jessica? Time for a professional riposte. "Maddie, I am on the road, headed straight for a pretrial. Call Lil and ask her yourself. That way you can resolve matters more quickly."

"Thanks, Jess. I'll pay her, of course."

"She will have to wait until after office hours, and she cannot use Triple O's phones. Colin checks everything." Jessica did not think he took the time to check phone records, but she was growing weary of doing favors for Dr. Madelyn Hendricks, especially when Jess suspected the reason for the psychologist's protracted absence lay with a man, not a potential conference. For that matter, Jessica could use a romantic London vacation. With Max. With Jeff. With Andrew. Dammit, even with the Eye Candy Bruce What's His Last Name who had rescued Cedric from the parking garage.

"How is my little baby? I miss my kitty. Is he eating?"

Daily contents from the Maine Coon's litter box served as concrete—yes, concrete—evidence that, indeed, the little dear was eating.

"Has he given you any problems? I know he can be a little difficult when Mommy is not around to play with him and kiss him."

Let's see: allergy attacks that caused lawyers from competing firms to jump to conclusions that Jessica was on a drunk, hiding under cars in a parking lot, hissing and spitting at Max's dog, chewing leather Louis Vuitton purse handles. Given time Jessica was certain she could spin off a few other examples. "No, he has been the perfect cat. I really have not done much except work. Cedric fits in well at the apartment where, as you recall, management rules forbid the keeping of pets."

Jessica distinctly heard a whisper, then giggles over the air, a distance of some four thousand plus miles. "I have to go. I'm driving. Call Lil. I will see you when you get home."

"Thank you, Jess. You are a true friend."

Jessica broke the connection before she heard any more drivel.

"Lil, it's me again. Maddie might call asking you to cancel her clients' appointments. Do what you want, but keep Triple O out of it."

Purchasing shoes online was one thing; conducting business for another company quite different. Jessica ignored any baser reasons.

"Jess, I just hung up with Colin. It seems your employer had to be in Columbus on another matter, so he wondered if you were free from four o'clock on. That way he will not have to drive up from Cincinnati next week for your usual meeting. I checked your schedule. It looks like you have an arraignment at two and a pretrial at three but nothing after that."

"Fine, let's get it over with. Call him back, but would you check the office and my desk to see if everything is in order? Colin likes to poke around. Then don't leave if he arrives early, even to use the ladies' room."

"Will do, Boss. Mr. Rhinesworth called wondering if our office had received the Articles of Incorporation yet. He asked you to return his call. Would you like his number?"

"No. He has mine. Let him sit. Change of subject. I am going to that family reunion with you whenever it is if Leonard Warren pays his bill beforehand."

"You should be able to dig up something there. My family is related to almost everyone in Southeastern Ohio, especially Hocking County. Besides, you will have fun that day. I promise."

By this time in her life Jessica had heard many promises, most not delivered on. A good time at a family reunion could be one of the first. Whatever disagreement drove Rachel out of the Warren house in Leonard's red pickup truck, whatever secrets Thumper attempted to dissuade Jessica from learning with his smoke and mirrors recipe for distilling moonshine, Jess promised herself she would discover. Unlike Andrew, she had not graduated from law school as valedictorian. Unlike Andrew, however, she had spent more than a year as a detective. The whole episode of the Languishing Liquor License could be fun indeed.

Speaking of fun, Jess checked her phone for a text from Max. Nothing. She almost, almost called Jeff. What next? Since she now had a long term feline house guest, she had better pick up more Precious Kitty. Why did the little darling balk at eating less expensive food? Jessica Feline Woods. No, Jessica Fooled Again Woods. Felines! Friends! A major four letter word came to mind. She almost yelled it out the open window. Best not to though. Forbearance.

She checked her watch. Run in quickly to a convenience store she recalled off Route 33. If the Duke and Duchess did not carry Precious Kitty, Jess probably had one can left of a brand she had purchased before a hungry Cedric registered his disdain by walking away from his bowl to hide under the potted palm in the apartment corner. The little dear not only hid, he sent out venomous stares directed toward what had then been his new caregiver. Now long forgotten by Cedric, the only participant who truly mattered in this scenario, Jessica could proffer the loathed second best food should necessity drive her to do so. Perhaps Cedric might think back into his past bad kitty behavior with his new caregiver, perhaps not.

There stood a convenience store straight ahead on the left right off Route 33 just as Jessica recalled. Screeching in, tires squealing, Jess would be late for the arraignment if she did not rushed; she leaped out of her car, then tripped over a concrete parking bumper. Someone had previously hit it, thereby knocking it at an angle

163

rather than horizontal with the others. Headfirst, she tumbled onto the hot asphalt. Cell phone flying out of her purse to skid along the pavement, Jess watched in horror as the leather handle on her ebony Gucci doctor's bag ripped almost in slow motion from the brass attachments. She stood up quickly, knocked the gravel off her scraped palms, retrieved her scattered possessions, and entered the store. They had better carry Precious Kitty.

In the pet food section paradoxically placed adjacent to the feminine needs shelf, Jessica noticed a familiar figure, back turned to her but definitely sporting a precisely detailed hair style, carefully maintained, but to an exact geometric shape. The style was perfectly chestnut colored, short at the nape, hugging the neck, textured on the sides to gently swing as the wearer tilted her head to read, my God, to read details on the back of an assortment of vaginal lubricants. Jessica recognized that haircut anywhere: the Honorable Susan Dial. Who the hell accompanied her, pretending to leaf through hunting magazines in the next aisle? Certainly not her husband.

No, the Honorable John Rentmore Dial, retired, tipped the scales at over 250 pounds and knocked on the wrong side of the age door at eighty something. Jessica checked her watch again. She might have a few more minutes if she pushed the Acura seven miles over the speed limit. Make that ten. In her haste to appear nonchalant if not invisible, she accidentally scraped her bloody palms against her Beach Bleached Blue dress. As she stepped back discreetly away from the aisle which did indeed contain Precious Kitty, she realized her J. Crew shoes had taken a beating in the recent tumble as well. The pale mint leather on both toes was hopelessly scraped. Maybe manicure scissors and nail polish could fix that later. If she zipped her bag as she should have in the first place and held it under her arm, she could exit quietly before Judge Susan Dial noticed her.

Jessica chided herself for always assuming a salacious side of other people, especially the ones she did not like much. It was entirely possible that the tall twenty something man with the square posture of a dancer or a military person was simply another customer with no connection to Susan. Best to scamper out anyway; she had wasted time here where the damned Precious Kitty waited, not to be purchased, only twenty-five feet from her grasp.

Whoever this knock out Should Be Banana Republic model with the slicked back sun streaked hair and piercing eyes blue as the spring sky could be, Jessica decided, there was no connection to Susan. Then glancing up from his magazine which he seemed to be leafing through to kill time, he caught the judge's eye as she chirped, "Ready to go, Sweetheart?" The Honorable Susan Dial approached the counter with her purchase of KY Jelly.

Just then Jessica's cell phone rang. Shit! Blindly scavenging deep into her purse, which was not easy to do, she failed to reach her phone within the four chime limit before voice mail. From near the convenience store cash register, Jessica heard a smooth self-assured greeting she feared, "Hello, Counselor." As poised and in control of the situation as she was on the bench, the Honorable Susan Dial nodded her head in recognition, then walked out the double glass doors, her blond tan companion trailing behind.

Oh, please, Jessica prayed, please do not ever let me appear before her ever again. Too rattled to pick up the Precious Kitty, Attorney Woods waited until the black Mercedes piloted by Surfer Boy maybe Banana Republic Model exited the parking lot, turned left, then headed east, the opposite direction from Franklin County where Mr. and Mrs. John Rentmore Dial entertained senior law school students in their historic stone mansion on the banks of the Scioto River.

Shaken, Jessica climbed back into her Acura, stepped on the accelerator and tore out of the parking lot, which had less gravel than when she entered. Back in Columbus on time she overcame her afternoon mishaps. The arraignment proceeded smoothly. Apparently the judge assigned for afternoon cases had been taken ill, so Jessica felt she knew more than the substitute who seemed mildly confused while attempting to appear knowledgeable. The pretrial occurred as well without problems. No one commented on Attorney Woods' uncharacteristically rumpled dress and somewhat shoddy appearance. The afternoon substitute did not know her, the bailiff had seen Jessica so many times in so many modes that she assumed nothing unusual, and the assistant prosecuting attorney secretly enjoyed Jessica's messy look. It might be added that a female, the assistant prosecutor, struggled unsuccessfully with weight issues, had, actually since high school. What harm was there to be inwardly delighted when someone looked worse than she? *Schadenfreude* the Germans called it.

As she left court for her office Jessica called Lil. "Has Colin arrived yet?"

Lil's guarded response could not be good news. "Jessica, Mr. O'Malley is here. You will be pleased to learn that the senior Mr. O'Malley has joined him."

"I know all the O'Malleys. Thanks for the heads up though."

A warble on her phone showed a text. It must be Max. Jessica would check much later, out of spite. Better check now, just in case her boyfriend needed her. No Max, but Lil.

"It's the *old* O'Malley. Grandpa."

"I thought he was dead!" she texted back.

"Not today. Here and smoking a cigar."

"Thanks. CU soon."

Jessica pulled into her spot in the parking garage, dragged a brush through her hair, hugged her bag next to her side, and scurried to the offices of O'Malley, O'Malley, and O'Malley. Before she entered the downstairs atrium, she scrounged through her purse to locate a possible container of nail polish for her badly scuffed shoes. Bubble Gum pink on the leather might hold it down if she applied a drop carefully. She quickly dabbed a few drops under the torn leather. Not bad if one did not examine the shoes too closely. Probably the old man had failing eyesight anyway, and there was every reason to believe Colin might be on his way to a drunk. She should be just fine.

As Jessica attempted to project a business like demeanor, she greeted Lil who turned her head just enough to roll her eyes out of sight of the two O'Malleys. Both men stood to greet her. Gentlemen.

"Jessica Woods," Colin stepped forward. No stale alcohol vapors but perhaps Gramps' cigar obliterated them. "Jessica, please allow me to introduce my grandfather, the Honorable Brendan

Colin O'Malley, retired, formerly of the District Court of Appeals, Kentucky."

"My pleasure, Miss Woods, I have heard so much about you. All good, of course."

Did he actually bow slightly? A true Southern gentleman.

"I am delighted to make your acquaintance, Your Honor." She liked him already. Too bad he wasn't her boss instead of Colin. With each visit she never knew which Colin O'Malley would be present: the lighthearted leprechaun, polymath and dilettante, or the cogent trial attorney: business first, social justice last.

"If you gentlemen will excuse me, I need to visit the ladies' room briefly. I'm sure Lillian has already taken excellent care of you, but can we offer you some water or some coffee?" Did Colin expect a drink? Was he on the wagon? At four o'clock would the judge like a Jameson?

Jessica hugged her Gucci with the ripped handle, which contained, thank God, her cell phone. Not that her iPhone hadn't suffered in the recent convenience store debacle, but at least the already cracked face had not shattered. Texting Lil, she sent, "Go down to Dempseys. Take cash out of the drawer. Buy a bottle of Jameson Irish Whiskey."

Please, please get the text.

"Will do, Boss. Getting nice glasses and ice too." Lil texted back immediately.

Thank God for Lil. Jess breathed in, checked her appearance in the mirror. Not bad, all things considered. The Bubble Gum pink polish on her shoes had long since dried. If she pulled her jacket just so, it would be difficult to see the dried blood on her dress. She washed her hands, took another deep breath, and stepped into the hallway to face, no, deal with Double O.

Where were they? Shit! In her private office. "Your secretary left on an errand. We made ourselves at home here. Hope you don't mind."

Of course not, especially since Colin accompanied would not have surreptitiously rifled through Jessica's papers. Hey, Lil had everything neatly arranged. Lemontinis tonight, for sure. Only two, though, and that was a promise she would hold herself to. You bet!

"Don't pay any attention to me," the elder O'Malley offered. "I'm an old man just coming along for the ride."

Jessica searched her memory from law school days. Hadn't Brendan C. O'Malley refused to hear cases, which negatively impacted, however minor, the practical application of social justice? Hadn't Judge Brendan O'Malley's recusance in other cases actually damned the reputation of hapless attorneys who thought they could ride their own personal comets only to fade miserably when colliding with the sun? It was years ago. Jessica could dimly remember the gossip but not the specific cases.

Colin interjected into Jessica's hazy memories, "On the way up from Cincinnati I was telling Grandfather here a little about you. Our firm has established a strong foothold in Columbus because of you. Speaking for all of us, we are pleased you represent O'Malley, O'Malley, and O'Malley."

After more pleasantries, Jessica and Colin reviewed her active cases. The Woolsey case, a holdover from her father's estate, was taking longer than she had predicted. Because it was no longer practical to drive to Upper Sandusky to work on the case, Jessica and Colin agreed that she would record her time away from firm business and pay one-fourth to the firm, the exact date to begin one year before. This worked out quite well for Jessica because she had been working on the case since joining Triple O.

Bartram Irving had brought her in on the Ompherous D. Oney case, so with his return from a professional conference he would resume handling One Eye's alleged felonies. He would also pay Jessica and therefore the firm for the time spent. Jessica planned to pad her hours. Infidelity with an intern disgusted her.

Although Ralph Edmonton had not referred work to her during his wife's surgery and recuperation, neither had Jay Rossford received any additional cases since Carolyn was recovering quickly. There would be no need of further treatment or chemotherapy.

A new client, Jeffrey Rhinesworth, could be a long term source of income. He had requested and would shortly receive Articles of

Incorporation for the plastics factory he was opening in Gahanna. Because he was relocating his family from Connecticut along with beginning a business, which he believed would eventually employ over two hundred people, the Rhinesworth client would be one to hold on to and to tend. Colin secured Jessica's affirmation that, yes, she would take good care of Mr. Jeffrey Rhinesworth.

As far as Colin's questions regarding Mrs. Rhinesworth, Jessica mentioned that Erin Rhinesworth, M.D., F.A. C.S. certified by the American Board of Plastic Surgery, was currently interviewing with three hospitals and expected to accept the offer from the Ohio State University Medical Center.

There was no need to mention Flaming Eric Stewart who had run into, no driven into, minor difficulties in a parking lot in Florida. Jessica had already referred him to her law school friend Kelly Rubinoff. No money would change hands. Personal cell phones were wonderful at times. However, Jessica anticipated a pair of coveted shoes she might have mentioned as she and her old friend talked one evening.

The case from which she had just returned involved a delayed liquor license, the reason for the delay Jessica could not determine. Her client, a Vietnam veteran, honorably discharged, no record of felonies, had purchased a building in downtown Canal Winchester. He retrofitted what had formerly been a hardware store into a restaurant and bar. Evidently obtaining the food service license had gone rather smoothly. However, the reason for the liquor license holdup, which should have followed quickly, remained a mystery.

Lillian, Jessica's assistant, had a connection to the client's family in Hocking County. The assistant planned on attending a family reunion in early June where it was anticipated that she might learn more about the client's background. For most of his life before moving to Canal Winchester, the client except for his tours to Vietnam, had lived and worked in the Hocking Hills.

"See if you can get an invitation," Colin interjected. "I want you to go with her and dig into this. Find out why those bastards at the Ohio Board of Liquor Control are holding up our client's desire to earn a legitimate living."

"I have already been invited. By the way, you used the same epithet that my client invoked."

"In addition to these that we have discussed, as I recall you have about seventy-five active cases, more than the asshole upstairs," Colin remarked.

"At last count I do. Do you happen to know Michael Ritter?"

"We went to law school together. I passed the bar the first time. I think it took the little shit three times before he finally passed. I've got to give him credit though. He just kept taking the bar and failing until he made it. Worked in the Women's Shoe Department I think at the old Lazarus. Everybody liked him." Everybody except Colin. Jessica could just imagine what happened. Probably a conflict over a woman or money or both, the usual. She had a rather good idea of who won.

"I would like to see you have at least 150 active cases, Jessica." Colin continued, "I know you think that might be a lot, but we expect a lot from you. In the Columbus legal community, you are regarded as among the top young attorneys. In fact, I have heard whispers that within a few years one or the other parties has aspirations of placing you on their ticket in a run for judge. Apparently the Democrats and the Republicans like you, so whatever you are doing, keep doing it. Now we don't want to lose you, of course, but our reputation and yours is certainly enhanced by all this positive chatter.

Jessica felt her face flush. Was Colin being truthful? Were the compliments meant to dissuade her from pressing for the bonus she had been promised at year's end but had yet to receive? Or was this Triple O's way of firing her, releasing her, so to speak, to be free to pursue a political career? Maybe that was why the most senior O'Malley had ridden with his grandson up to the capital city. Colin the Coward would feign some sort of excuse, leave, and the brains behind O'Malley, O'Malley, and O'Malley could drone on forever about cases he had heard in Kentucky. Then, when she was nearly asleep, strike the deadly blow that separated her from the firm forever. "Nothing personal," he would add, "just business. We want the best for your future."

A light tap on the already open door indicated Lil's arrival. Carrying a tray laden with old fashioned crystal glasses, a sizable bowl of peanuts, a small ice bucket already dripping water down the side, and, best of all, a liter of Jameson, the assistant deftly placed refreshments on Jessica's desk, then returned to the outer office. All three attorneys broke into smiles.

Jessica waited for the senior O'Malley to speak first. The Honorable Brendan O'Malley opened with "I believe, Counselors, that it is cocktail hour. Allow me to pour."

Thank God he was both gracious and well mannered. Using tongs he placed ice in Jessica's glass, then poured the amber liquid three quarters to the rim. "For the lady." He added a few cubes to Colin's, then poured. As for himself, no need for ice. "I like mine neat. Always have. The level of liquid was the same, but no ice disturbed the smooth flow of his favorite Irish whiskey. "To us," he toasted. "May we die and get to heaven before the devil knows we're gone."

If they were here to fire her, they had chosen an unusual method of doing so. A nervous Jessica gulped too quickly, then coughed.

"Too strong for you?" Colin chuckled.

"Just right. Smooth. Allergies occasionally bother me. I am keeping my friend's cat in the apartment, and I am very sensitive to cat dander."

"Try a little more medicine then. Just what the doctor ordered." Brendan filled Jess's glass to the brim. Colin drained his, then helped himself to a second round. Brendan sipped slowly, as if, instead of spending waning hours of an afternoon in the office of a very junior attorney, he were instead relaxing in the inner sanctum of the Louisville Country Club.

Jessica's boss mused, "Unless you would like to add anything, I believe our business today is concluded." Neither Colin nor Brendan rose to leave, however.

Lil peeked around the corner. "Jess, I am going to go. I locked the office door, so just pull it shut when you leave. Mr. O'Malley, it was nice meeting you. Colin, always a pleasure."

Both men rose, offering pleasantries along with goodbyes.

171

The Honorable Brendan O'Malley suggested, "Hate to let good Irish whisky go to waste. Drink up. Your ice is getting warm." Jess sipped as much as she could, trying to recall if she had eaten lunch.

"Your Honor."

"Call me Brendan. I appreciate the deference, but I retired five years ago. I loved the law. To be a judge, you have to. Some attorneys dance around the system. They get away with it for a while, call it a game and that sort of thing. It is not. The American legal system has its flaws. I'm certainly in the position to speak credibly about that.

"Here's the thing though. For all the people who slip by, and I will admit that they do, think of the people who are innocent, innocent, Miss Woods, until proven guilty. For the more than thirty years I sat on the bench, I did the very best I could to uphold our American freedom.

"I read case law in which you had a hand, Your Honor."

"Miss Woods, please call me Brendan. I will honor you with the same familiarity. It is very kind of you to remember some of my work." He poured two fingers of Jameson into his empty glass. "Let's talk about something less serious. It is, after all, cocktail hour."

"I promise, Brendan, if I can just add one more thought." Jessica's head was still clear. God, she must be turning into the archetypal trial attorney. Men, booze; all she needed now were the gambling debts, the divorces, and, for fun, a private plane.

"I may have been mildly hungover at my law school graduation, but I did not fall asleep during the speeches. The president of the Ohio Bar Association spoke at commencement, and to this day I act or do not act on his words to us."

Jessica hesitated, holding in sudden tears as she remembered that day: Andrew was still in her life after all the brutalizing effects of law school; Bob had died less than four months before. Jim and Alex were there though. And Robbie. How life changed; it crept up before you knew it, and you were in another place looking back down the road you had walked. No map. Just a mirror at the end of your path. Could she bear to look at her reflection and live with what she saw? Most days she could. Then there were a few. She supposed everyone felt like that. Tough to be an adult.

Jessica pushed her hair behind her ears. As she did so, she touched the pearl earrings Andrew had given her for graduation. Andrew. Best to focus. Despite her guest's insistence that she address him by his first name, she could not forget that Brendan C. O'Malley, one of the most respected judges in the Midwest, was sitting and drinking in her office.

"Brendan, when I listened that day I took the address to us newly minted graduates, not yet attorneys though, to heart. The speaker cautioned us that every time we allow criticism of a judge, every time we participate in or permit disparaging remarks about the legal system, we chip away at justice. We allow, in fact, we perpetuate the disintegration of our American freedoms. I believed him then; I believe him now."

"I had done a little investigating myself before the firm hired you," the older O'Malley commented. Colin tried unsuccessfully to avoid looking surprised at his grandfather's interjection. "Your dad was a good lawyer. You, Jessica, will be a great one. Perhaps, even though my sons and my grandson prefer to keep you in the firm, perhaps even a judge. How was that holiday gala at the Governor's Mansion last year, by the way?"

"Fine. As Colin already commented, I manage to have avoided either political party hating me, yet. I was lucky to be invited, but since you already know that, I do appreciate your asking."

"Come on, Grandfather, let's talk about the old days. Tell Jessica here what you did before law school made you upstanding," Colin urged. "We still have half a bottle left. You don't have another client, do you?"

"Not yet, still working on picking up the extra seventy-five you set as my goal."

"I can set a date certain," her employer joked, she hoped. "How about Halloween?"

"Can do." At least alcohol made her cheerfully compliant.

"So, Grandfather, tell our employee here what you did back in the day."

"Jessica, let me preface this by saying that I am very, very proud of my family. My boys grew up without me. I count myself a lucky man that time brought us together. I certainly do not deserve the honors. Time and my second wife, God rest her soul."

"Come on, Grandfather, divulge how you earned money for college." Colin could definitely be pushy. How was Jessica supposed to secure an additional seventy-five lucrative cases, not pro bono? Oh, no. Lucrative.

The elder O'Malley sipped his Jameson, closed his eyes as if retrieving visions from years before, then began. "I didn't always drink fine Irish whisky. I had to earn it although, Jessica, I do thank you for the drinks today. As you already know, I lived in Kentucky, grew up there actually. I wasn't the best behaved boy back then either. Got Colin's grandmother here pregnant, married her. She had the good sense to leave me and head up to family in Cincinnati. You probably thought the O'Malleys' patriarch was landed gentry. Far from it.

"My folks came from way back in the hollers of Kentucky. We still have family reunions down in Snake Holler in Greenup County. We have to have them in the spring because when it gets hot and dry in the summer, the snakes come down to the creek for a drink. Some folks don't mind the snakes, but the women and children, particularly now that many arrive from the city, prefer avoiding snakes if possible.

"Anyway, when I was a kid I helped my grandpa make moonshine. Everybody was in the business. It was in the 1930s, people were starving. Moonshine was the only way to earn money. To look at me now you might find it hard to believe that at one time my mother fed us kids with food she canned from the garden and a little chicken from the few that we had. There were plenty of times she didn't eat, said she wasn't hungry.

"We lived in Star Holler then. Dirt roads. They didn't have bridges in those days. When you came to a creek, either you'd drive right through the creek or cross it down a ways. Dad had a car, a Tin Lizzie. He didn't drive much. When he did though, he'd load up with a jug or two for the trip.

"I can remember one time I went with him to buy moonshine. He must have been out or we wouldn't have made the trip. Mom didn't drink herself and couldn't abide by Dad drinking, so like most farmers he kept a keg in the cornfield

"I was the youngest for sure. Everybody had a nickname. To this day I couldn't tell you what people's real names were. Anyway, that day I rode with Dad's pals, Junior, Gus, and Boomer. The Tin Lizzie was mighty old then but it got the job done. Just horse hair padding on a board, no seats in the back. But everybody had his own jug. The goal for the day was to pick up some moonshine, then head home. I sat up with Dad, Gus rode on the board in the back.

"See, Moonshiners were pretty smart. They let you sample their wares before you bought. Of course, the drunker you got, the more moonshine you bought. I tasted some myself although I was mighty young at the time. It was clear as water, and, Jessica, real good.

"So Dad and Gus and Boomer bought what they came for. They seemed pretty drunk but Dad maybe not so much because he knew he didn't drive too well and he wanted to get home without a wreck. We headed back down Schultz Road where we came from, got to the creek just like before, but instead of driving around it, Dad got really courageous and just gunned the accelerator and crossed.

"Gus and Boomer were hootin' and hollerin', having a good time. I was laughing too. Everybody drinking from their own jugs except me. We get down the road a ways and somebody thought to ask, 'Where's Gus?'

"Dad turned back looking for his buddy. Along comes Gus stumbling down the road. The board he'd been sitting on under his arm and carryin' a broken jug in his hand. His overalls were all wet. I bet his wife was mad as hell when he got home.

"Back in those days when you wore overalls, you wore them forever. People saved one pair, a better one, for church."

Both Colin and Jessica waited patiently, wondering too if they could stand up to the tough life Brendan O'Malley and his family routinely lived. Neither thought they could. Colin urged, "Come on, Grandpa. Tell Jessica about the mules."

The old man smiled, reflecting. "People had mules back then too. Mules worked out better for farming than tractors. Besides, folks didn't have the money. They loved their animals though.

"I remember one man, Forest. He was the most saintly man I ever knew. He was a gifted Moonshiner too. Helped Dad in the business so Dad paid him by allowing him to grow crops on a corner of the farm. Forest had two mules, Maude and Molly. They were huge.

"You know what a mule is, don't you, Colin? Jessica?"

Silence from both attorneys.

"A mule is one of God's multiple experiments that worked out very well. You see, a mule is a cross between a mare and a male donkey. A mule's head is bigger than a child's. Now a mule can outwork a horse over and over again, so Forest made a pretty good living with Maude and Molly by farming for folks around the area.

"I can honestly say that he loved those mules. Those beasts were beautiful, black as midnight. Both of them had harnesses, and they were the most expensive beautiful harnesses I have ever seen. I'm in my eighties now, and I still hold with my opinion.

"Anyway, those mules were Forest's life. Every morning he gave each of them a big handful of salt to make them thirsty, then walked them down to the creek to drink and drink. Forest worked them really hard so they'd get all foamy, come back looking white. At the end of the day he'd take them down to the creek again and give them a bath. It was probably the only time he took a bath too.

"Folks paid Forrest in eggs, and bacon, and salt. He did all right too, he and those mules." The Honorable Brendan O'Malley sipped his Jameson and smiled. "I wouldn't go back to those days, of course. Lots of bad things happened too, but I'm one of those men inclined to forget the bad and hold the good close to my heart."

Placing his glass on the desk, the older man concluded, "Colin, we're keeping this woman way past office hours. You can drive us back to Cincinnati. I just might take a nap on the way home." He laughed. "I promise not to fall off like old Gus did." He paused, centering his gaze directly at his grandson. "I don't know if you would come back to pick me up."

Colin looked appropriately distressed, although Jessica doubted his sincerity. The old man could very well be correct in his assessment. After they left, Jessica placed the glasses and empty bowl of pretzels on the tray, then threw the Jameson bottle into the trash. Her desk cleared, she decided to scan her messages before going home.

Annie Minter had called, asking for an appointment. Why call her at the office? Annie and Jessica talked frequently on the phone. As college friends and sorority sisters, Annie and Jess played intermural basketball together, worked side by side at the alumni office at Miami. Why did she choose to make a formal appointment? If Jessica were thinking clearly without the fog of alcohol interfering, she would have called Annie. Best to let that one go until tomorrow.

Might as well check her phone for messages. None. Jessica rested her head on her desk, closed her eyes to think without distractions, and fell asleep.

Wednesday of Week Three

"Wake up, Sleeping Beauty," Lil lightly touched her employer's shoulder. "Double O must have kept you out way past your bedtime."

Jessica jerked upright from her chair. Her back and neck ached; again her dry mouth felt as if she had eaten cotton. She just could not keep this pace up. "Would you mind fixing coffee, Lil? I feel terrible."

"Coming up," Lil chirped. "I heard from Craig last night, finally. He didn't have much to say, just that he had been out of the country on some sort of secret mission, which is why we lost contact. He should be coming home Christmas."

"You know I'm happy for you, Hon."

Lil busied herself in the back room as Jessica waited in a stupor at her desk. Her contact lenses cloudy due to yet another overnight wearing, she attempted to read her messages from the day before. Unsuccessful. Instead, in abnegation she dropped her head back onto her desk to wait for Lil's coffee.

"Do I have anything important today? I really need to go home, shower, and go to bed."

"No appointments, no court dates. Nothing major."

Lil served Jess a mug of hot coffee, sugar, and cream just the way Jessica liked it. She might be a vegetarian, but she had inherited her mother's sweet tooth.

"Thank you. You are indeed a life saver. And a friend." Jess pushed her hair back behind her ears. Somehow during the night she had managed to lose one pearl earring. Dammit. She was so over Andrew, but the earrings symbolized hope, plans they used to have. Those gone, at least she could try to hold on to the earrings.

"I cannot see a thing. Can you look for my earring and call me if you find it? One more request after which I am going home. Will you call Annie Minter and set up an appointment for later this week? I have no idea why she called the office, but if she wants to work it this way, we should comply."

"Will do, Boss. Now, go home and go to bed. I'll text you when I find the earring, and I'll call if anything urgent comes up. By the way, urgent does not include an unscheduled visit from Clara and Mel Woolsey. Or if I am not mistaken, from a Mr. Jeffrey Rhinesworth." Lil grinned what appeared to be a conspiratory smile, if Jessica could have seen better.

Oh, shit. Cedric. The poor little guy must be furious with her, not to mention starving. Granted, he had enough fat on his twenty pound body, but leaving him without dinner or breakfast must have constituted some kind of felony in his feline brain. Jessica fearfully opened her apartment door, expecting yowls of annoyance. Instead, silence greeted her. Was he dead? How to explain the demise of a pre-viously healthy two-year-old Cedric to his doting mother? Make that his negligent mother. Dr. Madelyn Hendricks should have returned by now from her conference to take charge of her little darling instead of cavorting at the Ritz with who knows who.

"Cedric, Honey. Auntie Jessie is home. Mommy might not love you anymore, but I do." Bad, bad Jessica. It was the hangover and terrible night that drove her to say things like that to a helpless ani-mal. "Come on out, Sugar. Auntie Jessie has a nice yummy breakfast for you." All of one can remaining of Precious Kitty Bacony Bities. Forget the other can if she expected forgiveness. Still no yowls either of outrage or of hunger. What if he was dead? Oh, no. What if the apartment manager had entered, illegally of course without a twenty-four-hour note, seen the cat, and confiscated him?

"Ceddie, Sweetie. Auntie Jessica is home. You can come out now." Still no meows, or howls, or purrs. Maybe twenty-four hours without food, well, there were dry kibbles he could have snacked on, maybe a day without wet food killed a cat. Jessica tried to reason with herself as she would a client. Cats roamed unrestricted everywhere she had traveled: Paris, Rome, London, Munich. No one fed them wet food daily, yet not only did they live, they procreated.

"Come on, Sugar. I am opening your favorite breakfast." She rattled the electric can opener. Nothing. It was then on the counter where, through cloudy vision, she noticed what appeared to be a handwritten note. Nearly scratching her eyes as she pulled her lenses out, she concentrated next on finding her glasses. Usually they were on the night stand if Cedric had not played with them. No, Cedric was dead. Shoving her glasses onto her greasy face, she read a message on official paper headed Columbus Buckeye Properties, Inc. *Refined living for our refined guests*: "Please contact us immediately regarding unapproved pets per contract restrictions."

Poor Ceddie. He must be hungry and scared but she hoped safe. Not, her heart stopped, at the Humane Society! Surely management would not have done that!

Leaning against the apartment door, she tried to think what to do next. She was a lawyer, for heaven's sakes. Be logical. Cedric was in custody somewhere. Even the Humane Society allowed people time to retrieve lost pets. It was then she noticed the slim business envelope under the door at her feet. Tearing it open she read,

May 6, 11:00 a.m.
Dear valued tenant.

During the next week we will be reviewing all apartments in this building so that we can continue to ensure safety and health issues for all of our guests. The units on Floors 1 through 5 will be reviewed on the second week of May during the business week between noon and 5 p.m. Thank you for your understanding and compliance. We continue to appreciate your choice of residences as we uphold our mission to provide *refined living for our refined guests.*

Yesterday. No wonder she had not seen the note. She was already on the road, about ten minutes away from Leonard Warren and a waste of time interview followed by a worthless long winded tale from Thumper on how to build a still. Dammit!

Think like a lawyer, not like a histrionic hysteric, she upbraided herself as she leaned her head against the door. The note requested that she, a valued tenant, call management, which is what she would now do. Avoid projecting without reason. Alex did stuff like that; not her daughter.

A familiar voice answered, although Jessica could not place the owner. "Columbus Capital Properties, Refined living for our refined guests. This is Bruce. How may I help you?"

"Bruce, this is Jessica, Apartment 5 *S*." At the time she originally signed the contract, she fretted over the letter *S*. Was it the albatross that kept her single? What if her home of two years were more appropriately named, *R*, for example, or *M*? To be fair, she *was* in a relationship; Max would surely cool off. For heaven's sakes, many people spent time in jail. He was only locked up for a few hours. He should not have been speeding so soon after his prior arrest anyway. Yes, his sitting in the Huron County Jail was definitely his own fault, not hers. She was tired of clearing up other people's peccadillos, without pay even. As for *M*, marriage, her mother had continually reminded her, would happen soon enough. Well, actually the reminder had come from Jessica to Alex if Jess were truthful. So far, no engagement ring yet. Best to avoid concentrating on same. Get the cat, wherever Cedric reposed. Then smooth things over with Max. The rest would follow, she hoped.

"Yes, Jessica, how are you?"

Had too much alcohol already destroyed her memory? How in the hell did this Bruce know her? How did she know him? Think like a lawyer. Calmly, logically. Let time work for you, she told herself.

"Hello, Bruce. How are you?" *Whoever you are.*

"I'm good, Jessica. Have you called about your cat? Cedric, I believe."

All those years of law school were worth it after all. Logical thinking worked every time. Bruce knew the cat's name; he knew hers. Therefore, Bruce was the one who had rescued Cedric a good long week ago as the dear little feline hid under a car in the parking garage. Do not, however, admit guilt. Ask the questions and wait for the response.

"Bruce, so good to hear your voice. I received a note from management requesting a call."

"Oh, yes, my brother can be a bit Pharisaic sometimes. You know how it goes, new job, trying to prove himself. He wanted to take Ceddie here to the Humane Society immediately. I covered for you. I said Cedric was a rescue cat and that you were planning to take the little guy over there yourself as your firm was a committed supporter of animal rights."

"Bruce, thank you so very much. Do you know where Cedric is now?"

"I have the little guy right here with me in my apartment. My brother took the day off to play paintball with his buddies, so he forwarded the phone. We're right down the hall from you. Just please don't say anything to management. Brother Bill is supposed to use a previously approved substitute from the Columbus Capital Properties list, but it's a hassle.

So, Jessica reflected, Good Old Bill had violated the terms of a contract with the same company as she. Hot Shit! No losses this time.

"I'm on my way, Bruce. What number is your apartment?"

"Five *D*. Down the hall and around the corner."

D for *Divorced?* Jessica had to stop thinking in semiotics. First, retrieve the cat. Second, shower. Third, go to bed. No, second, feed Cedric. Poor fellow was probably traumatized.

Bruce opened the door immediately as she knocked. He must be infatuated with her to be responding so quickly. "Come in. I believe I have the little house guest you are looking for."

Stretched out on his back, arms and paws reaching as far above his feline head as possible, purring so loudly Jessica heard him from the hallway, lay Cedric. Far from traumatized, he appeared to be more at home with Bruce than in the days the cat had spent with her. His head tilted back, chin up, eyes rolling back into his head, this animal looked like a possum at rest. "Oh, Cedric, I am so glad to see you, Little Fella." She stroked his ample stomach. "I see Uncle Bruce here has given you the royal treatment."

Scooping the groggy cat into her arms, she continued, "How can I thank you enough? My friend, not so much now I might add, my friend blindsided me with cat sitting at the last minute. She had a conference in London, the regular sitter backed out, so here we are. Maddie was also supposed to be back by now."

"Where are my manners? Please, sit down." Bruce gestured to the couch where Cedric had reposed. "Can I brew you some coffee?"

Jessica assessed her appearance in the mirror over his leather seating arrangement. Greasy hair, greasy face, bloodshot eyes. Smelling of last night's Jameson, she congratulated herself on reaching one of her all time worst personal presentations. She could accept the coffee or hurry out, feline parcel in hand. However, continuing to think logically, she realized she probably was out of coffee; tea would not do, and a very attractive man close to her age had invited her for coffee. Think how he will react another day when she presents her very best face.

"Coffee sounds terrific. Thank you." Cedric jumped out of her arms and strolled over to what looked like Villeroy and Bosch feeding dishes where he nibbled at kibbles.

"I felt bad when Bill told me about the cat he had confiscated in a routine safety check. The least he could have done was leave Cedric in the apartment, call you, and manage the situation after talking with you." Oh, the coffee smelled good. He brewed it in a percolator, just like the one Alex owned at the bed and breakfast. "I intervened.

The only reason I knew you were an attorney was through some of the television commercials for O'Malley, O'Malley, and O'Malley."

"Cream and sugar?" he asked from his Pullman kitchen almost an exact replica of hers in 5 S.

"Both please." Jessica nearly drooled.

Bruce brought a Villeroy and Bosch cup and saucer to her as she sank back into the couch. She sipped the hot brew, just the right mixture of sugar and cream. Heaven. "Jessica, I am sorry but I have to run. I have a class I have to get to. They keep us adjuncts on a short leash."

Placing her coffee on the cocktail table, Jessica jumped up, ready to leave.

"You can take that with you or finish it here. Whatever you wish. Just lock the door on your way out. Cedric probably wants to go home."

"Home is Reynoldsburg. He seems to be on an extended vacation with me though due to his mother's absence. What do you teach?"

"It depends on where you mean. Developmental English at Columbus State Community College. Beginning speech, oral communications they call it, at Ohio Wesleyan, and report writing at DeVry. I am an adjunct professor at all three."

"And I thought I participated in a shit show. My goodness, they keep you hopping."

"I would like to say it keeps me out of trouble, but my brother might say otherwise. Anyway, as part-time employees, we adjuncts are limited to the number of hours we can teach at any one college. However, I can teach at several colleges, which I am fortunate to do. Driving from one to another especially from a four o'clock class at one place to a seven o'clock class across town gets a bit dicey. I eat dinner, if that is what you call it, in my car while attempting to circumvent rush hour traffic."

As he talked, Bruce deftly tied his Brooks Brothers navy blue tie with pale blue stripes into a Windsor knot. *Oh, Jessica, do not even think about it,* she cautioned herself. The guy probably has a committed relationship with someone. Worse yet, he might have just broken up. Rebounds take months to get over, especially men, then right about the time I think about really liking them, I get the "It's not you, it's me" crap as they return to the bitches who dumped them.

"I'll just finish the coffee here." She eyed her scuffed shoes, the leather on the toes hastily glued on with bubblegum pink nail polish. "The way this week has been going, I most likely would drop your exquisite china. I love this pattern."

"I don't know what it is. It's rather flowery for me, but my mother insisted I take the set after my grandmother died. Evidently she believes English professors, even adjuncts, need to cultivate a refined life. There is a word for you, by the way, considering our management's slogan."

Jessica grinned. "Whoever dreamed it up, it's a doozy: *Refined living for our refined guests.*"

"Gotta run. Just pull the door shut behind you on the way out." Bruce hastily retrieved a navy blue blazer from his coat closet, grabbed his laptop, and left.

As she finished her coffee, she slipped back onto the couch to pet an already purring Cedric. "I am truly sorry, Fella. None of this is your fault. I left you enough dry food for two days, and water too. Still, it's not wet food, is it?"

Maine Coons can be talkative. Cedric blinked, then warbled a cat reply. Jessica hoped that meant, "I forgive you." He reached two long arms toward her, then kneaded his paws on her leg. Reeking of alcohol and two days' body odor, she probably smelled delicious to a male cat.

"We can sit here for a few minutes, I guess." She pulled the cat up to her chest, laid her head down briefly against the back of the couch, and closed her eyes.

"Hello, Goldilocks."

Jessica jerked to attention. Where was she? Bruce's apartment. No Cedric though. She turned her head toward the person who had awakened her. What time was it anyway?

"Sorry to waken you, Sleeping Beauty." The voice mixed metaphors poorly, juxtaposing two different fairy tales. Definitely not an English major. "Any idea where my partner is?" Whoever it was seemed rather hostile.

"He has a class. He did not say which university. He just left, I think." Jessica checked her watch. "That is, he left about two hours ago. I must have fallen asleep."

"I see. Well, tell your friend I stopped by to pick up some clothes." The intruder turned friend, albeit a hostile one, huffed around, gathering shirts, ties, pants, and belts from the bedroom. Apparently he knew his way around the apartment as the procedures took place quickly. Did he have a key or had Bruce left the door unlocked?

The interloper sneezed loudly. "There's a cat in here. I'm allergic! He set me up, the bastard! I told him I was coming by and he knows how allergic I am to cats!"

Cedric slithered out from under a leather club chair. Brushing against the man's legs, the cat purred loudly. "Get away!" The man shook his leg. "They always latch onto people who hate them," he confessed to Jessica.

"I'm sorry. I didn't catch your name."

"Because I didn't give it." He sneezed again. "I have to get out of here! Keep the cat away from me, and I'll leave as soon as I can." Then the man noticed the empty cup and saucer on the cocktail table. "I'll miss the china though. I sure as hell won't miss Bruce." Storming out with a load of clothes over his arm, he let the door slam loudly, deliberately so.

"Come on, Cedric. We have to go too. I'll write a quick note to Bruce first. If I can find something to write on." She considered tearing off a paper towel from a roll next to the kitchen sink, but then she could not locate a pen either. "There must be paper and pens or pencils in this desk drawer." She opened the drawer, then closed it rapidly.

"Cedric, you and I saw nothing. Absolutely nothing. Let's get out of here." She pulled the recalcitrant cat, paws gripping the carpet, from underneath a dining room chair. "After I feed you, we are both going to sleep in the right apartment, mine, and when we wake up everything will be just fine."

Back in Apartment 5 S Jessica rifled through her cupboard until she located one remaining can of Precious Kitty from the pantry. "Here, Dumpling, Munchie Lunchies. Tasty Tuna Tidbits just for you. Cedric sniffed his bowl, then walked away.

Just then her cell phone chimed. "Maddie, where in the hell are you?"

"Getting ready to board the plane. I'm in New York. I should be home in about two hours. I left my car at home. Can you pick me up?"

"Maddie, I am wiped out. I just finished a trial and I have got to go to bed. Do you mind terribly taking a cab? I'm sorry, but as exhausted as I am, I might fall asleep at the wheel."

So much for the favors Jessica owed her friend. She was finished. Maddie could term the denial anything she chose, from passive/aggressive to lying. Jessica had to go to bed.

"Sure, Hon. I understand. I'll call you when I get back, so I can come over and pick up my little baby. I hope he didn't give you any trouble."

"None at all. All I did really was work and sleep. The little guy was one perfect kitty house guest. I'll see you later tonight then." Cedric suddenly found his brunch intriguing.

"Hang on a minute, Jess." Maddie's tone shifted from matter-of-fact to excited. "I have a huge surprise. I can't wait to tell you in person."

Jessica, however, could wait. Especially if it meant leaving Cedric with her on a permanent basis. No, Dr. Madelyn Hendricks would never give her baby away. Unless. Unless. Yes, she would.

Whatever it was, Jessica did not care. The ID badge she had seen in Bruce's drawer meant nothing. Jessica would wipe the slate of her memories clean as she slept. She closed her bedroom door. "Cedric, I'm sorry, but I have to go to bed. Go rest under the potted palm. I'll see you soon. Night, night."

When Jessica awoke, a late afternoon sun shone through her bedroom window. She needed a good run, then a shower in either order. The run first. She already looked and smelled horrific, except to Cedric. Might as well keep going.

She grabbed her keys and some money for cat food she planned to pick up at the Kroger store across the parking lot after she finished her run. Forty-five minutes of pounding the path through Bicentennial Park heightened her mood along with her sense of well being. She might be sweaty and smelly, but Jessica F. Woods, attorney, felt terrific. *Fine* in fact. Ready for whatever came her way.

She breezed through the automatic doors at Kroger's, heading directly for the pet food aisle. Might as well check her cell phone for any important messages. None. Oof. She bumped into someone on his or her way out. "I'm sorry," she offered even without looking.

A cultured voice she already knew too well responded. "Counselor, nice to see you again." The Honorable Susan Dial. Of course, who else.

For Jessica F. Woods, attorney of record, the remainder of the week proceeded normally. A few pretrials, some arraignments, several potential new clients during regular business hours. In the evening, Pilates classes, some running. No distractions with phone calls from Max, no unexpected visits from Jeffrey Rhinesworth. Unfortunately, no calls from Maddie either. Cedric had managed to learn to open the door to Jessica's bedroom, so cat and newly adopted mother slept peacefully all night long. Apparently long, frequent, and personal contact with the Maine Coon had resulted in an immunity far less expensive and time consuming than allergy shots.

Jessica supposed she could call Maddie, but why bother? She had not heard of any plane crashes or horrific murders, so Dr. Madelyn Hendricks must be surviving somewhere. Evidently her clients were as well; no desperate phone calls from anyone in crisis. At least Lil who covered the psychologist's office in the evening, not on Triple O time certainly, had not reported anything.

Lil seemed content too. By now Jessie's assistant had reconciled herself to infrequent contact with Craig. A time difference of eight and a half hours interfered with romance as well as missions, which Lil's fiancé had mentioned kept him out of personal communications for security reasons.

With no plans for the weekend, Jessica spent Saturday at her office. Friday evening she had joined a few friends at the Westin

Hotel on High Street for drinks, then walked home to bed where she and her loyal cat slept companionably. No snoring, no hogging the covers, no extra towels to wash. Except for the deep loneliness that washed over her when she realized Max might not come back. Jessica planned to confide to a psychologist when she made an appointment that she was indeed happy.

Sunday of Week Four

In her apartment on Sunday morning after reading the *New York Times Review*, the style section, business, sports, and finally the front pages Jessica set the *Book Review* aside to check her appointments for the next week. Leonard Warren must have paid his bill because Lil had scheduled him for an office visit. Articles of Incorporation had arrived for Jeffrey Rhinesworth. Lil had him set up for a Monday appointment. Evidently despite Jessica's request, Mr. Rhinesworth had insisted that he meet his attorney in person. Fine. Billable hours. No word from Clara and Melvin Woolsey. It looked like another peaceful week. Knock on wood. For good luck, Jessica knocked twice on her cherry coffee table.

Jessica's cell phone chimed. Maddie. "It's your long absent friend," she greeted Jessica cheerfully. "I'm sorry I abandoned you. How is my little baby? Can I talk to him?"

"Where are you? Are you all right?"

"Perfect! Remember I told you I had a surprise? It's an even bigger one now. I just do not want to tell you over the phone. Can I talk to little Ceddie now?"

Jessica set her phone down on the coffee table, then searched in his usual places. First, under the palm plant, then under the bed, finally in the pantry by his dishes. No Cedric. Was he afraid he might travel again? Jessica eventually located him on a chair under her table. "Come on, Honey, your mommy wants to talk to you." He dug his claws into the cushion. She pried each paw out. "Here, Sweetie, it's Mommy." Cedric chewed the rubber casing around the cell phone.

"Hi, Baby, it's Mommy." The Maine Coon listened, then chewed again. "Mommy misses you. Have you been a good kitty?" Mommy, in Jessica's opinion, possibly Cedric's as well, had been a very bad mommy. Cedric jumped off the couch, then headed for the palm.

"Sorry, Maddie. He recognized your voice. I think he misses you too." Not quite the truth; if anything, Cedric evidenced cat annoyance. He turned toward the wall, stretched out, and began dozing.

"I'll be back tomorrow. Someone will be driving me from the airport, so you do not need to make arrangements." Jessica was not planning on doing so anyway. "I'm sorry about leaving Cedric with you for such a long time. He's fairly easy to take care of, so I hope you did not have any trouble." None at all. Everything ran smoothly.

Hiding under a car because Jessica had not been informed he was astute at opening his carrier door, a minor fight with Max's dog, temporary confiscation and near death. No, no trouble at all with Cedric. Not to mention the embarrassment she felt which would never have occurred had she not needed more food for her feline guest. Jessica sincerely hoped that months, years intervened before she had to face Judge Dial on the bench. The Honorable Susan Dial's escapades with law school students were private issues. However, Jessica hoped that accidentally surprising the judge and her paramour of the moment would not negatively influence legal decisions. Oh, Cedric had not caused any problems whatsoever.

"Listen, Maddie, Cedric and I are looking forward to seeing you tomorrow. We'll talk then. I have to run." Jessica clicked off before waiting for her friend's goodbye. Dammit, by now despite difficulties, she had grown attached to her furry four-footed guest. As with Max, she did not realize she cared until he might be gone.

Sunday night brought the usual phone calls from Alex and Rob as well as Jessica's touching base, she called it, with old friends and newer ones. Some were married now; married ones she told herself she should not call. Still, these fellows were friends from law school, mostly.

Alex called around nine. "Hi, Honey, did you have a nice weekend?" Alex always hoped that her daughter might hint about a forthcoming engagement.

"Yes, Mom. I just worked. Nothing special. How about you?"

"After our shopping trip I kept thinking about Oliver Oney, you know, the man I knew from college." Alex had a discreet way of substituting less specific words for potentially revealing ones. Connotative rhetoric, her mother termed it. "Anyway, he is fine, retired, living in Florida in the winter, still on the East Coast the remainder of the year. He has two sons, did I tell you?"

"I don't recall." Yes, she hoped Alex would not go on about One Eye.

"One of his sons lives in Columbus. He plays in a group of some sort but substitute teaches to supplement his income. I thought you might know him."

"Columbus is a big city, Mom. I generally don't meet substitute teachers unless they bartend or get into trouble and need a lawyer."

"Ollie seems very proud of both his boys, so I doubt you will meet them. Maybe at one of your brother's fundraisers though." Robbie definitely participated in a lot of fundraisers, and Columbus was certainly the city for them. All those golf outings, dinner dances, and reverse raffles eventually brought investors to Rob's financial firm. Besides, they were fun. Jessica had enjoyed many of them herself.

"Mom, I have a beep. I have to go. Love you." Jessica saw that the caller was Robbie; she clicked onto his call. "Bro, how are you?"

"I am really doing very well. I just wanted to check in with my sister to see how it's going. How's your love life?"

"About the same as yours, unless you've fallen in love over the weekend." Robbie had a tendency to remember all of Jessica's mistakes with men. Forgetting to call the prosecuting attorney, an error that resulted in Max sitting in jail for a few hours, was not a story

Jessica chose to reveal to her brother. Robbie liked Max; Jess would never hear the end of it. Besides, she might not ever see Max again, come to think about it. In the past, Robbie also asked too many questions about the extent of Jess's relationships as well as the progress. This time she had remained vague. Probably a good idea since now she did not need to confide that through her own negligence her relationship with Max may very well be no more.

"Actually, I might just have done that very thing. You are going to love Eleanor." Jessie doubted it. Robbie's choices in women were open to question. Except for Madelyn. Feline Fiasco notwithstanding, Jessica still wished she had Maddie as a sister-in-law.

Robbie, as the saying goes, wore his heart on his sleeve. "So tell me about your new love." As she half listened, Jessica flipped through the styles section of the *Times* again. When romances fizzled, best to buy oneself a consolation gift. The gold bracelet from Tiffany's might be just the thing. The Easton Shopping Mall had a Tiffany's; tomorrow she had an appointment with a client on Hamilton Road, less than two miles away. The interview could very well take a little longer than she expected, just long enough to purchase a gold bracelet.

"Eleanor is beautiful. She looks a lot like you."

I doubt it, thought Jessica, *but go on.*

"Slim, long sun streaked hair. Unlike some of my girlfriends in the past, she has a respectable career." Jess recalled some of those past relationships. Usually most of the women, all beautiful, fit one or both categories: married, their husbands didn't understand them, or they engaged in shady financial schemes of one kind or another.

A recent girlfriend of Robbie's lived with a man in his late seventies. He claimed he needed a caregiver, one who not only saw to his grooming needs but who also performed light housework and managed his checkbook. From what Jessica surmised, managing the checkbook meant generous pay for the caregiver/girlfriend. She had an idea that the old gentleman's grooming needs exceeded assistance into the shower. Assistance after the shower probably included any additional number of manipulations to ensure that the client enjoyed a restful night.

"She is an attorney, Jessica, just like you."

"Where does she practice?"

"In the Marion, Upper Sandusky, Bucyrus area. I'm surprised you haven't run into her. She's great, Jess. Her parents—"

"Robbie, I can't talk. On my way to court. Call me later."

She really did not want waste time listening about yet another perfect woman who walked into her brother's life, then for whatever reason scurried out the symbolic door or perhaps was thrown out, so to speak. Now there was a word: *defenestration*, throwing out the window.

"I'm sure if you like her I will too."

Again, she doubted it but no need to incense Robbie. This girl might be the one to settle him down once and for all.

"How is the job going? Are you bringing in the clients you had hoped?"

Like the gambler he was, Robbie discussed only his wins, never his losses. Hell, weren't they all gamblers?

"I'm meeting my goals. Remember Myron Steinhauser, a friend of Dad's? I'm having lunch with him Thursday. He wants to talk with me about a few ideas."

"Did you call him or did he call you?" It made a difference.

"He called me." Jessica hoped the best always for her brother. "I'll let you know what happens. I'm in a golf outing in a couple of weeks. A fundraiser. Do you want to join us? I have two already signed up. You would complete the foursome."

"Rob, I'm not that good. I haven't played since last fall, and those were basically lessons. I don't even have my own set of clubs. I've been using Mom's pink golf bag with fifteen-year-old clubs, at least."

"I'll get a set for you. You are an excellent athlete, Jessica. Your idea of how good you are and mine usually are very different. I'm signing you up with our group."

"Fine. Who are we raising funds for this time?"

"I have to look it up. I am doing a favor for one of my friends who helped me out a while ago." Robbie was nothing if not loyal. "Anyway, I have you down. The event is at the OSU golf course, so it should be fun. Take a day off from work and enjoy yourself. I have to go. Eleanor is calling. Love you."

Jessica checked her phone in case Max had called while she was talking to Robbie. Nothing. "Come on, Cedric, you can have a snack instead of me. In the bad old days I scrounged late night grocery stores for cherry pie. Any old cherry pie would do, although if I had one from Mom, that was the best."

As she shook a bag of Chicken Yum Yums, *It's party time any time* the package read, the cat raced to his dish.

"Now let's practice your numbers. When Mommy returns, if she ever does, you can show her how you count." Cedric raised a paw. "One. Good boy." She fed him one kibble. "Two." He raised his paw again. She fed him two kibbles. "Three." He raised the other paw. "Well, still very good." She opened her hand as he delicately nibbled each kibble from her palm.

"One more call, then bedtime for both of us. We have a busy week ahead. You might be going back with Mommy this week!" Cedric raised up on his hind legs, pulling at the treat sack she still held. "All right. I do not want to think about Mommy either. Here, these are from Auntie Jessie." She poured five onto the floor. "Eat up, Kiddo. I'll be over on the couch."

Admit it, she told herself. *You are lonely, and you have yourself to thank for it. Why not text Max and suggest you meet halfway. Be realistic. You messed up by forgetting to call the prosecutor.*

But her boyfriend of the moment, no, her boyfriend, messed up by speeding. As her own attorney, she grudgingly realized, she had a fool for a client. All right. Do not call Max. Who else? Bruce! Yes, Bruce.

It was too late to invite him for a drink. Whatever his sexual preferences were, and that angry man yanking clothes out of a closet could be anyone, 9:00 p.m. on Sunday night was no time to extend a social invitation to a person one hardly knew. She could, however, call. Just to be friendly.

What the hell? She still did not have his number. Dammit. Walk down the hall, knock on the door, be neighborly. By all means do not let on about what you saw when you opened a drawer you should not have opened.

Jessica checked her hallway mirror. Unlike a few days ago, she had clean hair. Her face was clean, and she did not reek of last night's booze. Good to go, so to speak. "Be a nice boy, Ceddie. Auntie is just going to run down the hall for a few minutes." She grabbed her keys and shut the door behind her.

Jessica knocked. No answer. She waited. Maybe he was gone. Packing more of his grandmother's Villeroy and Boch flowery dishes to bring back to the apartment. Perhaps he and the last angry man had reconciled whatever disagreement they had and were enjoying a repast in the pub down the street. Maybe he had joined his brother's paintball club. It was still light enough to finish splattering one another with lurid pigments. Or maybe he was in the OSU library reading Shakespeare. He was, after all, an English major. The last option was least likely only because Jessica was unsure of the university's Sunday night library hours.

Two more quick knocks, then she would go. Just as she reached up, the door opened. "Jessica, to what do I owe this pleasure?" Although feigning calm, he seemed mildly disconcerted. "Not missing a cat, are you?"

"I have been an awful neighbor. You saved a cat not mine from potential harm, served me coffee when I was badly hungover, I fall asleep on your couch, and I fail to write or call. I came to apologize."

"I would invite you in, but the place is a mess." He stepped outside into the hall.

Think like a lawyer, she reminded herself. Bruce had a woman in there, maybe a man, none of her business, or he did not want to see her. Best to retreat gracefully, especially considering what she had uncovered previously. "I can see you are busy. I'll call another time." Which without a number would be difficult. Have Lil check LinkedIn or Facebook.

"I can take a few minutes off." He smiled at her. "If you don't mind, I could bring a bottle of wine down to your place. Just give me about ten minutes and I will be down."

"Great. See you in ten." Delighted with herself, Jessica affected a calm stroll down the hall until she was certain Bruce was back in his apartment. Then she raised both arms in a victory gesture. Whatever his preferences, she would soon be in the company of one drop dead gorgeous man, an English professor to boot.

Leaving her apartment door slightly ajar so that her guest would feel welcome, Jessica checked the mirror again. She flipped her hair back in what she hoped looked like a carefree, tousled, youthful style. It never hurt to add just a little mascara, not much as Sunday evening called for casual. Maybe change her T-shirt for an Anthropologie blouse, one that was not wrinkled or ripped. Cedric meowed a greeting as she reached for wine glasses in the rack over the refrigerator. "Here, Honey, you can have another treat. We are expecting company." The cat raised one paw. "Good kitty. You can show our guest how well you count."

A light tap on the door, and Bruce glided in, carrying a bottle of Chianti. "I hope you don't think I'm cheap. When my wife and I lived in Italy, this was all we drank."

So he had been married at one time but to a man or a woman? Either way Jessica did not care; she hated to embarrass herself if she decided to make a pass at her guest, and he definitely was not interested.

"I see you chose the appropriate glasses. Wide mouth, stemmed, just right for the bouquet of red wine." Bruce poured hers first. The guy certainly knew his china and stemware. Didn't English professors sip sherry? He raised his glass. "A toast to a good neighbor. Thank you for inviting me, however circuitous the invitation."

"Some invitation. You brought the wine, all I furnished were the glasses." Jessica's phone chimed. Under no circumstances would she look; Max could just eat his heart out.

"Do you need to get that? It might be a client."

"I can check later. Right now I have a guest." Usually not tongue tied, Jessica felt at a loss for words. Widely read, an English major in undergrad, she could discuss authors, but which ones? English professors had their favorites; some loathed Stephen King, a former high school English teacher turned multimillionaire.

Alex had read almost all of King's books, owned several too, even quoted favorite lines from many. For Jessica's mother, for Jessica as well, the writer's themes and characters bridged from common appeal to academic culture. A critic examining archetypal patterns discovered to one's delight modern settings, rhetoric, and themes linked to great literature of the past. A twenty-first century Grendel's Dame mourned the loss of her son in more than one novel. In another, a modern young Arthur still pulled a symbolic sword from a stone as he prepared to become King, once and forever. Look for updated characters from the Bible to Chaucer to Shakespeare. Students and teachers found them all in Stephen King's novels.

However, a writer who could have been great but instead succumbing to the dark side, that being lucre versus literature. What to discuss instead? Jessica had strategically placed the current Sunday *New York Times* on her coffee table. She followed Maureen Dowd's controversial editorials; most educators were considered liberals. Maybe she should start there. By doing so, she decided she could be perceived as well read, current, and, she hoped intelligent. Start with rhetoric instead of issues, a safe choice, she decided.

Sipping his Chianti, Bruce glanced at the *Times*. "I see we read some of the same newspapers."

"I have to confess I look for Maureen Dowd's column first, then work my way through the remainder of the sections." She actually grabbed *Styles* first, but best not to appear meretricious. Oh, she drooled over the most recent advertisements for hand bags and shoes. Best not to mention that either. Nor tell her still new friend she planned on popping into Tiffany's tomorrow to assuage a taste for bracelets as well as to pick up an anodyne for a possible broken heart.

"Dowd's opinions aside for a moment, her diction delights me. Mom keeps a paperback dictionary by her chair. I look up words on my phone. I keep a list of words and definitions, which I go back over about every two weeks."

Sipping his Chianti, Bruce reflected, "One of my friends developed his doctoral thesis around a successful pedagogy of vocabulary in the classroom. No, I do not have my doctorate, if you wonder. I earned my M.A. four years ago. The possibility of a Ph.D. still looms, but student loans lurk out there too."

"I'm paying on loans myself. Would you then call us *impecunious*?"

"*Pecuniary* might be more accurate." Bruce chuckled. Jessica congratulated herself on secreting her Louis Vuitton bag in the closet. Adjuncts, even those with three jobs, earned less in a week than many of the designer bags cost. In addition, adjuncts paid for their own medical insurance, usually were excluded from many full-time faculty meetings, and from what Jessica knew of her mother's position, suffered even worse socially at their place of employment. Oh yes, they were invited to college and university holiday parties, but not to the ones that mattered: those private engagements hosted by department chairs and select administrators at their homes. Each semester adjuncts learned their class assignments a day or two before the semester started; it depended on class size, and all over the country class size on brick and mortar campuses was declining as online enrollment rose. Even then full-time faculty received the pick of the curriculum, with adjuncts expected to accept without complaint classes that remained. Adjuncts did so year after year. As with their counterparts in Grades 1-12 substitute teachers, adjunct professors knew all about placing last in the race. Still, hope drove these same instructors to believe that the next year might bring with it a permanent position. With that would come friendships with department chairs, committee meetings, normal office hours, maybe an office. But even as they dreamed about better days, adjuncts applied to other schools in other cities and states, updating their curriculum vitae every few months with added memberships to professional and social service organizations. It never hurt, right?

Jessica's phone vibrated. "Let me put this thing in the other room. I do not have much occasion to talk philology with an English professor."

"Thank you for the diplomacy. Three colleges and universities notwithstanding, I remain an adjunct, but I do appreciate your respect."

"I believe the term is *redoubtable*," Jessica toasted Bruce. "You, my friend, are worthy of respect."

"Again, Counselor, I appreciate your obeisance." Bruce raised his glass to hers. Fairly certain that the word meant *gesture of respect* such as courtesy or a salute, Jessica still felt it wise not to offer a definition in case she was incorrect.

"I leave tomorrow for a conference, which is why I did not invite you into my apartment. I have clothes everywhere, I trust you understand."

"Can I do anything for you? Would you like me to check occasionally to see if everything is okay? Water the plants, that sort of thing?" She remembered Bruce did not possess any plants, but it seemed the right transition.

"No, my brother will look in. The worst part about leaving for two weeks is arranging for substitutes at my jobs. I am fairly certain that all three department chairs are not happy with me. We have sixteen week semesters, and here I am, unexpectedly absent for classes. A statistics person could add that I am missing more than 11 percent of the semester. I risk being fired, whoops, not requested to return."

A reply seemed unnecessary, so Jessica merely nodded, looking sympathetic. Cedric materialized from his hiding place behind the potted palm. He jumped up onto the couch between Bruce and Jess, then settled in to purr and knead.

"Jessica," Bruce hesitated, "I am afraid you will have to find another home for your cat. I overheard Bill talking with one of the owners about terminating your lease. I saved the little guy once, but I will not be here if my brother decides to 'review your apartment again for health and safety concerns.'"

Jessica's cell phone warbled from its place on her bedroom dresser. A text. She ignored it. Apologetic or not, Max could just stew.

"I would offer my apartment as a temporary hideout for your furry house guest, but Bill will be checking in there occasionally. I am sorry."

Kneading and purring loudly, Cedric climbed into Bruce's lap, lay down, and blinked. Bruce scratched the cat under his chin as Cedric's eyes closed in utter contentment. Reaching into a side pocket, Jessica's new friend pulled out a catnip mouse. "Look, fella, I brought you a toy." The Maine Coon sat up abruptly as he sniffed his gift. Then he reached out, pulled the treasure to his mouth, and jumped down.

"We had a cat when I was a kid. Cedric here reminds me of him. Back then we awarded pets actual pet names instead of people names like now."

Toy in mouth, Cedric secreted himself behind the palm in case anyone wanted to steal his mouse. "I kept that Pretzel from kindergarten through college. He lived to be over twenty years old until we had to put him to sleep. Even now the day we took him to the veterinarian's remains one of the saddest days of my life."

Jessica nodded again, sympathetically. Bruce finished his wine, "I found the toy at the back of my desk drawer. The same one you looked in the other day."

Jessica felt as if her heart stopped. How did he know? She ended up writing a note on a paper towel, which she left on the kitchen counter. Unless, unless her neighbor about which she knew little except that he liked cats and taught English, unless Bruce had a camera. Why in the hell would an adjunct professor need to record activities in his apartment? Of course, to catch the angry former roommate/partner stealing.

Best to breathe in, then apologize. "I am truly sorry. I was only looking for a piece of paper so that I could scrawl a quick thank you note." She felt a deep blush creep from her face to her chest.

"I figured that much. No offense taken. Anyway, I have to run, still packing to do, not to mention e-mailing lesson plans to all the adjuncts panting to take over my position." As he set his glass on the coffee table, they both jumped at voices in the apartment.

Madelyn. "We tried calling from the airport, but you didn't answer. Then we texted, still no response. We just decided we'll drive right here first instead of to Reynoldsburg."

Jessica wondered how they got through the doors into the apartment building. Visitors needed to buzz the resident or, most likely, wait until someone left and ask politely for entry.

"We waited for a nice young man to exit, then explained we wanted to surprise you." He let us in. *Surprise* was an understatement. Try *shock*. "We knocked. I guess you didn't hear us."

"Maddie! You're back. I thought you were due tomorrow!" Jessica recovered enough to hurry to embrace her friend. "Craig, what are you doing here? You must have been Maddie's ride from the airport!"

"Bruce, this is Maddie. Maddie this is—"

"This, my friends, is my new husband. We met in London. We are officially Mr. and Mrs. Craig Washington."

"Pleased to meet you both." Bruce extended his hand. "Sorry to run off like this, but I have a plane to catch early tomorrow. Congratulations and best wishes. Jess, if you don't mind, I would appreciate using your bathroom quickly. I have clothes and supplies strewn all over mine. Makes it a lot easier.

"You know where it is. Same layout as yours."

A few minutes later with a hasty wave of his hand, Bruce soon closed the apartment door on a stunned Jessica Woods. Think like an attorney, she reminded herself. Ask simple questions, build on the respondent's answers, wait.

She addressed her returning friend and Maddie's new husband. "Would you like a glass of wine? We finished the Chianti, but I have a nice bottle of champagne in the fridge I just have had no occasion to open."

"No, no," Maddie declined, all the while circling Craig's waist with her right arm as he held his new wife closely. "We can sit down for a few minutes though, can't we, Honey?"

"Oh, my gosh, in the excitement I forgot about my little baby." Bleating delightedly psychologist Madelyn Hendricks hurried to the Maine Coon who was tentatively creeping under the coffee table from his hiding place behind the palm. "Mommy's home!" She knelt down to pull him out. Cedric hissed.

"Poor baby. You're mad at Mommy for leaving you so long. Craig, Honey, come on over." Still kneeling as the cat glared at her, she continued, "I brought you a brand new daddy. Craig, Sweetie, just offer Cedric your hand so that he can sniff to get acclimated."

Accustomed to following orders, Master Sergeant Craig Washington gently proffered his right hand. Cedric spit, then clawed him.

"All right, Sweetums." Did Dr. Madelyn Henderson now Washington mean the cat or her husband? "We can try this again later."

In an effort to collect her thoughts, Jessica gathered the dirty wine glasses she and Bruce had used and carried them to the kitchen counter. How to word the questions she most wanted to ask of her good friend and her assistant's now former fiancé? He, as she recalled, or she who talks first, loses.

"You probably would like to know how all of this occurred. It's a long story, but I'll make it brief. You work tomorrow." Which meant Madelyn would not be observing office hours. In addition, the psychologist would be interacting with Lil who would have to contact, if she had not already, the clients Madelyn had scheduled. Lil, who had figuratively been left at the altar, Lil who had been jilted by a man who left her for the woman Lil worked for. Make that did a big favor for.

"I thought you were in Iraq."

"Afghanistan. I was. Headquarters ordered me to London for surveillance work. That mission I cannot discuss. Which is why Lil lost contact with me for days at a time. I know you think that I deliberately deceived your assistant, but the truth is, even over here before I was deployed I had doubts about our relationship.

"Don't misunderstand. Lilly is a wonderful person. Jessica, I am so sorry. Wonderful as she is, Lil is a little too wild for me. In my line of work, I had the ability to check on some of her friends present and past. Much as I cared for her, still do for that matter, I realized I could not form a permanent relationship with her, let alone a marriage. I should have told her so before I left." He shrugged sheepishly. "Instead I dragged the whole thing out, hoping that by degrees I could let her down more easily. I was wrong."

"Have you talked with Lil?"

Just yesterday Jessica had noticed Lil scrolling through sites displaying arrays of wedding gowns.

"I plan to meet her tomorrow at noon." He hesitated as Jessica shot him a cautionary look. "Alone."

Adopting a genuine air of a caring professional, Maddie tilted her head as she added, "We thought it best, considering Lilly's situation."

Although Jessica wanted to chastise both of them for betraying Lil, she understood that keeping her temper in check was the preferred alternative. After all, Madelyn and Craig had met, fallen in love, and married; they certainly did not need the permission of Jessica F. Woods, attorney. And maybe right now, former friend.

"I had just finished my presentation, so a few colleagues took me to one of the many pubs for a pint, as they say in England. Poor old Craig was sitting at the bar looking so lonesome. I thought he was a Londoner until he opened his mouth to order another Guinness."

"My mouth gets me in trouble every time." Craig laughed as he draped his arm around Maddie.

"Your mouth gets me in trouble too, Sweetie. The right kind of trouble though."

"We get each other in trouble." Their suggestive remarks needed to stop. Poor Lil.

"So I sashayed up to him and asked, 'Where in the U.S. do you come from?'"

"Who would ever dream that we both could be on the other side of the world but both come from Columbus?"

Make that less than a quarter around the world, not half, Jessica argued silently.

"You know, maybe we will take you up on that offer of champagne." Maddie laughed. We haven't celebrated since we landed. I forgot to tell you, we were married in Las Vegas. I hope you forgive me for forcing Cedric on you.

"Craig used some leave to spend time with me after my conference. His commanding officer graciously allowed him to fly back to the U.S. with me so we could officially marry here. Less paperwork, you know."

Jessica did not, but suspected that Madelyn had deliberately extended her time away, using gratuitous approvals as an excuse.

"Let me get the champagne." Jessica had already decided enough was enough. She feigned searching for the bottle in her refrigerator, pushing it discreetly to the back behind a container of tofu and a bag of lettuce. "I'm sorry. I thought I had a bottle of Cook's, but evidently my brother took it on his way to one girlfriend or another."

"We'll celebrate at home, won't we, Sweetheart?"

Did Maddie allow Craig to speak for himself?

"You've got that right, Babe." He pulled her even closer.

Disgusting newlyweds. Jessica vowed when she married never to climb all over her husband. If she married. Perhaps she would remain single, apartment 5 *S*, not condominium *2*, townhouse *M*, or 1234 Primrose Lane.

"I'll pack Cedric's toys up while you two cuddle."

"Make that," she whispered to herself, "I'll throw up while you two make out."

As Jessica crawled underneath the bed, retrieving a very chewed wet catnip mouse, Maddie called from the living room.

"Jess, could I talk to you for a minute? You'll be all right by your lonesome self, won't you, Sweetheart?"

She must have addressed Craig because Cedric crouched behind some shoe boxes in Jessica's closet.

"Jess, I truly hate to ask you this, but could you watch my darling for a few more days? Just till my new husband and I go on our honeymoon."

Jessica stared at Maddie. *Sure, any plans in place? What about your practice? Do you honestly expect Lil to run it for you while you fornicate with the man she thought she was going to marry? Good luck with that one, Girlfriend.*

"Craig has to be in England next week. His commanding officer mentioned something about returning to Afghanistan once the London mission ends, so we only have six days together. I'm thinking New York, but Craig just wants to sit on a beach and drink rum punch with those little paper umbrellas in them. We can book a direct flight from Columbus to Mexico. Craig has privileges because he is in the service, so we can get a few discounts, enjoy each other's company, and relax before we both go back to work."

Holding a soggy catnip mouse, Jessica looked at the toy, gauging a reply. "I got into a little trouble with property management, so let me think about that one. We are not supposed to have pets, and the manager found Cedric while I was out of the apartment. He nearly deposited the little fellow at the Humane Society, but the man you met who just left talked the manager out of it. I really have to think about this, Maddie. I am sorry. Can you take Cedric tonight at least?"

"That is the problem. Craig already booked a flight for tomorrow afternoon. It seems silly to drive Cedric back to Reynoldsburg, then turn around and bring him back here."

"I wish you had told me that originally, Maddie. I thought you said you were still in the planning stages."

"I'm sorry. I'm in love and just not thinking."

Thinking too much, trying to lie to your attorney and getting away with it. "All right. I can take care of your cat. I just do not know where."

"Why not your office?" Craig suggested. "Lil mentioned you have a suite with some rooms still unoccupied. Until another attorney comes in, would you be able to keep Cedric there, just until my wife here returns?"

With a knock on the door, Bruce reappeared. Didn't anyone bother to consider the time or her inconvenience? "I forgot to ask you to water my plants. Would you mind?"

Jessica nearly blurted out that Bruce had already informed her he had no plants, but evidently he remembered he did, although she failed to see any. Best to agree rather than contradict.

"Certainly."

"Thank you. Here is my key. And your phone. You left it on my kitchen counter."

No, she had not. Whatever message her friend down the hall was communicating, she decided to acquiesce as she waited for more information. All she added as she looked at his expressionless face was "Have a good trip. I will see you when you return from the conference."

Turning back to the more pressing problem of cat storage, she delayed her answer to the newlyweds' request, "I honestly do not know about keeping Cedric in the office. O'Malley, O'Malley, and O'Malley have to approve it. I can only get away with so much."

"How about if I bring Cedric's litter box and food over tomorrow right before I talk to Lil?"

Perfect. A shit delivering a shitter. Fine. "Just take the poor little guy tonight. He should go home for a while."

Maddie reached down under the coffee table to pull her cat into her arms. Quicker than his negligent mother, the Maine Coon darted behind Jess's potted palm tree. Maddie crouched under the palm; Cedric backed into the corner. Maddie reached; Cedric raced through the great room into Jess's bedroom. On his hands and knees, Craig crawled around trying to coax Cedric out from underneath the middle of the king sized bed.

Jessica let him crawl for a while, out of spite. Watching a big man on his hands and knees was fun. After a few minutes she gave in to her kinder side. "Leave him there. You can bring his things to my office tomorrow. I hope you warn Lil before you break her heart completely."

"I am sorry. I will call her tonight." Hand in hand, hard to do as they walked side by side through the apartment door, Mr. and Mrs. Craig Washington departed.

Ah, peace. Cedric remained safely under the bed. Jessica's phone chimed. *Unknown.*

"Jess, it's Bruce. How about a late night glass of wine? I will meet you outside. We can walk down to Charlotte's Wine Bar. I think it's still open."

Ten minutes later, Jessica rode the elevator to the street. Although she usually walked the five flights even in spikes, by this Sunday night she had had enough racing around, figuratively and literally.

Bruce hugged her. Hmm. Real emotion or more subterfuge?

"Thank you, Jess. I appreciate your going along with this."

"Anytime. I would, however, very much like it if you let me in on what is occurring so that I can be a bit more helpful."

"Jess, I know you saw my ID badge in the drawer. I realize you were not deliberately searching, but you did see it, and I suspect you have some ideas. I need your assistance.

"First, I should not have kept it there. In the fracas with the man you saw in my apartment, I dropped the ID into the drawer and forgot about it. I have some personal issues, as you might have surmised."

Bruce gently folded his hand around hers as they strolled in the spring evening toward Charlotte's. "I am not attending a conference. I will be in place as a government agent. My ID, which you discovered, reads Joseph Johnson, Oklahoma City Janitorial Service. We are very, very concerned about the influx of the Ku Klux Klan and seemingly random acts of violence against lesbians, gays, bisexuals, and transvestites. In short, people with sexual preferences other than what the Klan describes as straight.

"I will be working as a janitor in an apartment building believed to be a KKK headquarters. Janitors do not get much attention. We have keys, we come and go. We can work in most states in property management with little or no background checks.

"How do I come in as your attorney?"

"I am fairly certain that my brother suspects I might be involved in a clandestine activity. He probably thinks it involves drugs. Actually, that I don't mind. What concerns me is that he might be nosing around in my absence. By the way, I took pictures of my apartment with your phone. Hence, the subterfuge there. I do have one plant which you can water. That gives you an excuse to enter my place. Just walk through as you normally would, check things out occasionally, compare what you see to the pictures on your phone. Call me if anything looks out of place."

"How will I know other than the pictures on my phone?"

"You are a woman. And you are an attorney. You'll know. Guys, in case you forgot, are not as careful as girls. You'll know."

Bruce reached into his pants pocket with his right hand. Then grasping both of Jessica's hands in his, he slipped a piece of paper into her palm. "Call me at this number if anything, anything appears to be disturbed. I will take it from there."

"Okay."

As they reached the entrance to Charlotte's Wine Bar, Bruce kissed Jessica on the cheek. "Thank you. Now let me buy you the glass of wine I mentioned."

Like two lovers on a late spring night, an hour later Bruce and Jessica walked arm in arm back to their apartment building. He kissed her in the elevator, walked her to her door, then left her after a final gentle kiss to her forehead. Whatever he did, whatever he was, she liked him.

Cedric greeted her. "Out from under the bed, I see. How about a snack before we turn in?" Cedric wound his body around her legs. "I know, I know. You were a little scared before. I do not know what to do with you, but for now food is the answer. Let's work on counting. One."

Together cat and mistress slept peacefully through the night. No phone, no texts, no more knocks on the door.

Monday of Week Four

On Monday morning Jessica awoke at 6:00 a.m., rested. Cedric had slept through the night as usual, so after feeding her furry companion, she dressed hastily in her workout clothes and ran the trail through Bicentennial Park. Quite a Sunday night, she reflected: a surprise visit from two people whose marriage would completely disconcert her assistant who believed herself to be engaged to one of the pair; a revelation from a neighbor regarding government intrigue; and, paradoxically, the nicest, a request to continue to care for a pet, not Jessica's, that had insinuated itself into a beloved role in her all too often lonely life.

She showered, washed her hair, and styled it. Spending additional time on grooming was not a preferred passion of Jessica's, but when she took the time, she congratulated herself on the result. Not that she dressed in a white Banana Republic suit accented by a pale blue Hermes scarf for anyone in particular. No, not that. Stretching up to the double layer of shoe boxes on her top shelf, she narrowly missed giving herself a black eye as a pair of powder blue Chanel pumps tumbled past her face.

Jessica remembered oh too well a bruised eye and swollen nose from a few months ago when, in her usual frenzy, she had not dodged a falling shoe box in time. At a meeting with her employers the following day in Cincinnati, Jessica refused to acknowledge Colin's snickering innuendos. Let him think what he wanted; he would anyway. In addition, from the gossip she had gleaned from other attorneys, her direct supervisor was in no position to judge. The pot calling the kettle black, as Alex would say.

At 8:45 a.m. Jessica drove into the Triple O parking space reserved for her. She dreaded seeing Lil, expecting a tearful breakdown as the poor girl deleted message after message from the office computer where she was not supposed to have e-mailed Craig in the first place. Upon entering the office, Jessica was disappointed to see Clara and Mel Woolsey plopped in the next room. No appointment, of course. Couldn't Lil have some peace as her life unraveled, without the Woolseys rubbernecking?

As expected, Lil's red eyes and stuffed up nose informed Jessica that Craig had called the night before. "Let's go into the back room. The Woolseys can wait till Hell freezes over for all I care." Jessica helped her friend from her seat, then walked her back to the conference area. "I'm sorry, Honey. They both stopped by last night. It was completely unexpected."

"He called about eleven last night. He said he wanted to talk to me today. By the sound of his voice, I knew we were through. I pushed until I got an answer. He said he met someone else. That he would explain more today when he stopped by at noon." Lilly pulled a handful of tissues out of the box on the conference table. "I guess I put too much meaning into our relationship before he left for the Middle East. I should have known better, but I really thought this one was for keeps." She blew her nose, sniffed, and wiped her eyes. "If things go badly, may I take the afternoon off? I have a few errands. One is to return the wedding gown to David's Bridal."

Poor Lil. "I brought it home yesterday on twenty-four hour approval. The store does not like to do that, but I persuaded them to allow me to do so. I said my fiancé was in the service and coming home briefly. I did not know how accurate I was."

"Take as much time as you wish. I can manage. Would you like to leave now? Clara and Mel aren't going anywhere, and any appointments I have can be handled without you needing to be here."

"I will stay until Craig comes, but thank you. You are a good friend." Lil excused herself to wash her face with cold water in the restroom down the hall, then, looking surprisingly refreshed, she returned to her computer where she continued to delete messages.

Jessica walked out to the waiting area. "Good morning, Mr. and Mrs. Woolsey. What a nice surprise. I didn't expect to see you here."

Neither Woolsey rose to greet her. No need to. They assumed they were the ones to be shown respect, not the other way around. Clara's squirrel eyes blinked; Mel remained in what appeared to be an almost comatose position. How did he get that huge bruise on his arm? What in the hell had happened to his walker? It looked like someone had duct taped the handles to the support bars. Was he in another accident? Surely he and his wife had not been foolhardy enough to ride the Super Bus again.

"Would you like to come into my office?"

"We have a few minutes. I suppose we can take the time." They exchanged what Jessica believed were practiced glances. What were these two up to now?

Through long experience, Jessica knew that for Clara and Mel navigating from the waiting room to her office consumed at least ten minutes. One or both of the Woolseys liked to use the bathroom first, then inch step by step toward her office. Still, caring attorney that she was, Jessica always offered assistance. As usual, both Mel and Clara declined. Good. She could check her e-mails in the time it took her clients, no client, to arrive.

Any number of messages offering free visits to spas and resorts. Some reminders about conferences. A few tiresome ones advertising private detective agencies ready 24/7, licensed and endorsed. One, whoops, one from Ralph Edmonton. Carolyn had an infection in her incision and had to be hospitalized. Nothing serious, but could Jessica be a backup if Jay Rossford needed her? Flattered that Uncle

Ralph placed her in such high regard, Jessica also felt terrible about Carolyn. Dammit. Bad things should not happen to good people.

The sound of shuffling and rolling wheels announced the Woolseys' approach. Mel should not lean so hard on what appeared to be a very unsafe walker. "Please, come in. How have you two been?" From the looks of Mel, not good. "What happened to you, Mr. Woolsey?"

"He was not paying attention at the mall and had a minor accident," Clara spoke for him. "Didn't you, Mel?"

Mel nodded his head obediently. As with child abuse, if officers of the court or other people in positions such as teachers, nurses, or family services, even anyone who suspected elder abuse, should report it. Jessica wondered if Mel's situation warranted a phone call.

"I am sorry, Mr. Woolsey. Is there anything I can do for you? I am your attorney."

Clara jumped in. "I believe you are *my* attorney. My husband accompanies me for moral support which, due to my ongoing pain not to mention the slow turn of the wheels of justice, I badly need." Mrs. Woolsey pointedly glared with those beady squirrel eyes. Mel remained silent.

"Mrs. Woolsey, you are correct. I am here though, Mr. Woolsey, if you need me." Jessica leafed through papers on her desk as she considered her next remarks.

Lil knocked on the door frame. "Ms. Woods, I am sorry to interrupt. These faxes arrived, and I thought you might want to review them. Mr. and Mrs. Woolsey, please forgive the interruption." Jessica's assistant reverted to formality when urgent matters demanded immediate attention.

What the hell? Trying mightily to appear professional, Jessica found herself staring at a faxed menu from Dempsey's Food and Spirits. The second page contained a solicitation for O'Malley, O'Malley, and O'Malley to advertise in the *Tampa Florida Free Press*, "Free for Floridians forever." In her shock over a broken romance, had Lil lost her marbles? The Woolseys shifted in their respective chairs. Clara reached into her oversized quilted bag for her knitting. Mel stared vacantly at the carpet under his walker. Bored, but, of course, concentrating on trying to read Jessica's faxes as best they could, upside down with tiny print.

What was this? A typewritten note from Lil attached with tape at the very bottom of the third fax. "Do not do anything. Jay called. Woolseys."

Retrieving tortoise shell framed round glasses from a side drawer, Jessica placed the faxes in a neat pile on her desk. In truth, she wore contacts almost every day unless tardiness or the effects of alcohol the night before interfered. She had found the glasses at Nordstrom's, no prescription, just plain lenses. Good attorneys, and Jessica was a good one, excel with props. The tortoise shell frames provided just the official professional appearance that came in handy when occasions merited it. This morning was one.

"Mrs. Woolsey, as you commented, you are my client. Mr. Woolsey, I am sure your wife and certainly I appreciate your moral support. Regarding your case, I have received some important information that with your patience I would like the opportunity to peruse. I strongly believe that we will be able to conclude your case in the very near future."

Clara busied herself with her knitting. *Good God, what unfortunate recipient would be gifted a ten foot neon scarf, stained by now, as Mrs. Woolsey had dragged the thing along to every meeting, scheduled or not, since her first appointment?* "That will be fine, Dear. It sounds as if things are finally working out." The Woolseys uncoiled themselves slowly, Mel last.

"Mr. Woolsey, you really should have that walker repaired. As it is, it looks very dangerous."

"He has one ordered. It should be in shortly. Right, Dear?" With the promise of money soon Mrs. Woolsey's doting wife and grandmother demeanor might fool a grocery store clerk, but not her attorney. "You know, Jessica, I believe I will have the scarf finished about the same time you wrap up my case. Won't that be nice, Dear?"

"Certainly, Clara. I will call you later this week. Lil, would you mind assisting the Woolseys?" Her assistant held the office door for them as they exited into the hall. Until Jessica heard them get into the elevator and descend, she avoided calling Jay Rossford. The Woolseys had a habit of sneaking back into her office with some innocuous question or other. She and Lil suspected this particular client and husband used the maneuver as an excuse to snoop, so attorney and assistant always waited until they were certain that the Woolseys were safely out of the building.

Lil presented a remarkably calm front for a person with a broken heart. Poor Lil. With Craig's disclosure at noon Jess's friend's mood would only worsen.

"Jess, Jay Rossford called. You need to talk to him immediately. Here is his cell phone number." Must be an early tee time.

"Jay, what's up?"

"Let me hit this tee shot, and I'll call you right back. Gorgeous day, isn't it? You should be out here." A few minutes later he called. "Thanks, I had the best drive in weeks. Landed on the green. One putt to an eagle. You should call me more often."

"Jay, you called me."

"Right you are, Kiddo. Hey. You have been very helpful with this whole SBS mess." Jess heard a distant "Go ahead, play through." Then Jay spoke more clearly into the phone. "My wife's cousin plays Bingo every Friday night at some Bingo place in a strip mall off West Broad Street. A game of chance, as you recall, that our little Violet gravitates to precisely every Monday, Wednesday, and Friday. A game, which, unfortunately, either she is not good at or Lady Luck has not been kind."

Jay, get over the bumptious tone and get on with it.

"I'm up. Sorry. Hold on."

Even hurtling to the green in a cart, Jay could not possibly be up that quickly. Golfers. Gamblers. A mulligan?

"Okay. I'm back. Now that was one terrific shot. Sorry about the wait. So my wife's cousin plays Bingo with Gardenia Pulchinski's daughter. The cousin knows nothing about the case."

Right. Jay's reputation as a blabbermouth always made for hilarious gossip among attorneys. "Anyhow, Friday Violet loses again, runs out of money, leaves, and about an hour later comes back.

"The wife's cousin thinks nothing about it until the end of the night. Cousin and Violet walk out to the parking lot together. It's getting lighter every evening, but by ten o'clock it's still dark out. Violet by now is acting a little cagey, like she wants to be friends with the cousin but has to get away.

"Sorry. I'm up again." Did Jay stop counting strokes past seven? He had to be quite a distance from the green, and he still had to putt. "Now that was a good one. Thanks.

"So the cousin says goodbye to Violet but watches her walk to the far corner of the parking lot. You'll never guess what she does next." Jessica heard Jay talk to someone probably his caddy. "Get my sand wedge. This should be an easy out.

"Creeping at a snail's pace a white older model Cadillac pulls up. Violet climbs into the passenger side. At this point it is terribly difficult for the cousin to see who is driving, but she starts her car, then pretends she is going in the direction of the Cadillac. She follows, not too well but apparently close enough.

"Violet's all over the driver. Kissing, hanging onto his shoulder as he's driving. Of course, the guy is going a good five miles under the speed limit. Then a few miles later Violet's head disappears. The cousin seriously doubts if our little girl had fallen asleep.

"Just a minute." Jessica hears, "Not that one. Get the other wedge. This new one isn't worth crap. Sorry. Lousy day. The first, as they say, is the worst."

For Jay anyway. Jessica hoped the fundraiser was for a worthy cause. Jay's interests encompassed raising money for splinter political groups as well as the opera and the Columbus Zoo. Jessica hoped today was for the latter two. Betting on holes among foursomes was also part of most fundraisers. The way he was going with the first few holes, Jay could be expected to lose a lot.

"So Cousin finally gets to a stoplight behind the white Cadillac. No sign of Violet but she's still in the car because car hasn't stopped anywhere and no one has jumped out. It's really hard to see, but Cousin persists. You'll never guess who is driving that monster."

"Not Gardenia."

Jessica had lost patience with the dragged out story and the botched golf game.

"No, of course not. But someone we both know and love. I'm kidding. Someone we both know."

"Finally. You guys go ahead. I'll catch up." Jessica heard, "Pick the damned ball up. Write down a six. Here." That caddy should do well by Jay. Money already and they were only on the second hole.

"Our boy Melvin Woolsey is hurtling his Caddie through the night. Serviced by Violet Pulchinski, and I don't mean the car. Gotta go." He clicked off.

Jessica called back. Jay had better answer. "He'eeeeeeeere's the Jayster!"

"Jay."

"Call me Ishmael."

Christ, English major inside jokes, this quip from *Moby Dick*. Jess took a deep breath. "Jay, where did you say the Bingo game took place? I am going."

"The West Broad Bingo Card on the west side of Columbus. Gardenia's little girl got fed up with the Legion or most likely they banned her. She moved on down the road, so to speak. It's a long way to drive for Violet, for Mel come to think of it. Anyway, Friday night Bingo pulls them in. When you go, don't dress like you just stepped out of Nordstrom's. Violet doesn't know you, so you can probably get away with it. Just act like one of the new players which you are. Take your assistant with you. You will be less noticeable. I'm up. Gotta run. Glad you got to talk to me."

Shaking her head, Jess heard a distant "Who's in the john, Milton?"

God, another English major joke from the Jayster. Way to go or, as she considered an unspoken riposte, John Donne, Ann Donne, Undone. Fun for all in that fun filled Seventeenth Century England.

Jessica checked her watch. A few hours before Craig's planned arrival at the office; therefore, she could reasonably expect some work still out of Lil. Making plans for the future, even a Friday night Bingo game, might get her assistant's mind off looming romantic troubles. "Lil, do you have plans for Friday?"

"Not now. Why?"

"How about a Bingo game on the west side off Broad Street? That phone call from Jay was extremely important, and thank you for letting me know. Evidently Mel is involved with the Pulchinski family, Violet to be exact. I would like to see for myself, and two of us are less conspicuous than one. Besides, I haven't played Bingo since elementary school."

"Got it down, Boss. My aunt and grandmother play occasionally. I used to go with them, so I have some idea what to do. Wear tennis shoes, a T-shirt, jeans, no makeup, leave your Coach bag at home. I have a couple of vinyl purses I picked up at a garage sale. My nieces play dress up with them. We can carry our wallets and combs in them. Don't bother getting your nails done. No, come to think of it, go ahead."

"Why, do most women at these things have perfect manicures?"

"To tell you the truth, I cannot remember. After today, however, I would like one. I would also appreciate some company. Who do you go to? I'll schedule appointments for both of us."

"Maureen at Ultra Nails on Henderson Road. I haven't seen her in awhile. We can go together, then get dinner afterward."

Friday of Week Four

Friday night at the Bingo hall with her secretary, make that her personal assistant. No call from a boyfriend. No Saturday night plans with anyone male, married or not. Eighty-five open cases for O'Malley, O'Malley, and O'Malley, but not enough to satisfy the boss and therefore not enough to receive the year's end bonus she had been promised when hired. Everyone had plans for the weekend, hell, outlines in place for the future. Even her formerly footloose fancy free brother seemed to be serious this time. Wedding bells rang over the pot of gold at the end of the rainbow for everyone, everyone, it seemed, but Jessica F. Woods attorney of record and her faithful sidekick Lilly Dawber Taylor. At least their gel nails, Lil's painted Scarlet Haira Bewara and Jessica's glistening in Sunset Siren, at least their nails looked fabulous.

Finding the West Broad Bingo Card, *Winnings nightly. Be In and Go!* proved easy enough. All Jessica and Lil had to do after exiting from I-270 was to follow the slow moving line of cars ahead of them as they made their way past the old Westland Mall toward a strip mall with abandoned buildings. All abandoned, that is, except for the concrete block edifice with the flashing red sign promising "One dollar a card, five cards for three dollars, everybody Bingos." Clutching their plastic purses, Jessica actually planned to keep her flamingo pink one with the molting feathers, the two women entered the hall. Even though the games started at 7:00 p.m., apparently most people arrived at least an hour ahead to, as one elderly woman of a certain weight confided, "Get a lucky seat."

Jessica and Lil trooped between wooden chairs pushed far out to accommodate occupants' girths as well as accompanying walkers, canes, umbrellas (it could rain any time on the west side. You just never knew these days.) and lavishly decorated totes overflowing with water bottles, lotions, tissues, and dry markers. Jess and Lil spied rickety seats in the far corner of the room just as the caller introduced himself.

Wearing a nametag that proclaimed her as Evelyn, a stout woman with newly permed hair meant to adumbrate Afros of the 1970s reigned over a long table with an old fashioned cashier's box and several hundred well used Bingo cards. Her husband or partner or boyfriend for that matter—nattily attired in ankle length brown polyester pants, tennis shoes, and a T-shirt that read "I have multiple personalities and none of them like you"—barked out greetings to steady customers.

"I'll get the cards," Lil offered. "You sit down and save our seats." She returned with ten cards. It looked impossible to keep track of all the numbers, but Jessica noticed some people lined twenty or more cards in front of them. This was big business!

The caller who may very well have been Madam Afro's twin brother stepped to the microphone. With a "Hey there. Ho there. What do you know there!" he reminded the players of the rules.

The assembled players cheerfully roared back, "Whoa there. Ho there. Let's BIN-GO there!"

With that, the caller's lovely assistant, cranked the Bingo ball.

"B 5," Mr. 1970 boomed into the microphone, and the games began.

After five Bingo games the caller took a break, allowing people to use the restrooms, purchase beverages, or go outside to smoke.

"Let's split up and see if we can find Violet," Jessica suggested. "I forwarded you a picture Jay e-mailed me this afternoon. Check your phone. I know you vowed not to look for messages any more ever, but this is a job, so help out the firm."

The image Jay Rossford had sent might not be one of the most flattering but served the purpose of identifying Gardenia Pulchinski's little daughter, now possibly Mel Woolsey's nearest and dearest. A very tan woman in her early forties, messily teased blond hair, close set heavily lined black eyes crinkling into a suspicious stare, glared out at them.

"Lovely, isn't she?" Jess commented as Lil retrieved her phone and the subsequent image.

"Mom used to say there's a mate for every skate. Besides, for our Mel, love is blind," Lil whispered. "I'll hang out by the restrooms."

"I'm going outside by the smokers. We'll text if we see her." Jessica hurried out.

The cool night breeze of a late spring evening helped dissipate the dense nicotine fog that sent a sharp sudden pain into Jessica's lungs as she pretended to dig in her bag for cigarettes.

"Here. I know what it's like to leave your cigs at home," a deeply tanned woman with leathery hands offered Jessica a generic cigarette.

Now what? Best to refuse politely rather than make a fool of herself trying to light up when she had not smoked since college, make that law school and that only after Andrew left her. No, she left Andrew.

"Thank you. I really am trying to quit. I think forgetting the cigarettes was God's way of telling me not to smoke."

"I'm Violet. Most people call me Vi though. You're new. You live around here?"

"Actually, I'm from Niagara Falls. I'm visiting my sister, so we thought we'd try out Bingo tonight. No dates. You know how that goes."

"Slim pickings around here," Vi inhaled, taking her time to add. "Unless you're into old guys."

"Not particularly. My sister is married, and I am, as we say, in a relationship, sort of."

Vi nodded not so much in agreement as in understanding. What woman had not landed in similar life situations wondering how in the hell she got there and where in God's name she was going. Jessica's mother termed this *vicissitudes*; Vi simply lived through them and endured.

Her new friend checked her phone. "Time to head back in. Good luck with giving up smoking. I've been trying to for five years. I quit for awhile, then something happens and back I go to the first pack I can find." She smiled sheepishly. "Once after a bad breakup I rummaged for an hour through drawers in the house till I found one of the many packs I hid from myself. I swear the pack was a good year old, but I didn't care. Stale, strong. I lit up anyway."

This time Jessica nodded. She had not smoked long enough to appreciate the come hither omnipresence of nicotine addiction, but she certainly understood upheavals, which drove a person to grab for solace in some form or other. "Thank you for the offer." She did not know if shaking hands was appropriate in this situation with Violet. Among attorneys, yes. Here? Instead, Jessica patted the other woman's arm. "Nice to meet you."

Back in her seat she spoke quietly to Lil, "I found Violet. Let's hang around afterward to see how it goes."

"Hey there. Ho there. What do you know there? Get your cards, folks. We've got some more fun right ahead there!"

Once again the collective group cheerfully broke into verse two of what Jessica assumed consisted of *The Bingo Song*, "Whoa there, Don there, let's move on there!"

The retro Sonny Bono, evidently named Don, stepped up to the Bingo ball. "My friends, our first number in this brand new game is G-17."

At 10:00 after the final cries of *Bingo!* the game ended. People packed their talismans, from scraggly neon trolls to Cabbage Patch dolls to Ohio State coffee mugs and trailed out to their cars. Jessica located Violet doing the same. Her new friend had not walked up to claim any winnings, although Jess noticed that she regularly purchased twenty cards. Poor Vi. If she gambled elsewhere as well as online, it was very conceivable that the push behind Gardenia Pulchinski to settle the SBS case came from her daughter: unlucky in love, unlucky at cards.

By 10:15, almost everyone had left the hall as well as the parking lot. Jess noticed the Sonny Bono Don type toss his briefcase behind the driver's seat and get into his car. He started the engine but let it idle. What was he doing?

"Lil, act like you are having trouble finding your keys. I'll use my cell phone. We have to stall."

"Right, Boss. Anything you say." She dug through her oversized blue plastic bag.

Bright headlights announced a large car pulling into the parking lot from Broad Street. Someone probably needed a ride home. Stepping out of the shadows at the far end of the Bingo Card, Violet waved her hand to the approaching hulk of an old Cadillac.

The driver pulled up next to her, but instead of waiting for Violet to enter, he idled and made noises with the door. A younger person would have leaped out of the vehicle, so furiously was the door on the driver's side then flung open, but the driver was not a young man. Instead, Jessica recognized the hunched slow moving form of Melvin Woolsey as he meticulously extricated himself from behind the wheel. Not only did he retrieve himself, he wrestled with a walker, which eventually gave in to his furious pulls and yanks. With one more vicious tug, which nearly sent him tumbling onto the pavement, Mel had his walker. A steady diatribe, Jessica and her astonished personal assistant noted, accompanied the retrieval.

"Where is the asshole? I know you're meeting him! Come out, you coward! Be a man!" Mel raged into the darkness.

Violet scurried up to the old man. "Hon, there's no one but you." She gently placed her hand on his forearm as she tried to calm him down. "Let's get into the car. It will be all right."

Leaning heavily into his walker, Melvin refused to be consoled. "I know he's out there. I see the bastard's car!"

"Honey, that's the Bingo caller."

"I know damned well who it is. He's the one you're two timing me with!" Mel hung onto his walker with his right hand, raising his left into a clenched fist. "Come out, you bastard!"

Lil pulled on Jess's arm. "Look, Mel's car is moving! What the hell?"

Both women gazed into the darkness as, sure enough, the dented old Cadillac slowly but steadily backed up. All that yanking and pulling must have shifted the old gears into reverse.

Violet begged, her urges falling on deaf ears. "Mel, Honey, please, please, don't make it like the last time. Please, Honey, there is nothing going on." Then she too noticed the Cadillac inching its steady progress backward toward the West Broad Bingo Card. By this time in his anger Mel had accidentally maneuvered himself into harm's way, right behind the eventual path of the old vehicle.

A small woman, Violet tried mightily to pull Melvin out of the way of the approaching car, but recalcitrant as ever, Mel refused to budge. "Help!" she yelled to what she believed was an empty parking lot except for the caller's car at the far end which, evidently, was unoccupied although Jess and Lil had seen Mr. 1970 get into the driver's side a few minutes earlier.

"I'll get the car; you grab Mel!" Jessica ordered her personal assistant. "The hell with confidentiality."

Without taking time to reply, Lil ran up to Violet, both women shoving Mel out of the way. He landed with a thump and an "Oof" onto the parking lot. Fortunately in his anger and haste he had left the car door open. Jess jumped into the driver's seat, turned the ignition to off, and with an earsplitting grind, the old Cadillac lurched to a halt.

Other than swearing, Mel seemed to be intact. His walker, however, had suffered. Violet knelt next to him.

221

"Honey, you did it again. I don't know if I can fix it this time, but I'll try. At least you are okay. That's what matters the most."

Adjusting her eyes to the darkness, she recognized Jessica. "Thank you, Hon. He thinks I'm having an affair with Don." She must have meant the Bingo caller. Violet gestured to the lone car in the far corner of the lot, almost obscured in the darkness. "He's over there with Evelyn. Those two have been getting it on for years. She tells her husband she has to drive separately so that she can stay to help her boss lock up. You can guess what I mean by 'lock up.'"

"Would you mind handing me my purse? I need a cigarette." Jessica and Lil retrieved the purse, the contents of which had spilled onto the parking lot in the fracas.

"Thanks." Violet inhaled. Looking at Lil, she said, "You must be the sister. Sorry to meet you under these circumstances, but I do appreciate your help."

"Mel here is a little jealous, aren't you, Hon?" She petted his leg. "You're the only one Mama loves. Just you."

Violet inhaled again, then blew smoke rings. Three, Jess counted. "Ladies, since you're here, could I persuade you to help me get Melvin into the car?"

Melvin grunted what sounded like an "I'm okay." Although it could have been "Damn you" or "the bastard." He mumbled more to himself than to anyone else.

The three women helped Mel to the passenger side. Jessica placed the now crushed walker in the back seat. This time she did not think duct tape could effectively repair Mel's handiwork.

A calmer Mel waited as Violet turned to thank Jess and Lil. "I appreciate what you did tonight. Maybe I'll see you next Friday. If you're into Bingo there are any number of good games around. When we get together next week, I'll tell you where." She flicked her cigarette out onto the nearly empty lot, stepped into the Cadillac, turned right onto West Broad, and headed home.

As Jessica and Lil climbed into the red Acura, they both noticed a stout woman with an Afro emerge from the back seat of a late model Taurus. In the dark it was hard to identify the man getting out of the other side of the back seat, although his large framed glasses and longish hair definitely spoke of an earlier era. Well, Don got his Bingo tonight too, as did his loyal employee Evelyn.

"Nothing quite like a free space," Lil quipped, "to make your evening a winner."

Hurtling north on I-270 Jessica and Lil settled into comfortable silence, each absorbing the events of the evening. After more than fifteen minutes, each woman lost in her own thoughts, Lil spoke first. "Would you care to tell me what the hell just happened?"

"I'm figuring it out, although I think I know. Violet and Mel are having an affair. My guess is that one is as avaricious as the other."

"While you're figuring it out, would you please use words your poor assistant can understand?"

"One is as greedy as the other. Somehow those two met which makes sense since Clara and Gardenia have become thick as thieves over this damned lawsuit. Mel and Violet fully expect to reap the benefits that come from four million dollars: two million for Clara, two million for Gardenia.

"First of all, neither acknowledges that their long suffering attorneys, in this case Mr. Jay Rossford and I, are entitled to and will collect fees, which approximate 50 percent of the settlement. Nevertheless, one million dollars for Mel's little wifey and one million for Violet's beloved mother make a damned good nest egg. We will have to wait and see, although I am inclined to wonder if Mrs. Clara Woolsey even has a case. I received a phone call this afternoon from her primary physician, which causes me to question the whole damned scenario.

"Anyway, when those two were in the office recently, a too proud Clara lied about the origin of the damage to Mel's walker. He most likely ran over it himself in the same stupid maneuver he pulled tonight. Although tonight it would have been he who was run over, not his walker. After that previous episode, somebody repaired the damned thing with duct tape, I don't give a shit who, but somebody fixed it.

"Our dear Mel is not the subservient husband he portrays in the offices of Triple O. Most likely he and the termagant, sorry, *bitch*, Clara have long ago deteriorated from loving husband and wife, if they ever were, to hated and hateful partners, each silently waiting for the other to die first. Talk about Deus ex machina, God from the machine, a bus accident out of the blue presents itself. Clara is injured, or says she's injured. Mel hangs on now for dear life, spotting a pot of gold at the end of the lawsuit rainbow if he can just hang on.

"Dad may or may not have been on to Clara before he died, which is why he dragged out the case as long as he did. Dad most likely suspected that the Woolsey pair were lying. He needed proof though, and you know how physicians and lawyers can be."

"Oil and water," Lil added. "It's tough when both play God."

"I hope I'm not like that. Ralph Edmonton isn't. Jay sure as hell can be though. Dad wasn't. He just wanted be certain of the truth. We'll see what this week brings, but I have a feeling we are about to see the last of Mr. and Mrs. Melvin Woolsey."

As they reached the familiar streets of Columbus, Jessica added, "It's not too late for a drink. How about a Lemontini? I owe you that as well as overtime for your help tonight."

"It was fun. And yes, you can keep the purse."

Jessica passed a few of their favorite bars, then pulled into the parking lot of one they had not tried off High Street, the Green Dragon Martini Bar. "I suspect, my friend and colleague, that the offerings here might be just to our liking."

Although by 11:00 the bar was definitely crowded, it was not overly packed as it might be with an after work clientele. Jessica and Lil found two seats at the polished wood bar. The plastic purses they both carried as well as their less than uptown attire could be an embarrassment if they unintentionally ran into to their usual colleagues and acquaintances. Nevertheless, Jess and Lil wanted a drink. The hell with their appearance.

As the bartender delivered their Lemontinis, Jessica and Lil toasted each other on a mission accomplished. "Thank you, Girlfriend." They clinked glasses. "I'm afraid Dad's estate won't get much of a fee, but at least we will be rid of the Woolseys once and for all."

They chatted about men and life in general. Lilly announced that she had put herself on a diet and exercise regime beginning, as it usually did with her, tomorrow. Jessica revealed that Max was possibly no longer in the picture. Still, that could change. She confessed to her good friend that she might very well love Max more than she thought. Now that she might be losing him, she realized possibly too late, the kind of man she wanted to marry might not want her.

Some talk of Cedric emerged. It seemed the Maine Coon adapted rather well to his new home at the office. If only Colin allowed the little guy to live in one of the empty rooms at least until a new tenant arrived. Wasn't he interviewing attorneys or accountants anyway? Surely it would not be long, just long enough for Jessica to find a home for Cedric or for Madelyn and her husband to return from whatever resort in Mexico they had run off to on their honeymoon.

Jessica ordered a second Lemontini for both of them. The two then settled into a discussion of plans for the approaching Dawber family reunion in Hocking Hills.

"Isn't Blue Something a state park? We can't drink."

"We do, though. Everyone brings plastic cups and coolers. As long as we don't get rowdy or fight, which we don't, the rangers turn a blind eye. Most of them are related to us anyway, so we are fine."

"Should I bring something? I mean, I have never been to a family reunion. Mom and Aunt Kate get together often, but their side of the family aside from those two is small. I am inclined to think whatever relatives Mom has do not care to see each other. Dad had a big family but except for funerals and weddings, they don't see each other much."

"Bring dessert. You have a huge sweet tooth, so bring something good. My family loves desserts. Remember, whatever you bring will be sitting out, so your Watergate salad is not a good idea. You bake an excellent Coca Cola cake. Bring that. I may still be mourning the loss of my former fiancé now married to your good friend, so chocolate will be most appreciated."

"A good anodyne for a broken heart," Jess reflected.

"That too, whatever your long word means."

"I think we both have had one hell of a week. Some shit show, huh?" Jessica drained her Lemontini. "I am going home. Do you want me to drop you off or are you staying?"

"For what? A drop dead good looking man who might walk in, go out with me a few times, tell me he's being deployed to Afghanistan, ask me to marry him, and leave? Been there, done that. Bought the T-shirt." Lil patted her woman's plus sized just-right-for-travel top embellished with faded palm trees. Where she bought this crap, Jessica failed to ask. The uniform of the evening worked well for the Bingo Card; however, maybe they should have changed before gracing the Green Dragon Martini Bar.

"I'll drive you home, Hon. Two city blocks is two city blocks, and it's late. Come on, Sweetie." Quickly wiping a few tears, Lil bent down to retrieve her purse from the hook underneath the bar.

A man's voice Jessica should have recognized sooner than she did, she blamed the two Lemontinis for that delayed reaction, authoritatively addressed the bartender. "I'll have a Tanqueray martini up, two blue cheese olives, drag the dry vermouth across the top. And get these ladies another drink whatever it is they are having." Jeff Rhinesworth dropped onto the barstool next to Jessica. "Waiting for someone or may I join you?"

"We were just leaving," Jessica demurred. Unfortunately, not with enough resolve.

"Come on, girls, it's Friday night. Time to celebrate the weekend." Jeff's charming smile dissolved what willpower remained. It was the Lemontinis; no, the long work week. She was tired. What could one more drink hurt? Besides, it was, after all, the weekend.

Too much a gentleman to comment on their current dress, Jeff sipped his drink.

Their Lemontinis arrived. "Thank you, Jeff." Jessica raised her glass in a toast. "To friends."

"No, to old times. And to the future."

"I received those Articles of Incorporation," Jessica replied. Keep it all business. "You probably wonder why Lil and I look like this."

"I figured you were on some kind of job adventure. Ten years might have passed, but the Jessica Woods I met at O'Malley, O'Malley, and O'Malley wore Kate Spade spikes, not orthopedic sandals with athletic socks.

"You are right. We can't talk about it, so thank you at least for not mentioning it. In fact, you never saw us tonight."

"I can do that." Jeff took a long sip of his martini.

"Where is Ellen? Come on, it's Friday night Date Night. Your wife should be with you."

"*Erin* is home with the kids. She had a terrific interview today with Riverside Hospital. In fact, they offered her a job."

"So why aren't you home celebrating?" Lil joined in.

"I'm taking her to dinner tomorrow night. Any suggestions other than the ACC?"

"Jeff, I have to tell you, it's a little weird. You here in Columbus late Friday night, your wife in Bucyrus, you buying us drinks, your wife sitting home. Fess up. What are you doing?" The trial attorney in Jessica asserted itself. "Besides, what is wrong with the Athletic Club of Columbus? I take it you belong or know someone who does."

"It is a beautiful club. I met some potential investors there this evening. In fact, one of them is recommending me for membership. Consequently, Miss Trial Attorney, I am not yet a member and cannot therefore treat my wife to an excellent Saturday night dinner." He grinned. "Next question."

Lilly conveniently stared into her drink. "Folks, as much fun as this is, I am going home to bed. Jess, I can walk. It's a very safe area."

Jeff stood. "At least let me order a cab." Before Lil could object, Jeff turned to the bartender. "Will you call a cab for this lovely lady?" He laid ten dollars on the bar. "Thank you."

Lil gulped the few remaining drops of her Lemontini. As Jeff escorted her to the arriving taxi, he turned back to Jessica. "Wait here. I'll be right back." He smiled that old smile she remembered from a much younger man so very long ago.

"Can I get you another?" her old boyfriend asked as he returned to his seat. Although it was somewhat past midnight, a light after theater crowd had drifted into The Green Dragon. As much as Jess longed for a fourth martini, at this point the "I'm not drunk" stage had set in, so she declined.

"I have to go, Jeff, but thank you." She reached for her purse. As she stood, she turned her ankle ever so quickly, more a brief stumble that she hoped went unnoticed. It did not.

"Sweetheart," Jeff said, as he took her elbow, "let me take you home. Did you drive?"

"I'm fine, Jeff. But yes, I had better leave my car in the parking lot and take a cab. No more DUIs for this attorney."

"Why don't I drive your car, then walk back to mine? Your apartment is only a few blocks away, isn't it?"

How did he know unless he had looked it up? Well, fine. He was an old friend who cared about keeping her safe.

Leaving a crisp hundred dollar bill on the bar, Jeff gently placed his arm around Jessica. "Now, where, Ms. Woods, is your car?"

Nothing would happen. Driving her home was the gesture of a gentleman. That was as far, Jessica vowed, as it would go.

Jeff pulled the Acura into the dark parking garage, turned the ignition off, and handed her the keys. He opened the door on the driver's side. Did she feel disappointed? Did she expect a good night kiss? She had set the rules; she refereed the game.

He opened the passenger door for her, waiting gallantly as she stepped out onto the pavement. Did he move toward her first? Did Jessica lean toward his arms? Who pressed closely into the other's body first? Who brought lips toward the other's mouth, familiar, oh, so very familiar, as comforting yet heated as their passions so many years before. Stillness except for a night bird's call somewhere behind them in the wooded lot. How long did they embrace? Time did not matter. Once again it was a field after the prom their senior year, the stars shining, Taurus rising, Scorpio gleaming.

A cell phone chimed. Jessica let it go. Another phone belted out "Hang On Sloopy." No one cared.

Saturday of Week 4

Sharp, insistent poundings on her apartment door woke Jessica Saturday morning. Her head pounded; she had to use the bathroom.

She pulled the pillow over her ear, turned onto her right side, waiting for both hammerings to cease. "Jessica, it's me! Wake up!" A key turned in the lock.

Max.

"I missed you. I don't care who was right or wrong. I missed you." He lay down next to her in her king sized bed, the one Alex insisted that as a single woman she did not need. Max nuzzled next to her, his warm big bear body pulling her tight. "Whew, you smell pretty rank, Honey. I do not know where you have been, but you sure as hell could attract moose."

Jessica groaned. "Lil and I had to track down a client and friend in their lair. Just another hunting trip in the shit show called lawyering." She turned to kiss him. "I missed you too, Max. I'm sorry about jail. I should have called the prosecutor."

"And I should not have been speeding. So, Jess, let's kiss and make up." He began unbuttoning the oversized blouse she had fallen asleep in. "Where did you find this get up?" He tugged at her culottes. You must have attended a Grandma party."

"Bingo."

"That is either the event or the correct answer." He moved on top of her. "I don't care. Wear all the polyester pants you want as long as I'm the guy that takes them off."

In her shower an hour later Jessica considered remonstrating herself. Didn't Marilyn Monroe pull stunts like this? Look what happened to her. Well, best not to think about it. Better yet, avoid confessing to Dr. Madelyn Hendricks. Oh, shit! Cedric.

"Now that I am here, what should we do today?" a very content Max Edwards asked as he brewed coffee for them both.

"For starters, I have to go to my office and feed Cedric. What did you do with your dog? Is he in the car?"

"Actually, I ran into a guy last night who lives in my apartment building. He has to work this weekend, so he said he would walk Charles for me. Come to think of it, I'll call to see if he got in all right. The key I gave him is the one with a burr on it, so he might need to get another from the manager."

Jessica retreated to the bathroom to attempt to find at least four ibuprofen. She should have closed the door. Instead, she heard, "Hey, Andrew, did you get in okay?"

Way to start the weekend. Best to practice the realtor's motto: saying nothing. He or she who talks first loses.

A cup of coffee, four ibuprofen, and a shower cleared her head enough at least to get through the morning as well as to revive her memory. "Max, I forgot. Cedric is in transition. Right now he's at my office. He goes back and forth when his mother manages to be at home. I know, I know, you missed a lot. See what happens when you don't call?"

"Good Lord. When did that happen?" Jessica recouped the histrionics of the past five days, while Max shook his head in disbelief. "Miss a week, miss out. I'll remember that the next time you mess up."

Jessica glared. "We mess up."

As the two considered plans for the weekend, Jessica's guilt feelings disappeared along with her hangover. By noon she felt energetic enough to run through Bicentennial Park with Max. Restored clear conscience aside, Jessica considered it judicious to avoid Columbus restaurants or the ACC. They dined that evening in the apartment; Jessica broiling a chicken for Max, tilapia for herself. Maybe a taste of juicy white meat, just a taste, at her counter, just to test if it was done. Well, the chicken breast could be removed from the bone, what remained that is. Plate that with the remaining leg and thigh. It looked better that way, come to think of it.

Sunday of Week Five

Sunday morning they read the *New York Times* together; then Jessica remembered her promise to her neighbor to check his apartment for interlopers. "Hon, I need to run down the hall to water some plants. I'll be right back." She dropped her cell phone along with Bruce's key into the pocket of her cargo pants in case she needed to take pictures.

"You planning on being gone long?" Max asked as he observed her secreting the phone. Max's tendency to be suspicious annoyed Jessica; of course, there were occasions when he had a right to be. Oh, well. Smooth it over; for the moment their relationship was solid.

"Hon, I have a client. I am sorry, but this is business."

As the apartment door shut behind her, Jessica wondered if her riposte could have been less trenchant. Allowing a man to cool down, her mother had offered unsolicited advice some months before, was often the best option.

No unusual smells greeted her, no rifled through drawers, no fires or stabbed pillows, no dead plants—make that no singular dead pot of ivy. A paranoid Bruce should have left his fears in his apartment; everything seemed in order for the one occasion she had visited. Still, he had requested the help of his attorney, which Jessica assumed she was. She opened the drawer where she had discovered his ID—missing. That was to be expected. Her neighbor's assignment required him to work for Oklahoma City Janitorial Service as Joseph Johnson. She ran the water in the bathroom and kitchen; no explosives, no leaks.

Might as well water the ivy. Where did Bruce/Joe keep his watering can? Not under the sink. Maybe above it? No, a man perhaps did not even bother with that. Just use a glass. She opened a few cabinets to begin the search. Uh-oh. Something was missing. A lot of somethings. No dishes, cups, nothing. All the Villeroy and Boche was gone. She glided her cell phone icons to Camera, snapped some pictures of the empty cabinets, then wondered what to do next.

A ping from Max. "U OK?"

"No. Come down." Keeping her foot in the door, she waited for Max as he ran down the hall toward her.

"What's up?"

"I think someone broke into the apartment and stole some china. I shouldn't bring you in, but I am a little rattled. Would you mind looking around with me?"

Max peered under the bed, poked around in closets, crawled behind the couch. "Having not been in here before, I cannot tell if anything has been stolen. You said some china was missing?"

"Yes, the Villeroy and Boch."

"I have to tell you, Jessica, I have no idea what you are talking about, but if you mean the cupboard is empty of tableware, you are right." Max chuckled. "Find the villain, you'll find the Villeroy."

"I am not laughing. I think I had better text Bruce. No, he said to call."

"Call him back at your apartment. If somebody is stealing things, we really need to get out of here in case the thief returns."

Back in 5S, Jessica called, leaving a message on Bruce's voice mail, which was answered as Joseph.

Max gathered his clothes and grooming kit. "Listen, Hon, do you want me to stay with you? Should we call the police?"

"No, I don't think Bruce wants the police. I'm fine here. You probably need to get back to Cleveland. Don't you have a big meeting early tomorrow?"

"I can cancel it, Jess." Max lightly kissed her on the cheek. "You are more important to me than my clients."

Oh, Jessica. What was the name of the fragrance she still wore, occasionally? *Guilty*, that was it.

"I'm fine. I have to go to the office this afternoon and will most likely work through the evening. It acts like it might rain, so you might as well head out before I-71 gets slippery. You know how those trucks race along spraying water onto the windshield. Drive carefully." She kissed him back. "And call me when you get home."

Max left as thunder boomed somewhere in the distance, probably a huge storm over Dayton heading east. As she collected her briefcase and laptop, her cell phone chimed. Maddie.

"Hey, Hon, how are the newlyweds?"

"In love," Madelyn purred. "Stop that, Craig." She laughingly cautioned. "I'm trying to talk to Jess." Silence.

Newlyweds. Disgusting.

"Back on again. Sorry about that. I know I've asked a lot of you already, but I have one more huge favor and then we're done. I promise."

Jessica waited. Giggles. Then silence. She almost clicked off.

"Craig received his orders. He is being sent back to England. He wants me to go with him. But I cannot take Cedric."

Silence. "Will you?"

"Maddie, you know perfectly well if I bring him back to the apartment I most likely will be required to leave for violating the lease. Colin refuses to allow him to stay at the office. I just cannot keep your cat. I'm sorry."

"What about moving into my house? We will be out of the country for a year. You and my little baby can live here?"

Some baby. A man comes along and the baby gets thrown out with the bath water.

"No, Maddie. Not this time."

"I probably should not ask Lil, although she might agree if I pay her."

"Dr. Hendricks, use your professional compassion. Give her some time."

"I do not have time. Craig and I fly out tomorrow evening. Can you think of anyone else who might take Cedric? I love the little guy. I know, I know, I have not acted very considerately. Can you forgive me?" Jessica halfway forgave her friend. Halfway. Men and romance, sex come to think of it, reached into the most resolute of reasonable people and turned them into thoughtless fools. Then there were guilty fools too. Jessica could name one or two herself.

"Let me call my brother. He lives out in the country in Wyandot County. I have not talked to him for a few days, so asking him to take Cedric off your hands is a good excuse. Robbie clams up when he thinks I am checking up on him. I will let you know as soon as I know."

"Thank you, Jess." Madelyn sighed. "I am fully aware of what a terrible friend I am right now. I really do have a conscience. I just fell in love when the right man came along."

"It happens." Jessica's right men seemed to line up like bowling pins. The problem was, they knocked her down instead of the other way around.

Jessica reached Rob's voice mail. Unusual for her. Oh, Alex could call and call her son, leaving message after message. Her mother accused him of holding the phone, ignoring each and every call. However, when his sister called, he almost always answered. What did he mention about a new girlfriend? Everyone, it seemed was in a relationship except Lilly Taylor and Jessica Woods. Some, if you counted Bartram Irving, Jeff Rhinesworth, and, my God, even Mel Woolsey, successfully juggled two relationships. Then there was poor old Max who thought he was solidly entrenched with his loyal sweetheart.

Jessica shook her head. Best to ignore Friday night's escapade. It was, quite frankly, almost forgotten. She should go for a run, but a storm threatened. What she could do to forget about her slip-up with her boyfriend of years before would be to work it off in the exercise room the apartment complex provided. Dr. Madelyn Hendricks could stew for a while about foisting her beloved cat child off to anyone willing to care for him while she traipsed halfway, make that one quarter way, around the globe.

First stop on the way to the exercise room, however, would be Bruce's apartment. It did not hurt to check in again in case his thieving ex-partner returned. He had to be the one who stole the Villeroy and Boch, since he was the one complaining about how he would miss the china but not Bruce. Jessica retrieved her phone from the charger. It would be fun to snap a quick picture to send along to Bruce.

Shit! A low battery message reminded her of her failure to plug the phone in for most of the weekend. Messages from clients along with two previous phone calls had nearly drained her phone. Well, no matter. The ex-partner whoever he was, probably was not in Bruce's apartment anyway. She took her phone more out of habit than anything else. She doubted Jeff, whoops, Max would call. Or Robbie.

Jessica unlocked the door to Bruce's apartment. Dammit. A clap of thunder, then lightning. The apartment went dark. Why the hell had Bruce closed his blinds? That stupid ivy plan needed sun. She banged her shin hard against a footstool she had overlooked as she moved to open the blinds. Oh, God, that hurt.

What was that? Someone turned a key in the lock.

"Looking for Bruce, Miss Woods?" a man's menacing tone sounded. "I believe he is out of the state." Jessica turned to see whose voice came from the hallway. In the dark she had difficulty making out the face. Definitely a man; she recognized the voice. Her shin throbbed, probably bleeding. Hard to concentrate.

"Miss Woods, is there something I can help you with? You seem a little distracted." What did he have in his right hand? A gun? Settle down. The guy was a property manager. He probably had a flashlight. Still, flashlights swung hard enough could knock a person out. Kill them. Stop it. Think like a lawyer, reasonably, calmly.

"Is that you, Bill? Bruce asked me to water his plants while he was gone. The lights went out, so here I am in the dark."

"You're in the dark in more ways than one, Miss Woods. I could have watered the plants. The little shit doesn't trust me though. Surely he knows I have a key to every apartment in the building. I come and go whenever and wherever I want." Bill advanced toward her, carrying what looked like an Army Surplus Store flashlight in his right hand.

"He asked me, though, so here I am. Just following orders." She forced a chuckle which, even to her, sounded contrived.

Keeping his flashlight off, Bill kicked the apartment door shut. What the hell?

"Miss Woods, you have been a very busy girl."

Did he have a video of her Friday night garage episode with Jeff? She kept quiet, hoping her fears had gotten the best of her. And her guilt.

"I don't know what you mean."

"Look, whatever I have or do not have on you is my business. What I want right now is my grandmother's china. I got most of it, but my beloved brother hid the serving pieces, which is why I'm here. I personally do not give a crap about Grandma's china, but my fiancée loves the pattern. What I make as an apartment manager sure as hell will not finance the place settings she wants. Half of that is mine anyway, a factoid I am sure my brother neglected to tell you."

A key turned in the door. A regular Grand Central Station this place was getting to be. Jess felt secure in the comparison; she had been there often enough both with Aunt Kate and on her own. As with Grand Central, Bruce had a bar, no oysters though.

"Hello, Bill. Anything I can do for you? I believe my rent is paid up."

Bruce. Jessica sat down on the footstool as she grasped her bleeding shin.

"Bro, Miss Woods here claims she is watering your plants. I'm here for Grandma's china, half of which belongs to me."

"You could have asked instead of this cloak and dagger move. What's with the camouflage?"

Just then the lights came back on. "I'm on my way to paintball. I thought you were on vacation for another week. I wanted to surprise my fiancée with that china you have. She saw the pattern online. I remembered cleaning out Grandma's house with you after she died. I kind of remembered it looking like what Annie wanted, so I decided to help myself. It just seemed easier."

"Your paintball buddies are messing with your head. You can have half the china. I just did not think you cared, so I kept it here rather than in storage. You have to admit your apartment décor, and I use that term politely, hardly adumbrates an atmosphere for fine china."

As the brothers clasped their arms around each other, Jessica waited silently wondering if Bill's previous comment about her activities was a veiled threat. She decided to begin a conversation, hoping that by being friendly, Bill might refer to his earlier comments.

"Bruce, I thought you were out of the state."

"I move fast, Jessica, but not that fast. I never left Ohio. When I got your message, I figured I might as well check in. By the way, my vacation went well. I just needed some R&R close enough to home so that I could still teach. Adjunct work is tough. I found two substitutes but the third backed out, so I had to return from Cincinnati sooner than I had planned."

He turned to Bill. Do you want to load up some boxes now? I have a few good ones stored in the top part of my closet.

"Mom always brings me some too," Jessica offered. "I can go get them while you guys 'kiss and make up.'"

"I'll go with you. Bill, the rest of the china is in the pantry above the washing machine. There is a stepladder too. Just don't drop anything." Bruce laughed. "Any plates that break come out of your half."

Bruce shut the apartment door behind him, then walked side by side down the hall with Jessica. "Thanks for your help and for your discretion. I really was on assignment, but not in Oklahoma. In all fairness, I do not know you well enough to trust you completely."

Jessica looked chagrined.

"Sorry. It never hurts to be careful. For the time being, I think we have a handle on the activities of the KKK in the central Ohio area. That's about all we can do right now, but they know we are watching. Thank you, Jessica, for your silence.

"Oh, if you are worried about my brother, he likes to rattle people's cages occasionally. The only cameras he has are those in the hallways. He just likes to pretend he is more important than he is.

"I have to tell you though, Jess, the people I work for have cameras in quite a few places. You might want to be a little more discreet with your romances." Bruce grinned. "Don't worry. I erased Friday Night at the Movies. Your secret is safe with me."

Jessica gulped. Nice to have friends in high places. And friends who liked their plants. "Thank you, Bruce. I had a moment or two there."

As she unlocked her apartment door, she heard her phone chime. Either Max or her mother. Alex usually called on Sunday night to check in on her daughter's weekend. Whatever her romantic or professional vicissitudes, Jessica usually mentioned them to some degree but not to the full extent. Her mother loved her; best to gloss over most situations that usually worked themselves through anyway. Best to avoid mentioning others entirely.

Alex. "Hey, Mom, how are you?"

"Hi, Honey. Just calling to see how your weekend went. Anything I should know? Any events to plan for?" Alex pushed sometimes a little too hard.

Jessica ignored her. "Just working. Max came down Saturday, so we went to dinner last night. He just left."

"Your Aunt Kate is flying into Columbus this week. Some kind of window treatment convention. I know you would offer for her to stay with you, but she is rooming near the convention center with friends in the business. I do, however, plan to drive down and get together for dinner. Can I stay all night with you?"

"Anytime, Mom. I will check my schedule, but next week in the evening is free, so we can all get together for dinner. It's been a while since I've seen Aunt Kate. Is everything all right with her?"

"I have a very strong feeling she might be announcing her engagement."

Of course, everybody was married or getting there.

"Anybody I know?" Jessica asked conversationally rather than expecting an answer.

"I don't think so. The only reason I know is because I went to college sort of with her fiancé. Remember the Eye Candy we saw at Crocker Park?"

"Mom!"

"Anyway, as you recall I lingered after you left. I introduced myself. We started talking, and the young good looking man is the son of your Aunt Kate's soon-to-be husband Mr. Oliver Oney. Small world, isn't it?

"Your aunt has been heavily involved in dancing, various places, all kinds of clubs, new steps, all of that. No one drinks either. They have soft drinks and water, snacks like pretzels and potato chips, but that is it.

"Kate goes for the exercise and the social interactions. I suspect too she likes dancing because it keeps her mind active."

"Mom, neither of you is that old. Still, if she likes it, it is good that she continues to stay young and mentally on top of things. I take it she met the man of her dreams at one of these."

"She did indeed. So many of those men, she says, are retired divorced men or widowers with grown families. They have enough money to enjoy life. Dance lessons, the whole scene, dues, admissions, are not cheap, so attrition takes care of the social bracket.

"Kate has been rather reticent about the fellows she meets. Unfortunately, apparently these fellows make the rounds; more women, you know, than men. Besides, everyone carefully protects his or her finances. No prenuptial agreements for them unless, of course, people fall deeply in love. Apparently, my old college friend, Oliver Oney, Senior was out hunting. A few dances with Aunt Kate, and the love bug bit.

"And you know all that from your sister?"

"Most of it."

"Mom! Oliver Oney the Second is not a boy toy! You haven't been talking to him, have you?"

"Only occasionally. I worry about your Aunt Kate."

"I see. Well, I am happy for everyone involved. We'll have dinner this week, whoever appears. Now I have to go, Mom."

"See you Wednesday or Thursday, Honey."

"Bring Jim. Leave Junior Oney at home."

"Yes, Your Honor."

Alex clicked off.

Jessica showered, then climbed into bed with a book. All right, late afternoon was rather early to go to bed. The weekend's events had worn her out. She drifted soundly asleep until her cell phone chimed. Robbie.

"Hey, Jess. What's up? You called."

"I am just peachy. How are you doing?"

"Great, Jess. Pumped up after lunch Thursday with Dad's old friend, Myron Steinhauser. We drove down to the G & R for fried bologna sandwiches. Mom hates that place, but Dad and he evidently sneaked away quite a bit. All the way down to Waldo he kept talking about the good times he and Dad had: golf, OSU football games. The guy has had season tickets for the last thirty years."

"As I recall, he called you. What did he want?"

"Well, originally, I had called him to see if he wanted to invest in the golf course idea a group of developers and I have revived."

That old scheme. It had brought only heartbreak years before. "Who are the developers? Are they from around here?"

A few, some of my college buddies too. At age thirty-five Rob was getting a little too old to chase rainbows. Leprechauns, even those graduating from Notre Dame, were impossible to catch and even less likely to tell the truth. This sounded like another missing pot of gold. "Well, good luck, Robbie. I hope it works out for you."

"Thanks, Sis. This time I think it will. Steinhauser turned me down on the golf course investment. Said it was too risky for him personally and certainly a poor decision for his clients. However, over sandwiches and a couple of drafts, he got around to what he really wanted."

Jessica looked at her watch. How often had she listened to her brother excitedly sketching out his plans. She was tired. Move this one along or click off. Jessica waited.

"Myron Steinhauser offered me a job!"

Mowing lawns? Most people, Alex included, had a tendency to inflate opportunities.

"I have another call, but we'll talk all about it when we get together. How does lunch sound later this week?"

Lunch sounded fine if a certain cat were involved, that cat being transferred indefinitely to a house in the country in Wyandot County.

"Robbie, don't hang up. I have a short but serious question to ask you. Would you take Cedric for awhile? Madelyn got married, and she and her husband leave for probably a year in England. I will get evicted if I keep the cat, and my boss refuses to allow the little fellow to camp out in the office."

"Fine. Bring him with you. Lunch Tuesday?"

"Okay. I have to wind up a few details from one of Dad's old cases, so I will stop by your house with your new pet. Make sure I do not have to encounter any of your other two legged pets."

Robbie laughed. "Don't be so hard on me. I have given up all that catting around, so to speak. Wait till you meet my new girlfriend. You will love her. I'll call and have her come along Tuesday."

Great. Jessica preferred a root canal. Come to think of it, a root canal stopped tooth pain. Maybe this new girlfriend was just what the dentist prescribed. What Attorney Woods could use in a big, big way was a dentist/boyfriend. Or a dentist in the family. Without thinking, she touched the jagged molar way at the back of her mouth. Another old filling on the way out. She had her mother's teeth for sure.

A knock at the door followed by a familiar booming male greeting announced the arrival of Captain Craig and Dr. Madelyn Hendricks Washington. "Sorry it's so late," her friend apologized rather breathlessly. "My phone has been acting up, so I assumed you called and did not get an answer. We brought little Ceddie over because we have to be up early to catch a plane."

Captain Washington. God Almighty, he must have been promoted in the field. Two ranks up from master sergeant and so damned fast. Whatever he did, he was good. Jess admired him for that, if not for his personal missteps.

Glaring at her from his carrier, Cedric appeared supremely annoyed. What happened to the loving feline who had purred his way into her bed? *Cats, like men,* she thought, *conveniently enjoyed selective memories.*

"Can we come in? Are we interrupting anything?" Madelyn grinned conspiratorily.

"No, I was in bed for the night. I would offer you some wine, but I have a busy week ahead and I know you want to get back to pack." Jessica had no intention of dragging this out. She did not like being manipulated; psychologists knew all the tricks.

"Thanks, Hon." Madelyn gently placed Cedric's carrier down, then opened the cage. He balked. "Come on out, Sweetie. Auntie Jessie is going to babysit you for a while while Mommy and Daddy take a little trip."

"What about vet appointments, shots, food, that sort of thing?"

"Let me give you a check." Madelyn hastily scribbled out a check for two thousand dollars. "That should cover your expenses for the year we are gone. If you need more, you have my e-mail. I am keeping one account here open, so I will send you more if you need it."

Jessica did not feel it necessary to tell her friend where Cedric would spend his time. She accepted the check, seriously considering doling out the funds for lunches and dinners with her brother.

"Thank you, Madelyn. I'll stay in touch." But not for a very long time, not until the newlywed psychologist took a long guilt trip down the Bad Behavior River. Lawyers too had their tricks. Timing, Dr. Hendricks, was one of them.

As the newlyweds closed her apartment door, Jessica knelt down to speak softly to a cat who deserved more than a merry-go-round of changing parents. "Come on, Little Fella." She tried to stroke his back. The cat cowered. "You are going to have a happy life out in the country. I promise." To herself she hoped it was a promise she could keep.

Monday morning, Jessica woke up with a start, forgetting about the provenance of that weight next to her. She reached out to stroke a sleeping Cedric's ample stomach.

"So you remembered me, huh, Fella? Good boy."

The Maine Coon's steady purrs answered her question. Following a breakfast that they ate together, one from the floor, the other from the counter, Jessica left an explanatory note on her desk in case a prying Bill happened to need to investigate yet again for Columbus Capital Properties. Cedric would be traveling to a permanent home in Wyandot County on Tuesday. Given Madelyn's uncertain professional and domestic situations, Jessica did indeed believe the best resolution for the cat would be a permanent one with Robbie.

An unexpectedly cheerful Lil greeted Jessica. "Your first client arrived a bit early. I believe she mentioned you were friends from college."

Right. Annie Minter. Jessica wondered again why her old friend preferred an office appointment rather than lunch, dinner, or a phone call. From the couch in the waiting area Annie rose, rushing to hug her. She looked wonderful, glowing, for that matter. Tall at five feet eight inches, slim, with expertly blunt cut black hair that graced her shoulders, Annie appeared settled and confident. Whatever the reason for her visit, Annie's self-esteem had skyrocketed from the diffident freshman days at Miami.

"Hey, Hon. You didn't need to be so formal. I am happy to talk with you any time. But come on into my office. What can I do for you?"

"Jess, I like a show. You know that. I wanted what I have to tell you to be special." A professor, newly promoted from adjunct into fulltime faculty, Annie taught chemistry at Dennison University in Granville. Perhaps she wanted to arrange for a title check on a house now that her position was secure. Jess waited.

"I met the most wonderful man over the winter. No, he is not a professor, not a lawyer, just a regular guy who loves me, and I love him."

Jessica shrieked joyfully. "Whoever he is, he must be wonderful to have caught you. Tell me all about him!"

"I can do better than that. He is waiting in my car. I'll call him to have him come up to meet you."

A few minutes later Jessica heard the elevator doors open, then the office door. Together she and Annie hurried out of her private office to meet the regular guy who loved Ann.

Jessica hesitated, then stopped as she gazed at the fiancé of one of her best friends. Leaning against the door frame, keys dangling from his worn leather belt, name tag clipped to his uniform pocket, was her very own property manager, Bill.

Good lawyers are nothing if not good actors. Extending her hand, she smiled at him. "Bill, congratulations. You have a delightful lady here as your bride." Annie would also have a delightful gift in wedding china, the source of which was not Jessica's job to divulge.

Annie broke into the polite conversation. "Bill tells me he knows you from his job, but I wanted to surprise you." Some surprise. Jessica hoped Annie could adjust to her fiancé's peculations. She probably could; all men had their faults. Pick the ones you can live with. Appropriating dinnerware from his brother's apartment did not fall high on the list of crimes. Mild bullying, however, was another matter. Jessica decided to term Bill's behavior as bumptious rather than bullying. Annie could handle him. Maybe he just needed a strong woman, which from her demeanor Professor Ann Minter indicated she was. The happy couple could probably use a Villeroy and Boch salt and pepper shaker set from Nordstrom's. Jessica did not recall that being among Bruce's now Bill's collection. She would have Lil call to have the set wrapped and delivered.

The office phone rang; Lil apologized for interrupting the friends. "Sorry, Jess, do you want to take this call? It's from Dr. Schultz of Northwest Medical."

Clara Woolsey's physician.

"We have to run," Annie offered. "Wedding plans, picking out dresses, china, silver, you know. And Bill has to go back to work, don't you, Honey?"

No need to pick out china, but that remained Bill's little surprise.

"I'll take the call, Lil. Thanks." Jessica waved goodbye to her friends, then grabbed the office receiver.

"Dr. Schultz, thank you for your call. What can I do for you?"

"I am just following up with a few remaining cases before I take a sabbatical. I'm too young to retire, but I would like a few months off. This Clara Woolsey case has been bothering me, so rather than e-mail you, I wanted to talk. Do you have a few minutes?"

She sure as hell did for a case that had dragged out far too long from her father's estate. Carrying the phone, she hurried over to Lil's desk. Scribbling a note to her assistant, she wrote, "Anything right now? Clara's doctor wants to talk."

Lil scribbled back, "Nothing urgent. Leonard Warren called. Sent a check. Wants an appointment later but for now everything on hold."

"I have plenty of time, Dr. Schultz."

"I looked back through Mrs. Woolsey's files. Years ago, you were probably in a playpen, we used to keep records in manila folders. My secretary, yes, we used that term for our assistants back then, my secretary remembered a much, much younger Clara Woolsey among my very first patients.

"Between my secretary who will retire when I leave for my vacation, whoops, sabbatical, and me we decided we had better review older records. I still keep them in huge file cabinets. We didn't have designer colors like we do now either. Those damned old things are Army olive green.

"I can't remember the name of the poor bastard that had to move the cabinets when we built my new offices. He most likely still visits a bone doctor, but it sure as hell isn't me. He probably hates my guts.

"Anyway, Christine, my secretary, located the Woolsey file. She took Polaroid photographs of patients back then so I could go into the waiting rooms and call people by their names instead of 'Sunshine' and 'Big Guy.' She figured rightfully so that this way was more professional.

"So Christine hands me the Woolsey file. A much younger but still mean looking woman stares out at me. Same gal. In my years of practice, I have never had a patient so angry, so caught up in hate. Actually, that is what kept bothering me. We never resolved her first problem so why did she return after more than thirty years?

"It was a little late to sue me for a diagnosis she felt had gone wrong back in 1984. So what did she want?"

Jessica waited. It was usually never too late to sue. A greedy client, *avaricious* was a better word, and an unscrupulous attorney could always find a way. In her years of practice, Jessica had met only one questionable attorney; she knew plenty of greedy clients.

"Then I rifled through the records. I had better handwriting back then, I'll tell you. Stapled to a sheet of notebook paper was a phone message my secretary took from Clara's primary physician. I went to med school with the guy, so he didn't bother to type up a formal letter.

Patient diagnosed as schizophrenic. My advice, get rid of her. More trouble than she's worth.

"I did just that. Either she forgot, or she wanted to cause me trouble. Whatever her reasons, I wanted you to know."

"Dr. Schultz, thank you. This confirms what I suspected. The woman is a liar. I guess that concludes this case at least. I'll call the insurance company and tell them it's over. Enjoy your sabbatical."

"I might not come back, Miss Woods. I just couldn't let this case dangle. You have been professional, and I have to say polite with my office and with me. Call it extending the Hippocratic Oath."

"I appreciate it, Dr. Schultz. If I may ask, where are you going?"

"Italy. Need I say more?"

"You, Dr. Schultz, have more than earned it. Graci. And Ciao."

Jessica, it could have been *Firenza* were she in Italy herself, clicked off.

Case closed. "Hey, Lil, would you check out some Italian wines online if you happen to be shopping on the Internet? Send three cases to Northwest Medical ASAP. Make sure one case is all Chianti. On the message put 'Buono Ventura. Jessica F. Woods, Attorney of Record.'"

Because she felt wonderful and because she truly did love him, Jessica texted Max. Thank you, God, she prayed as Max texted back, "I love you too."

Today at least, as Robert Browning wrote, with the year at the spring, the day at the morn, all was indeed right with the world.

Robbie texted. "CU lunch tomorrow. bring cat."

Jessica spent the remainder of Monday as she should: two pre-trials, arranging meetings with clients, returning phone calls. By four thirty she was ready to leave early. A file pushed off to the side of her desk reminded her of one more issue.

"Lil, would you drop these Articles of Incorporation into the mail? I think you have Jeff Rhinesworth's local address."

Lil closed out the shopping site. "I have several. Which one do you want?"

"His personal one, the place he resides with his wife."

"Will do, Boss. Anything else?"

"Yes, if our Mr. Rhinesworth calls or stops in, please tell him I am in court. If I happen to be here, please let him know that I apologize, but I cannot see him. I am expecting a client."

After a long run in Bicentennial Park followed by a shower Jessica felt energized enough to review her e-mails. From the comfort of her couch she scrolled through her messages quickly. Most continued to be the usual advertisements for private investigator services or reminders of upcoming conferences for required CEUs. Those in Las Vegas and San Francisco sounded wonderful; same conference in Columbus, of course but, oh, the opportunity for a vacation, whoops, for the chance to listen to a skilled trial attorney. Almost automatically Jessica repeatedly pressed delete until, until, she read a heading from Lil marked *Urgent*.

"Hey, Jess. Mel Woolsey called. He needs to see you ASAP. I pushed him for a reason so he and the little woman did not waste your time yet again. Clara died this morning of a stroke. I checked your calendar. Didn't want to bother you. You have nothing tomorrow morning till lunch. Mel is coming in at 9:30. If it's not all right, text me, and I'll change it. Lil."

Dead. Mrs. Clara Woolsey, the last remaining client in Robert Wood's estate; in fact, Jessica's first real client. Dead. A termagant, a liar, perhaps even a husband beater. Out of Jessica's life this morning as a client, now out of her life forever.

Jess called Lil. "Holy shit!"

"I take it you are calling about our now deceased client," Lil replied. She sounded mildly distracted. "I can't believe it either. No more clicking knitting needles an hour before the appointment. No more hauling that twenty-foot neon scarf out of the God awful filthy quilt bag. No more trying to listen in on office calls. Still, I imagine we'll miss her. Our first client to die. I guess it's a milestone of some sort."

"Is someone with you? You seem a little distant."

"I have a date. He is setting up for a gig here at the restaurant, so I have a little time to talk. Is the appointment tomorrow all right?"

"Of course. I feel sorry for poor old Mel. He has certainly had his ups and downs, and of course there is Violet. Still, for a marriage as long as he and Clara endured, he will miss her."

"I am glad, though, that you, my friend, are moving ahead with your life. Who is your date? Anyone I know?"

"I don't think so. Gotta run. He's coming back to the table. We'll talk tomorrow."

Missing Max more than she expected, Jessica called him. Instead, she got his voice mail. Probably playing intermural basketball. She remembered he usually had a league game Monday night. Yes, that was where he was. He would never. Jessica stopped herself from speculating.

At midnight a ping on her phone woke her up from her deep sleep on her couch. Max. "Love you. Out with guys. Night."

Too sleepy to fix even a light meal since she had missed dinner earlier, Jessica dragged herself across the living room and into her comfortable, roomy king sized bed. "Good night, Max," she whispered to the dark room. "I love you too."

Tuesday of Week Five

At 7:00 a.m., a purring furry body nudged her awake. Poor Cedric. Thank goodness the little guy had dry food in his bowl and a watering station jerry rigged from an upside down empty liter of root beer.

"Poor little fella." She hugged him. "You need a decent breakfast. Come to think of it, so do I."

Jessica scooped extra Precious Kitty Eggie Baconies into his dish, then scrambled some eggs for herself. Since no prying eyes could see her, she pulled a package of thick cut bacon out of the freezer and fried that too. "If your ship was sinking," she quieted her vegetarian conscience, "you have to have baggage to throw overboard." A little meat now and then with no one the wiser remained her stowed emergency cargo. Six slices later she felt rather bloated; at least she had blotted the grease onto paper towels.

Guilty conscience assuaged, Jessica washed her breakfast dishes, then opened her bedroom closet. For her first official meeting with a newly bereaved client, she selected a conservative charcoal Ann Taylor suit with white blouse. However, the Chanel pumps she had picked up a few weeks before complemented the outfit so well, it was a shame not to wear them. Besides, Mr. Woolsey in his state of grief would never notice. Anyway, she had a lunch that noon with Robbie and his newest girlfriend. Best to dress to impress. Just make it on the less flamboyant side.

Lil was already at her desk when Jessica arrived at 8:30. "You're here bright and early," Jess greeted her.

"I thought I would catch up on a few things." Lil darkened the desktop screen. Shopping again. "Before you ask, yes, Jeff Rhinesworth called. I think he was a little surprised when I answered and repeated the message you gave. You also have an e-mail from the senior Mr. O'Malley."

"The old man?"

"One and the same. He has a speaking engagement in Columbus the third week in June and wants to meet with you. He said nothing about bringing Grandson Colin along. Sounds official."

"He is either going to fire me or promote me," Jessica countered.

"Should I preorder some Jameson?"

"Yes. Call Nordstrom's too and ask them to deliver half a dozen Waterford old fashioned glasses, Colleen pattern. Bill it to Triple O. Make that eight glasses. If Brendan fires me, you and I will divvy up the Waterford on our way out the door."

"Will do, Boss."

"Don't you have a laptop at home? What's with the early arrival?"

Sheepishly Lil responded, "I do, but I didn't want to disturb my guest. Late night gigs wear him out. I went home, but he had to stay and pack up. It was too far for him to drive to his place, and I offered him the couch at mine. I have never dated a musician before, so the hours are very different for me. At least I got some sleep, more than he did."

"As they say in England, where Dr. Madelyn and Captain Craig Washington soon will reside, 'Carry on.' I have a few phone calls to make before Mel comes in. One of them to Jay Rossford." Jessica closed her office door in case Mel arrived early, which he usually did.

"Jay, it's your old friend Jessica Woods. How are you this lovely Tuesday morning? Everything good on the golf course? It's Men's Day, isn't it?"

"My God, you have a mind like a steel trap. You will make something of yourself yet in this old world of attorneys." Jay's voice suddenly sounded muffled, although Jessica was certain she heard, "Pick the damned thing up. Just go on to the tee. I'll be with you in a minute." Back more clearly, "Hey, Good Lookin', whatcha got cookin'?"

"My end of the SBS case is dead. Literally. Clara Woolsey died yesterday morning of a stroke. Her husband notified our office. I just wanted to let you know."

"Too damned bad, Jess. All that work and your client dies. Shit happens, huh. There goes your fee." He must have covered the phone again, but not too well. The Jay Bird really needed to learn how to manage his cell phone. Did he still carry one of those flip phones? "You hit it for me. I'll catch up."

"I was not going to get much anyway. Clara's physician called me yesterday probably about the time she died, although Dr. Schultz did not know about her demise. He told me she was a schizophrenic. Most likely a hypochondriac as well although he didn't say it. Schultz came by that information via Clara's primary physician years ago. Schultz's assistant kept damned good records. The guy sounds like he is retiring, although he told me he was going on sabbatical to Italy no less. Anyway, I was planning to notify the insurance company and the Super Bus people. Just thought I would let you know first."

"That's a Big 10 Four, Good Buddy. Damned shame though. Hate to have a client die before we get paid. Thanks for the heads-up." As Jay Rossford put his phone away, Jessica heard him yell, "Hit that one too. What the hell? Those guys are on the next tee already. What they don't know won't hurt them."

Jessica's cell phone chimed: Robbie. "Hey, Sis, we still meeting for lunch?"

"Rob, good morning to you too. Yes, you said the G&R at noon."

"Let's change that since you are giving up your newborn for adoption."

"Cedric is two years old. He is not my baby. He was placed in my care by one of your many former girlfriends, a woman, I might add, I had hoped you might marry. The least you can do after you broke up with her is take care of her cat."

"Jeez, Jess, lighten up. Just bring the cat to my place. We can have lunch then at the Dew Drop afterward while your former charge, if I am using the correct rhetoric, acclimates himself to his new home."

"Fine. See you at noon."

Jessica heard the elevator doors grind. It could not be Melvin Woolsey as no walker bumped steadily along the hall. The office door opened; she heard Lil greet someone. "Hello, Mr. Woolsey. I am so sorry about your wife."

What the hell? No walker? Trying successfully to overcome a curious urge to run out to view what could be a miracle cure, Jessica held herself back as she calmly opened her office door to her client. Instead of a walker, he carried a cane. Instead of fraying overalls with a much faded Conrail emblem, Mr. Melvin Woolsey arrived attired in a black suit befitting, Jessica assumed, his role as grief stricken husband. Hair newly cut and, surprise, washed, the new widower scorned his usual seat as he took his wife's former one, directly next to Jessica's desk.

"Mr. Woolsey, I am so very sorry about your wife. If there is anything I can do for you—"

"Stop right there. Clara and I were miserable. You knew that. Don't mince words. I am not. She's dead. I'm alive. Now let's get down to business."

"Of course, Mr. Woolsey." Jessica retrieved her now deceased client's file from her desk as she waited for Mel to continue.

"I have a caregiver now." My goodness; he worked fast. Or the caregiver did. Poor Clara had just died yesterday. "My wife inherited some farmland from her brother in Wyandot County. Most of it went to his wife, of course, but before he went to prison he deeded a hundred acres to his little sister. Clara was the baby of the Whitaker family, I guess he felt sorry for her and bad about what he had done. A murder and all. That's a story for another time. I would like to place the acreage up for sale. I'm hoping you can handle it."

Mel pulled an envelope from the inside pocket of his suit coat. "I brought a copy of the deed with me." Placing the deed on her desk, he reached into his coat again. "When we were first married, we took out life insurance policies on each other. We planned on having kids, but that never worked out." He sighed. Too much fighting, probably, gradually cooling into silent hatred. "Back then I had a good job on the railroad. I paid for both of the policies, half a million dollars on Clara, the same for me. We figured if something happened to either one of us or both of us for that matter, the children we left behind would at least have a good start in life."

Did Jessica see tears as he lowered his gaze to the carpet underneath her desk? Poor Mel. Years of living with a woman he realized too late he did not love. Then age creeping in, making it foolish to separate. At least one could care for the other if illness struck. Otherwise, caregivers and homes cost money. Mel probably had an excellent pension from Conrail, now CSX. Who could fathom why he and Clara stayed together. Certainly not Jessica, no expert at committed relationships.

"Kids did not arrive, as you know. I actually forgot about the life insurance." Right. That was why he had made an appointment with his attorney the day of his wife's death. "My caregiver suggested I look into Clara's estate, so here I am."

Mel smiled. "I do not know if I have the term right. Violet, who will be taking care of me, said the lawyer who handled an estate was called the executor. I do not know any other lawyers. Clara called quite a few, but you are the only one I know. Would you consent to being the executor?"

"Of course, Mr. Woolsey, I would be honored." Jessica hoped she appeared professionally distant yet caring. Let's see. Years of work deteriorating into no case for Clara Woolsey. Then client unexpectedly dies. Fee gone entirely. Client's husband requests Jessica as executor in what could turn into a lucrative estate, given the escalated prices of farmland. Yes, Jessica Woods would be happy to serve as the attorney of record.

"I believe there is some commercial interest in farmland in Wyandot County. I will look into that as well as your other matters." Jessica stood, indicating the appointment was concluding, at least for now.

Mel reached for his cane. "Thank you, Jessica. My wife and I gave you a hard time. With her gone, I plan to treat you much better. My caregiver has given me a new outlook on life, and I intend to enjoy the years I have left."

You bet. Just keep her away from the Bingo parlors. "I will be in touch, Mr. Woolsey."

Mel tap tapped out the door, but before he reached the hallway, Jessica buzzed Lil. "Find out where Mrs. Woolsey is being shown. Send flowers to the funeral home. Not too ostentatious. Just enough to show we care." She was sounding more and more like Jay Rossford. "A hundred dollars should do it. Have the card signed 'Jessica F. Woods.'"

Jessica returned some phone calls, responded to a few e-mails, then left for her apartment and Cedric. "Come on, Fella. This time you will have a permanent home out in the country. I know we have made the right decision. I can't keep you, but my brother will." Cedric seemed unperturbed; he trusted her. She pushed a purring cat into his carrier, then began the trip which she hoped for Cedric would be a good long life at his final happy home.

About an hour later, phone at his ear, Robbie waved a welcome in the driveway to his sister. Blinking in the sunlight a tall young woman with a rather familiar physique and face waved too. A much younger version of someone Jessica already knew; she could not place her, though. Whoever it was, Jessica liked her instantly as the new girlfriend ordered Robbie, "Put the damned phone away." If she could get him to do that, she was already Number One on Jessica's list of favorites.

He actually put the phone in his pocket! "Jess, this is Eleanor. Eleanor, my sister, Jessica Woods."

Jessica expected to shake her hand. Instead, Eleanor hugged her. "I am so very pleased to meet you. Robbie has told me so much about you."

Despite herself, Jessica felt flattered.

"She is an attorney, Jess, like you." Robbie laughed. "No competition though. Most of her work is in Wyandot and Crawford Counties. She can give you referrals though. Right, Ell?"

"Of course. I wonder if you have had the opportunity to meet my mother? My dad is retired, but my mom is still working in Franklin County. Judge Susan Dial."

That was it—the familiar physique. Good old Susan Dial, close friend of law school students. Very close indeed.

"I grew up in Columbus, but after law school I could not get a job down there, so I interviewed around the Columbus area. I started as an assistant for the Crawford County prosecutor. Now here I am on my own. I am actually starting to get several good cases, but you probably know how it is up here. From what Robbie has told me about your dad, as a new lawyer you take just about anything that comes your way."

"Yes, yes, you do and he did. Congratulations, though, for having the courage to jump out on your own. I'm still part of a shit show for a big Cincinnati firm. My boss expects an unreasonable amount of cases, and sometimes I wonder from day to day if their monthly or weekly visits will result in my being fired."

Robbie intervened, "Where is the cat I am supposed to take care of since you as usual take on a pet and then send it my way?"

"This is only the second time. The first time does not count since Andrew gave me a kitten, which I did not expect and could not take care of where I lived. I have to add that the same thing has occurred with Cedric. One of your former girlfriends, my apologies here, Eleanor, that you dumped largely because she refused to put up with your crap, one of your girlfriends without my permission shoved the cat my way while she took off to England. You should be glad it was only a cat and not a baby the way you carry out your socialization."

"Just open the carrier and let the damned cat out." Robbie backed off. Just as when they were children and fought, when one child realized the other might truly get hurt, that child retreated. Jessica's and Rob's parents' divorce brought brother and sister closer, although they had already been close. With Bob's death and Alex's remarriage, Jess and Rob realized even more how very much they needed each other. They understood each other; they loved each other. On many occasions, because of their past, their relationship was all they had.

Robbie gently placed the carrier on the ground, then opened the wire door to find Cedric crouched in the back, hissing. "Come on, Little Guy. We won't hurt you." He tried gently to reach in and stroke the frightened animal's chest. Cedric cowered, then hissed again.

"Should we give him some water? Maybe he is thirsty as well as nervous," Eleanor suggested.

"Yes, water, definitely," Rob agreed. As Eleanor hurried into the house to pour water into a small bowl, she accidentally left the back door ajar. Delicately but definitively a Maine Coon marked with tabby stripes and a white medallion on its chest stepped out onto the deck.

"Mary Alice, come back," Eleanor beckoned. As felines do, Mary Alice ignored the command, continuing oh, so gingerly toward the carrier.

Water sloshing over the glass custard bowl, Eleanor hurried out to join Robbie and Jessica as they froze in place, waiting for Cedric or Mary Alice or both to make a move. Mary Alice tiptoed to the carrier's door, took her time peering in, as if doing so were the biggest decision of her life, then sat down and waited. Slowly, slowly, Cedric emerged.

The two cats stared, then gradually eased toward each other. First they hissed. Then they sniffed, delicately touching noses.

"Ceddie, please be a gentleman. That is not how you impress a lady," Jessica interjected as Cedric moved to sniff Mary Alice's rump.

"Come on, Jess. That's how I meet the ladies too." Robbie laughed. "Besides, just like my dates, the little gal seems to enjoy the attention."

"Should we leave them alone while we go to lunch? I really do not think that is wise." Eleanor judged.

"Okay. Order a pizza from the Dew Drop, and I will go pick it up. These two look they are falling in love, but we do not want a fight in case the romance goes sour," Robbie offered.

After mutually getting to know each other, the two cats strolled toward the screened in porch off the deck, Mary Alice in the lead. "It looks like she is showing him around, including where the food is," Eleanor observed.

"Another wise decision in what could have been a delicate custody matter," Robbie quipped.

Jessica pulled her checkbook out of her white Louis Vuitton bag. "Here is your first payment for cat support. For now a hundred dollars should take care of food. Let me know about vet bills, and I will reimburse you there too."

"Thanks, Jess. You always do the right thing."

Yes, yes, she did. No need to tell her brother where the funds came from. Timing, silence, and a little drama worked well as efficient respected tools in the lawyer's belt.

Following lunch, a vegetable pizza for all three humans and Precious Kitty Chickie Lickie for the newest romantic couple, Jessica drove back to Columbus.

Her phone chimed. Robbie. "Don't forget about the charity golf tournament. I signed us up. You should be getting a letter soon."

"Thanks, Rob. I like your girlfriend. Fingers crossed that it works out for you this time."

"Jess, I'm a different guy already. Steinhauser brought me in. He doesn't do the hiring and firing with Edward Jones. He can recommend, of course, which is what he did. He has been in the business since before 1985, and he told me at this time he has so many clients that he feels he is not servicing them as well as he could.

"Our family name is good in the community. I know, I know, I have a few traffic violations and a DUI, which he knows about. He also knows that people like me. I am a Notre Dame graduate, which carries weight, and I do have a head for finances."

"Mr. Steinhauser and Dad were good friends. I am glad he believes in you, Robbie. Stay legal," Jessica cautioned, "you will do fine."

"Of course I will, Jess. FINRA sees to that."

"Jargon. I can't remember who they are except that they are watch dogs with securities."

"Financial Industry Regulatory Authority. It's a private corporation whose role is to watch over and protect investors. They have a very strict rule book, which I am reading now. Myron told me it may take three to five years for me to realize a profit, but I have time. As I develop a clientele, Edward Jones grows too."

"Jay Rossford would call it a win-win situation, one of the many terms he likes to invoke from 'back in the day.'"

"Rossford is playing in that charity tournament. In fact, he is one of our foursome! I got to know him at a few of the other golf outings I have played in. He's not very good, but he is a lot of fun. How do you know him?"

"Professionally through Uncle Ralph. We worked on some cases together."

"I have to go. I have a meeting with a potential client. Love you." Jessica's brother clicked off.

The remainder of Tuesday unfolded smoothly with routine work. Lil had returned to stealthy Internet shopping which, Jess noted from the history, centered mainly on wedding gowns. Poor girl, her assistant must be discouraged from reminiscing about marriage to a man who no longer was available, either romantically, legally, or even geographically. Jessica planned to talk with her friend and moral compass over Lemontinis. No, make it more casual, a beer or two at Dempsey's Food and Spirits after work soon. One of Sean's loaded burgers would go well too. No need to remind him she was a vegetarian; sometimes, oh, sometimes, a huge beefy burger medium rare, lots of cheese and mayo was, as Jay Rossford might comment, just what the Old Doc ordered.

Wednesday of Week Five

Wednesday morning's mail brought a letter from the Linda and James Katzen Fifth Annual Golf Tournament to benefit research for insights into autism. Jessica opened it before court to see the date of the event that her brother had strong-armed her into participating. June 12, her mother's birthday. That might get her out of it yet. Alex insisted on celebrating with her children if at all possible.

As Jessica read the list of teams another road block to her participation appeared. Team 8 of fifteen listed Rob Woods, Jeff Rhinesworth, Jay Rossford, and Jessica Woods. Absolutely not!

Instead of Robbie's usual voice mail, he answered on the first ring. "Rob Woods Investing. How can I help you?" Of course Edward Jones had to approve his hiring; then he needed to go to school for training. Until then, it was still *Rob Woods Investing*.

"Dammit, Robbie. Get me out of this!"

"You got the letter. Mine arrived yesterday. I thought you would be pleased." Robbie sounded hurt. "Your old boyfriend called a few weeks ago. I needed a fourth, and he volunteered. You have to play. Your name is in the letter."

"I do not have to play, and I will not. Find someone else!" Jessica clicked off without saying goodbye. Jessica huffed out of her office toward the hall. She turned back to a surprised Lil. "I'm so mad at Robbie right now, I'm going to walk a while before court."

As she rode the elevator to the courtroom where her client was to be arraigned, Jessica heard her phone ping with a text. Robbie: "i got eleanor's mom to play. chill out."

"Thanks. Luv you," she texted back.

Yes, the Honorable Susan Dial would certainly have fun that day. More power to her, Jessica thought. She even considered asking the woman where she had her haircut. Best to keep the lines of communication open. A girl never knew what was around the corner, or who might be there.

Wednesday evening Alex called with a reminder of dinner Thursday night. "Hi, Honey, what restaurant did you choose, so I will know what to wear?"

"Hi, Mom. I thought Aunt Kate would enjoy Lindey's Restaurant in German Village. I made reservations for 7:30. As far as what to wear, you always look good in St. John knits. Wear the orchid suit with the Carlos Santana shoes Robbie and I gave you last Christmas. Aunt Kate has a hotel room, you said, so you can stay all night here in my apartment."

Jessica reserved a circular booth at Lindey's, semiprivate but still very much a part of the busy upbeat atmosphere that drew diners to the restaurant and beckoned them back.

Alex arrived on time Thursday afternoon in the orchid suit Jessica had suggested. Whatever procedures her mother had done on her face, Jessica promised to allow herself the same when the time came. As she recalled, Botox followed by Restylane, both administered in the offices of a plastic surgeon, appeared to be the right combination. Botox paralyzed the skin; Restylane filled in the wrinkles. Come to think of it, Jessica might not wait for age sixty to start a few restorative practices. More for her professional appearance, of course, than for vanity. Eliminating a few wrinkles on her forehead might do the trick.

At 7:30 Jessica and her mother, seated at the circular booth Jess had reserved, sipped a glass of Pinot Grigio as they waited for Kate. "Mom, you look fabulous, of course. Tell me, how is Jim?"

"Still farming, still selling insurance. Farming, Honey, is in his blood. If he ever sells his acres, I expect he will keep the barn. That,

Jessica, is in his soul. He needs a retreat, just as we all do. He might keep a few acres for himself and get into cattle again. I know you are not interested, but for us meat eaters, a good steak on Saturday night from a cow we raised comes very close to heaven."

Alex jumped up. "Kate! Over here!" A hostess led Alex's sister and Jessica's aunt to their table. "Welcome to Columbus! I'm so glad your convention brought you here!"

As always, Katherine King Madison looked superb. Dressed in an Escada suit accented with a blue Hermes scarf, Kate looked both professional and feminine. Jessica's aunt carried a navy shoulder bag purchased on the trip she and Alex had taken to Italy the previous year. For travelers who relished places, Ponte Vecchio in Florence stood out as a favorite place for jewelry and leather. As a daughter and niece, Jessica had been a fortunate recipient of both when her mother and aunt returned.

"Ladies, what are we drinking?" Katherine asked.

"Right now we have Pinot Grigio. Tell us about your kids Graham and Mandy and of course Kate's Interiors. Then anything else you would like to add." Jessica tilted her glass in a polite toast to her aunt.

"Graham, Mandy, and my grandchildren are fine as are the spouses. As far as the window treatment business, that is why I am here. I won a trip to Buenos Aires! I had already planned to attend this convention. What I did not realize was that I had had enough sales with one of the biggest companies to join the Gold Level.

"Last year I missed the Silver Level by a thousand dollars, all because one client canceled her order and bought blinds from a big box store. You should see her house. A three million dollar stone facade Tudor, five bedrooms, totally renovated. She doesn't work; her husband is in banking in the city. She decides to save money by 'just going to the home decorating store in the next town and ordering something temporary for now.' Can you believe it?

"Then she has the nerve to call me and ask me to come over to measure her master bedroom in case she wants to order fabric from me after Christmas! She said she sews a little, so she planned to make the draperies herself after the holidays. It was all I could do not to tell her to go to hell. Instead, I told her I was sorry and referred her to another dealer. One whom, I might add, stole a customer from me last year."

"Every business has its jerks, does it not," Jessica said as she sipped her wine.

"As does every career," Alex added. "Enough shop talk. Tell us about your love life!"

The server appeared to take their orders. "Would you mind returning in about five minutes? I think we should be ready by then." Jessica looked at her menu for the first time.

Kate leaned forward. As she did so, she placed her left hand on the table. What looked like a 1 carat emerald cut pink diamond engagement ring sparkled on her ring finger. Surrounding the iconic stone, a double row of what Jessica remembered as bead-set diamonds enhanced the setting. Jessica and Alex gasped.

"It's beautiful! Congratulations!" They both hugged her. "Tell us all about it."

Jessica motioned to their server. "A Dom Perignon, please and three glasses. We're celebrating!"

A busser placed a champagne bucket filled with ice next to their table as the server retrieved a bottle of Dom Perignon. The three women waited silently, breathing in the joy that an engagement brought. Katherine Madison had been waiting years for the right man. Now that he had come into her life as well as asked her to marry him, she deserved the best champagne Lindey's offered.

"To you, Aunt Kate." Jessica toasted her. "You deserve all the goodness life provides. You have earned it."

"Thank you. You do too, Jessica. I hope the right man comes along just as he did for Alex. Jim is a terrific guy. Jessica, you are next."

"Maybe. Now tell us about your ring. Did you go to Tiffany's to pick it out? Did Oliver present it in some other way? Tell us everything."

"First of all, you know I met Oliver dancing. For him it was love at first sight. I had my doubts. You know how these men at dances float from woman to woman. I assumed he would date me for a few times then move on. After all, what did he have to lose? Retired, a widower, wealthy with his pension and investments that increased over the years, he certainly did not need me.

"However, as he told me later, he most certainly did need me." Katherine blushed. "He said the women he had met in the East had sharp edges to them that I did not. During those first few dances he did not even know I had grown up in Ohio. I don't really talk about it since so many people think all that is out here are cornfields."

"Soybeans too. And winter wheat. What do they know?" Alex piped in.

"Cattle," Jessica added.

"He just thought I was genuinely interested in him. As we got to know each other, no I waited three dates before I went to bed with him, we both realized that we had connections in the Midwest, in fact, in Ohio. Even to the same people. Good omens.

"We liked the same things: tennis, dancing, the ballet. We understood each other. One weekend we drove to Maine to Bar Harbor where we stayed in a perfectly delightful bed and breakfast. The weather was cold. We were the only couple in the place, but the innkeepers treated us like royalty. I guess it was there that we fell in love.

"We drove back home that Sunday night. Oliver had a meeting Monday morning, but he called me to meet him for dinner that night. He sounded a little distracted, so I naturally assumed he might have second thoughts about our relationship. I dressed carefully, not too ostentatiously so I would not feel like a fool if he gave me the old 'It's not you it's me' routine.

"I met him at that quiet seafood place in Larchmont. He was already there, two vodka martinis, up, on the table."

"The drink of the brokenhearted," Jessica commented.

"We toasted each other, talked about our day. I had a terrible one thanks to clients. Then as I chewed my blue cheese stuffed olive I tasted something other than blue cheese. Paper. I spit it out into my hand. Thank God I didn't bitch."

The women waited.

"It looked like something was written, so, curious, I opened the note. On it, of course, Oliver asked, 'Will you marry me?'"

"Oh, Kate, how romantic. I wish Jim had done something like that!"

"He proposed, Mom, on a parade field with the 'Battle Hymn of the Republic' playing. He was an elected official at the time. How much more romance did you want?"

"You are right, Dear. Go on, Kate. So when did you go to Tiffany's, which I assume you did, considering a bauble of that size and beauty."

"Here's the crazy thing about it. We called his kids. As you know, he has two sons, both living in Ohio. Ompherous actually teaches in Columbus. He also plays in an upscale small ensemble, the Tuxedo Bandsmen.

"Anyway, Ompherous, weird name, I know, but he is named after Oliver's father. Ompherous suggested we wait to purchase the ring. He had some connections with jewelers in Central Ohio. My Oliver flew out two weekends ago to see both his boys. They met for dinner either in Cleveland or Columbus. I forget. Ompherous was so happy to have found this ring for me. Oliver paid him, of course. But isn't that a romantic story in itself?"

"It certainly is. Ompherous seems like a very resourceful fellow," Jessica commented. Ah, good attorneys, good actors.

"I haven't met him yet, but I agree with you. I look forward to many interesting family get-togethers.

"So where do you plan to get married? The city?" Alex asked excitedly. "It will be fun to fly out for an extended visit. Jim loves it as much as I do."

"Since both of his sons live in Ohio, and since he fell in love with me because of my roots, we thought we could fly out here. The decision is more Cleveland or Columbus. Or somewhere in between."

"Fischer's Beach!" Jessica intervened. "My cottage! You're getting married on the beach!"

"Fantastic! I'll ask Oliver, but it sounds wonderful! Now, the next bottle of Dom is on me!"

Friday of Week Five

"Mom, wake up!" Jess's headache pounded as she shook her mother's shoulder. "Don't you have a class at noon?"

Alex bolted upright from her side of Jessica's bed. "Like the old days, right, Honey? College roommates drinking too much, then sleeping too late? What time is it anyway?"

"Mom, it's 8:15. I have to drive to Cincinnati for a firm meeting. Coffee is made, just unplug the pot when you go. Drive safely. I will too."

It was difficult to drive safely when both women suffered champagne hangovers as well as late rising, but they would try. Jessica hoped a nosey Manager Bill would not detain her mother who was mildly notorious for problems with locating the parking garage. Bruce had mentioned something about Bill's capturing a video of a much older version of Alex navigating the delivery access to the garage via a vacant lot filled with trash and dead weeds. Still, Jessica's mother was a big girl now with a doctorate; she ought to be able to remember how to descend the elevator to ground level.

Jessica kissed her mother on the forehead, then hurried out the apartment door to her car. Thirty minutes into the trip, Jess's phone chimed. Lil.

"You are at the office early again. I should give you a raise. Should. I'm continually scrutinized by Dear Colin, whose presence I will be enjoying shortly. However, I promise to mention a salary increase to him."

"Thanks, Jess. There is a message on the answer machine. Don't we usually forward calls? I'm relatively sure I did last night to your phone, but I confess I was in a hurry, so I most likely didn't. Anyway, Leonard Warren called. He wants to bring his uncle in next week; he did not say why. Do you need his number?"

"No, I have it in my phone. Thanks, Lil. Did you have a nice evening?" Lil rushed out of the office for only two reasons: men and shopping for clothes and shoes to wear with men.

"I did. My plan to mend my broken heart seems to be working."

"Hon, you cannot rush into a relationship so soon. Take some time to sort things out."

"Good advice. I will take the matter under consideration, but for now, I am having fun! He had a gig last night in the Short North, so I joined the groupies. We're getting to be friends. The girls said they have never seen David so serious about anyone, and so quickly."

"David, huh? Sounds like a good solid name for a good solid man. Does he have a job other than playing in the band? Just so you know, unless it is a big-name group, local bands don't pay much. Shoes and bags cost; take it from me."

"He does all right. He works for several school districts as a substitute teacher. He also was just hired as a bus driver for one of the districts, so between those and his band gigs he manages to acquire a tidy sum. You should see his closet!"

"Touring his closet means touring his bedroom first. Be careful, kiddo."

"I will. Have to go; the phone is ringing."

Jessica knew of only one person who fit the description Lil so enthusiastically proffered: Ompherous Oney, also known as One Eye and apparently now David as well. Thanks to that damned philanderer Bartram Irving, Lil's new love was also one of Jess's clients, former clients really, by default. Ah, a little knowledge, as she recalled from Alexander Pope, was a dangerous thing. Best to keep this eighteenth century truism to herself as well as her former client's escapades. Come to think of it. Ompherous David Oney was back in the well manicured hands of Bartram Irving.

Jessica called Leonard Warren, reaching his answer machine. Evidently people still had those. "Hello, Mr. Warren. I'm returning your call about your uncle. I'm also working on procuring a liquor license for you. Call when you get a chance."

Her phone beeped. "Hello, Miss Woods. I thought we agreed you would call me Len or Leonard. Sorry about not picking up. I dropped the little woman off at a church bazaar and just walked in the door. I know you're working hard. I assume you received my check."

At three hundred dollars an hour with already six hours billed, yes, Lil had deposited the check last week. Jess planned to bill her client for some of the time too at the Dawber family reunion, an event which Colin mentioned required her presence. He expected her to learn the background of Leonard Warren from the Dawbers who, according to Lil, knew everyone in Hocking County including all the family details. There must be some reason why the Ohio Division of Liquor Control was holding up acquisition of a license. Jessica knew they did not have to offer a reason, but it would be nice to find out what had caused the delay and fix it.

"Miss Woods, I trust you. You met my uncle John Henry Warren at my house on your last visit."

"Thumper."

"Yes, Thumper. He never had a will, and he liked you. The guy is eighty-six and survived Korea. You met him; he's one tough man. Still, even he realizes he may not live forever. He still drives, which he shouldn't, but he is a little nervous about making the trip to Columbus alone. He asked me to make an appointment with you and bring him in."

"Of course. I appreciate your business. I will have my assistant Lilly call with a time next week if that is suitable for you and Mr. Warren."

"We might have good news about the liquor license by then too."

Jessica doubted it since there was nothing to do until the Dawber reunion, but best not to dash her client's hopes. "We just might, Leonard. Fingers crossed for a right outcome."

"What?"

"Crossing my fingers for good luck. We'll see you next week."

"Lil, check my calendar for next week. Then make an appointment for Leonard Warren's uncle to prepare a will."

"With Memorial Day on Monday you have only four days next week, you know. How is Wednesday?"

"Wednesday it is. If I am still talking to Max I most likely will not leave the cottage until Tuesday morning, so Wednesday works out better."

"Lovers' quarrels," observed Lil, a veteran of them. "You and Max belong together. Your only problem is distance."

"I have another call. See you tomorrow." No call awaited. However, Jessica chose to avoid the Columbus/Cleveland conundrum. Summer was coming. Hardly a time to break up when two jet skis awaited along with boat trips to Put-in-Bay for beers; swimming, and, face it, the joys that swim suits and sun offered for couples. No, best to think about the here and now.

The meeting with other attorneys and staff at the offices of O'Malley, O'Malley, and O'Malley proceeded as smoothly as Jessica expected. No mention was made of Gerald's impending divorce from his third wife. Seated around the conference table, his personal assistant greeted Jessica warmly, complimenting her on her summer Louis Vuitton bag; Jessica noticed the assistant's bag as well, exactly like hers but with five charms, each one costing at least a hundred dollars. Did she have a monogram on her bag? What the hell? When did she change her last name? The damned thing had VHO inscribed. Oh, Gerald.

Ever the business man, Patrick conducted the meeting. Colin arrived about fifteen minutes late, apologizing for taking extra time to drop his kids off at school. Jessica wondered whose children those were, since Colin had none. Perhaps he was involved with Big Brothers and Big Sisters at the Y. Probably not.

As the meeting concluded, the door opened to a surprise visitor, Brendan Colin O'Malley. Simultaneously, everyone rose in obeisance.

"Please, friends, be seated," the older man responded to their gestures of respect. "I happened to be in the neighborhood and thought I'd drop by to see how things are going." He just happened to drive in from his horse farm in Kentucky, two hours away. "Actually, I am meeting some friends, retired judges, for lunch. We old folks make lunch plans now instead of dinner engagements so we don't fall asleep during the meal. Some of us still nod off, but a little liquor might be the culprit there." He winked.

He turned to Jessica. "Miss Woods. Congratulations on winding up the Woolsey case without too much outlay from the firm's accounts."

"Thank you, Mr. O'Malley."

Jessica was not one to slough off credit, misplaced though it may be.

"I am sure you are aware that Mrs. Woolsey has died. The firm sent flowers."

"Excellent gesture. That is why my boys hired you. You think ahead."

"Mr. Woolsey has also requested that our firm execute his wife's will. I believe that with the value of farmland in Wyandot County, which Mr. Woolsey wants to sell, the estate is worth about half a million dollars."

Colin looked up from texting under the conference table. Gerald's eyebrows lifted almost imperceptibly, and Patrick smiled. Jessica glanced at her pen, the firm's motto scripted in gold: *We make it right for you, because whatever the case, we are right, for you.* Perhaps Colin would decrease her case load requirement. Probably not.

At the conclusion of the meeting Brendan approached Jessica. "I have to be in Columbus next week. Do you suppose we could move the meeting up from June something or other to Wednesday?"

"Of course, Mr. O'Malley."

Patting her on the shoulder in a fatherly gesture he continued, "Thank you for your flexibility." Then, "Not all of us retired judges are men." He turned quickly and walked away, very quickly for a man in his middle eighties. Ah, love, what it does for one's health and life.

First Mel Woolsey discards his walker in favor of a cane; then Brendan Colin O'Malley practically sprints out the door. Aunt Kate dances years off her age; she looked fifty-five, not sixty-six. Robbie had a legitimate job, not a trumped-up one reflected in smoke and obscured with mirrors. Even Cedric forgot his state of neglect as he wandered off toward food and, shudder to think it, other activities with a lady love he had met only a few minutes before. Then there was Lil, online shopping yet again for wedding gowns. Learned as she was, Jessica reminded herself that she could, as Alex sometimes hinted, take a page from any of her friends' and families' books.

Declining Colin's invitation for lunch and some hair of the dog at the Cincinnati Club, Jessica returned to the road, arriving back at her office by four. "Anything earth shattering while I was away?"

Lil flipped quickly from a screen which appeared to display dresses more suitable for attending a bull fight in the eighteenth century than a wedding. What was she planning? Still, with Lil, there was no accounting for taste.

"Jeff Rhinesworth stopped in. Evidently he had just received his Articles of Incorporation in the mail and had some questions."

"Call him back. Tell him to call the Secretary of State. If he still has questions, refer him to Jay Rossford. Those two will be playing golf together at a charity event my brother nearly forced me into. You might soften the blow by adding that I have a rather large case load at the moment and cannot provide the attention that he deserves."

"What about the company business you stand to lose when you lose his account?"

"Mr. Jay Rossford will owe me a referral fee, of course. He does pay his bills; I just have to put up with the silliness along with it. Anyway, I have a feeling our Mr. Rhinesworth will be back in this office in a few years anyway if he continues to strew rocks along his primrose lane. I'll get his divorce. Or his wife's. If it's easy, I'll take it. If it's child custody, another referral to Bartram Irving, Esquire with, of course, the ensuing fee."

"Anything you say, Boss. I set up an appointment for the Warren will on Wednesday at ten."

"See if you can change it to 9:15 or 9:30. Brendan O'Malley wants to come in for some reason I cannot fathom before he has lunch with his friends."

"If there is nothing pressing, Jess, do you suppose I could leave early? It is a holiday weekend, and David and I were hoping to get out of the city early." Lil grinned. "I am taking him to meet my family. We camp every Memorial Day at Hocking Hills State Park. This year we are going zip-lining too, which should be fun."

"Of course you can leave early. No one calls on a Friday of a holiday weekend. We just won't tell Colin. If they do, I will forward the phone to my cell when I lock up. I'm leaving early myself to go to the lake. I take it Om/David does not have any gigs this weekend?"

"How did you know his real first name?"

"I believe your boyfriend was a client of mine briefly when I took over for Bartram Irving. As you recall, our Mr. Oney ran into a few difficulties with law enforcement officers. Mr. Irving should have sent a fee for bringing me in on the case while he whiled away his time with his assistant at the Greenbrier Resort."

"I do not have any record of that yet. Should I e-mail him?"

"Better yet, Lil, why not call on Tuesday if there is no check? You can also follow up with a letter. As I recall, Bartram's wife presides over the office, opening all his correspondence as well as answering the phone. In fact, now that I think about it, why not call now? Mr. Irving and his assistant may be out of the office, but if his wife is suspicious, particularly since I have heard our Bartram has pulled similar stunts before, she will field all calls. After that, my friend, hurry out and enjoy your weekend."

Although Jessica had hoped to get out of the office herself before the five o'clock rush hour, which promised to be worse for the holiday, after responding to e-mails and returning phone calls to attorneys, none of whom were in their offices, she finally managed to lock up by 5:15 and be on the road to Fischer's Beach by six. Stuck for thirty minutes on Route 23 between Columbus and Delaware, she texted Max. "CU soon. Love you, Jess."

A message from Robbie beeped into her phone. Messages from her brother she usually looked at later when she was settled, which was usually after Rob had overcome the difficulty that first drove him to text for advice. This one, however, she opened, along with the picture.

Her stomach dropped; her hands sweat and she felt sick. Max and Eleanor, smiling, holding hands. What kind of damned photograph was this?

Think like a lawyer, Jessica: logically. When was the picture taken? It could be today, probably not, or yesterday, or a year ago. Wait. Eleanor's hairstyle looks different, shorter, caramel streaks, not blond. The hell with logic.

Robbie answered immediately.

"Thanks for ruining my weekend. Why the hell would you send this picture!"

"Pull yourself together, Jess. It was last year, maybe more than that. I thought you knew or I would not have sent it. Max and Eleanor were engaged. She broke it off, I forget why. I assumed he already told you but evidently not. I think Max slept with somebody other than Eleanor. She found out, end of engagement."

"Well,"—Jessica's heartbeat slowed as her stomach returned to its proper place—"I guess people are allowed a few missteps along the way, a double life occasionally. You might have been a bit softer about revealing the information, though."

"I'm sorry, Sis." Robbie paused. "You seem remarkably understanding, however. Either you are in shock, or you are one forgiving woman."

"*Forgiving* is my middle name. Jessica F. Wood, how can I help. As I commented, everyone is allowed a few mistakes."

Traffic started moving again. "I can drive up past your house on my way to the lake if you want me to pick anything up. Are you coming up for the weekend?"

"Eleanor invited me to her family's house on the river. I think you already know her mom. Her dad is a retired judge, but her mother still works. Anyway, the Dials always throw a big party over the weekend: a picnic on Saturday for law school seniors, a huge party on Memorial Day for family and friends. They rent a tent, hire a band. Sounds fun."

Robbie sounded distracted, which meant he was either checking messages on his laptop or reading his mail, which Jess hoped did not include past due bills. "You know, Jessica, if things go as I hope they might, we could be one big happy family."

"Such as?"

"You, Eleanor, me, the Honorables Susan and John Rentmore Dial."

"My battery is low, I have to go. Your last comment was dropped."

"Have a good weekend even though you can't hear me," Robbie shouted unnecessarily. Of course she heard him. She just did not want to think about family events with the Dials. Well, best not to speculate.

Instead, she shouted back, "You too, Bro. Love you." After clicking off Jessica reflected, wasn't she dating Max at the time he was engaged to Eleanor? Yow. Well, let that one go.

A familiar dog bark woke her shortly after midnight: Charles, her boyfriend's dog. A few minutes later Max climbed in next to her in the king sized bed at Fischer's Beach. "Surprise!" He held her close. "I gave everybody the weekend off, including me. I missed you, Honey."

"Max." Jessica turned into his big comforting embrace. "I missed you too."

"Good thing no one else was here since you thought I was coming up tomorrow."

"No one else would be, Dummy." The remainder of the night passed pleasantly well into a late Saturday morning.

Sunday of Week Six

Alex stopped by briefly at the cottage on Sunday afternoon with Jim. She offered to help Jess plan Kate's wedding. Kate wanted a very small ceremony on the beach as the three had discussed. Graham, Robbie, and Jim would be ushers, with Graham giving his mother away; Alex would serve as matron of honor with Mandy and Jessica as bridesmaids. Jessica and Alex drove over to the North Coast Yacht Club to make arrangements for a dinner reception after the ceremony.

Returning from the club, Jessica and her mother joined the men outside in the yard at the cottage. "Do you have a minister yet?" Jim asked, pouring himself a beer as the four lounged on deck chairs. Charles gnawed contentedly at a pig ear Jim had tossed him.

"Kate has yet to choose a date, so we have to firm that up before we contact a minister and possibly arrange for music," Alex replied. "I do not know any musicians up here, but an ensemble of say three might be enjoyable." She turned to Jessica questioningly.

"Do you know anyone in Columbus?"

"I will have my assistant Lil look into it. I believe she knows a few people who would be honored to be asked." *Assuming Ompherous/ David/One Eye is available and behaving himself.*

"Why don't you call your aunt to see if she has a date for the wedding yet?" Max offered.

Jessica called, placing her phone on speaker so that everyone could participate. Jim jumped in first. "Congratulations, Katherine! We are so happy for you!"

"Jim, thank you. We're excited, aren't we, Oliver? Here, you can meet your soon to be brother-in-law now on the phone. Thanks to FaceTime you can be as close to shaking hands as you will get until we fly out there."

"Hello, Jim," Oliver replied pleasantly. "Looks like we will meet in person if not before June 12, at least then. Katherine tells me that is also your wife's birthday."

"Right you are. I look forward to it." Jim handed the phone back to Jessica then returned to his beer and relaxing on the lawn chair.

"My birthday! What a terrific gift!" Alex exclaimed, delighted. "All we need now is a minister, Kate. Do you have anyone in mind?"

"I don't know anyone, Sis. Do you? Or Jess?"

"If Uncle Ralph can come up, I believe he can marry you. I'm pretty sure he is licensed in Ohio. I will have to see how Carolyn is feeling, but if he is available, I will ask."

"Ralph Edmonton. You have told me so much about him. How wonderful for him to preside at our wedding. Please do ask. Thank you, Jess."

"Are you flying in or driving?" Alex intervened.

"Oliver and I are flying into Columbus on the Wednesday before the wedding. Where could we all meet for a casual dinner Thursday night?"

"Dempsey's Food and Spirits. I will arrange it. In fact," Jessica suggested, "the dinner will be my wedding gift to you. I insist. I will make appointments for you, Mom, and me at Ultra Nails on Henderson Road. Mo is terrific. We can have our hair done in Haines Landing on Saturday morning, but the manicure and pedicure Friday will be relaxing." Jess added to herself, and all of this will knock Robbie out of the golf tournament which he didn't need to be in anyway, especially with Jeff Rhinesworth.

"Mom, you can bring the Dom," Jessica ordered.

Her mother obediently nodded in agreement. "I was going to anyway. As long as I do what you tell me, I'm in good shape."

"Right, Trickster. Keep that in mind, and I'll keep you out of jail." Mother and daughter exchanged smiles. Jessica, of course, was correct yet again.

Monday of Week Six

Sunday afternoon and most of Monday Jessica and Max delighted in the activities that being on the shores of Lake Erie on a sunny warm weekend offered. They rode jet skis to Kelleys Island for beer and pizza, mushroom and avocado for Jess. They parasailed off the north shore of Kelleys Monday, and on Monday afternoon they rode the Miller's Ferry to Put-in-Bay where, with most of the tourists already departed, the two talked over their week and their plans.

"I wish, Jessica, that we lived in the same city," Max wistfully lamented.

"I do too, Hon," she held his hands as a deep pink sunset graced the western sky over Toledo Monday evening. "I do too."

Tuesday of Week Six

Tuesday morning at 6:00 a.m. a red Jeep Cherokee with an Indians sticker on the left side of the rear window and a Browns sticker on the right backed out of the grassy parking area at 5863 E. Peach Tree Lane, Fischer's Beach to head east toward Cleveland. At 6:15 a red Acura with a dented rear bumper backed out of the same grassy area and headed south toward Columbus. Ten minutes later, as she crossed the Edison Bridge over Sandusky Bay, Jessica answered her phone. Max.

"I miss you, Honey, already."

"I miss you too. We will have to do something about this distance."

"Yes, Max, we will. See you in two weeks. I love you." Jessica clicked off.

Arriving ahead of Lil, Jessica unlocked her office door. She bent to pick up a simple white business envelope slipped under the door, the name handwritten, addressed to her. A woman's writing, she could tell, from the loops and flourishes. In it was a plain blue business check from the firm of Irving and Irving, LPA, Inc. for 1,500.00 written not to O'Malley, O'Malley, and O'Malley but to Jessica Woods, Esq. Nice way to start a short week.

Too many e-mails stared unopened in her mailbox, the consequence of a long weekend away from the office. By 9:00 a.m. Jessica had opened and returned all her e-mails as well as read the accumulated mail from the US Postal Service. Lil arrived chipper at 9:15, apologetic but happy.

"Yes, we had a wonderful weekend. David loves my family and they love him. I know, I know, we're moving too fast for you."

Jessica held up her hands in mock abnegation. "No one, my friend, is getting any younger. I am happy for you, Lil. That really is all I am going to say on the subject. Is David teaching today?"

"One of the districts called him. However, he already has a job driving on a field trip to Cedar Point for another district. I told him he is supposed to let the districts he works for know in advance when he cannot teach, but he forgot. Anyway, the kids and he should have fun. The trip is a reward for all the students who had no behavior referrals for the last six weeks.

"There are three buses of kids, all high school, so Cedar Point I hope is prepared. All that pent-up bad behavior from the darlings might erupt at the park."

Jessica and Lil laughed together, glad they were not chaperoning.

Jessica spent Tuesday as almost every professional person does after a holiday weekend. Along with accumulated mail and e-mail, phone calls from clients filled her voice mail. Two potentially good cases caught her attention. First, a young woman had been injured when brakes failed in the rental car she was driving on a job assignment. Jessica hoped that the young lady's reasons for selecting a rental car rather than driving her own were not precipitated by necessity, that being a previously wrecked personal vehicle with the owner, the young lady, at fault. The second case involved a severe burn at a tanning salon. Evidently from the message, the manager of the salon had failed to alert the victim when the time was up although the timer in the tanning booth should have worked first. Both cases required research, depositions, and time: all billed by O'Malley, O'Malley, and O'Malley. Colin et al. would be pleased.

Another phone call from a hysterical mother centered on child custody and visitation. Long weekends brought out the worst in separated and divorcing families. A father might keep a child too long, responding to the inquiring attorney that the child was having so much fun, he hated to tear the little girl away from a family gathering. Likewise, a mother might apply the same excuse. Who suffered always? The child. Jessica so far refused custody cases; her own childhood experiences still plagued her like a dormant bad tooth. No, she referred these cases, collecting a modest fee or not. She wanted no part of other people's miseries, which mirrored her own not so long ago.

By Tuesday afternoon Jessica had attended a pretrial, an arraignment, secured the two personal injury cases that had interested her, and referred the hysterical mother to Bartram Irving's office. Perhaps a direct encounter with divorcing families might teach him a lesson. He had two young children of his own who deserved much better than a philandering father and a subsequently suffering mother. Most important, the innocent victims, kids.

As she shut her computer down, gathered her Louis Vuitton summer handbag, and checked her phone, Jess looked up sharply as Lil tore in. Eyes wide with fear and concern, she handed her cell phone to Jessica. "It's David. You had better take this."

"David, it's Jessica Woods. What's up?"

"Jessica, thank God you are still in the office. I need your help. There has been an accident with two of the buses, not mine, thank God again. Most of the kids seem to be relatively fine but shaken up.

The highway patrol is on its way, but I wanted to let you know. You do this kind of thing, don't you?"

"David, what kind of thing?"

"Personal injury. We are on Route 4 coming back from a day at Cedar Point. The driver of the first bus must have suffered some kind of seizure. I don't know if it's epileptic or diabetic, but the bus veered off the road and turned on its side. The bus right ahead of me crashed into the first bus, knocking kids and driver around but not overturning. My bus got caught by a traffic light, so we were far enough behind to stay out of the accident.

"David, I'm glad you are safe, but I feel terrible about the children. Are any of them badly injured?"

"I think mainly broken arms, legs, lots of jarring and knocking around."

"What do you want me to do, David? How can I help you?"

"Here's the thing, Jess. People like me in the district. I've played a few gigs, and, Jess, behaved myself if you were thinking of my other ventures. Lil said she would drive up here. She has your business cards. If you are willing, I am relatively sure I can convince most of these people to choose you to handle their cases. I have no idea of the nature of the lawsuits, but if you are game, I will send them your way."

"David, I have to ask. How many people are involved?"

He paused, then counted out loud on the phone. Alex termed that self-regularization. "The buses are fairly new, so each bus seats forty-eight people plus the driver, which is forty-nine. There were two buses. You might have close to one hundred people if everyone comes to you. If not, I imagine you most likely will pick up about fifty to seventy-five, and that is a modest figure."

"I'm shaken myself, David. For all the children's and family's sakes I'm glad that no one was severely injured. However, as you mentioned, there will be lawsuits. Yes, I'll take them. And, David, thank you."

In mild shock, Jessica slumped heavily into her chair. More than anything she prayed that the accident victims, and they were victims, suffered only minor injuries if at all. True, so many potential lawsuits brought her active cases close to the quota Colin had set for her. However, she loathed the physical and emotional suffering that drove her clients to her. Worse yet, these were children. Broken arms healed; by midsummer broken legs would have recovered enough so that the victims could swim in pools and even camp with families.

What though would lasting effects entail? Could quarterbacks return to the football field in August to lead their team to victory against long standing rivals? Would a less affluent family who had counted on a tennis scholarship for their daughter to attend a prestigious university drive her instead to a nearby community college so that she could start at least on pursuing her dream of a career in medicine? Would the child who complained of headaches now learn months later that she had a brain injury? Yes, Jessica would take the cases. As she quietly opened her lower desk drawer to pull a tissue out from the box she kept for unexpected client meltdowns, she reminded herself again that she embraced the law as a career. Tears were for other people. Jessica sniffed, stood up, then resolutely walked to the outer door.

"I think we both have had enough for the day. Go home, Lil. I am. See you tomorrow."

Together they turned off the lights, locked the door, and headed toward the elevator, today with its troubles left behind in the offices of O'Malley, O'Malley, and O'Malley.

Momentarily forgetting that no furry four-footed admirer would greet her, Jessica unlocked her apartment door as she wondered if Cedric needed more Precious Kitty, any variety would do. Of course not. The little fellow now resided in Wyandot County with his lady love Mary Alice who had never ever shared her food before. Now the two ate together out of the same bowl.

Tossing her handbag onto the couch, Jessica lay down on her bed for a short nap before going for a run.

Wednesday of Week Six

Wednesday morning at 7:00 a.m., her phone chimed: Max.

"Jess! I called at least ten times last night. No answer. Are you all right?"

Groggily Jessica smiled into the phone. "Hi, Hon. I'm fine. I guess I fell asleep right after work and slept through the night."

"I love you, Jess. I was worried about you, that's all. I'll let you get ready for work. Big day?"

Max knew not to inquire about specific cases, although Jessica did let him know when some days brought more events than others.

"I meet with the old man today, Brendan O'Malley. Either Colin is too much a coward to fire me himself or Mr. O'Malley merely wants a complimentary Jameson. We keep Waterford old fashioned glasses now on a top shelf for when the O'Malleys come calling."

Showered and dressed in what Jessica viewed as conservative attire, she unlocked her office. Because of her employers' Irish heritage, Jessica thought it best to select Kelley green spike heels and delicate emerald and diamond earrings to accessorize her simple beige Banana Republic sheath. One wanted appropriate clothing if one were to be fired or, for that matter, unexpectedly slightly drunk should the occasion arise.

She was sorting through her mail as Lil arrived, about ten minutes late.

"Sorry, Jess. David played later than we expected. People kept collecting money for him to continue, so he did and I did."

"You're fine. Just hold the calls until I finish with Mr. Warren and his uncle. When Brendan O'Malley arrives, you know how to be ingratiating."

"I take it you mean a cross between polite and obsequious. You see, David has been coaching me in vocabulary."

"Well, then, you, David as you call him, and Mom should get along just fine at Aunt Kate's wedding. You can talk five dollar words when a nickel word will do."

Jessica returned to her office just before the door opened for the Warren pair. Lil greeted them. "Ms. Woods expects you. Please go on in."

Jessica rounded her desk to shake hands with them both. Apparently the men felt they had dressed for the city; both wore suits, white shirts, and ties. Their shoes shined, their hair cut and waxed military style, they looked more like lawyers than some of the lawyers Jessica worked with. Their speech, however, reflected their rural background. Real, though. Not fustian, one of Jess's new words, not high blown, just down to earth.

"This is one hell of a place, Jessica," Leonard offered. "I am impressed! To think, Uncle, that she took the time to drive out to Canal Winchester to see us. You're a big-city attorney, all right. Hey, we've got ourselves one smart gal. She's even got a corner office!" Leonard's tone was one of amazement and admiration.

Jessica blushed, although she wished that as a fairly experienced professional she could hold her emotions and reactions in check the way some of her female colleagues did. "Please, sit down. These are trappings only, but I appreciate your compliments."

"Miss Woods," the older man interrupted. "My nephew here has been kind enough to drive me, so I won't take up much of his time or yours. I'm eighty-six years old. I believe it's high time I had a will other than the one my lawyer now deceased wrote up for me before I headed off to Korea in 1950."

"I am honored, Mr. Warren."

"Call me Thumper like we talked when you drove out a few weeks ago."

"Fine, Thumper. But for legal purposes, what is your formal name?"

"John Henry Warren. I'm a widower. I've got no kids to speak of. My son was killed in Vietnam. My daughter lives out in Oklahoma somewhere. The last time she talked to me was ten years ago when she wanted me to co-sign on a house she and her boyfriend were buying. A house, mind you, she never bothered to send pictures of."

Jessica shook her head. People and their shit shows.

"I want Whizzer here to inherit my estate such as it is when I'm gone."

"Uncle Thumper, I did not bring you to Columbus so that I could inherit. You told me you were leaving everything to your daughter, and I am fine with that," Leonard protested. "Jessica, I'm sorry. I did not expect this."

"I'm an old man. That's what I want and that is what I expect my attorney, which is what you are, I believe,"— John Henry Warren nodded in Jessica's direction—"to do."

"All right, Mr. Warren and Mr. Warren. Let us proceed."

Although the general form for preparing a will was easily accessible on her computer, for older clients Jessica preferred to fill in the appropriate information on paper. The specifics took more time than most clients anticipated because Jessica included questions about a living will, power of attorney, and organ donations. Nearing conclusion, the intercom hummed, a signal both Jessica and Lil used to indicate that it was time to draw matters to a close. Jessica could do as she wished, but it helped clients to understand too, a tacit reminder, that their appointment was almost over.

Jessica thanked both men, then accompanied them to the outer office where the Honorable Brendan O'Malley, retired, rested comfortably in a chair.

The two old men acknowledged each other, nodding briefly. Then together, they stopped, staring in disbelief. In a commanding voice he had last used on the bench, Judge O'Malley spoke first. "Sergeant Warren. My God, it's good to see you!"

"Colonel O'Malley."

John Henry Warren straightened his back, held his head high, and saluted. Briefly Jessica glimpsed the face of a much younger man, a man who years before had served under a commanding officer in a war the government called a conflict. A conflict where at least 34,000 Americans died in battle.

As Jessica Woods and Leonard Warren stood aside out of respect, a commanding officer and a man who served in his unit sixty years before embraced each other as brothers and equals.

"What brings you here, old man? A divorce? A paternity suit? I always wondered where you wandered off to those nights you managed to arrange leave," Brendan joked with his sergeant.

"I could ask the same of you, Colonel. Before the women find us and begin demanding half our pensions—"

"And usually getting them," O'Malley added.

"Which is why I stayed a bachelor after my wife died ten years ago. My nephew here has Jessica as his attorney, so considering that I haven't bothered to update my will since Korea, I thought I'd better get on it."

"Tough as you are, Sergeant, you'll outlive me. I'm pleased you chose my sons' firm, though. Ms. Woods is one of our finest lawyers."

Jessica blushed, staring at her shoes.

"That's what Whizzer, sorry, Leonard tells me. The damned state is giving him one hell of a time with a liquor license. Jessica has it handled though, don't you, Hon? You're giving those bastards a what-for."

Jessica shifted only slightly, just enough for Brendan to notice. "We are doing our best. Mr. Warren deserves it, for service to his country and for grabbing life and hanging on. I hope to resolve matters as soon as possible for him."

"I know you will. Whizzer should have found you a year ago instead of screwing around with the damned computer on his own. Come on, Boy. I'm taking you to an early lunch. Any good places near here? I could use a drink, and my nephew needs to see how a bar in the big city operates."

"Try Dempsey's Food and Spirits down the street. Lil will call to let them know you are arriving. I recommend Sean's Special: a burger grilled to perfection with the works."

As uncle and nephew departed, Jessica ushered Brendan into her office. "I know it is somewhat early, but would you care for a Jameson?"

The Honorable Brendan O'Malley winked. "As long as you have one with me."

So far her meeting with the grandfather of the firm O'Malley, O'Malley, and O'Malley was proceeding smoothly. Surely the old man would not carry out plans to fire her if he was smiling and drinking with her. Lil unobtrusively brought in a tray with two Waterford glasses, a liter of Irish whiskey, ice, and small white linen cocktail napkins.

"Skip the ice. It's much too early for cocktails. Just pour the Jameson."

Jessica did as she was told. Now what?

"Jessica, I'm an old man. I do pretty well with the two legs I've got. It's the third leg that doesn't cooperate the way I'd like."

It was one hell of a morning for blushing, Jessica mused, staring yet again at her shoes.

"Come on, Jessica, a toast to good health, such as it is." They touched glasses. "I've got a lot to be grateful for, but I'm not here to talk about me except as it applies to you."

Jessica allowed the whiskey to glide smoothly down her throat as she waited for her employers' father and grandfather to continue.

"First, not that it is my business, just nosey. Why was my old sergeant here with his nephew? Is there anything I can do to help the man who saved my life?"

Jessica swallowed another sip, too quickly after the first.

"That man dragged me wounded out of a nasty situation. I made sure he was awarded the Purple Heart. Sergeant John Henry Warren is not the kind of man to tell you, so I am. Whatever he needs, I will move heaven and earth to get it for him. Because of him, I am alive and walking.

"Those North Korean bastards shot me in both legs. If he hadn't pulled me to safety and shoved me into a helicopter, I would not be here. He nearly lost his leg in the process. He won't tell you that either. Without his risking his life to save mine, the firm of O'Malley, O'Malley, and O'Malley would not exist."

"Well, really, all the senior Warren needs is a will. It appears to be fairly uncomplicated, although I will of course have to do some research. The problem is not with him, it lies with his nephew who originally contacted me about obtaining a liquor license."

"Any felonies, annoying misdemeanors, encounters with the wrong people that might hold up his obtaining his license?"

"From what I have determined, except for a few speeding tickets, Leonard Warren has a clean record. He served in Vietnam, was honorably discharged, returned to work for years in Hocking County, then moved a few years ago to Canal Winchester. He bought a hardware store downtown, converted it to a bar, the local Board of Health granted a certificate. All he is waiting for is his license.

"I do not know how well he and his wife get along, although that is not the issue. It looks as if someone on the board is deliberately stalling."

Jessica set her glass down. Drinking Jameson with a retired judge was just too pleasant; she had to maintain a professional attitude.

"Whether someone had an affair with someone else is not our business. Most likely, however, that may be why a monkey wrench got tossed into the machinery, so to speak. Now I just happen to be having lunch with a few judges and other people who can move things along. Let me see what I can do."

The Honorable Brendan O'Malley finished his drink, then waited expectantly.

"Shall I pour you another, Your Honor?"

He winked again. "We can't very well fly on one wing."

Two of the best-selling Irish whiskeys in the world before noon. *Excellent work, Jessica.* What the hell, the eponymous brand did indeed owe its name to John Jameson, a lawyer, a colleague, albeit one from long ago, the eighteenth century to be precise.

"May we get to heaven before the devil knows we're dead," the judge offered. "Now for the reason I arranged this meeting. I do thank you for altering your schedule, Jessica, to suit an old man's social calendar. And,"—he paused—"his romantic one, God willing."

"I love my sons and grandson. They have their difficulties as you have witnessed. Colin got into a little trouble at the neighborhood Memorial Day parade, but people seemed accustomed to his holiday escapades. By now he should be out of jail and back in the offices.

"Of my two sons, Patrick is in control of the firm. Another divorce along with a girlfriend who is the living definition of effrontery has temporarily skewed my other son's thinking. Still, the firm is doing well.

"To come to the point, Jessica, I like you. Even though you are still very new as an attorney, you are one of the most intelligent, ethical, considerate lawyers it has ever been my good fortune to encounter." The judge emptied half his drink with one large swallow. "People talk. As you know lawyers are some of the worst gossips around. Believe me, I know quite a lot about you."

As long as this is the morning to blush, Jessica thought miserably, I might as well keep blushing. Speeding tickets, several towings, DUIs, romantic bunglings. She supposed the Honorable Brendan O'Malley was well aware of most of her peccadillos. Still, best to remain silent.

"Did you ever let Max out of jail?" He chuckled. "Here is my advice, from an old man who sometimes still has his mind. Stay with Triple O, as you call them."

Shit. He knew that too.

"You and I know that you will never make partner. My family has enough relatives in law school or in the firm already to see to that. But, Jessica, stay where you are. Here is why.

"The people I stay in touch with, in fact, those people I am having lunch with today are as impressed with you as much as I am. You love the law. Granted, you have made a few mistakes. Hell, we all have. Allow yourself four more years with the firm. I am well informed that within four years or no more than five at least two judges are retiring. One may die well before that. The men and women I have the pleasure of working with professionally and engaging with socially will approach you about a judgeship. We need you, Jessica."

"Your Honor, I just do not know what to say."

The Jameson had not hit her yet, thank God, so she did not slur her words.

"Then do not say anything. Think about it." He looked her directly in the eyes, just as he must have done to attorneys where he served the state of Kentucky for so many years. "I urge you, Jessica, to consider my proposal."

"I, I will, Your Honor."

"Brendan. Now, one more nip before I meet my friends." He poured for both of them.

After the retired judge left, walking as briskly as he had an hour before, Jessica slumped into her office chair. Slurring only slightly, she asked Lil to close her door. "Call me if anyone or anything needs my attention. I have got to take a nap."

An hour later Jessica's intercom buzzed.

"It is Mr. O'Malley. The senior Mr. O'Malley. He sounds drunk, but I think you should take this."

"Jessica, you really ought to join us at the Athletic Club after work. That is, unless you have other business. Call your client, I can't say who because people do listen. Call your client and tell him to expect to drive to Reynoldsburg on Friday."

"I will, Mr. O'Malley. Thank you."

Jessica's head pounded, but her mind, like her mentor's, was clear. The office of the Liquor Control Board was in Reynoldsburg. Sergeant John Henry Warren's nephew Leonard Warren could pick up his new liquor license there.

Preparing to go back to her apartment for the remainder of the day, Jessica collected her handbag and scrounged through it for some ibuprofen. Her intercom buzzed again.

"Ms. Woods, I am sorry to interrupt, but Mr. Eric Stewart is in the outer office. He does not have an appointment although he says that you will be happy to see him. He added that he has no legal difficulties, just something for you."

Flaming Eric, the eBay King. Out of jail, of course, back from Florida minus the planned and paid for cruise. "Tell him to come in."

Carrying a large plain brown tote, a cheerful man with curly blond hair and twinkling eyes stepped into her office. "Ms. Woods, this won't take a minute. I just wanted to thank you for your assistance during my recent run-in with the Ft. Lauderdale Police Department."

"Glad I could help, Mr. Stewart."

Jessica pushed her hair back. That hour nap helped considerably. Maybe she should just order lunch and keep working at her desk.

"Call me Flaming Eric. Everybody does." The eBay King pulled a brightly colored box out of his tote. "I brought you these. I hope they are your size. In my business I've acquired a fairly good ability to ascertain women's sizes. From your television commercials you look like about an eight and a half medium." He handed her the shoe box. Dolce and Gabbana.

Jessica caught her breath. Delicate floral brocade pumps, 845.00 retail, before tax.

"Oh, Eric, these are beautiful. I really just referred you to my colleague Ms. Rubinov. I know her from law school. You did not have to do this."

"You got me out a difficult situation, and, Ms. Woods, on a Saturday night when you did not know me at all. I believe in paying my debts and in appropriate thank-you's."

Flaming Eric paused. Somewhat hesitantly he continued, "I do have to ask if you handle divorces. After what I refer to as my Lauderdale Looniness, my wife threw me out. She went on the cruise, of course. As things happen, she met somebody in the casino onboard ship. The guy owns a bar with an Irish theme in Columbus. Allyson gave me the address. I think it's down the street from your office.

"Anyway, if you handle the divorce, I would appreciate it. My wife and I, soon to be ex-wife I guess, are on friendly terms. She is in love, and I deserve what I got. Actually, she makes more money than I do. She is a psychologist, and she will be working for a woman on sabbatical or something for a year while the lady joins her husband in London.

"Of course, Mr. Stewart. I will be happy to help you out." It sounded like spousal support for Flaming Eric as he continued his eBay reign. Hmm. "Set up an appointment with my assistant, so that we can take care of you." Even before her new client closed the outer office door on his way to the elevator, Jessica had her new Dolce and Gabbana shoes out of the box and on her feet. They matched the beaded floral Mary Frances handbag Kelley Rubinov, Esq. had sent. Perfect.

Saturday of Week Seven
June 12

"A heartfelt welcome to everyone present as you participate in this most joyous ceremony of love," the clear, bell-like voice of Carolyn Edmonton rang out over the sounds of gentle waves lapping onto the shore at Fischer's Beach

Robbie elbowed Jessica, rather hard, Jessica judged. "I thought Uncle Ralph was lined up for the ceremony."

"Carolyn is in what is expected to be complete recovery. She is the minister, not Uncle Ralph. He has applied for his license from the state of Ohio, but even if he had it, he would defer to Carolyn. Out of gratitude for a return to good health, Carolyn is donating all her fees for one year to the Susan G. Komen Breast Cancer Foundation. This is the first wedding ceremony since her release from the hospital."

Shaded under an aqua canopy, the Olivier Oney String Quartet, renamed for the occasion, struck the chords for the familiar *Bridal Chorus* from Richard Wagner's 1850 opera *Lohengrin*.

Whispering, Lil sidled up to Jessica. "Thank you for allowing me to tag along with David. He is so talented."

"Yes, yes, talented he is. Who is Olivier?" Jess whispered back.

"That's his professional name."

"I see. Very fitting." So, Jessica mused, was the much less flattering epithet "One Eye." Depends on which profession currently engaged Mr. Ompherous D. Oney. Jessica affectionately touched her friend and moral compass. "You look beautiful."

"Thank you, Jessica. I love my dress. Mo and I drove to Cleveland last week. Her mother manages the Ann Taylor store in Crocker Park, so she gave us a huge discount. I'm glad she and her mom have gotten back together. Divorce is tough. People say and do things they wish they hadn't. Her mother seems happy, as does her dad. This time it all worked out."

"Rats! I'm sorry." Lil shifted her whisper from friend to personal assistant. "I forgot about these. I checked the office phone before I left the city." She shoved a phone number and name into Jess's jacket pocket.

Then, more conspirator than employee, she continued, "Did you miss a dentist appointment or what? The guy called five times, Jess! Doctor Halberstrom's last message seemed pretty insistent. Something about working on your smile. What in the hell have you done now?"

Jessica looked down at her rose pink Chanel shoes. "Nothing, Lil. He probably just wants to discuss incorporating. These matters require time."

Carolyn Edmonton's high, bell-like voice continued, "We are gathered here today to celebrate the marriage of Katherine King Madison and Oliver Martin Oney. Their union is both a pledge of enduring love and an expression of their commitment to each other."

Kate had chosen a conservative trim St. John knit jacket and skirt in aqua. Oliver, a white tuxedo with an aqua bow tie he had, Kate confided, tied himself.

"He appears to have talent with his hands," Alexandra inferred at the bachelorette dinner Kate's daughter Mandy, Jessica, and Alex gave Kate two nights before at the North Coast Yacht Club.

"Yes, Alex, he does." Kate's New Yorker style confirmed her sister's innuendo.

Robbie nudged Jessica again. "I thought you were going to be a bridesmaid. Why aren't you up there with Mandy?"

"For the same reason you are not standing next to Graham. This is a second wedding for people both mature and with good taste. Having her son and daughter only in the wedding party keeps it simple yet elegant. Graham looks handsome in his cream colored tuxedo, doesn't he? You look good yourself, Robbie."

Next to him, Eleanor smiled gratefully at Jessica. "I persuaded your brother to get a haircut. I imagine you notice too, no cell phone." She pointed to her purse. "I promised him I would take good care of it."

"What if potential clients call?" Robbie whispered somewhat loudly. "I'm missing a golf tournament and a chance to network because of this damned event!"

In unison Eleanor and Jessica, responded, "*Your potential clients* can call back. Besides, you'll have the number in the phone."

Robbie grinned, looking somewhat both chastened and, in Jessica's view, accepting. Ah, love.

The Reverend Carolyn Edmonton continued, "Katherine and Oliver request on this day of celebration that each of us gathered here give freely of our loyalty and our support to their union."

Standing next to Jessica, Max patted his breast pocket yet again for the small velvet box that caused him so much worry, excitement, and joy.

"Marriage is an embracing of souls. It is the promise of hope between two, who love one another and trust that love."

Gentle waves on the beach provided Nature's background music as Carolyn spoke the words that would unite Katherine and Oliver.

Max longed to reach into his pocket, just once more, to check the contents, a two carat canary yellow engagement ring, nestled into the box that burned into his chest. Through a connection with a jeweler, Lil's new boyfriend had offered a very good deal on rings, but the conservative side of Max politely declined. He preferred an established store rather than dealing through people who, David had mentioned, "Worked out of their homes."

"With this ring, I thee wed. Receive it and treasure it as a token and pledge of my love for you."

Oliver Oney placed a Tiffany band with two rows of diamonds on Katherine's left hand."

"I now, with the Love of God, vested through me, pronounce you husband and wife. You may seal this union with a kiss."

As Katherine and Oliver melted together in an embrace and a kiss on the sandy beach where Jessica had played as a child so many years ago, Max pulled her close to him.

"I introduce you to Mr. and Mrs. Oliver Martin Oney."

The small group of friends and family applauded.

Max pulled Jessica closer to him. "Jessica, Jessica."

She cuddled under his arm, then stretched up to kiss him on the cheek. "I love you, Max. So very much."

She promised herself not to think beyond the moment. That was best, all things considered.

As the Olivier Oney String Quartet broke into the joyous chords of Mendelssohn's *Wedding March*, Max patted his pocket one last time, anticipating as he did so, one of the most significant questions of his life.

"Happy birthday." Jim kissed his wife.

"You are my birthday present," Alexandra whispered back. Arms around each other's waists, they smiled at the new Mr. and Mrs. Oliver Martin Oney exuberantly raising their joined hands as they walked back down the canvas which formed an aisle on the sand at Fischer's Beach.

In a pub in London, Captain Craig and Dr. Madelyn Washington raised glasses of Guinness in a toast to each other and their new marriage. It was nine o'clock in the evening London time, three o'clock in the afternoon in Ohio.

Scratching his head at his desk in downtown Cleveland, Andrew reviewed the few cases he had landed and wondered if joining one of the largest firms in Ohio had been a wise decision. Their idea of billable hours and his differed significantly. On a perfect Saturday afternoon in June, the thermometer hovering in the midseventies, he and Jessica could be sunning, hell, on the way to Put-in-Bay on her wave runners. Anywhere but here. Who had broken up with whom anyway? God, running into her at Crocker Park shook him deep down to his soul. What did she used to say in law school? Yeah, life could be a shit show. It sure as hell could.

At Crocker Park in Westlake, about thirty minutes south and west from downtown Cleveland, maybe less as the crow flies, Nancy Murphy delicately wrapped a white pashmina in tissue paper. She had planned to mail a package to her daughter in Columbus, but Maureen called earlier in the morning, inviting her mother for the night and shopping the next day. As manager at Ann Taylor, Nancy hastily rearranged her hours so that she could leave by five that afternoon. There was so much for mother and daughter to catch up on. Nancy had been a fool, a fool, to throw her family life away for a dead-end romance. She thanked God that time and heaven allowed her a second chance.

About an hour south down I-71 from behind the bar at Los Palmas Grande in Canton, Ohio, Mike O'Donnell served Budweiser to the regulars from the old days when the place used to be the Canton City Tavern. Maybe he should never have quit his construction job. But he reminded himself, he was getting too old for all the heavy lifting. Still, he might be too old to bartend too. He had one hell of a time with the younger folks, Generation Xers he read somewhere. Shots were okay, but piña coladas, hurricanes, and chocolate martinis? What was this world coming to? It crossed his mind to call his old friend Sean Murphy to see if he needed a bartender down Columbus way. Best not to though, all things considered.

A good hour and a half south off I-71, then west on Route 30 in Bucyrus the Rhinesworths piled their in-laws into a pearl white GX Lexus SUV. On a warm summer day midafternoon, Jeff had hated to drag the kids out of the country club pool to go to dinner with Grandma and Grandpa Howard, so he sent his wife to do the deed instead. Besides, the reprieve allowed time to check his messages; Jessica would call any time soon. He just knew it. Dammit, the years fell away. He never should have…

Twelve miles farther west on Route 30 at the Dew Drop Inn, owners Wayne and Deb Holenborg asked each other why in the hell a Dr. Erin Rhinesworth from Bucyrus called to make dinner reservations for six people at four o'clock on a Saturday afternoon. It was a bar, for heaven sakes, not a five-star restaurant. Well, give the doctor what she ordered, they agreed. You never knew when you might need a physician; best to be on the friendly side with one close by.

A short drive from the Dew Drop, really only five minutes or less, Myron Steinhauser unlocked the door to his office in Upper Sandusky. A tastefully lettered maize and ebony sign read Edward Jones Financial Services. Investment advice had been Myron's life for more than thirty years. He looked forward to sharing that life now with the son of one of his best friends. Oh, Robert Woods, Junior, had grown up the hard way, too soon when his father died. Still, Myron had confidence in his old friend's son. Robbie was a good person, smart, kind. "He will do just fine," Myron murmured, "just fine."

About thirty minutes or so down the road, Melvin Woolsey placed his newspaper on the floor next to his recliner in the family room. There was not much to do in Ostrander, although he and Violet had been plenty busy during the brief time she had moved in. He worried now though; where was she going all dressed up?

"Do you have a game tonight? I thought you just played Bingo during the week?"

"I do. You and I are going to dinner. You like to eat early, so I thought on this nice day we could drive up to Delaware or even Upper Sandusky. I'll get your walker."

"You know, I have been doing rather well with just my cane," Mel replied. "Speaking of cane…"

"Or we could just stay home and take care of your other cane." Violet laughed.

"That we could! Bingo!"

To the east of Ostrander, then farther south off Route 23 at his home in Worthington, Jay Rossford shoved his golf bag into the trunk of his 2013 Beemer. In their bedroom his wife Cindy tied her golf shoes, readying for her first golf lesson from the new pro at the country club. Her friends had already briefed her on the fellow's drop dead gorgeous looks. Golf lessons, paid for of course by Jay, promised to be such fun. Maybe more.

In downtown Columbus Sean Murphy taped a *Closed til Sunday noon* sign on the door, and locked up Dempsey's Food and Spirits. He had a date! Allyson called with specific descriptions of the picnic she had packed for them to enjoy at the Hoover Dam. Cold ham sandwiches on homemade bread, potato salad with plenty of eggs, and chocolate chip cookies she had baked herself lay snuggly in a Nantucket basket she had learned to weave on the cruise ship where she and Sean first met. It hadn't been too many weeks ago, but Sean reflected, he could have met the woman he just might marry. His bachelor days, make that years, had stretched out far too long.

From his command post, Bill Majors liked to refer to his computer at Columbus Capital Properties as that, the apartment manager reviewed a rather interesting video of the tenant and visiting boyfriend in 5 S. She annoyed him all right, but saving the damned movie wasn't worth the effort any more. Bill pressed Delete/Delete. There. Done. He had better things to do with his life now that he was in love. Fancy china wasn't his thing, but if Annie liked it, so did he. He had eaten dinner off much, much worse tableware; that was for sure.

Up in his apartment Bill's brother Bruce graded student essays. At least they were submitted electronically, so printing, marking, and possibly losing the damned papers no longer posed problems. He gave himself until four o'clock at which time he planned to stop work for the day. Thoughts of that wine bar down the street offered incentive until another assignment with the government came his way. He could wait. Truth to tell, he liked teaching.

Sorting through files in her new if temporary office in Reynoldsburg, Dr. Allyson Stewart happened across a manila folder from the 1980s, which her predecessor must have tossed into a desk drawer and evidently forgotten. Another psychologist may have sent it to Madelyn, from the looks of the dog-eared and aged paper. Allyson considered reading it but quickly rejected the idea. People and their problems. She had a boyfriend!

A few miles farther east of Reynoldsburg, in the little town of Canal Winchester Leonard Warren tapped a new keg of craft beer. Wearing a spanking clean white apron, his wife Rachel served a nice cold glass of the brew to Uncle John; she refused to call him Thumper. The old sergeant reached into his pocket for his wallet.

"You know your money is no good here, Uncle," Rachel reminded him. "You brought my husband and me back together again. We owe you, not the other way around."

The old soldier smiled, watching as his niece by marriage scurried between the kitchen and the bar. Not only was Rachel happy, she seemed to be losing weight too. He hadn't done much for Leonard or his wife, he thought. Years before, courage and loyalty between two Marines, one a commanding officer, the other an enlisted man, had done that.

On the west side of the capital city just off Broad Street at his desk among the piles of eBay treasures, Flaming Eric Stewart scrolled through online dating sites. He wished to hell he had not lost his temper down there in the Publix Parking Lot in Lauderdale. Damn. Eric shrugged. Hey, he still reigned as eBay King. Things could be a lot worse, like disparaging comments on the Internet causing the collapse of his monarchy.

He minimized the site, then returned to a previous one, Statement Jewelry. What was this? A diamond tiara in an estate. He entered a bid, then waited. Ah, the head that wears the crown, always, always thinking.

At their home in New Albany, Linda and Jim Katzen opened a bottle of Dom Perignon. A bit early for cocktail hour, but they needed sustenance to prepare themselves for dinner with the Schultzes and the Dials. Whose idea had it been anyway to suggest a bon voyage party for those two couples? Richard and Eugenia Schultz were fine; in fact, their decision to live in Italy for at least a year as they researched Eugenia's heritage was excellent. Dr. Schultz could use a sabbatical. As for their Honors John and Susan Dial, Linda and Jim agreed that the old man would not be able to keep up with his wife. She may have planned it that way, come to think of it. Send the old guy home while she cavorted with those romantic Italian men. Yum.

Linda and Jim toasted each other. "We don't need that kind of carrying on, do we?"

Jim's handsome face broke into a wide smile. "I could use some carrying on tonight, but just with you, my pet."

"Happy to be of service, my dear." They toasted again.

About twenty miles south of Columbus, Bartram Irving and his newest intern hurled along in her red Maserati toward the Greenbrier. Although the car belonged to her—a gift, you might call it, from her soon-to-be-former husband—Bartram drove. The previous intern had just not worked out, wanting marriage as she did. Fortunately, Bartram Irving, Esq. had collected enough credit card rewards to apply them to his reservation at the West Virginia resort. No need to let on to his protégé why he was already so familiar with the layout.

In Southeastern Ohio the Dawber family reunion proceeded as scheduled but without Lilly Taylor. The collected relatives agreed that it was a shame her boss had called her into work, but that was how you got ahead in the world of attorneys. Lilly had mentioned something about a nice young man too, a musician, they thought, and a teacher as well. Perhaps an engagement ring might come out of it everyone hoped.

At another family get together, the annual O'Malley picnic, always held as close as possible to June 12, Brendan O'Malley's birthday, Colin, Gerald, Patrick, along with assorted wives, children, and girlfriends celebrated in relative calm. As everyone knew, Flag Day on June 14 was only two days away. Then, of course, Fourth of July loomed ahead too. How unfortunate that Grandfather O'Malley had called to regret that his presence at the event in his honor was not possible. They all missed him; they did indeed. Perhaps someone should call to check up.

On the night stand alongside his king sized bed, Brendan O'Malley's cell phone chimed in his penthouse suite in Louisville. "Should you answer it?" his companion asked.

"Sweetheart," he replied, "you and I in our jobs on the bench and off have answered a lifetime of phone calls. "We can let this one go."

"I concur with your decision." She smiled. "We do indeed have more pressing cases."

One Year Later

"Jess, sorry to interrupt but this package just arrived. I thought you would want to open it before you left."

Lil bustled into the office with as much energy as she could muster carrying, as she did, a beautifully wrapped box for Jessica. Jessica had to admit that her friend, unabashedly pregnant with a baby due any day, was beautiful. Lil didn't waste time. Her wedding band still fit although even Lil might have to acquiesce to her obstetrician's strong advice to take it off before they had to cut it off. Truth be told, Lil was proud of her marriage, hasty as it was, to David, formerly One Eye.

Jessica assumed the substitute teacher also musician also now husband and soon-to-be new father had given up at least one of his pastimes. Maybe. Lilly Taylor Oney seemed a bit circumspect about discussing David's work. Well, it wasn't Jess's business to pry. What she did not know she did not have to worry about. Bartram Irving had assumed that little task.

"Thanks, Hon. You feeling okay? You look ready to pop any day now."

"The doctor told me to have my hospital bag prepared, but next Wednesday is still Baby Day. I'm working till then. Who else would keep the office going when my boss is on her honeymoon?"

"Lil, you're always my good friend and my moral compass. We've been through a lot. But honestly, if Baby insists on seeing her mother face to face, the temp we arranged for can manage. I'm leaving my laptop here. Ralph Edmonton is covering for me, and even Triple O insisted I leave my work where it should be: at the office."

"That is exactly what I plan to do."

Jessica smiled as she gazed down for the thousandth or so time at her wedding ring. A two carat pear shaped emerald set in a simple band of gold caught the morning light. What a difference a year made.

Both women heard the outer office door bang open, a familiar cheerful male voice yelling, "Anybody home?"

"We're in here, Ken," Lil responded first. "Your wife is almost ready, aren't you, Jess?"

"Come on in. Let's open this package together!"

"You don't think I'll hurt my hands?"

God, dentists. If they were so worried about their hands why in the hell did almost all of them subject themselves to the frequent abuse of the golf club? Still, those hands had made her wedding ring. Dentists were good at that too. And other things. Very good.

A girl just never knew how a cracked filling could bring about anything positive. Still, there it was. An emergency visit to an office where she had never been a year ago just because, rushed, she didn't have time to drive back to Upper Sandusky to her childhood dentist.

Then, the right side of her face still numb from Novocain, Jessica speaking like a drunk or a stroke victim stumbled out into the hot late May sun to her car, which, dammit, wasn't there. Towed again. Nobody on this quiet neighborhood street in Worthington, nobody paid attention to the *No Parking* signs by the school. Christ almighty, the buses didn't come until three, so why the brouhaha over a temporary parking place? Thirty minutes at most, maybe forty-five. Nobody except the municipal police.

As she blinked at her phone in the noon heat wondering which towing service to call, Kenneth G. Halberstrom, DDS pulled out of the driveway next to his office. Rolling down the window, he asked, "Ms. Woods, are you all right?"

No, she was not. Her jaw was numb, she truly had no idea where her car was, she had an arraignment at one downtown. No, she was not.

"Jump in. I think I know where your car is at least. They're sticklers around here for parking violations. Any number of my patients have suffered the same treatment you are. One guy in the department seems to have nothing to do but ticket and tow. Come on, I'll give you ride. The impound lot is on my way to the golf course."

So a phone call that night from Dr. Ken Halberstrom inquiring about her well-being was both courteous and professional. And the phone calls later into the week, which, Jessica had to admit, flattered her. No need to tell him about Max. Ken was just being friendly.

Well, distance and time contravened on a relationship, no, a brief engagement. No wedding plans, no set date. Max knew it too, but, gentleman always, honestly nice man, he accepted the breakup for what it was, the best for both of them. Jessica could not start all over in Cleveland, and Max couldn't leave his expanding business, now with family members as well.

Still friends, she and Max sometimes talked, but those occasions entropied, gradually diminishing as weeks, then months passed. If Ken hadn't been so insistent, like those phone messages Lil relayed to Jessica at Kate's wedding, maybe nothing would have happened. But it did.

Good old Robbie managed to play his part too: a fundraiser with Jessica and Ken half of a foursome. The Old Jayster and Rob the other half. Best ball, shotgun start at Muirfield. Ken persuaded Jess to arrive early to practice putting; her drives were terrific. Robbie sneaked in ahead, placing a golf ball wrapped with a message into one of the cups in the practice green. Putting clockwise with Ken as her golf teacher, Jessica eventually reached into the hole to retrieve the question that changed her life.

"Yes, yes, yes!" She laughed and cried at the same time. "I'll marry you, my love. Yes, I will."

That day even the Old Jayster played well; handicaps definitely deferred to, their team placed first. Rob and Jay stayed for the prime rib dinner. Jessica and Ken excused themselves to celebrate, but first Ken had to stop by the office.

"Dammit, I can't remember if I put my clubs in. Just let me check while we're here," he added as he stopped in the parking area behind his office. Ken retrieved a bottle of Dom Perignon from the Styrofoam cooler stuffed at the back of the trunk, along with two Waterford champagne glasses. Returning to Jess still in the passenger seat, he poured the first of what would be many celebratory drinks later with friends and family. "To us, Jessica, where it all began."

"Are you going to open the gift or stand their day dreaming?" Ken cheerfully pulled her out of her reverie. "Robbie's going to pick us up in ten minutes."

Jess ripped open the tastefully wrapped pink box, Victoria's Secret. As she lifted out a frothy pastel confection, nightgown and robe, a note fluttered to the floor:

Light of my life, you waited for the right man.

All my love, always,
Mom.

Jessica wiped a few tears. She couldn't help but cry. Then, "Jess, look, there's an envelope in the box.

"You open that, Ken. I just can't."

A gift certificate for 200.00 for Graeter's Ice Cream. And another note.

Now that you're eating for two, you deserve the best.
Love, Jim

"Come on, Hon, Robbie's down there already. We stopped at the house and put your suitcase in the trunk, so we can head right to the airport."

"Let me visit the ladies' room first. You know us expectant mothers. I'll catch up."

As Ken clattered down the steps and Lil returned to her desk, Jessica gazed around her office one last time before shutting off the lights. There on the library table, the congratulatory note from the Supreme Court justice. There too a framed picture of a much younger Robbie and her with their mother and dad at Christmas, the kids in red plaid, Alex in red taffeta, Bob in a tuxedo.

Hard not to cry. Jessica walked over to the Waterford framed picture of her dad. So long ago. Bob as high school quarterback, confidently holding the football, his whole life in front of him.

"Dad, Dad, I miss you so."

She picked up the picture, clutching it close to her heart.

"Jess, is this a bad time?"

Lil knocked discreetly on the already open door.

"No, Hon, just reminiscing."

"Sorry, but Dr. Rhinesworth called. She wondered if you handled divorces. What do I tell her?"

"Call her. Tell her I'll get back with her when I return. If it's ugly, they have children, Ralph Edmonton can handle it. If it's relatively amicable, I will take it."

"One more thing. Then you really need to go. Robbie, bless his heart, gets impatient, I know. These white roses were down in the lobby, addressed to you. They must have just been delivered. Do you want to read the card or should I open it?"

"You read it.

Best wishes for a happy life. I remain as always your biggest fan, your friend, and, Jessica…

Andrew

"Well." Jessica wiped her eyes. "That is certainly quite a bon voyage."

Her cell phone chimed. "Jess, come on! We're going to miss the plane!"

"Be right down, Sweetie. Just closing out a few details here."

One last beep, which she promised herself she wouldn't take. Still.

"Counselor and now Mrs. Halberstrom. Congratulations. Your wedding was absolutely perfect, and take that from an old man who has been to a lifetime of weddings: many of them my sons." Brendan O'Malley.

"As you recall, I urged you to be patient, stay with the firm until one or more of the judges in this area retires or dies. Anyway, I figured four or five years at best. Turns out one of my lady friends, a bit younger than me, mind you, has decided on an early retirement. Seems she wants to spend more time with her husband. My loss, of course. I liked the excuse of CEUs but, there are always more fish in the sea.

"So I know you are probably headed out but do keep this in mind. Both the Democrats and the Republicans like you, even the independents. Think about it. Justice needs you. I'll let you go, but it would be a great privilege to call you, *Your Honor*."

"Your Honor, I mean, Brendan, thank you. I will certainly think about it."

Jessica shut her phone down. She picked up the picture of her dad she had temporarily placed on her desk. Wait. She shook her head. Was this the wrong picture? Robert Woods grinned back at her, fishing vest decorated with brightly colored lures, fishing pole in his hand, canvas hat tilted to the right, sunglasses dangling from an orange cord around his chest.

Did she hear, did she imagine?

"Hi, Sweetheart. I'm so proud of you, my beautiful, accomplished daughter. Good luck. You know I am with you always, just, just on a different plain."

Jessica blinked through tears. She looked again at the framed picture she knew so well. A high school quarterback gazed out confidently, squinting ever so slightly into the sunshine of forty-seven years before.

Lil knocked politely. "Jess, sorry, but Robbie called me on the office phone. He's going ballistic!"

"I'm on my way."

She hugged Lil, then took the elevator to meet her husband and her brother.

Loud honking from a driver in a red Mercedes. People can be so rude! It was Robbie!

"Hey, Sis." He jumped out. "Over here."

"Robbie, what did you do? This is one beautiful car!"

"I got a bonus. I've been lucky this year, Jess. Myron thought it was time that I ought to reward myself. So here is my reward, which you can see I am driving. Don't fret. Eleanor and I will still lease Fords, but I have to tell you, a Mercedes is mighty fun."

"Congratulations, Robbie." She hugged him. "I knew you could do it."

Jessica stepped into the car and slid so close to Ken she almost sat on his lap.

Turning the ignition, Robbie scratched his head. Newlyweds. When he married Eleanor—and he would—he promised to restrain himself. He swore he would not glance back into the rearview mirror, but he did. There they sat, holding hands and kissing. God.

"Hey, Jess, you told me Cedric was fixed! Mary Alice just had a litter, and they all look like your little charge!"

"He was neutered. Or so Madelyn said. Take the proud father to the vet, and I'll cover the procedure." She certainly would, with Madelyn's money. "You had better take Mary Alice in too as soon as she finishes nursing."

"Okay, folks, let's hit the road! Bahamas, here we come!" Ken chimed in.

"Columbus," Jess added, "see you in two weeks!"

On the second floor in the offices of O'Malley, O'Malley, and O'Malley a sedulous Lil juggled online shopping for baby clothes with sorting office correspondence. She swore she heard a low chuckle from Jessica's office. No, it must have come from upstairs. The blinds at her window rattled oh so slightly; then all was quiet. As it should be.

About the Author

Victoria King Heinsen is familiar with the world of attorneys and appreciates their ongoing service to justice for people from all walks of life. She holds an earned doctorate of education and continues to teach English and education at colleges and universities. Victoria lives with her husband, Ed, along with their Maine Coon cat, Lockwood, in Port Clinton, Ohio. She is a graduate of Ohio Wesleyan University, Ohio State University, and Walden University and is a loyal member of Delta Gamma sorority. In addition to writing and teaching, Victoria works with her husband as together they operate their bed and breakfast, The Marshall Inn, located near the shores of Lake Erie. *Jessica F. Woods, Attorney of Record* is her third book.